The Stable Boy

by Sisco Polaris

ISBN 978-1-945247-18-7

THE STABLE BOY

A Thurston Howl Publications Book
Published by Thurston Howl Publications
thurstonhowlpublications.com
Knoxville, TN

jonathan.thurstonhowlpub@gmail.com

Edited by Sean Gerace
Cover artist: Rov

Printed in the United States of America
10 9 8 7 6 5 4 3 2 1

Preface

Wow, it's hard to believe that two years ago this whole book was nothing but an idea mulling around in my brain while I rocked along on my bus ride to work. Some ideas take such strong root in a writer's mind that they have to be planted on a page to see what kind of plant they grow into. When I first came up with the idea for *The Stable Boy* I knew it would be one of those stories. What I didn't expect was for it to turn not just into a plant but a bloody full oak tree. It was a lot of fun to write, I have loved working on this for the last two years and seeing this book completed is both a joy and a slight sadness. It is done, and all there is left to do is put it out there and see what everyone else thinks. I truly hope you enjoy reading this work as much as I have enjoyed working on it. I do want to say a quick thank you to my ever patient husband Brazz, my gang of friends, and the patrons who have helped support this polar bear. My thanks also go to the editing team, who have helped prune the tree into something fit for your eyes.

Chapter 1

TEST, TESTS, AND MORE TESTS? If there is one thing company guys love, it is testing things. BioCorp, the genetic research branch of the Iris Corporation, had at least two pints of his blood by now . . . Kyle couldn't help but muse on that fact as he sat in a small chair in the third examination room he had been in that day. The room was exactly like the others. Conformity — the watchword of all company architecture. What works once works every time; innovation and personality were not needed or welcomed here. A small gurney opposite the door, a desk beside the window, two chairs beside the desk. They were all the same color as the previous rooms, arranged in the exact same pattern, for maximum efficiency. The rooms even smelled the same, that unpleasant chemical stench that kills all bacteria and slowly drains the souls of those who inhale. Though Kyle was sure the last part had nothing to do with the disinfectant the company used (their own brand, of course).

Kyle knew the facility was located by the foothills of the Rockies somewhere. He hadn't seen the exact destination when the company car picked him up, but he saw the map and where in America he was being taken. The drive had been an exciting one; he hadn't left the city since he was in school and he was taken out of the city for a trip. That plus the thrills of traveling almost twice the speed of sound, the sonic boom had made his heart race.

The young man glanced out the window, catching sight of his own face reflected in the glass. A serious look on his ebony features, black hair kept short (less for someone to pull on). He never liked his ears; he always felt they stuck out far too much. His mouth showed no trace of mirth. This wasn't a club or somewhere he could relax and enjoy himself. It was company turf, and he was an independent; no company owned his soul, none of them paid his way. Of course, that had made his way far more difficult and less pleasant. However, with only a basic education, his options within the companies were extremely limited. Custodian of the porcelain bowl? Ha! Not Kyle's style. He was his own person, or so he lied to himself when life was so unpleasant that only the lies could convince him to keep going.

Growing bored by the wait, Kyle stood up and stretched, his frame lithe and trim. He was careful to make sure he didn't put on any weight. Dempsy wouldn't tolerate his clients being overweight; it made finding work for them far more difficult. Kyle had no wish to upset him, not for a second time anyway. A company job was a new one for him; they usually stuck to their own soulless, mindless minions. How Dempsy had brokered this deal, Kyle had no idea. Of course, he didn't know what the deal was. He had been sent, along with a bunch of others, to some selection day.

It hadn't been like any other audition Kyle had been on in the six years he had been with Dempsy. It had taken just a few minutes: Walk in, smile, and give a full turn, and then leave. He had found out that evening he was shortlisted; he didn't know how many others there had been or even how many positions there were. Hell, if it came right down to it, he had no idea what the job actually was, though he was sure the mystery would be worth it. Dempsy had canceled all his other work and paid on those contracts 'out of my own pockets, dear boy.' That told Kyle this was a good job with a high payout, which Dempsy would pocket at least fifty percent, or fifty percent of what his agent claimed the payout was.

Just as Kyle finished stretching, in stepped a man in a labcoat. He wasn't the nurse who had taken the last blood sample, and Kyle gave him a quick scan, sizing him up in a heartbeat. Silver hair, neatly trimmed, along with an expertly trimmed beard and clearly manicured hands. The man was careful to maintain his appearance. His eyes looked tired and yet in control. He had no apprehension of approaching a stranger; that spoke of confidence. His body was thin and yet not overly so; he ate well but exercised often. The labcoat covered his clothes, but Kyle already knew what would be under there — an expertly ironed dress shirt, tie, and suit pants and waistcoat, their jacket counterpart no doubt in some office somewhere. This room wouldn't be one this man spent a lot of time in; he was a higher executive of the company.

The man gave Kyle a warm smile, but the boy noticed he was smiling with his lips only. The man's spectacled blue eyes were cool and made the hair on Kyle's neck stand up. He had seen many smiles like that before, most often on the face of his agent. It was a smile to trust at your peril. There was no friendship or bond offered. Sitting at the desk, the man quickly took charge, waving for Kyle to sit down.

"Right, Kyle; your test results are all clear. There is just one more thing to do before I confirm your contract." The man's voice was clear, each word formed precisely and with no hint of an accent. Kyle couldn't guess where he had been born, but it was clear he had been educated in the highest-tier company schools. Accents were hammered out of pupils there along with individuality and souls. He was at least a second-generation executive, probably a lot higher generation, as there weren't many lower company employees promoted each year.

The elite, at the top of the companies, ensured their soulless offspring prospered first before considering others. The monarchy had returned to rule all, the kings of old now in suits of gray instead of robes of ermine, stepping on the penniless serfs below. Millennia of human civilization had passed, and still the rule of the few over the many held strong. Only a fool thought the government had any power. The companies ruled this world and ensured peace. War is bad for business . . . in the long run, anyway.

The man — who hadn't even bothered to introduce himself, as if Kyle should know him already — glanced back at the forms in front of him and frowned slightly. For a moment, Kyle worried there was a problem, and he felt a slight panic at the thought of informing Dempsy everything had fallen through. Then he received another hollow smile as the man said, "I need to explain what the job is and what your duties are. First, of course, you need to sign this standard NDA."

Kyle frowned and replied, "I already signed two of those forms." He wondered how many non-disclosure agreements were needed and if the first two were flawed in some way.

"Ah, yes — paperwork, the bane of us all, I'm afraid," the company man replied with humorless mirth. "However, those previous forms covered the interview and testing process; this one is far more inclusive about the rest of the work. After this, no more forms or signatures needed. You can get to work. Assuming, that is, if you want the job once you have all the details".

It didn't take much thought for Kyle to sign; it was just a piece of paper, and it probably wouldn't stop him talking about anything he wanted to. After all, if Dempsy asked (and he would), there was nothing Kyle would hold back from him. All the company could do was sue him into oblivion. There were far worse fates. "All right, so what's the gig?" he asked, trying to hide his impatience. After all, insulting clients was bad for business.

"Have you heard of the Dr. Moreau children?" The man asked, his eyes expectant, and Kyle got the feeling he was definitely being judged.

Of course, he had heard of the Moreau Children — some company scientist messing with mixing human and animal DNA to create a mixed race. Something about making better humans, not morally or mentally, just physically more able. Kyle wasn't really sure what the motive had been, probably to create soldiers or something equally as unimaginative. It was all about profit for the company. Imagination was only needed in very small doses; after that, it was all marketing.

"Yeah, I heard about them, the horse kids or something. The religious nut jobs go on about them in the news vids every other year." It probably wasn't the most intelligent of responses, but then Kyle wasn't being paid for his brains, and in Kyle's line of work it never hurt to let the boss underestimate you. At least he vaguely knew about the Moreau Children; a lot of religions were opposed to their creation and continued existence, claiming they were an affront to God, or Allah, or whomever they prayed to.

With a nod of his silver head, the man acknowledged the response, giving a patient smile like a teacher suffering the answers of an idiot child. It was a look Kyle had rarely received. While not well-educated, he was intelligent and had a keen eye for details and people. It helped him play the audience, and right then he had his audience measured — the man liked to feel superior, and he could easily feed that desire.

"Yes, well, that's just one part of the story," the man replied, and Kyle leaned back in his chair, giving a slight nod in the assurance that the other parts were about to be told to him in detail. If there was one thing he knew, it was how to listen to a client who wanted to talk. "Twenty years ago, I and my team managed to create a new technique for gene splicing. Do you know what a gene is?"

Kyle forced himself not to roll his eyes at the insulting question and just gave another slight smile and nod.

"Our technique allowed us to combine genes in sequences that previously could never have been stable. It allowed us to blend different species. We had some successes with lower animals; we made a cat-dog, because you know even us science types have a sense of humor.

"Our aim was to take a bunch of attributes and create a new type of human for one specific goal. You have heard of the Mars terraforming project, I assume?" Kyle nodded again, wondering who on Earth hadn't heard of the plan. It had been a hundred years since the first colony on Mars had landed. The companies had boasted that their efforts would soon turn the red planet into a lush Eden. One hundred years on, and those promises sounded like the hollow empty shells they were.

"Well, the atmosphere we have managed to create there is far too thin for us normal humans, and it will take another hundred years or more at the current rate to make it so our colonists can step outside. However, the 'horse kids' I created could breathe and survive, if not all that comfortably, on the seven percent oxygen in that atmosphere for days at a time. You see, the horse appearance was just a side effect of using some equine DNA to enhance certain muscle use. In fact, most of what we did was reactivate genes and sequences that we all have which have been dormant for millennia. I had intended to perfect the mix to remove the equine appearance. However, those, as you put it, religious nut jobs saw my research as an affront to God." The last word was spat with bile; for the first time, the man hinted at an emotion beyond contempt.

For a moment, they sat in silence, and then, as if suddenly startled from some daydream, the man jumped slight and muttered, "Sorry, I got a little sidetracked there." Kyle shrugged. He didn't care, really; he was being paid for his presence, and the man could lecture him on the wondrous world of yeast or Morris dancing for all he cared. The scientist continued his slightly more interesting tale. "Well anyway . . . gene tampering on such a scale was banned, and some people thought that would be the end of it. Of course, that is the limitation of shortsighted politicians; they can't see beyond the next election. As a scientist, I have somewhat better eyesight. I saw a potential loophole. You see, because of the technique I use, the children I had created could, in theory, breed true with one of several species used to create them. The ban stops me splicing any further, but it does not stop me increasing my laboratory stock by breeding new test animals."

Kyle tried not to react to the rather disturbing revelation as he wondered momentarily if this job was worth the pay, whatever that turned out to be. The scientist didn't notice anything, too lost in his own success at avoiding the law. "Sadly, with just three animals, breeding them is slow business. Only one in a thousand pregnancies have resulted in a birth, and only one in twenty attempts results in a pregnancy. However, the value of these animals is beyond measure. Imagine what they can do for the colonization efforts. They can go anywhere, set up new equipment with ease, take samples, increase mining efforts . . . They will speed up terraforming efforts tenfold. In thirty years, man might be able to truly live on Mars."

The young man blinked a little in shock. He had never seen any higher executive expressing himself with such passion. He clearly believed his crackpot scheme was some amazing leap forward. However, Kyle couldn't stop his lips as they asked impatiently, "So, what does my job actually entail?"

Reeling back a little, the scientist finally realized how far off point he had strayed. "The three subjects are eighteen now, and one of them, Aden, has a preference for male companionship. That is your job: you are to keep him company."

"That's it?" Kyle asked cautiously. Life had repeatedly told him anything someone said was "simple" was either a lie or a con, more often usually both.

"That's it. We had some issues with his last companion, a young scientist named Brian Charles. He no longer works for the company." Kyle winced in sympathy; nobody ever left the company, and those who were thrown out . . . He felt a deep pang of sympathy for Brian. The scientist didn't notice the look and continued. "Anyway, you will have an earpiece on at all times, and my colleague, Dr. Ramon, will feed you your lines."

There it was. The job: glorified puppet and pretend friend for some laboratory animal. It was easily in the top three of the weirdest contracts Kyle had taken. However, he had to admit it was far less objectionable than some of the jobs he had taken in his time.

The unnamed man asked him, "So . . . do you accept the job and the limitations of the contract?"

Kyle had no hesitation. He reached out and added his thumbprint and signature to the contract. If he had refused, he would have to explain to Dempsy, and whatever this beast was like the job couldn't be that bad. The scientist smiled. "Excellent. Please wait here, and my colleague will be along shortly to collect you. You will be briefed, and we will arrange a short introduction to Aden today. He is looking forward to seeing you in person."

The man didn't wait for a response before he stood up and left. Kyle couldn't help but note he didn't even bother to offer a handshake of welcome, but then he was just some puppet toy friend for the man's lab experiment. How much respect did he have a right to expect?

As he sat in his chair and waited for the next in the long line of company people, he found himself wondering what the creature would be like. Apparently, it liked men, whatever that really meant. Kyle had noted the scientist had mentioned 'seeing him in person.' The implication was that the creature had seen images or video of him. The beast might even have had a hand — or is it a hoof? — in selecting him for the job.

Being a companion, he could handle, even to some weird animal, but he wondered just how much autonomy he would be given. Having someone in his ear all day telling him what to say sounded tiresome. If they also told him what to do, maybe even right down to the details of how he should stand, that would be annoying. If he had wanted to be a company guy, he would have signed up with one of them a long time ago. Dempsy was a pain who stole more than his share of every payout, but he just gave Kyle the job; he rarely got involved with how he pulled it off. That was left between him and his client, and Kyle had quickly learned how to control his clients.

This would be a challenge; he would need to learn to control not only the creature, but the man in his ear as well. That would mean making a good impression as soon as he arrived and building on that, gaining some trust. As he heard the door open, he turned to syrup, his least-threatening smile spread over his chocolate face.

The man who entered was clearly a lot younger than the first, un-named scientist. Kyle assumed it was Dr. Ramon. His nails were unmanicured, slightly chewed in fact. His hair was neat, but Kyle knew how to spot the difference between a standard company barber's cut and a high-priced stylist's work. The first scientist had been the latter; this guy was the former. However, the smart shoes and the dress pants were not exactly cheap. That all added up to someone mid-level with ambitions of promotion.

"You must be Dr. Ramon," Kyle said, putting as much enthusiasm behind his voice as he could and standing up quickly to offer a friendly shake. He kept his shake light and easy, letting the other man feel like he had the stronger grip. Letting this guy think he was in charge would be the key to making sure he wasn't. "I hear you are going to be my guide and mentor for this job."

A slight flush came to the man's pale cheeks. Kyle wondered at the paleness of the man. It had been a beautiful summer, and the laboratory was in an idyllic location; was the man working so hard to earn that promotion that he barely stepped outside to breathe the fresh mountain air? It wouldn't surprise Kyle to find out the answer was yes.

"Guide, mentor . . . judge, jury, and . . . guy who writes all the exciting reports," Dr. Ramon replied with what Kyle felt was a genuine attempt at humor. Of course, the joke had been designed to establish just who was the puppet and who the puppeteer. Kyle had no problem dancing to this tune. He noted a vague Spanish hint to the man's accent. Clearly, he had been to a good school, but not early enough. Kyle guessed he was born to lower-level company types, but natural talent had him selected for further and detailed education.

"Hey, the man who writes the reports is the man who rules the laboratory, right?" Kyle quipped with a friendly chuckle of encouragement.

Dr. Ramon laughed, and, as he replied, Kyle noticed a slight thickening of his accent. "Not quite, but I won't say I don't hope to be that man someday . . . making some other lower-level scientist write my reports and . . ." the man paused and glanced at the door guiltily before adding, "Taking all the glory."

Kyle laughed openly and gave another warm friendly smile as he said, "It is the way of the world; the only thing that changes is who is on top, hogging the glory."

"Ha! Very true in the world of science anyway. I imagine it is hard for your agent to take credit for your performances," Dr. Ramon laughed at his joke, and Kyle laughed along on the outside. There it was: the kind, joking doctor had just shown him exactly what he thought of the actor.

"So, the other guy is your boss?" the actor asked with a smile as he enjoyed watching Dr. Ramon's smile fading. As an ambitious company guy, Kyle knew he would hate being reminded who was on top, and he wanted to show he could put the scientist in his place just as easily.

"Dr. Salter is my superior, yes. He insists on interviewing all employees who have direct access to our . . . subjects," replied Dr Ramon in a far more serious tone. The pleasantries were clearly coming to an end, and Kyle knew he had probably slipped up. Putting the guy in his place had been fun, but now he would have an uphill battle to gain his trust. Inside, he derided himself for letting the man provoke him; it didn't matter what the man thought of his profession as long as he liked and trusted Kyle. Though he did note the name of the original scientist, and he squirreled it away in his mind for later, when he would start to research. Know your enemy and know yourself, as the old saying went; Kyle found it worked just as well with clients.

The pale, thin man took a step towards the door, saying, "Well, if you follow me, I will get you set up, and we can start your final checks before you meet Aden." Getting to his feet, Kyle felt a huge mixture of emotion: gratitude for the change of topic, apprehensive that the work would start soon, and annoyance at hearing that there were more checks and presumably tests for him to take. Kyle followed him out into the corridor.

"Do you need any more blood samples?" he asked.

With a slight chuckle and shake of his head, the doctor replied, "Not today; just stool, urine, semen, and mucus samples." He paused as he saw the slight look of disgust and annoyance that Kyle was rapidly wiping from his face. The doctor gave a shrug of his shoulders and an evil grin. "Just kidding, although for every trip here, you will need to give a blood sample to be tested before you will be permitted to see Aden."

As infuriating as that little bit of information was, Kyle knew he couldn't do a single thing about it, so he laughed at the terrible joke as jovially as he could. After all, he still had to work his way into the good doctor's graces, and he clung to the good news of no more needles that day.

He was led through a maze of corridors, the doctor talking all the while, explaining why they had chosen such a remote location and the troubles they had getting the environmental permits to build. Fortunately, a large injection of cash from the company to the government had 'compensated' for the impact to the environment. Kyle knew that kind of arrangement happened all the time; no doubt some Senator spent a fraction of that cash on a few parks or something, then pocketed the much-larger remainder. Less than three percent of the population voted at the last election. It didn't seem to matter whom you voted for; all you got was some corrupt rich politician, all smiles and long words on the outside and hollow on the inside. The young man shivered; political clients were, by far, his least favorite.

Dr. Ramon led him through a door, and a surprising sight met his eyes: a room with a different arrangement. The desk moved away from the window, a bench instead of a gurney. There was a small poster on the wall; it had a picture of a planet that looked like Earth on one half and a brown world on the other. At the bottom was a message that read 'Ten Years and two months closer because of your efforts.' Kyle assumed it was hinting at their efforts to speed up the terraforming of Mars. Though he wasn't sure where they got the two months from or why they felt the need to add that.

Both the desk and bench were covered in a mess: a scattered pile of papers on the desk and a host of different gadgets on the bench. Kyle had no idea what most of the equipment was. He was impressed to see actual paper. It was rare; everything was electronic these days. Of course, paper had one advantage left: it was completely un-hackable and easily destroyed. He smiled to himself, as it confirmed everything he had always believed about the companies: they were far more corrupt than people.

Dr. Ramon waved at a seat. "Okay, have a seat, and we can go through all the equipment checks and get you set up, and then I will give you a briefing on Aden before you meet."

Kyle did as he was asked and sat down. He had never needed a briefing prior to meeting a client before; he found the getting-to-know-you phase of an appointment to be the best part of his job. After all, until he knew who they were, they could be anyone, anything. He had met very few genuine people in his career so far, but some of his clients had actually surprised him delightfully, and that was a rare and wonderful gift.

As he sat, the doctor rummaged on his bench, muttering to himself. Kyle found himself wondering what his new client would actually be like. He knew the briefing would be wrong; people are far too complex to be summed up in a briefing with any real accuracy. Of course, that made him wonder if his new client was even technically a person. Supposedly, he could walk and talk. A few concerns started to run through his mind; he had seen enough sci-fi movies to know that creatures grown in the lab rarely turned out well, in the movies at least. The creature might be some near-human brute, barely able to speak or comprehend him. He shuddered as he imagined what he might have to do as the companion of something halfway between human and animal.

He was awakened from his rather disturbing thoughts by fingers on his ear. Jerking his head away from the cold digits on reflex, he glared at Dr. Ramon. Then he quickly remembered himself and his need to keep on the doctor's good side and muttered an embarrassed, "Sorry . . . Reflex. Your fingers are cold."

"Ah, yes, sorry. Poor circulation, I'm afraid; bit of a family curse. My grandmother had fingers like ice. Here, why don't you place the transmitter yourself?" As he spoke, the doctor offered his index finger. On the tip was a tiny dot. Kyle couldn't help but notice the color was very similar to his own skin tone. "Just take it and place it as close to the auditory canal as you can."

The actor took the device, trying not to notice the man had to say "auditory canal" because "ear hole" would have been far too unscientisty. It was a mere couple of millimeters across and as thin as skin. The actor carefully placed it on the tip of his finger and then very carefully placed it in his ear. The device seemed to stick easily, but then it was probably very expensive tech.

Dr. Ramon picked up another device and said in a clear voice, "Test."

Kyle's hand flew to his ear as he dove out of his chair, his eardrums almost blown out of his skull. "Fucking hell!"

"Oh, shit, sorry! I guess I had the volume up a little too much," the doctor said with genuine concern and embarrassment.

While he pulled himself back into his seat, Kyle forced a smile onto his face; inside, he wanted to retaliate, but outside he gave as friendly a smile as he could with his ears still ringing. "Maybe more than a little," he observed slightly dryly.

"I am really sorry; how are your ears?" The tone of his voice (well, what Kyle could hear over the bells chiming twelve repeatedly in his brain) seemed to be one of genuine concern.

"Not too bad, though it might be a while before the ringing stops," he replied with a shrug. "No permanent harm done, I think."

"Okay . . . well, let's try this again, a lot lower." As he spoke, Dr. Ramon pressed a few controls on his device and then spoke again, much softer. "Test." This time, the word was whispered into his ear so quietly, it was hard to know if he actually heard it or if he was just hearing the man in front of him.

"I think I heard that, but maybe you should step outside and turn it up a little." It was a polite suggestion, but it was Kyle's own test, asking the man to leave his office. By rights, it should be him as the employee and subordinate who left, but, after the previous test, Kyle figured the doctor was on the backfoot. To his delight, the doctor stepped outside into the corridor, and he heard a soft "Test" whispered into his ear. "That's about the right volume," Kyle observed out loud to the empty room.

"Oh good, the mic's working, too," Dr. Ramon's voice whispered into his ear rather surprisingly. Kyle hadn't realized the device was a two-way transmitter. Luckily, he hadn't said anything more offensive while he thought he was alone. Of course, he realized this would probably mean he would never be truly alone with the device in his ear.

The doctor returned with a triumphant smile on his face, which Kyle thought was a bit over the top for testing some simple communication equipment. "Okay . . . next up is the camera. Can you just lean back in the chair a bit . . .?" As he spoke, the doctor picked up a small pipette from his bench. "Left or right eye?" How generous of the man to let him choose which eye he would be observing everything through. Kyle would have to keep that eye closed on his next toilet trip. After all, he knew far better than most just how depraved company guys could be, and he wasn't being paid to put on that kind of show for Dr. Ramon.

"Left eye," he said leaning back in his chair and opening his eyes wide. Dempsy had made him wear a camera on several jobs, though he didn't know why, and he definitely wasn't going to ask. He got paid a little extra for it, and it didn't hurt. The tiny device would float around his vision. Some of the fancier models could even project back onto your retina, allowing two-way video without anyone else knowing. Of course, it could get confusing seeing out of one of your own and one of someone else's eyes at the same time. Kyle had never done this, as that kind of equipment was out of Dempsy's budget. He blinked after the drop of liquid hit his eye. He could see a tiny black dot in his vision.

"Okay, now let's just see . . ." muttered the doctor as he turned on a small desk monitor and was treated to a view of the back of his head. "Oh dear, is my hair that messy?" It wasn't, and Kyle could see the feeble attempt at humor for what it was and so chuckled along.

"It isn't that bad," he replied, adding, "So, now you can see and hear everything I do or say." It was an observation, not a question.

However, the doctor was clearly a person who liked to explain things, or maybe just liked the sound of his own voice. He proceeded to explain that it was all part of the job. Of course, he insisted that he could rely on the doctor's discretion about anything he said or did of a personal nature. Kyle thanked him for that, while on the inside he had to bite back the knowledge that anything he did or said would be in Dr. Ramon's no-doubt very thorough reports. The man clearly thought the actor was an idiot if he thought Kyle would believe the doctor would omit anything from his report. To do so would mean taking a risk. Company men who took risks don't last long or never make it to the top, and the doctor had made his ambitions clear. Kyle made a little joke to show how relaxed he was about the monitoring of his every word and movement.

"Right, now . . . about Aden," the doctor said as they finished discussing the camera and transmitter. Kyle had been paying reasonable attention, as any bit of information could prove useful. He also guessed rightly that it would help put the doctor more at ease; he left wanting to feel in charge and intellectually superior, and Kyle wanted Dr. Ramon to feel comfortable with him. "He is a bit unique, obviously, but not just in appearance. He is far more observant than his brother. Bruno is the only other subject here; the final subject is in . . . another place. Aden was the last one, born about two months after Bruno and a year after the first subject. To be honest, he was almost aborted, but Dr. Salter managed to convince the board that he should be carried to term.

"I can't tell you how much has been invested in Aden; however, I can assure you the sum of money would shock you. It certainly shocked me." Kyle nodded in acknowledgement of that, although he was pretty sure he wouldn't be shocked. A place like this establishment had to cost billions alone. It seemed insane to him to be spending so much; the idea of these creatures colonizing Mars was ridiculous, especially with just three subjects to start with. The actor assumed that, eventually, someone higher up would see the bill for this project for the black hole of a cash drain it was and put an end to it. Until then, it was a cash cow, or he hoped so anyway, and he would milk it for every last credit he could get.

"His previous companion was with him since the age of ten and had considerable freedom with the activities they undertook. We have learned from this and would like to . . . keep Aden's attention on the task at hand." The doctor was suddenly unable to look Kyle in the eye. "He has an inquiring mind, especially about the outside world, and his previous companion told him far too much. Quite frankly, I think it is rather cruel to poor Aden to know so much about the world he will never be able to explore . . . for his own safety, of course."

Kyle said nothing. In school, he had learned about lots of places he would never get to, Mars being a primary example. He had heard of thousands of experiences he would never enjoy. Of course, some he would, some experiences he could choose to try or places he could visit if he worked hard enough, earned enough. Maybe it wouldn't be safe for the horse kids to go anywhere. He knew the church was still dead set against their existence. After all, God made man, and if man made another man, did that make him God, or did it make God a man? The existential dilemma passed through his mind and then was dropped; he didn't really care. The company wanted their subjects to stay put, be happy, and not think too much about what they are missing out on. That was something he could live with, as long as they paid him.

"I will be in your ear at all times, and I will let you know if you stray into a topic area we don't want him discussing. I suggest you keep it light, especially on your first day. It would be useful if you could promote the pleasantness of his surroundings." Kyle nodded again. They wanted him to sell his captivity to Aden. Selling, he was used to, and he certainly had no qualms about bending the truth. "We don't plan on trying to get a sample from him today, as he has been refusing to co-operate, and we want your first meeting to be a pleasant one for him. We will have you bring his lunch to him, as we want you to form a bond with him. The meal will be quite a sweet one, mainly a selection of fruits. He is particularly fond of mango and watermelon, so plenty of both will be provided. It would be good if you could join him in the meal; it will help him to think you like the same things."

Kyle couldn't help but smirk as the doctor told him this. As an actor, he had learned a long time ago that imitation was the best way to make someone feel comfortable around you. He had been echoing the scientist's body language since the moment they met. With most of his clients, he did the same, sharing their food and drink, ordering the same or similar meals; all to make them relax and feel at home around him.

"You will be with him for approximately an hour today, and, assuming everything goes well, eight hours a day, with an optional half hour break, for the week. You will get one day a week off, you will be taken back to Chicago the night before, and a car will pick you up the morning of the day after. Do you have a preference for the day?" Dr. Ramon asked with a smile, and Kyle saw a golden opportunity to advance his friendship.

It didn't matter to Kyle what day he had off. Hell, he had never had a real day off since he signed up with Dempsy. Clients' needs came first, and they called any hour of any day. The idea of a day with sixteen hours to himself was pure, unadulterated luxury on its own. The sickly sweet, glazed cherry of a day off on top was almost too much. Of course, he wasn't above using it to his own ends. "Well, since you are going to have to be in my ear all the time, what day is good for you?"

The doctor's expression was a mixture of delight and surprise; Kyle knew he had scored a direct hit and was edging closer to making Dr. Ramon think of him as a friend. "Well, I would love a Wednesday so I could go down to the city and see my sister on her day off. She always complains that I don't spend enough time with my nephews."

"Ah, well, it is not your fault. I mean, everyone has to earn a living, right?" the actor sympathized, putting as much sincerity into his voice as he could, which was easy as he did mean it. One thing he had learned in life is you need money; it rules all. No money means no food, no place to live, no healthcare, forget entertainment, travel, culture, or God. All bowed down to the almighty credit; your bank balance spoke volumes about you. Hell, it could predict your future, be it a happy holiday or a trip to the pawnbroker to try and get some cash from whatever you have that you can live without.

"Yeah, exactly. I mean, it's not like this is an easy job, either. I have to monitor twenty different research projects, procure new mares when we need them, and hire new consorts for Bruno, after he . . ." Suddenly, Dr. Ramon paused mid rant, aware that he was about to go too far. Kyle's curiosity screamed at him to find out why Bruno needed new consorts regularly. However, he knew that the doctor would not let that slip willingly. The actor filed that away in his mind for later. It was only his first day; there would be plenty of time to find out all the little secrets of Dr. Ramon, and everyone else, for that matter. There is always extra cash to be made if you know where to look and are willing to screw someone. As an actor, he knew what it was like to be screwed, and that it was always better to be the one doing the screwing.

Taking another chance to score some points, Kyle kindly steered the subject back by saying," So, how old are your nephews?"

"Six and ten," the scientist replied with obvious relief in his voice and a small, grateful smile.

"That is a great age! I was sixteen when my sister was ten. I used to have to look after her while my mother worked. It was fun. She could be hard work sometimes, though." A little shared pain was always good for building a bond.

The doctor didn't need to know all the real details, though he probably already had them somewhere; given the level of scrutiny he had received, his mother's criminal record and his years in and out of social care must be in the files somewhere.

A buzzing sound broke through their conversation, and the scientist checked an incoming message. "Ah . . . We have to move on; I'm afraid we are twenty minutes late for Aden's lunch. I will show you to your room where you can get changed."

"Changed?" Kyle asked in genuine shock; this definitely had not seemed like a job where he would need to dress up.

"Yes, change and shower. Your own clothes cannot be worn, as they may contain contaminants or infections which could be transmitted to Aden. While staying in this facility, you will be provided with sterile clothing. Did nobody mention it?" Sterile clothing had not been mentioned to him, nor had anybody 'mentioned' he would be moving into a research facility. Suddenly, those sixteen free hours now spelled sixteen hours of sitting around in his room. After all, he was just a paid-for friend for a really big lab rat; they were hardly going to give him the run of the place. He could catch up on his reading, which he had been meaning to do ever since he was eight; all he had been needing was a complete lack of alternatives. Kyle just shrugged; he wasn't about to refuse the job, and, if he complained, he would probably achieve nothing but annoying several people.

His room turned out to be quite well furnished. He spotted a rather expensive entertainment system in the corner; it was certainly more advanced than his home system and was linked to a holo display that took up a good section of the wall. It seemed that he would catch up on his reading some other time. A pile of light blue clothing sat on a comfortable bed. There was a single poster on the wall; Kyle had spotted a few other posters placed mostly at intersections. This one had a picture of the Earth and a graph, a steadily increasing line to represent current population predicted into the next one-hundred years. There was a message along the top, 'The answer to over-population is colonization.'

His window looked out over the Rockies, unlike his one at home, which looked out onto the fifth floor of an office block. It might take a while, but he could probably adjust to not accidentally flashing 'Maureen from accounts' every few days when he got out of the shower. Of course, she often gave him a smile when she saw him at the coffee shop on the street below and had bought him many muffins over the years. Not bad for 'accidentally' forgetting to close the blinds once a month. Every little bit helps, and a free muffin every couple of days is nothing to sneer at.

Dr. Ramon said he would wait outside but advised that Kyle hurry; they liked to ensure the subject's meal and exercise times remained regular to ensure their biological systems remained functioning at the proper efficiency. Kyle interpreted this as scientist-speak for wanting them to crap often and on schedule. He stripped quickly and jumped in the shower, determined to be quick. As the jet of water hit him, he cursed the timetable; the jet of water was wonderful, so powerful, he could feel it massaging his muscles as the droplets drummed on his black skin.

He turned the temperature up as high as he could stand and grabbed a handful of the industrial soap they had provided. The stuff stank and clearly had been chosen for its cleaning properties and not its fragrance. For a moment, he wondered if it was safe to use; soap this strong might make him sterile, not that he planned to have any kids. Though he had noted life didn't really care if he made plans. In fact, it seemed to take perverse delight in pissing on any plans he did make. His employers wanted him clean, a common request and more pleasant than the possible alternative, so he would be spotless.

Taking no longer than a few minutes to scrub clean, the actor promised himself he would spend plenty of time later lingering under that powerful jet. Back home, he could only shower for two minutes before he was over his water allowance. He had seen no water meter or warning signs about water usage in the room, so Kyle assumed he was at liberty to use as much as he wanted, so long as he was clean enough not to infect the subject with anything. He had often noted that his more affluent clients didn't worry about such trifles as water bills. Sometimes, he had been permitted to use their facilities; however, abusing them too much while on the clock could lead to complaints. The one thing he didn't want was to ever give Dempsy a reason to be upset with him.

Fully cleaned, he dressed in the hideously unflattering blue scrubs — light cloth with no style. Normally, he wouldn't have been seen dead in something so bland unless he was being paid to wear them. At Dempsy's suggestion, he had worn a plain white T-shirt and jeans to look respectable . . .ish. They covered up his tattoos anyway, which Kyle always felt was a waste; why get ink if you can't show it off? Of course, Dempsy was right — company types are afraid of ink. It robbed people of their uniformity, and that was bad, apparently. The scrubs covered up almost everything and were far too loose; the arms flapped around as he walked, making him feel like some sort of ridiculous bird. Not what he wanted for a first impression. He had wracked his brain trying to remember any images of 'the horse kids', but he had been too young when they were big news.

Emerging from the room, he found a rather impatient-looking Dr. Ramon with a large plate of fruit in his hands. Kyle noticed the excess of mango and watermelon. Fresh fruit was a rare treat; land is expensive, and transporting food is costly. Most food tended to be processed on site and most people didn't bother cooking. After all, a kitchen took space, and space was at a premium . . . everything was at a premium, except people. They were commonplace and easy to replace.

The doctor pushed the tray into his hands, saying, "Here you go. Feel free to eat some while sharing a meal. However, try to keep it hygienic." Kyle took the tray without a word and pushed back the urge to pick every single bit of fruit on the tray out of pure outrage. 'Keep it hygienic', how did they think he ate? He may be an actor, but he was not an animal, unlike their precious test subject. He was careful not to let his outrage show; instead, he gave a nervous smile. The nervous part wasn't an act.

While he was escorted to the door, which apparently led out to the garden where Aden could be found, he found his stomach churning a little. What if the creature didn't like him, what if he was violent, what if this was all some lie? These and a hundred other questions started to rattle through his brain, coupled with many unpleasant scenarios. It was clear that the creature was valuable; he was not. If anything happened, their concern would be for their creation, not for his hired pet.

His heart leapt into his mouth as the door opened and he looked out at a green lawn. He could see a figure framed against the warm sun. Looking to Dr. Ramon as his only possible friend and support, he waited for him to head out. However, the doctor shrugged and muttered, "He doesn't like me since I explained why he couldn't see Brian anymore. I will be nearby, watching, and I will help you if you get stuck."

With that, the scientist gave him a pat on the shoulder as he beat a retreat. Kyle took a deep breath, his only potential ally gone, then he took a step forward. The late afternoon sun was in front of him, and all he could make out was a vague human shape sitting on the grass. Holding the plate out in front of him as if it would provide a defense, he advanced on the shadowy figure, wondering if this was really worth the money or if Dempsy would care if he was killed by some out-of-control science experiment. Probably, until he made the company pay for his silence; after that, nobody would notice his passing. Maybe a couple of his former clients would remember him fondly.

Chapter 2

As Kyle approached the subject, he walked slightly around to one side, moving so the sun was no longer blinding his eyes. He wasn't really sure what he had expected – some sort of hideous, mutant creature, maybe all weird skin, teeth, and a vague horse-shaped head. The sort of beast who would have been at home sitting in a labyrinth, with virgins being thrown to him on a regular basis. Of course, he was one of the furthest things you could get from a virgin. Which was fitting, as Aden was no hideous, terrifying creation.

What Kyle saw was covered in blonde fur, a sort of golden color. Kyle had seen a video of wheat fields blowing in the wind in some lesson long-forgotten. As he saw the wind stir the golden fur, the memory of that video sprung to the forefront of his mind. The creature was big, maybe seven feet tall; it was hard to really tell, as it was seated. His feet were huge and very definitely not human: dark brown hooves, polished to a shine. The musculature was more human, though, and quite prominent. Given the care the company people took to make sure these creatures were healthy, the fitness of the beast didn't surprise Kyle. His mane was a far lighter color, the long cream hair running down his back. His fetlocks matched his mane in color and wildness, his wild hair blowing in the breeze.

What did surprise Kyle was the lack of clothing; the creature was completely naked. Kyle wasn't sure what he should have expected: a tuxedo and top hat, or maybe a lab coat and a small badge saying, 'Aden: Overgrown Lab Rat and Proud of It'. Wearing nothing seemed wrong, even to Kyle, and he had worn some outrageous outfits. That had all been for a job, though. You got the gig, you wore the clothing, and you tried not to judge, at least not to their faces.

Speaking of faces . . . Kyle found himself being looked at by the horse. It was silently watching him from its seat on the grass. Its golden fur covered most of its long, equine face, except for a small patch around his mouth. Of course, what Kyle really noticed were the eyes. He had expected something more equine than human. However, what he found himself looking into were two golden pools, far more human than any animal he had met. Kyle could see trepidation in those eyes, a hint of fear, and yet determination as well.

That was when Kyle realized that he was standing and staring at the beast like it was a circus sideshow while holding out a tray of fruit, as if trying to tempt an animal closer. With a blink, his demeanor changed; he relaxed his muscles and pasted the sweetest smile he had on his face, pulling the tray back into a natural holding position. "Hi." Okay, it wasn't the most erudite of openings, but it broke the silence in a friendly enough way.

"Hello." The reply was shockingly clear. Kyle had wondered if the beast would have the right combination of vocal cords and tongue- and lip-dexterity required to speak English clearly. Apparently, Dr. Salter and his team did good work.

Kyle took a few steps closer, saying, "I'm Kyle." Again, not an award-winning speech, but it got the main point across.

"I know," the beast replied with a little bit of a smile, if that is what it was; his lips went up, anyway. Kyle took it as a good sign. He had guessed that the horse had been shown pictures of him, but he didn't know how much they had shared. Hopefully, just the picture and his name; he didn't want this client knowing his full past. Or any client, really.

"You're Aden." Kyle had meant to phrase it to ask a question, to try and get the creature to introduce itself; however, it slipped out more like a statement. The creature turned its head slightly and gave him a curious look as it examined him further.

"Who else could I be?" it asked, and Kyle was sure he saw a twinkle of mischief in its eye. It was enjoying his discomfort. Somehow, that helped the human relax a little; an animal able to tease was able to enjoy a joke. His fears of babysitting some barely-conscious mutant creature began to fade.

"Well, I don't know. I haven't been introduced to the janitor or cook yet; do you know what's for dinner?" Not his strongest joke, but he was treading carefully, trying to feel the client out. It did, however, draw a short . . . well, what could have been called a chortle from the beast.

"Well, my nose and eyes say watermelon and mango, although I can also tell you where to find a mop and bucket," Kyle joined the creature in a laugh. He was shocked to hear it joke back with him. Somehow, just sharing a joke dispelled a large chunk of his worries about Aden.

"Before you show me where to get the cleaning supplies, how about we eat?" the actor replied with a grin, lifting the tray up a little.

"We?" Aden asked cautiously.

"Well, I guess you can just eat and I could watch, but I don't get real fruit often, so I was hoping to steal a slice or two," offered the human, hoping he hadn't stepped too far. He had assumed someone would have told him they would be having lunch together. His stomach was definitely not happy with any suggestion that he not eat; it had been a long day, and his breakfast was nothing but a pleasant, but all too distant, memory.

"No, it's fine; just I haven't shared a meal with anyone since Brian left." As he spoke, the horse lowered his head a little, and his tone held more than a hint of pain and longing.

"Get him away from talking about Brian!" Dr. Ramon's voice demanded suddenly in his ear. Kyle jumped just a little; for a moment, he had forgotten that they were not alone.

Kyle had to bite back his natural reaction to such a demand, to ask more detailed questions on Brian. He long ago learned to mostly control that side of his nature; Dempsy had seen to that. Still, inside him somewhere was the little boy who would always do the opposite of what he was told, just to spite the person giving the order. Sometimes, his little voice won out against years of holding back.

This was not going to be one of those times. Glancing around, he observed, "This is a very nice spot." It was a rather poor attempt to change the subject, but the shout in his ear had rattled him, and it was at least a true observation. The Rockies extended for a thousand miles in front of him and behind, too. Clouds were spinning across the sky. Before his feet was a tableau any artist would struggle to capture: fields, trees, and a small stream, all dancing together across the horizon. Part of him wanted to just run down into it. Of course, he knew he would not get far; he could see the large perimeter fence in the distance.

"It is nice, though too close to home for me. There is a spot down by the stream that I like," replied the subject, and his smile returned as he thought of his favorite place. "It's on a little rise, so I can see further. There's a small town a few miles away. I can't see the people, but I can see the houses. I like to look out there and wonder who lives in each building, what do they do, and why." Aden's eye caught the slightly cynical look on Kyle's face, and he muttered an embarrassed, "It's just a silly thing. Telling stories to myself to keep myself entertained."

Inside, Kyle felt a slight twinge of something; maybe it was pity, or guilt, or both. Maybe it was sadness, because he knew there were no more small towns anymore. They all grew up and became cities, or they died. The automation of rural industry had seen to that. Some people had clung on for years, decades even, stubbornly ignoring the tide of reality. The only people living away from cities now were the rich, those who could afford the tariffs of living away from a city. The countryside was beautiful, but nearly empty. The only towns left were work colonies, those men who repaired the machines, and they were few and far between. The town Aden spoke of might be one of those, each building a dorm housing a dozen or so workers or vehicles; more likely, it was a shell, a remnant, the last bastion showing that one day people had lived and loved there.

He had no desire to tell that to the poor creature; let him keep his hope. Kyle wished someone could give him the same gift. "That sounds nice; maybe you could show me . . ."

"You are to stay in the yard today; we do not want you wandering further," Dr. Ramon announced in his ear, and Kyle had to think quickly.

" . . . Sometime, but . . . I don't know about you, but I am hungry," he finished after a brief pause. He saw a slight hint of doubt in the horse's eyes. Aden seemed to be inspecting him far more carefully than before. Kyle made sure his warmest, friendliest smile never wavered as he awaited the creature's decision. Inside, he knew this was a crucial moment; if Aden rejected him now, he would probably be kicked out. Some other actor would be chosen. Ha! That poor bastard could suffer the same battery of tests, blood takings, and insulting conversations as Kyle had; see how much he liked it. It was a small thought, a comfort to himself, a small lie to reassure himself that if he was rejected, it was their loss and not his, even though any fool could see the real truth.

"I think I would like to eat," observed the horse, and Kyle exhaled a deep breath he hadn't even noticed he had been holding. Smiling, he passed the creature the large tray of fruits. Aden waved at the ground beside him. It was strange to see such a human gesture from something so very clearly not human. However, Kyle was too relieved to dwell on that; he just slipped down to his knees and then onto his rear. His legs stretched out in front of him, the Rockies extending beyond his feet for what seemed like forever.

He turned and rolled slightly onto his side so he could face the horse. The beast had already devoured a slice of watermelon and was working on a second. His cream muzzle was flecked with spots of pink. Kyle reached out and snatched up a piece slightly cautiously, wondering if the creature would stop him. If he did, the actor would wait; he could skip a meal at his client's pleasure. However, as his fingers touched the ice cold fruit, Aden did nothing but continue to munch on his own.

With a smile, the man brought the fruit to his lips, and he bit a huge chunk off. The sweet, watery taste hit his tongue with an unexpected punch, the juice flooding his mouth and dripping off his chin. He had forgotten how much he loved the taste, how the processed food packs never quite tasted the same. It had been months since his last taste of fresh fruit, but watermelon . . .

It brought back older memories – sitting on a balcony, looking out over New York . . . the strange green-and-red fruit, it had been almost as big as he was . . . the baby in the basket sleeping beside him . . . Where his mother had gotten a whole melon from, he tried not to think. He had just eaten slice after slice, his face, hands, and clothes being soaked by the sweet, wonderful juices. He had shared a tiny bit with his sister when she woke; it had kept her calm as the sun set, and he wondered just how much longer before his mommy would return.

The memory hit him hard, and he struggled for a moment before swallowing both the memory and the melon. "Mmmm . . . Oh, it has been too long since I had watermelon. I forgot how good it tastes . . ." As he spoke, the juices dripped off his chin onto his shirt, and he added with a chuckle," . . .and how much of a mess it makes."

"It is my favorite, so juicy and sweet. The seeds are crunchy, too," the horse replied as it picked up a third slice. "Who wouldn't eat it every day?"

Kyle couldn't stop the laugh escaping his lips; it was far too bitter for his liking, but Aden didn't seem to notice. "Well, most people I know can't afford to eat fruit every day, not real fruit like this." Remembering his role and what Dr. Ramon had said about trying to make the horse want to be there, he added, "You are very lucky to be here, where you can get fresh fruit daily."

"Nice, well done," whispered an overjoyed scientist in his ear. However, for a moment, Kyle thought he saw a flash of disappointment cross the horse's face. He had spotted the comment for what it was, and he said nothing in reply. Maybe he had scored points with his employer, but he had lost them with his client. This was going to be one tough balancing act; he knew in that instant he would need to walk a fine line. Stray from it one way, and he would lose his job for not following company orders; too far the other way, and he would lose the horse and ultimately be replaced. Either result would leave him explaining to Dempsy exactly why his lucrative contract had ended early.

One good thing about fear is it can be a powerful motivator. It can force you to do things you never thought possible, take risks you never dreamed of taking. Right then, Kyle felt highly motivated to walk that line as if it was the rope strung across Niagara Falls and a billion credits was waiting for him at the far end. All he had to do was put one foot in front of the other, tiny step after tiny step.

"Well, I don't have your appetite. I doubt I could manage another slice, so I think I will try the mango instead." As he spoke, he popped a couple of slices of the orange fruit in his mouth, savoring the sweet taste with audible delight. "Mmmmm, sweet and tart, perfect," he observed, sucking his sticky fingers with every indication of enjoyment, something he was far too adept at showing, whatever his feelings.

"Yes, I agree . . . though I prefer my mango slightly less ripe, so it is far more tart and it crunches," the horse observed as it grabbed another slice of watermelon.

"Ah, then you might be disappointed to hear this mango is soft and sweet. Apparently, I fail at fruit-picking. I may need to study at the feet of a master." Kyle took the blame for the soft, sticky fruit; it was a minor fault, but he knew that contrition worked best with most of his clients. Take the blame for minor transgressions, and they will learn to trust you; people like it when others take the responsibility for failure, especially their own. The truth here was probably that whoever prepared the tray had selected the softer, sweeter fruit, thinking the sugar would be the equine's preference. That told Kyle they were far more adept at providing nutrition than caring for the enjoyment of the food.

"Or maybe the hooves of a master," snorted Aden with a slight wave of one huge, hoofed foot.

Kyle couldn't stop the genuine laugh escaping his lips; he hadn't expected the joke, and the timing was so perfect, just as he had a mouthful of sweet mango. The fruit mush sprayed from his lips, and he looked on in horror as some flecks of orange dotted across the golden fields of Aden's chest. "Oh my God, I'm so sorry!" His hands immediately rushed to his pockets, but the scrubs he had been given had nothing in their pockets. No napkins had been provided with the fruit, either. In a moment of desperation, he pulled his sleeve over his hand and reached out to try and brush the dots of mango of the horse's chest.

"What the hell did I say about hygiene?" exclaimed a disgusted scientist in Kyle's ear.

The growls and threat of his disgruntled employee did little to help Kyle; if anything, they proved that Dr. Ramon wasn't there to help him, but to watch him and stop him saying something he shouldn't. Then he felt a strong hand grip around his wrist, and he looked up into two warm, friendly golden eyes. "It's okay; I am not so fragile that a little spit and fruit is going to kill me."

There was little Kyle could do but blush. Inside, he felt ashamed. For all his experience and all his skills with people, he had broken down over something so simple. He had never expected that he would cave to the pressure like that. However, all he had seen was the look of shock on Aden's face, of mild disgust, and then he had seen his future: going back after he was fired, standing in front of Dempsy and admitting how he had failed. There were always consequences for failure.

"Sorry; I just didn't want to offend or upset you on my first day," he admitted with absolute honesty and sincerity.

"Well, you haven't. I am not so easily offended." Aden's eyes glanced around the rest of the yard to make sure they were alone before he leaned a little closer to whisper, "You don't need to fear me."

Kyle couldn't help but smile. He had known after a few seconds of meeting the horse that he did not need to fear Aden. It wasn't the creature that scared him, but his employer's rejection and ultimately his own agent that drove terror into his heart. His hand was still held against the creature's firm chest. The fur was softer than he thought it would be and warm to the touch; beneath his fingertips, he could feel the soft thump of a heartbeat. "Thanks," he muttered as he pulled his hand back, the horse releasing his wrist easily, though the memory of his touch lingered.

The two sat and were in slightly awkward silence as the moment passed, and then a rather impatient voice muttered, "We are not paying you to not talk." Kyle tried not to sigh too audibly; apparently, Dr. Ramon may know a lot about science and genetics, but he was sadly deficient in his understanding of people. Silence was part of any relationship; it was just as important as words. Kyle knew its importance, that it was in the silent moments you could exchange looks and signals that gave messages far too deep and complex to trust to simple, clumsy words. He decided to push his luck and ignore the comment for another minute or two, gazing at the beautiful vista.

When he had panicked, Kyle had moved closer to Aden. He hadn't backed off afterwards, deliberately staying inside the horse's personal space. Aden had shown no intention of moving away. Kyle gave him a slightly embarrassed and yet warm smile. The smile was returned, and, out of the corner of his eye, he saw the horse's hand slowly moving across the grass, inching closer to where his right hand sat as Kyle leant back on his right arm.

"Look, just tell him how much you like the place, say it is safer than where you live," Dr. Ramon demanded in his ear. Kyle tried once more to ignore it; he knew he was pushing his relationship with the scientist, but he needed to make a connection with his charge. "We are paying you fucking good money; say something now, or I will find someone who can listen."

With a deep sigh. Kyle's rebellion ended, and he made a point of looking directly at Aden; he wanted the scientist to see what was about to happen. "This place is really wonderful; such a beautiful view, good food, good company, and no worries about being mugged. It doesn't get much better than this." Even using his own words, he knew he had just taken a huge, screaming leap backwards in Aden's opinion of him.

Aden broke eye contact immediately, his hand stopped moving, and, after a few seconds, he moved, removing the actor from his personal space. Kyle tried to keep the smile on his face as he watched everything he had been trying to achieve being torched by a scientist with a microphone and no people skills. "Happy now?" Kyle was as shocked as Aden was confused as the actor spat the question. It was aimed at the moron in his ear; the actor had followed his cues and fucked up the budding relationship.

"Happy? I don't know, I am well fed, healthy, and protected here." Aden's reply was quiet, and Kyle could hear sincerity in his voice, a tremble of doubt and worry. "I have never left this place. I know every building, every tree and stone. But beyond that fence, I have seen nothing. I have never seen the ocean or the desert or even a city. Maybe I am happy; I hardly have enough experience of the world to know. The only person who really cared for me is gone, and I have been told I will not be able to see him again . . . Does it sound like a happy life to you?"

The actor froze as the horse turned his question back on him. His mouth felt dry, and the voice in his ear was thankfully silent. Kyle's mind raced as he tried to think of a response; he knew he had to think it and say it before the moron on the mic fed him some more rubbish about how pretty the horse's gilded cage was. "I don't know. It is not like getting beyond that fence will make everything better. Life sucks most of the time; anyone who says otherwise is trying to sell you something. If you were to get outside, you might find no more happiness than you have here. There are no guarantees in life; you pay your money, and you take your chances, and hope like fuck you have what it takes to make it. Many do, some don't. Pity those of us who fall short . . . Don't ask me what a happy life is; I am just as clueless as you on that score."

The horse regarded him carefully, as if digesting his words. Kyle didn't smile, and he kept his eyes low. He was lost in his own thoughts, wondering where those words had come from. He had an apartment, enough food not to be hungry, a few friends, and a boss that terrified him to his very soul. Was he happy? He had long ago lost track of when someone else had cared about his happiness. Kyle couldn't even remember the last time he had looked at his life and asked if he was happy with it. It wasn't like he had any options to change it. Pay the bill, do the job, don't piss off Dempsy, and don't think of the future. There was nothing good there anyway.

"What the fuck was that?" demanded Dr. Ramon, and Kyle had to fight the urge to respond directly. "Look, we can pull this around; just tell him you think you could be happy here with a friend like him."

Kyle knew the scientist wasn't far from the mark for once. Aden was clearly aching for company and to trust someone. His honest outburst had hit home, Kyle was sure of it; he just needed to capitalize on that now, use the moment of confusion to cement himself a spot in the horse's mind. However, just for a moment, he hesitated. Something didn't feel right about using Aden's loneliness against him. Of course, Kyle knew if he didn't, they would find someone else who would. There were plenty of other actors out there. More than a few Dempsys, too.

Reaching out, he placed his hand on Aden's shoulder and squeezed. "What I do know is that it is truly good to meet you, and I hope we can maybe help each other figure it out."

Then he got the reaction he expected: an embarrassed and yet happy smile, eyes more hopeful and accepting. He had got his foot wedged in the door of the horse's heart. It was going to get easier from here on in to get close, and that is all his job required of him. Aden nodded his head in response, the gesture far more equine than human. Kyle wondered why he felt guilty. All he had done was to make contact with a lonely person; in his heart, he knew there was going to be more than just being friends. He was an employee now, almost a company man; next, he would have his own parking spot, corner office, and spot on the five-a-side soccer team. The company would want more. It is their nature: once you give a little, they want just a little more, taking and taking, until they drain everything you have, telling you all along that your job is worth it.

Not letting any of his doubts show, Kyle waved at the tray of fruit. "We should finish our meal." As he spoke, he picked up some of the mango, finding it sickeningly sweet and soft again. He left the watermelon to Aden, who crunched through the fruit with every indication of enjoyment.

"Well, it wasn't the most ideal first outing. You got there in the end." Faint praise from the idiot in his ear who almost ruined everything. Kyle knew the doctor would take any glory from a job well done as his own. After all, Dr. Ramon was his boss now; in the companies, your boss always took the credit from your achievements. "We are going to pull you out in a few. I think we shouldn't push too far on your first meeting. You will be debriefed, and then you have some time to yourself."

A little flutter of relief passed through Kyle. It had been a rather intense half hour. He knew he had made real progress, but things were still fragile. Aden had accepted him, but something told the actor that the horse hadn't just forgotten the slip-ups of the idiot doctor. The horse seemed far too intelligent to fully trust him; that would take time and removing Dr. Ramon from his ear.

"So, what do you do for fun?" Kyle asked in as casual a tone as he could manage as he finished the last piece of mango.

"Not much. I have a daily exercise routine; Bruno and I work out together most mornings, when he isn't having fun with his companion. Then I sometimes run the fence. I like running, but I really would like to try a new route," Aden replied, sighing at the end, his eyes looking at the horizon.

"Get him off the topic of outside!"

"I like to run, too. It feels good – music in your ears, just yourself and your thoughts." It was an honest statement, though Kyle never ran outside. The streets of the city were usually packed with people except late at night, and he had no desire to run in the dark. Some of his most affluent customers had houses with gardens big enough for a brief jog. Mostly, he ran at the gym, closing his eyes and forgetting everything for a moment but the music, the beat of his heart, and the rhythm of his steps.

"Yeah." Aden gave the human a slight smile and then added with a sigh, "I used to read, but, since Brian left, they haven't given me any new books."

"Well, maybe I can do something about that." Kyle wasn't sure he would be able to do anything, but if he could convince them to let him be the hero by bringing him some fully vetted and approved reading material, then he would be able to make some large strides with the equine.

"We don't want him reading," the fool on his shoulder muttered in mild annoyance.

"Really?" asked Aden eagerly, and Kyle could see the near hunger in those eyes.

"No promises, I don't make promises unless I am sure I can keep them. However, I can ask and see what I can get you." A simple truth. He was going to ask and push for it. Even if the only book he can bring in was *Spot and the Big Red Ball*, he could turn that into a victory.

"Thanks. I appreciate whatever you can get me," replied the horse with genuine enthusiasm and warmth.

"Hey, I'm here to be your friend, and helping each other out is what friends do, right?" This time, Kyle realized he had pushed too far; he had been too trite. No blaming the fool in his ear on this one. Aden just nodded, but the human could see mistrust in those eyes. He had said it himself: life sucks, and anyone who tells you otherwise is selling something. The horse wasn't in a purchasing mood.

"Why did you pick me?" Kyle asked suddenly, changing the topic quickly to try and get Aden's mind off his slip up.

The horse shrugged. "Not sure. You just seemed nice." Kyle wasn't sure if it was just paranoia messing with his mind, or if the horse had slightly stressed the word "seemed".

"I guess it must be hard to know who someone is from a video and a file," the human replied. At least he knew who had some say in it.

"Yes, but you were my third pick out of fifty." The horse gently tore the human's ego to shreds. He hadn't even been the first choice, just top three, a bronze place actor.

"What happened with the other two?" Kyle tried to ask the question casually. If they were Dempsy's boys, too, he knew they would not have gotten off lightly, given how much stress his agent had put on him.

"They . . . turned down the job, I am given to understand." The human could detect more than a hint of pain in that voice. It hurt to be turned down; to have your friendship refused by two paid actors, that probably stung.

"People are stupid. Try not to take it personally. Their loss, as far as I am concerned." Probably a little too trite again, but Aden reacted with a smile. Sometimes, a little sugar worked; other times, you got rotten teeth. It all took trial and error to know the right level with each client.

"Why did you take the job?" Once again, the question came out of the blue to smack the human in the face with a splash of ice cold water.

The voice in his ear had been silent, and, as he opened his mouth to respond, Kyle saw why. Dr. Ramon was just heading into the yard; the scientist had left his post to come collect him. The last few minutes, he had been unsupervised, although he knew he would have been recorded. "Honestly? I need the cash, and this job seemed like it might be worthwhile." Another honest answer, though not the complete truth. He accepted the job, worthwhile or not; saying no was far scarier than yes. Though if Dempsy hadn't been a factor, the job was interesting enough that Kyle probably wouldn't have said no. There were far less pleasant jobs out there.

Aden accepted his reply with a simple nod. "Looks like our time is over." As he spoke, the horse shot a rather malicious look at the approaching scientist.

"Hello, Aden. I have come to collect Kyle; he will be back tomorrow," Dr. Ramon announced as he reached them both. Kyle noticed the horse's ears twitch. Aden didn't respond, turning his back on the doctor silently instead. "Still not talking to me, huh? I thought after I got you a new friend, you might have changed your mind."

The actor bit his tongue as anger rose inside him. That stupid fuck had come out to try and score points with the horse, at the same time reinforcing just who Kyle's employer was. The moron was pissing over Kyle's hard work. It was a stupid, infantile attempt to regain something that he was never going to get. Aden was no longer a child; you couldn't give him a shiny new toy and expect him to forget you burned the old one he loved.

"Well, I suppose we had better go, then," the doctor added and made a gesture for Kyle to follow him. The horse remained stationary, not glancing in their direction.

"I will see you tomorrow," Kyle muttered softly and then lowered his voice to add, "Alone." He knew that the doctor would replay the recording and hear it. He didn't care; let the fool complain about it afterwards. Right then, he saw Aden's ears twitch, and the horse turned ever so slightly to look at him. The actor took it as a good sign and gave Aden a wink, making sure to use his left eye so it would show on the recording. Then he left, following the scientist mutely as he hoped things would get easier soon.

However, "easier" was not in the stars for the next half hour, as the good doctor debriefed him on his performance. Kyle took most of the critique calmly. He knew it would do no good to argue; the only reality a boss cares for is the one they create in their own minds. He did his best to gently point out how he had turned things around, he had made a connection; he bit his tongue to stop it adding, despite your best efforts to make him hate me. It was clear the scientist had a selective memory. Maybe when he reviewed the recordings, he might actually realize it was Kyle that had saved things.

As the debriefing was drawing to a close, Kyle made a request that apparently was akin to kicking a sleeping bear: he asked if he could select a few books.

"Don't you listen? I have already told you several times: we don't want him reading." Dr. Ramon positively growled at the actor with the exasperation of a not so patient teacher talking to the idiot child who has knocked over his paint pot for the third time that day.

"I heard you, but surely, if you guys select the books, it'll be okay," Kyle replied, appealing to the scientist's vanity and challenging him in one quick retort. If the scientist said no, he would be admitting he wasn't clever enough to find a suitable title. "I mean, I'm just an actor, but you guys are some of the smartest guys around; you could figure out which books could do no harm, right?" It was a heavy-handed hammering of his point, but Kyle was proud of it as he watched Dr. Ramon's face twist. He particularly liked the use of smartest; it sounded child-like, implying the other was his superior in Kyle's mind.

Sure enough, the doctor smiled and shrugged his shoulders. "Well, look . . . maybe. I will give it some thought, see if I can come up with something you can take to Aden. I would need to get it approved by Dr. Salter first, though; no promises."

No promises. That was exactly what he had used on Aden. It was, at its heart, a simple way to actually imply that you promise something while leaving yourself the ultimate get-out clause. However, Kyle knew it was also the best he could get, and he had no intention of pushing his luck or the good doctor any further. Well, not that day anyway. He thanked the scientist and retreated back to his own room. Dr. Ramon said someone would be along "at some point" to give him a tour of the areas of the facility he would have access to.

Chapter 3

Kyle sighed with relief as he sank down into a chair. He had slipped back into his own clothes and out of the company scrubs. After a few moments of reflection, he reached up to his ear and lightly rubbed the transmitter; he closed his left eye and very carefully peeled the device off. He didn't know what he could expect to learn from looking at it; he wasn't a techy, but he had friends who were. They would probably love to get their hands on company gear like this. Of course, he was not going to be so stupid as to let them see it. He knew exactly whom he could trust, and he looked at them all every morning in the mirror.

His mind slowly turned over the day, Dr. Salter, Dr. Ramon, and Aden. He wasn't sure what to make of it all; it was an opportunity too good to back out of. There was one thing for sure, it wasn't going to be a simple job. Nothing about the last few hours had been simple. What was worse, he was going to have two full days more before he got to go home. With a grimace, he realized he hadn't brought anything more than the clothes he was wearing along his credit chip and comm device, both of which had been confiscated on entry to the facility. Company guys, they trusted just as many people as Kyle did, maybe even one fewer.

Aden. What a strange creature; he seemed like something out of a cartoon, so unreal and yet very, very real and present. Alert, too; earning his trust was going to take more than a tray of fruit, even without Dr Ramon shackled to him. Pulling that fool's deadweight would slow Kyle's progress a lot, and he knew it. He had to find a way to get out from under the scientist. There would be a way; he had to be careful, though, company guys were tricky, and, if he did it the wrong way, he might end up replacing one deadweight with another, heavier one.

The actor's thoughts were disrupted by a loud knock on the door and a female voice shouting out, "Room service, I have a mint for your pillow." Kyle glanced around the room, except for the pile of his scrubs on the floor the room was pretty much spotless. Then he remembered Dr. Ramon had mentioned someone giving him a tour of the areas he was permitted to use.

With a sigh, he replaced the device in his ear and pulled himself to his feet. A few seconds after the knock, he opened the door. A grinning face was the first thing he saw; the knocker was far shorter than him, maybe five and a half feet if he was being generous. Dressed in a lab coat hanging open to show a t-shirt with a print of something Kyle vaguely recognized as from a band he struggled to remember the name of.

She was also wearing jeans around her slightly pudgy hips. The actor was impressed; very few people who could afford treatment were confident enough to keep a few extra pounds on. Most people caved to the social pressure to keep their figure at the more socially acceptable trim size. A couple of quick treatments, and all those pounds could be gone, but then, in the second he had to look, Kyle had figured out a lot about her.

First of all: her joke, very un-company like; humor is tricky and what is funny to one person is offensive to another, save it for your friends, not your co-workers. Her accent had been almost non-existent, so she had gone to a good school, which told him her parents were high up the company. Jeans and a small band t-shirt, he was sure she would love the band and their music totally spoke to her, however, her clothes spoke to him she wanted to be a rebel. He was willing to bet somewhere she would have either a butterfly, dolphin, or maybe a tiger tattoo, somewhere she could hide it easily but see it when she wanted to remind her that she was her own woman and a free spirit.

Kyle couldn't help but smile; a free spirit, but only lightly brushing against the confines of freedom permitted by the company. She was a rebel in her mind only, maybe sometimes she bent a rule or two, but she hadn't ever seriously broken a rule. All of this information, Kyle absorbed in a heartbeat or two before she said, in a voice far too perky to be a real rebel, "Hey, so you are the new stable boy, huh?"

The actor smiled; he understood the reference to his job, he had guessed someone would have given it a joke name, but he gave a fake look of confusion. "The what?"

"The bloke who looks after the horses," she announced with a chuckle. Kyle joined in with her laughter; it was a weak joke, but she seemed friendly enough, and he could use a friendly face or two if he was going to work there for any length of time. Her use of the word "bloke" surprised him; he'd only ever seen that in vids, but it hinted at either a British or Australian upbringing.

"Ah, yes . . . I suppose I am, name's Kyle." She would already know his name, but it was good to offer information freely even when it was already known or unimportant; it helps establish trust quicker.

"Well, Kyle, I'm Becky, nice to meet you," she replied with a warm smile. "So how did you find Dr. Ramon?"

Little alarm bells rang in the actor's head. He knew everything he said or saw was being recorded. "He seemed nice enough, though, I am still getting used to him and all of this," offered Kyle with a small shrug of his shoulders.

"Ah, personally, I find him to be a bit of a cold fish, a pervy fuck, though. I mean, my face is a clear foot above my tits, but he isn't ever looking above the shoulder, you know? The dirty fucker." As Becky went on Kyle's eyes went wide, and he pulled a few faces as he tried to let the woman know about the transmitter without saying it out loud. "Oh, that reminds me, I have this for you." As she spoke, she pulled a small tin out of her pocket. "It's for your transmitter so you can have some form of privacy while off duty. Though we will have to leave the eyecam in, it'll dissolve in about a week, until then . . ." The little woman stepped closer and looked directly into Kyle's eyes as she finished. "No looking at him in the shower; you dirty fucking cunt. Oh, and don't forget to sign the card for Raymond, his daughter's name is Alice. I put it on your desk, a few creds for his gift would be nice, too, you cheap cunt."

Becky laughed as she saw the look on Kyle's face, a cross between admiration, shock, and concern. He quickly realized he had gotten her wrong; she wasn't someone willing to just push things up to the line, she was willing to run up to the line, squat down, and take a piss on it while swearing at you. He took the tin from her hand and quickly pulled the transmitter from his ear, locking it away before the short, dumpy woman could drop another atomic c-bomb; the casual use of the c-bomb confirmed his suspicion about her origins.

Still a little flustered, the actor placed the tin on the small bedside table in his room, noticing that Becky wandered in uninvited. "So, you were going to give me a tour?" ke asked as he finally got his voice back.

"Oh yes, of all the areas you are allowed while off duty. Well, this is your room, you are allowed in here." The woman waved at the room vaguely. "Now, if you will follow me, I will give you the grand tour, and please keep your arms and legs inside the facility at all times." Another terrible joke, but Kyle smiled to hear it; the woman was clearly completely unfazed by the insults she had been recorded throwing at a guy, Kyle assumed, was her superior. It meant one of two things: Becky's parents were very high up in the company, or she was just plain insane. Kyle wasn't sure which, and he wasn't sure which one he preferred either.

As they walked through the corridors, Becky kept up a long monologue, a mockery of tour guides everywhere. She swore almost constantly and never stopped with the bad jokes. Kyle didn't have to pretend he liked her, because by the time he reached the mess hall, he had already developed a good dose of affection for her. It was too mesmerizing not to like her; she spat in the face of social convention with a smile, she introduced co-workers by her own personal nicknames for them; they always introduced themselves again as Dr. Such-and-Such. Kyle stored their names and noticed which ones smiled and who grimaced at Becky's behavior.

As they passed the fifth poster Kyle had seen along a very small corridor, the actor couldn't stop himself commenting on it. "How do they know they've knocked off ten years and two months from the Mars terraforming efforts?"

Becky rolled her eyes and shrugged her shoulders. "Oh, there is a lot of really vague math behind it. Really, this one-hundred years away thing is all just bollocks. The truth is, we are between one-hundred to three-hundred years away. If you want to start a fight in this place, just ask any two scientists to give a figure and watch them try and defend their theories. At least this one is kinda positive, you should see the shit we have in our lab. I mean, you can't, you aren't allowed in there."

The dumpy lady leaned a little closer and lowered her voice, "I spilled half a tube of a sample once, and, the very next day, there was a poster on the wall saying that 'one spill delays full colonization by one month, be vigilant'. Personally, I don't buy into the whole overpopulation problem. Birth rates across the world are falling, so I think we'll level out before we wipe ourselves out . . . probably."

The actor looked at the poster and the one next to it. This one had a family sitting on some grass with the Earth in the blue sky behind them, 'We can colonize Mars if YOU make it happen!' Feeling suitably motivated, the two moved on, although the motivation was more a desire to never read another poster than to put in an extra hard day's work. This, of course, is the traditional result of any workplace poster designed to motivate the work force.

"Alright well, this is the mess hall where you can eat. Through that door is the garden, where you can sit out should you want to, assuming it isn't fucking raining. Right, now the tour is over. I'm going to grab a bite to eat, if you want to join me," Becky announced, making her way past the tables towards a long counter that Kyle could see a selection of high-end food packs on.

All processed, of course; it made food last longer, cheaper to transport, and cut down on bad things like food waste and food taste. Too much flavor was a bad thing. It gave people the false impression that life could be good, and companies didn't want to get people's hopes up; they might start asking questions and wondering if they really needed that new, upgraded super deluxe entertainment system.

Kyle followed Becky, grabbing a couple of protein packs and a fruit one, only for the woman to dump several sweet snack packages onto his tray. "You need the fucking sugar and fat, it's good for you . . . well, not good, but come on. It is your first day, and this shit is free. Take some back to your room. I do all the time, despite the cunty emails they keep sending."

Free, unlimited food? There was a perk Kyle could literally get his teeth into. Food wasn't cheap; in the harsh, densely populated cities, it was not uncommon in the poorer areas for enough food to live on to be more expensive than your rent. He picked up a few extra packages. Some jobs had offered free food before; however, Kyle had been looking his employer in the eye, well mostly the eye, and it was hard to take advantage of someone fully when they were looking right at you. With a company, the actor didn't feel guilty or even uncomfortable doing exactly what Becky recommended.

With food packages piled on their trays, the two found a table and sat down, and Kyle took the opportunity to ask a question that had been sitting in his mind since they arrived in the mess hall. "So, the tour is over, there is nowhere else I can go when not on duty?"

Becky shrugged her shoulders and replied, "Pretty much everywhere is off limits; top secret work, you know. Of course, I am sure you could always spend more time in with Aden. They have a full gym and a huge outdoor area for the subjects. I suspect they might want to try and get some free extra hours out of you. It's a company job you've taken. They have people whose job is to try and figure out ways to get extra work out of others for free. Human resources," Becky pulled a face, "Ugh I hate that term, but let's face it: these days, humans are the cheapest resource available. "

There wasn't a word of that last part that didn't ring true to the actor. He picked up one of his food packages and took a bite. They really were high-end quality: they had almost no chemical sting on the tongue and minimal aftertaste. However, after a lunch of real fruit, Kyle really couldn't enjoy them. Instead, he decided to see if he could get some more information out of his tour guide. "So, what is it you do here when not giving such comprehensive tours?"

Becky gave him a smile as she finished chewing her mouthful. She paused for a second, and then, just when Kyle took another bite, she replied, "Oh, I'm a sperm sucker." Kyle snorted and almost choked on the small mouthful. He could see from the mischievous look in her eye that she had planned that. At least he hadn't spat over a second person that day, he told himself as he swallowed. Spitting over employers was bad for business; well, unless they specifically asked for the service.

"A sperm sucker?" The actor had gotten used to Becky enough to know this would be a nickname and that she would need very little encouragement to share the details.

"Okay I am a research associate whose main function is to take and ensure the samples taken from our specimens are appropriately preserved, diluted, and I spent a huge portion of my day mixing sperm with ova." She replied with a smile, clearly content that her joke had worked. "I check for conception and monitor for deformity. Should things go well, which they almost never do, I get the vet in to implant it in one of the female horses. Not exactly what I thought I'd be doing once I got my second PhD, but hey, as Daddy says, 'working with Dr. Salter will look good on your CV.' That's what most of the lab staff are thinking. Well, that and free fricken food."

"Well, I must say the free food is one perk I hadn't expected," Kyle admitted as he finished his first package and opened a second, a far sweeter, less healthy one, a nice mixture of honey, chocolate and nuts. It was indulgent, but he rarely got to indulge, and there was something about sitting with Becky that made him want to say "fuck you" to the rules and especially his diet.

"Oh, there's Kazzy. She is Bruno's current companion. I should introduce you, you will definitely be around her a lot." Becky waved at a woman who had just entered, and Kyle turned to see whom she was waving at. Kazzy stood out as much as he did, the only two not wearing a labcoat, possibly in the entire building. Well, except the security guards on the gate. She was a tall, attractive woman, chestnut hair matched perfectly with her hazelnut skin. Dressed casually in a deep V-neck T-shirt that just so happened to show a little of her ample cleavage and some shorts that were cut off just ever so slightly shorter than was normally socially accepted. From one actor to another, he could see she was trained; nothing about her appearance was accidental. It was all designed to be attractive and suggestive. She achieved the perfect balance needed to separate herself from society without giving the appearance of being easy. Her appearance was an invitation to look but not touch, at least not yet.

Kazzy gave a smile that was far warmer in appearance than Kyle sensed it was. She glanced at him, and he felt it. He was being examined. She no doubt was reading everything she could about him. To some, it might seem disturbing to be inspected that way. It lasted only a second or two; to Kyle, it was nothing more than two professionals getting the measure of each other. Fortunately, there was no conflict here; they both already had the job. Something about the look in her green eyes told Kyle that was a good thing. He had fought dirty more than once, and he sensed so had she. This was not a woman to piss off. She would smile, oh so beautifully, while she slipped a knife into your back.

She was also heading their way. Becky greeted her with such genuine warmth that, for a moment, Kyle wondered if it was an act. Surely, nobody was that accepting these days. "Kazzy, it's great to see you. Please join us. This is Kyle, he is Aden's companion."

"Nice to meet you, Kyle, it's Cassandra to you," the woman said. Her voice had a soft accent, a gentle Hispanic twist to it. It also held enough edge to it that Kyle had no doubts that calling her Kazzy was not a good idea, for him anyway. No handshake was offered, but then none was expected. Kyle had no doubts that this woman was going to be highly professional. Which, given their profession, meant that she wouldn't hesitate to plough through him should she think there was an advantage to it. He returned her warmthless warm smile and gave a slight nod in acknowledgment. He knew that he would go right through her if he needed to as well.

Fortunately, neither of them saw any advantage to it then. They also wanted to retain the friendship of the seemingly oblivious scientist at their table. After another bite of her food pack, Becky asked, "So, how is Bruno today?" Just for a moment, Kyle thought he saw a softening of the actor's expression.

"Energetic as usual, in a good mood, I believe," Cassandra replied, taking a nibble from the edge of her food pack. Kyle spotted her nibble for what it was; a practiced motion she was trying to be endearing. He had done the same when eating with some clients, once he had the measure of what they were looking for in him. Small things, tiny aspects of body language. They made the difference; they turned a one-time job into a repeat client.

"Oh yes, that horse has a lot of . . . energy to waste." Becky replied with a laugh. "I remember after his last companion left, we had a week before Kazzy arrived. Poor sod got so lonely, he started flirting with me. Well, if you can call what he does flirting. He is very . . . direct."

"He is gentle, though," Cassandra replied quickly to Kyle's slight surprise. He detected a note of defensiveness in her voice, maybe even protective. "A simple client to deal with and very easy to please, added to a good contract with some ample bonuses, and you have the best assignment I have had. Hell, with the money I have earned so far, I will be able to buy out my contract in a year."

For a third time that day, Kyle almost spat out a mouthful of food, an unforgivable sin in such austere times. For a moment, he remembered him, Esteban, the warmth of his smile and the sweetness of his poisoned whispers. His moment didn't go unnoticed; Cassandra had her eyes fixed on him, a smile on her lips, the same smile a lioness has while her teeth are in your throat. She proved her willingness to bite down with her next question, "So, how long do you have left on your contract?" Becky couldn't know how big an insult that was; in their profession, there were some questions you just didn't ask.

The scientist was looking at him, expecting an answer, and then Cassandra gave a fake gasp and put her hand up to her mouth. "Oh dear, you're a lifer, aren't you? I'm sorry." Anger rose inside the young man. He forced a smile onto his face and shrugged his shoulders. She had said "lifer", what she meant was fool, sucker, mug, idiot, and moron. He had been young and abandoned, Esteban had known that; hell, he had looked for it when picking him. His first love, he'd used Kyle just to escape his own lifetime contract with Dempsey. A life spoiled for a spoiled life.

"What's a lifer?" asked the oblivious Becky with honest curiosity.

"Most agents' contracts have a set period where your services are theirs for exclusive trade; a lifer has a contract with no end date," explained Cassandra with a whisper, hushed enough that a fool or innocent might think she was trying to be kind by not letting them be overheard as she shared out his misery. "You could try recruiting."

"Indeed," Kyle replied curtly as, internally, he swore that Hell would raise to Earth, the oceans would boil, and civilization would burn before he ever went out recruiting for Dempsy. He would find a way out of his contract; hell, the old man couldn't live forever. Unlike Esteban, he had standards and morals, maybe low ones, but there was a line. Finding some young, lonely boy just about to hit manhood and showering him with praise, gifts, and attention. Building up his confidence, only to burn it all the second he got what he wanted . . . Fuck them all, he would never do it. "I think I might go get some sleep. It's been a long eventful day." He got to his feet as he announced his departure, signaling to Becky that she could stay seated; he would find his way back.

Before he left, he nodded at the slightly chunky woman. "It was nice to meet you, Becky." Kyle didn't give her a chance to reply. He avoided any eye contact with Cassandra. Another complication he could have done without. From what Becky had said, he would probably end up spending a good chunk of his time with the other actor while doing his job. That was fine by him, he could bite his lip and keep his opinion to himself while on the clock. He had no doubt she would do the same. Just like him, she wanted to keep her client's opinion of her as high as she could.

He flung himself at his bed when he reached his room, placing several food packs on the small bedside table for later. It felt like the end of one hell of a long day, he had started at 5 a.m. over a thousand miles away in his tiny apartment. Not quite ready to sleep, he roused himself from the comfortable mattress and pulled his clothes off. Without a moment's hesitation, he jumped into the shower, turned the heat up as high as his skin could take, and closed his eyes. The room filled with steam as he blasted the dirt of the day away. Washing away the confusion, fear, anger, and awkwardness of the last few hours. Tomorrow, he would be on again, earning his crust. He would be whatever he sensed Aden wanted him to be.

The wrinkles on his fingers told him he had probably abused the shower enough, and reluctantly he turned the flow off. Just as he finished drying himself, there was a knock at the door. He struggled to pull his pants on in a hurry. Kyle guessed it would be Becky. She probably wanted to know why dinner had ended so abruptly. While he was pulling on his shirt, he pressed the door button, only to come face to face with Cassandra. For just a split second, the two stared at each other, her eyes dipping low to his exposed chest. She wasn't interested in him, that much he was sure. She knew how to get what she wanted if she had an iota of interest; she would have been sweeter than honey earlier. No, she was just checking out the competition again.

"Is there something I can help you with?" Kyle asked, his voice cool, and he had no intention of adding any fake warmth.

"I just wanted to apologize for earlier. I know it's rude to ask. I just . . . Well, the other girls this place has hired all came from my agent, so I assumed you had as well." As an explanation, it was lacking. Kyle assumed her agent never asked for unlimited contracts. There were a few who didn't; they said the practice was a little immoral. Like the dealer who sells pot and E, but, oh my god, they would never push crack, and, just like them, the hypocrisy was unpalatable. It also was no excuse. Cassandra clearly had known what she was doing, she had pushed him to see how he would react. "Look, we are going to have to work together for a while . . . most likely, anyway. So, I just hope you can accept my apology and we can get on as professionals."

Kyle pondered the pause and the slight question of the length of their working relationship. The implication that he might be on shaky ground was evident, then the penny dropped. She was scouting for her own agent, trying to get a little extra by pushing out a competitor and claiming a finder's fee. He gave her his best beaming, shit-eating grin and shook her hand firmly. "Absolutely, as professionals." He put as much fake sincerity into his voice as he could, laying it on as heavy as possible to ensure she heard the fakeness. He looked her right in the eye and held her gaze confidently; this was competition he could handle. It was business as usual when dealing with other professionals.

He could tell by the look in her eye she had received his clear 'I'm not going anywhere, bitch' message. For just a split second, he thought he spotted just a hint of respect in her eye and smile. Then it returned to the business-as-usual fake warm smile. "I look forward to working with you. Now if you'll excuse me, I could use some sleep. Good evening."

"Good evening," Kyle replied as he closed the door. As soon as he was sure she was out of earshot, he let out a laugh of relief. It was nice to end such a strange day on something so familiar, something he could handle, even in a strange situation and uncomfortable environment. He would be careful around Cassandra. He wondered if she was smart enough to be careful around him. Dempsy would pay one hell of a finder's fee if Kyle landed him another lucrative contract.

With that happy thought running through his mind, he laid down. His mind began to wander as he thought about what would happen the next day. It was strange to realize that of all the people he had met that day, the one he was most looking forward to seeing again was his client. Aden had seemed genuinely lonely and sweet; the best and gentlest of clients often were. Good people who were just looking for company. He knew that it wouldn't be easy to fully earn Aden's trust, but he had made a start today.

There was a connection at least, even if it was tenuous at the moment.

With a little work, he could secure it and make it stronger. However, there was one obstacle in his way: the idiot in his ear and ey., If Dr. Ramon continued to help him, all might be lost. It was going to be a tricky balancing act if the idiot doctor was going to keep making suggestions. The man clearly lacked people skills. Probably not something you develop easily in the lab, where it is all down to equipment and precision. There is little given in those situations, you get it right or wrong, unlike people where there is a world of grayscale between the black and white.

It was with thoughts of the next day, of what he could and must do, that the actor finally fell asleep.

CHAPTER 4

NIGHTMARES; THEY WERE nothing new, and yet that somehow made them worse. It had been a few weeks since Kyle had last suffered from them. That was his own mind, letting him think he was free, just to ensure that when they returned, he would feel the full brunt of their ghastly glory. His comfortable mattress was tossed in, absorbing the pressure of a squirming human perfectly, as you would expect of a high-quality soft furnishing. His sheets absorbed the sweat pouring off the human as he ran in his dark dreams.

There is no escape, you cannot outrun yourself, your fears never tire, and facing them is not so simple as the parents and psychologists of the world imply. Kyle had learned young standing up to your bullies did not earn their respect; if anything, their contempt for you grew as they showed you how weak you are, how insignificant.

With a cry, Kyle woke, sitting bolt upright, panting and shivering. His hands clenched the sheets tightly, and then he turned his wrists slowly, he tried to resist, but he knew he would have to look, he always did. Eyes moved unbidden down to his clenched hands and then across his right arm to his elbow and just above inside the series of marks, black, circular scars. They were easy to cover, but then that had been the point; just a T-shirt was needed along with empty promises and something sweet.

His hand snatched up one of the food packets he had placed on the nightstand, and the sweet, processed goodness calmed him down. Within a few seconds, he was able to bury the panic once more, focusing back on the present; the past was unchangeable and the future malleable. It was the potential of the future that had kept him going these past years, since he grew up and signed his contract.

His eyes caught the clock; it was just seven in the morning, early, certainly early for the young actor. Most of his work was in the evenings, late nights and later mornings had become his habit. It wasn't healthy according to the newsvids, but then what was? Much like any industry, medicine and health were filled with millions of professionals working to further one goal, increasing their bank balance. Look hard enough, and you can find the answer you want, some justification, and then it was simply a matter of ensuring the newsvids took the one key conclusion of your research and ran with it. Nobody who mattered would read the rest, everything was bad for you, everything was good for you. The information piled up, contradiction was rife until it was all white noise. A man could go mad trying to figure out what was truth in a jumbled mess of science and pseudoscience.

In a world where nothing is certain, there was a wonderful, secret freedom: there was always someone saying something you want is right. Kyle had found that freedom and had decided just to ignore all the advice. He exercised to keep himself fit and because the simple physical exercise gave him a clarity thinking rarely did. The actor couldn't afford to overeat, although some of his clients indulged him it was not often enough to be an issue. Something he knew he might have to keep an eye on in a long-term contract like this one.

As he got to his feet, he realized nobody had given him a time. He knew he was expected to spend eight hours with Aden, but which eight hours? For a moment, the actor wondered if he was actually free to choose. However, as he showered, he realized that Dr. Ramon was hardly one to give an employee that much freedom. Every aspect of these creatures' lives was planned out in detail. He might just be some playmate, but his role had been carefully scheduled; of that, he was sure. He would have to find out that schedule and then see just how much of it he could change to suit his needs.

When he finished his shower, he realized he didn't have a clean change of clothes. Had they bothered to tell him the job started today, he would have brought some with him, not to mention made arrangements back home. Of course, he wasn't rich enough to own a cat. He would just have to hope Venus could survive without water for a few days. The only other living object in his small personal world, a Venus fly trap plant. A client had given it to him. Kyle had received many trinkets over the years, but the plant was a rather weird one. Sadly, not even in the top ten of the weirdest gifts he had received, some of them made him shudder.

It hadn't been a gift, it was an obligatory 'here, try and keep this alive'. A challenge for someone like Kyle, yet he had managed, getting it enough light and water; he'd even fed it a couple of flies. However, Venus had shown him she could catch her own; it had been a strange thing, watching a fly struggle hopelessly against the crushing weight until it succumbed to the inevitable.

With a shake of his head, the young man pulled on a clean pair of horrible scrubs. They were clearly intended for him anyway. Then he wandered out into the hall, he could see the security cameras on every corner, and he knew he was nowhere near alone. So, he found it easy to resist the temptation to explore, usually a giddy, secret thrill when left unattended in a client's house. He was always careful, and he never stole. Dempsy had strong opinions on stealing from clients He would rather steal from his employees; it was risk free to skim a large chunk off the top.

However, Kyle still liked to look; pictures of loved ones, treasured gifts, trinkets, and gewgaws. One day, he had found a series of hand-painted cards, not just hand painted; finger-painted. It was strange to imagine his client as a loving or loved father. The discovery had shown the actor a side of the man he would never know. Strangely, it helped; seeing his clients as people made his job more palatable. There would be no looking today, the cameras were visible for a reason. These days, they could be tiny pin pricks, yet security cameras were deliberately visible. They were there to say, 'someone is watching you, don't get any ideas.' A pity; one rummage around Dr. Ramon's office might have helped him seem like a human, not a moron.

Kyle made a direct line for the mess hall. Nobody follows the rules better than someone being watched; individuals that break the rules in full view were rare, although he did know a few. Those individuals were ones he treated with caution. People who no longer care if they got caught tended to bring others down with them. Becky was such a person, or close to one anyway. Although, so far, she only seemed to be breaking rules of etiquette and behavior, no actual laws. Kyle knew it would only take the right situation or opportunity, and she would break a law or two.

The actor was disappointed to not see her when he arrived in the mess hall. She may have made him nervous, but she was friendly and open in a place that felt anything but friendly or open. Instead, he took a tray and helped himself to some food packets and an apple. Oh, what a glorious treat it was, to see a bowl of the fruit just sitting on the end of the counter. Leftovers from Aden or Bruno or just a treat for the staff, he didn't know which. Free, fresh fruit, it was like finding a winning lottery ticket, not the jackpot, just a few credits. One apple costed roughly what the actor would spend in a single day on food; the free food job perk had just been upgraded in his mind.

Biting into the fruit, he found it sweet and crisp, the natural sweetness so much better than the slightly chemical, fake taste of processed food. He chewed slowly and thoughtfully, savoring the taste and texture of the fruit. Just as he swallowed his second mouthful, he spotted Dr. Ramon hurrying in. Or more accurately, 'definitely not hurrying' as his hair was a slight mess and his clothes were not smoothed down. He was trying not to pant, putting on a decidedly fake air of nonchalance.

It was clear, despite the rather poor attempt to look natural, to Kyle that the doctor had gotten ready in a hurry, say for example because security alerted him to the actor emerging from his room. The company was obviously desperate to get Aden happy and productive. No doubt the second his face had showed up on camera, his boss had been roused and pushed to work, pushing Kyle to work.

It was still a hard concept for the young man to grasp. Not the physical concept, but just the "why" this would be so valuable. He suspected there was something else hidden, driving the need to keep this project alive. That, or Dr. Salter held more sway over the board than Kyle thought likely. It was possible, he had heard before of vast sums being spent on projects with no tangible benefits, especially research and development. He remembered a news article he read once which said a large number of research and development projects don't make a profit. However, it was difficult to know which ones will and which ones won't as the practical uses of research may not be fully known for years or decades afterwards.

The doctor made a good show of getting breakfast, though he proved it was a show when he missed the bowl of apples. Kyle had seen every other member of staff take one when they went up, the good doctor had just a few food packets. The actor took another bite of his green, crisp apple and kept the smirk firmly off his face as he watched the doctor give a fake shocked look as he 'caught sight of the actor'. A six-year-old could have pulled off the show with more conviction, the doctor clearly wasn't going to commit to the role.

Still, he did give Kyle a smile as he sat down opposite. "Good morning, how did you sleep?" Kyle had to award the doctor a point or two for not starting with 'so, ready to get to work, we have a horse to milk', although the latter half was more of a Becky line. The good doctor would never say anything so direct; he would use the words "extract" and "sample". It was amusing to see the science types trying to dance around such a basic biological concept.

"Very well, thank you," the actor replied and took another bite of the apple. It was a challenge to not smirk as he saw the doctor's eyes focus on the fruit and then dart back in the direction of the food selection. Apparently, fruit was not a daily occurrence, and the actor could see the inner battle between the desire to get a free treat and the need to do his job raging in the doctor's eyes.

"Aden is already up and breakfasting as well. If you are an early riser, then it could easily be arranged to have the two of you breakfast together from now on." Apparently the job won the battle, the doctor choosing to push Kyle to see if the actor would do more.

It was actually an appealing prospect. Aden and Bruno were clearly well looked after, and Kyle was sure their breakfast didn't contain any processed, baconish-flavored food packets. "I don't mind, but you guys are the client. We have a contract, so whatever you want." Just because it was appealing was no reason to let them think they were doing him a favor. Though, as he finished off his apple, the actor found his mind wandering back to the horse. Aden had seemed nice. If it hadn't been for the doctor's voice in his ear, he would have probably enjoyed himself, at least a little.

"Well, I definitely think it will help him bond to you to eat together more, so if you don't mind . . ." Dr. Ramon replied. It wasn't too unusual for the actor's employers to be nervous about giving him a direct order, at first. It was the honeymoon period, or more like the first five date period; when you have just met and are desperate to leave a good impression. Kyle knew he should make hay while the sun was shining, because it wouldn't be too long before that period ended and Dr. Ramon got comfortable telling him exactly what to do; most clients got there in the end.

"For today, maybe I should start soon," the actor offered, partly because it was clear the doctor was desperate to ask him to get to work, and it was getting uncomfortable to eat with someone with such a clear agenda. Although in his mind, he was wondering if there would be any more sweet treats. Having found the best perk of the job, the actor wanted to find out just how deep the well of fresh fruit went and was it just fruit; some vegetables or nuts would be nice, too. Hell, with the money the company was spending on this project, there was a prospect of actual meat.

The environmental cost of raising animals in land and methane production meant that all meats were highly taxed. It was rare that Kyle would splurge out on something like a burger or some deep-fried chicken. Though he had been fortunate to have a few clients who took him out to places he could order a burger. Those were good days and jobs, he usually put a bit more effort in for those clients. Both as a thank you and as incentive to ensure repeat business and the chance at further perks.

"Wonderful, I will get the equipment ready," Dr. Ramon replied as the tension left his body. Well, some of it, anyway. A man like him was always under pressure, Kyle could see it in his eyes. A man trained to think too much; he never stopped thinking, making the future an endless maze of pitfalls and problems. It could be both a blessing and a curse, really depending on the individual's confidence. Confident people planned, and less confident people just identified the problems and worried about being blamed for them, usually by confident planners.

The doctor grabbed his tray and turned to go. Kyle gave a friendly nod of acceptance of the plan. However, the actor remained fixed to his chair. He knew he would have a long and weird day ahead, and he intended to face it one a full stomach. Or at least an unhungry stomach. "I will see you in your office once I have finished." It felt good to say no, to tell the doctor what would happen. It was even better when the man nodded his agreement and walked off. Dr. Ramon was oblivious, but Kyle had just taken a tiny element of control from him.

There was no hiding the chuckle he had when the doctor reached the door and suddenly turned and walked quickly to the food counter and snatched an apple from the bowl. The man glanced around as if to see if anybody would challenge him for going back. Nobody cared or noticed beyond Kyle, who finished his own apple and then started in on his food packets.

Kyle finished the rest of his breakfast quickly in peace. Then he stopped by his room, replacing the earpiece and bemoaning the scrubs he was stuck wearing. He didn't even have a change of underwear with him. No, he was wearing some horrible company-issue boxers that had been lain out for him. It wasn't the first time a client had provided underwear for him to wear, but the others had really wanted him in them. The actor was pretty sure the company didn't care how they looked on him. Somehow, that made Kyle feel worse.

Shaking such thoughts from his mind, he headed out, reaching Dr. Ramon's office quickly. The door opened just as he arrived, and Dr. Ramon stepped out. "Great, there you are. Are you ready?"

Once again, Kyle couldn't help but notice how desperate the scientist was to push him to work. No pleasantries, no 'how was your breakfast? Did you sleep well? What did you think of insert name of sports team games last night?' Just a very simple 'get to work.' Although Kyle knew it could be far worse, and the truth was he was actually slightly looking forward to it. Aden had seemed interesting and interested in him, too. Except for Becky, he got the distinct impression the rest of the staff wanted as little to do with the actor as possible. No doubt due to the job he did, nobody wanted to discuss the obvious and straightforward role the actor was there to fill.

"I have my earpiece in," Kyle replied. There wasn't really any more he could do to get ready, unless the scientist asked him to do something more specific.

"Ok great, Aden is still lingering over his breakfast. We are going to try and get a sample today. I will warn you before the tech arrives." Kyle braced himself for what he expected next. Good jobs with nice perks usually have a grim side. The more they pay, the more they expect you to do, to give, to sacrifice. It was simple business, you get what you pay for, and you damn well pay for what you get. The only part Kyle struggled with was how the more money you had, the easier and cheaper everything seemed to get. "We really need you to do your best to encourage him to co-operate."

'Encourage him to co-operate.' The actor mulled over those words and the tone the scientist used. He was surprised at the lack of double meaning. He could read nothing more into the expression on the scientist's face than he wanted Kyle's verbal support. "You want me to . . . help take the sample?" The actor put as much suggestion into the subtext as he could. Given his line of work, that was one wordy subtext.

"Oh no, we have technicians who use a device for that," Dr Ramon replied with what Kyle interpreted as a reassuring smile. "You don't need to do that . . . unless you want to, that is. I mean, your contract pays a small bonus for each sample he gives. So, if you think you could . . . expedite matters, then you may try to."

"So, you really just hired me to keep him company?" The words came out far quicker than the actor's brain could edit then.

"Well . . . yes. I mean, Bruno has shown a preference for his companions . . . taking his samples, more directly. Aden has not previously shown any interest in . . . giving his samples that way." The doctor's blush as he spoke of such things amused Kyle. It wasn't entirely uncommon for some of his clients to feel nervous about talking directly about such things.

Taking pity on the man, Kyle changed the topic to something more comfortable. "Okay, I am ready. When do we start?" Although in that back of his mind, he wondered what he would do if he ended up taking a more active role with Aden. Maybe he could close his eye, protect the poor, blushing man from seeing something that might upset him. Although the devilish part of himself would probably want to ask the guy some questions. As Kyle's current employer and boss, it would be amusing to watch the scientist squirm if he asked him for a performance review.

For a moment, Kyle found himself wondering at how little the idea bothered him, but then he shrugged it off. A client was a client. You did your job, and you tried not to let it bother you. At least until you were out of the room and had time to shower. The prospect of helping Aden make a donation to the Mars colonization effort was surprisingly low on the list of his job concerns. Okay, the guy might be part horse, a claim most human males would kill to have so long as they could pick which part, but he had seemed shy and gentle. The latter part was an ideal in any client. There is something wonderful to be said for a gentle man; not to be confused with a gentleman, who in Kyle's experience were often anything but gentle.

"Right now would be best. Aden is still alone, and you can have some time together before his exercise regimen and then his afternoon run." The relief was heavy in Dr. Ramon's voice; talk of anything even marginally sexual seemed to make him uncomfortable. Kyle wondered how he had managed to get assigned to a project which involved so much uncomfortableness.

"Okay, which way do I go?" Kyle asked, ready to get on with his first day, grab the bull, or horse, by the horns, as it were.

"Back to where you met yesterday, then the door on the right." The doctor replied, adding for good measure and as a not so subtle reminder, "I will let you know if you go the wrong way."

The actor nodded and left without a further word. It didn't take him more than a minute or two to get to where he had first met Aden. He took just a moment to enjoy the vista. Another perk of the job, one he doubted the company employees truly appreciated. However, he was ever aware of his boss on his shoulder, and he didn't linger.

Locating the door on the right was as easy as it sounded. Dr. Ramon was quiet in his ear, something the actor was grateful for. He stepped inside a smaller version of the staff mess hall. There, sitting at a small table alone, was Aden. Kyle noticed Aden's ears perk up as the human entered, a curiously cute gesture. The animal gave him a smile, just a small one and a nod of acknowledgement.

Kyle took that as an invitation and approached quickly. "Good morning, did you sleep well?" He asked as he slipped into the seat opposite the equine.

"I did, how did you sleep?" Aden asked before he took a bite out of an apple. Kyle couldn't help but notice a couple of apple cores on a plate in front of Aden. Kyle had eaten the core of his apple, why waste good food? Of course, he knew plenty of his clients were far more accustomed to fresh fruit than he was. He made sure not to stare at the waste.

"Not bad, it took me a while to fall asleep, new place and everything," the actor replied casually. Small talk, it was important to make it feel natural and not forced. It put people at ease and eventually led to far more interesting conversations.

"I . . . have never been to other places," the horse was staring at his apple as he spoke, the subtext of the whispered statement was so obvious, it was practically jumping up and down in Kyle's face.

"Stop him thinking about other places," the voice in his ear demanded. Dr. Ramon may as well have asked the actor to pull the moon out of its orbit. Kyle was just as unable to do that; one of the few things you can't do is control a person's thoughts. However, if you are careful and clever, you can guide them gently to new thoughts.

"I have seen a few," observed the actor, savoring the frustrated 'hurmmmpphh!' sound the doctor made in his ear. The actor was confident he was on the right path, though, as Aden's ears had perked up and the horse was looking at him, practically begging with his eyes. He had a way in, all he had to do was share a little bit of himself. Normally, Kyle avoided that, but special circumstances demanded special reactions.

"You have?" The words 'tell me more' may as well have been painted over Aden's forehead.

"Yes, when I was growing up, we would move around a lot," as he spoke, the human leaned back in his chair, relaxing. He was surprised that Dr Ramon wasn't screaming in his ear. It was possible the scientist wanted to see where Kyle was going with this. Of course, it was also possible he was just giving the actor the rope to hang himself with. There was little anyone could teach Kyle about the perils of being hanged. "I lived in New York for a time, Boston and Chicago as well."

"Oh wow, that must have been amazing." The horse enthused, and Kyle couldn't help but smile a little. He had the animal by the curiosity. He knew he could lead this horse to water; the question was can he make him think or stop thinking.

"I suppose, well not really. There is a difference between being a tourist and living somewhere," replied the actor. "I never got to see the Statue of Liberty, the Empire State Building, or any of it, really. All I saw were crowded, dirty streets." Kyle knew he was dangerously close to losing the pony. You have to tread careful when stamping a person's dreams; they tend to hate you for it. "Don't get me wrong, I had a lot of fun, just life is never what you expect it to be. Same goes for places. What you read about is usually one person's opinion, and yours will be vastly different." Kyle heard a grunt of approval from the scientist in his ear, at least he took it as such.

"I suppose, I just want to make a few opinions myself, make my own choices like everyone does," Aden couldn't help but look crestfallen. "I've never even left the compound; this cage is all I have known."

"Cut down all the trees and put them in a tree museum. Then you charge the people a dollar and a half just to see them." Kyle muttered softly, looking at his hands as if struggling with internal thoughts. He looked up into a confused equine face. He knew the sudden change had been enough to get the pony by the curiosity, a dangerous grip on any male. "It is the words from a very old song. My old English teacher used to quote it. It was quite prophetic, really. It was three years since I last saw a tree, walked on grass. My last school trip. I know I could visit any of the nature parks at any time, but it costs credits, quite a few. So, I don't go. I live in a room about a sixth the size of this, in a block of hundreds. Your cage is far prettier than mine."

"Ah, but you are free to leave your cage at any time. I am a prisoner," retorted the pony with a knowing smirk. Kyle smiled, he could see the knowing smile of someone who thinks he has won.

"Oh indeed, I can walk out anytime I want, except where would I go? You cannot just walk out of the city. It costs. If you stay outside too long, the police track you down by your biochip, they fine you, and take you back home. I could move cities, trade one tiny cell for another, I suppose, but that would mean breaking my contract, an expense I might never be able to afford. Which in turn means I couldn't work." The sadness dripping off his tone was all too real for Kyle, but he knew it would stimulate sympathetic feelings from Aden. It was another way in, the fact that his words were too close to the truth for comfort was merely something he would have to live with. "Which would mean I wouldn't be able to pay rent, buy food, and soon would end up on the streets. Then I would be taken away and put on a work program. Less than five percent of those who start a work program ever get off one; living in a dormitory, bedtime, worktime, meal times, all dictated for your own good. It's the *humane* way."

Aden was stunned into silence, and Kyle took this moment to reach out; he put his hand on Aden's. The pony jumped a little but didn't pull away. Kyle looked him in the eye and said with absolute sincerity, "I don't blame you for hating your cage, but, please, don't hate me for looking at your cage and saying I wish it was mine."

The horse didn't say anything in response, but he did place his other hand over Kyle's and squeeze. Kyle looked up into the equine's friendly eyes. He could see the genuine concern and contrition there, and a little bit of him felt ashamed for using his life to manipulate someone who seemed to be a good person.

"That was just perfect!" Dr Ramon crowed in his ears. The actor knew he had scored points with both the horse and his employer. It was a masterstroke, and maybe someday, he would be able to forget the dirty feeling he felt for it.

With a soft sigh, Aden eventually took his hands off Kyle's and stood up. "It is time for my daily exercise."

Kyle sprang to his feet and forced a smile onto his face. "Great, I could use a workout, too, if you don't mind me joining you."

"Of course not, it would be . . . nice." The actor couldn't help but notice the slight pause in the sentence. Aden seemed to be warming to him, so he was sure the sentiment was mostly genuine. However, there was something worrying the horse, possibly to do with the others who were going to be exercising with them, the horse's brother Bruno.

Bruno turned out to be everything Kyle was expecting and a little more, certainly in size anyway. He was a good few inches taller than Aden, broader at the chest, and far bulkier muscles. His fur was pure black, not a hint of any other color. He reminded Kyle of an Arabian stallion he had seen in a movie once. His eyes were dark green, and they stared at the actor with malicious intent from the moment he and Aden stepped in the gym.

It was clear to Kyle the dark horse would try to confront him in some way and soon. Kyle also noted Cassandra dressed in some rather tightfitting, stretchy running shirts and a sports top that barely contained her assets, though he made sure to do no more than glance in her direction. Just a slight nod between the two actors made the black horse's nostrils flare. Bruno was using a weights machine next to the treadmill his companion was running on.

The gym was as well-equipped as Becky had claimed. He could see almost every bit of equipment he had seen at his gym and a few extras. Each machine was sat by an identical twin, clearly just in case the subjects both wanted to use the same equipment, or maybe so they could always be near their companions. Aden made for a rowing machine. Kyle followed, suddenly realizing his loose scrubs were hardly fitting for this sort of exercise.

Pausing for a moment, he wondered if he could ask one of the techs, observing from behind two desks in the corner of the room making notes on electronic pads, if they could get him some clothes he could work out in. Then a flash of memory came back to him, of the last time he had forgotten his sports gear. It had been at school. His coach had but one line to say, "If you've got no kit, you will have to do it in your pants." It was a bad idea, with Bruno clearly acting like an alpha male, but part of the actor wanted to rise to that challenge. He may not have muscles like the horse, but he had turned more than a few heads and more in his day job.

Aden froze as he grasped the handles of the rowing machine and looked up to find his companion almost naked in front of him, a pile of scrubs around Kyle's feet being kicked to one side. The actor could feel the hatred of Bruno's eyes boring into him. He desperately wanted to turn and wink at Cassandra; he knew the actress would be as businesslike as ever and would not have batted an eyelid when he stripped. However, he also knew he was treading a fine line, and that if things got physical, Bruno would make minced human of him, while the company would probably sue him for potentially damaging their property.

Still, it was nice to see Aden pause and his jaw drop. Kyle's body was a damn fine specimen of the male form; after all, it was what his customers paid for, and he liked to pride himself that he provided quality. At least it was something he could be proud of. He did give Aden a warm smile and a wink that he was sure Bruno couldn't see. Then he parked himself on the rowing machine next to Aden and quickly set in a program and started pulling, Aden started his own workout a few seconds later. In the corner, the technicians made some notes on their pads, and Kyle couldn't help but wonder exactly what they were noting down.

Less than two minutes into the rowing program, and the sun was blotted out by the shadow of a large, muscled equine towering over him. "I want this machine now." It wasn't a request, it was a demand. Bruno's voice was far deeper than Aden's. Like him, he didn't have a strong accent. His pronunciation was clear and crisp, like someone who has had a lot of elocution lessons.

Kyle knew exactly what this was, the alpha male desperate to exert his superiority. It was almost caveman-like. How strange it was to see such a base human reaction in someone not human. Kyle gave a friendly smile. "Okay, I'll finish my set after you." He knew most likely this would not be the end of it. It all depended on how far the alpha male wanted to push things. Looking into those wild green eyes, he saw someone who got his way almost all the time. A base animal like Bruno wouldn't care about leaving and new experiences; he would want food, fun, and companionship. All three of which were happily provided for him by the company. Still, he had to try.

The actor climbed off the machine and made for the generous set of free weights provided. "Bruno doesn't like you." Dr. Ramon's brilliant comment was as useful as it was insightful.

"Yeah, I think we all noticed that. Got any ideas on how to make him change his mind?" Kyle asked. His expectations were rock bottom with the doctor, but it was just possible they had dealt with this situation before and learned from it.

"He's a bully, just stand up to him, and he will back down," a useless platitude from the General Custer approach to bullies. Sure, that might work if they were both twelve and the bully was about his size. They were both fully grown, if not matured, and Bruno clearly was looking for a reason to match up physically, to show everyone his superiority. Standing up to him would be to give him what he wanted. The actor could let him chase him all around the gym, but that idea didn't sit well with him.

When he bent down to pick up a set of dumbbells, an all too expected shadow fell across him. Kyle turned to see Bruno towering over him, the sweaty beast stank of a mixture of horse and human musk. It was both unpleasant and oddly attractive. He always did have something for large, powerful men; he enjoyed the feeling of a large protector around him. Of course, Bruno was a threat, not a protector.

"Let me guess, you want the dumbbells, too?" He asked with a friendly chuckle. The horse didn't return it and just nodded grimly.

With a choice of fight or flight, Kyle chose to go for secret option number three. It was a trickster option, and its success would depend on just how much the black horse wanted him out. "Alright, you can have the dumbbells, too. I get the feeling, big guy, can I call you big guy? I mean, you are the biggest guy I have ever met." The sudden change of tack momentarily confused the larger male. He wanted to say no, and yet the name 'big guy' definitely stroked his ego in the right way. So, he didn't resist it, nodding his head.

Taking the momentary confusion, the actor stepped up to the horse and leaned up to whisper, "Look, it's okay, I get it, she is yours. I mean, it makes sense, right? You like women, she's a woman and your companion. However, did you ever think why she was chosen for you?" Bruno blinked, his eyes flicking to Cassandra who was watching the exchange with ice cold eyes. Kyle knew she would get the horse to tell her everything he said to make sure he wasn't undermining her. Still, the horse was no longer glaring at him, but staring at her, with little love-stricken puppy eyes. Kyle put a friendly arm around the horse's back. Physical contact, it was important. It established a bond quicker, and Kyle knew time was of the essence.

"It's because she likes men, like you. Now Aden, he doesn't like women, not like you do, right?" Kyle asked, knowing the answer. He could see the wheels turning in the black horse's mind. They were slow and rusty from lack of use. Typical alpha males never use the muscle between your ears, and all the other muscles work so much better. "So, why do you think they chose me to be his companion?"

The large horse gulped; it had been years since his last lessons from his tutors. They had stopped trying to teach him years ago. "Because . . ."

"Yes, go on," Kyle whispered, his voice as cheering and encouraging as he could make it. He sounded like a father cheering his child to start riding his first bike without support, pressing him to make it on his own.

"Because you . . . like . . . Aden?" Close enough, the actor thought.

"Yes, exactly! Damn, strong and smart, Aden is lucky you like girls, or he might have a challenge on his hands." the actor's voice was pure honey as he patted the pony to celebrate his triumph, letting his hand slip ever so slightly too low on his buttocks for Bruno's comfort. The black male shuddered, and Kyle pulled away his arm with a smirk. "What I am trying to say is, I am not interested in stealing her. She is all yours . . . so long as you just want women." He gave Bruno a suggestive wink as he said the last part and was rewarded with a look of pure confusion. A direct confrontation, he could handle, but flirting, he wasn't mentally prepared for, so he chose the flight option and gave a contrite, embarrassed nod before fleeing to his own companion for comfort.

Kyle's parting shot was possibly a little too much, but he couldn't help himself. "Talk to you later . . . big guy." Bruno didn't turn. He just trotted a little faster back to the far less confusing presence of Cassandra, who pulled him aside to whisper fiercely at him. The black bulky beast stood in front of her, shuffling his hooves like a tiny, confused child telling his mother what the other nasty children had done to him.

The rowing machine being free once more, Kyle returned to Aden, flashed the blonde pony a triumphant grin, and returned to his exercise program. A few minutes later, Cassandra and Bruno made a quick exit. Kyle knew the actress would want to confirm Bruno's devotion to her, and the horse would want to affirm his own masculinity. The actress was likely to be a little annoyed, but he was certain the large horse would stop treating him as a threat, and that made it worth it.

With the gym now theirs, Aden and Kyle worked out in peace. Although the actor couldn't help but notice the horse stealing glances at the actor's body as they worked up a healthy sweat. Kyle would have to admit he found himself admiring the equine's form, elegant lines and tight muscles rolling over each other and glistening in the sunlight. The shine from his glossy fur and the rather cute way he flicked his mane in triumph as he completed each set made it hard to keep his eyes away. The doctor had said little in his ear beyond a minor well done on his dealing with Bruno.

There wasn't much talk, a few words about exercising. Though Kyle felt comfortable in the silence, Aden was definitely accepting him; despite his fears and the doctor's useless dead weight around his neck, he had been successful.

As he approached the treadmills to finish off his workout with a run, Aden grabbed his wrist slightly hesitantly. The pony looked at him a little shyly. "It's a nice day, I normally run outside if it isn't raining." It was as clear an invitation, or maybe even an instruction, as the pony had given his companion since they had met.

"Okay then, let's go run outside. You show me the way," Kyle replied with a smile.

Aden led him outside quickly and then paused. "If you can't keep up, let me know, and I will slow down for you." The pony said sincerely, and Kyle's masculine pride brindled at the implication he might not be up for the challenge.

"Alright, and once I know the circuit, you let me know if you need me to slow down for you," the actor replied with a good-natured smile and a challenging wink. He could see a gleam in the horse's eye. It would seem that, despite being the gentler of the two, Aden was just as capable as his brother of being a macho male. Not that Kyle minded; a little good-natured competition between friends was a good thing. He could let the pony win and feel much bigger and stronger. It would help their relationship grow.

With a snort of delight, Aden took off at a challenging pace. Kyle followed, hot on his heels. He had to admit, following the horse had its perks; in the form of two wonderful golden mounds rolling against one another as he ran. The swish of Aden's tail serving only to keep his attention down low on those naked buttocks.

The circuit was rather pleasant; the facility's outside had a generous, fenced-off area covered in meadow grass and wildflowers. There was even a few trees, no charge for looking this time. With the warm noonday sun starting to beat down, the actor was glad he just had boxers on, the fresh air keeping him cool. He hated to admit it, but the pony was setting a difficult pace. However, as they completed their first lap, he pushed himself a little more. It was time for him to run in front and for Aden to stare at his tail, metaphorically speaking anyway.

The second lap at the increased pace was a warning to the young male. His legs were already starting to ache, and he had no idea how many laps Aden usually ran. He could hear the soft clop-clop of the equine's hooves on the dry dirt path they ran on. The actor knew nobody else used these grounds. Aden had set his own circuit the circumference of his world, and the pony ran around it several times every day. Just him alone, maybe sometimes with Bruno, cutting a dirt path in the grass through years of running. Maybe the cage wasn't as nice as it first appeared.

Any thoughts of the circuit evaporated when those clopping sounds suddenly grew louder and Aden trotted past him, barely breathing hard. Kyle gritted his teeth, refusing to accept defeat. His adrenaline surged, and he caught a second wind. It blew him past Aden a few seconds later, taking them into their third circuit.

Aden neighed out loud and snorted as he charged passed the human again; it was no longer a friendly run, it was a race. Kyle had no idea where the finish line was, but, even with his muscles on fire and his lungs burning, he was not ready to concede defeat. He rose to the horse's challenge, charging after the equine, grunting through gritted teeth.

Round and round they ran, passing each other again and again. It was Kyle who would fall first, quite literally as his tired foot missed its step and he slipped over. Aden stopped as he heard the human cry out in pain. The horse trotted back. "Are you ok?" Kyle had the satisfaction of hearing the heavy panting in the horse's breath. He knew even if he had lost, he had pushed the equine to his limits.

"Nothing damaged but my pride," Kyle assured him, taking the offered hand and standing up, only to feel some pain as he put his foot down. "Owww, I think maybe I have a mild sprain."

"What do you want me to do? Do you need me to get help?" The concern in the equine's voice was heart-warming. Kyle couldn't remember the last time anyone had genuinely cared about his well-being.

"I'll be ok, I just need to sit down for a bit and get my breath back," the human replied, smiling at the concerned horse.

The two hobbled onto the grass beside the dirt path, and Kyle sat down, Aden joining him in the grass a few seconds later. The equine sitting down right next to him, Kyle leaned against the horse almost on instinct. Blonde fur scratching lightly on his sweaty skin. It wasn't an unpleasant feeling, far from it; it tickled and tingled. He enjoyed the warmth of the body next to his, and he didn't notice Aden put an arm around him. It was just so natural and expected, he laid his head on the equine's chest.

Leaning more and more against the strong body, Kyle closed his eyes. The strong scent of sweaty equine musk filled his nose; much like with Bruno, he found it comforting and in no small measure arousing. The more he leaned into Aden, the more the horse pulled him close, holding him with both arms, his furry palms lightly stroking the human's stomach while Aden nuzzled his hair and neck, hot equine breath flowing over his exposed flesh.

His own hands had slipped down onto Aden's legs, stroking over the muscles, still hot from their exertion. With gentle strokes along Aden's thighs, Kyle explored the texture of the fur, the feel of the skin. He could feel the equine stirring behind him, and, more than that, he could feel something stirring inside himself.

It was a wonderful moment, a connection, and Kyle knew that a connection had been formed between them. However, before they could see where the connection led, a voice interrupted them. "Okay, Aden, it's time for you to give a sample. Are you going to be a good boy?"

Kyle felt the pony tensing under him, and their moment was shattered by two ill-timed buffoons and a sample cup.

"Help them get a sample," a voice he had forgotten about instructed in his ear. Aden had already pulled away and gotten to his feet, backing away, his hands held up defensively. Kyle knew there was no way to take a sample, not without destroying everything he had achieved over the last two days. So, he did nothing.

"You know I won't until you bring him back," Aden stated, his voice quivering with a mixture of doubt and anger.

"Oh come on, we got you him, didn't we," the lead technician said, much to Kyle's pure fury. The buffoon of a tech was destroying his connection right in front of him. That kind of statement might work on Bruno or a child; however, with Aden, all it would do is highlight Kyle's real purpose.

The lead technician was a middle-aged man, balding but with a comb-over that showed he hadn't accepted it yet. His body was rather thin, and he was supported by a young woman half his size. The two of them clearly couldn't force Aden to do anything. So far, they had showed that Aden and Bruno were valuable to risk injuring, but Kyle wondered how long it would be before they sent in someone capable of extracting a sample by force.

"Hey, come on, he doesn't want to give a sample today. Why don't you two just leave the container, and, if he changes his mind, he can provide one?" It was hard to know who was more shocked: the technicians who gawked with slack jaws, Aden who gave Kyle a look of pure gratitude, or Kyle who was trying to figure out if he would be allowed to gather his clothes before he got fired. Still, he had stepped in now, and there was no backing out.

With his choice locked in, the actor stepped forward and held out his hand, "Just give me the cup." He took the plastic pot from the unresisting hand of the lead tech. The female held up a device Kyle was all too familiar with, although this was a larger version.

"In case he needs it," she muttered as Kyle took it from her. The two beat a hasty retreat, leaving the horse and his new hero.

There was no time for Kyle to revel in the horse's adulation as an ominous, deadly serious voice spat in his ear, "I think we need to talk, now!" Kyle knew that the choice was hardly his; it had been a spur of the moment decision, one made on instinct. Not that it would matter, not to his employers or to Dempsy if he lost this contract. With a sigh, he dropped the cup and device into the meadow grass, crushing several flowers as they thunked to the floor. It had been such a good start to the day as well. He had had an apple for breakfast, it looked like crow for dinner.

Chapter 5

Home, it's where the heart is. Kyle had often wondered on that saying. If his heart wasn't at home, did he still have one. Maybe, the events of the last day certainly proved he had something left. He wasn't sure it was heart, more like stupidity crossed with stubbornness. Protecting Aden had not gone down well. Dr Ramon had been really pissed off when the actor got to his office. Kyle hadn't even been allowed to dress. It had been many years since some had given him such a dressing down. Well, who wasn't a client enjoying a part of his service.

Looking out of the window of the company car, he wondered how he had let things go so bad so fast. "What the hell do you think we pay you for? Do you have any idea what you have done? You think we are going to get a sample anytime soon when he thinks you support him? You know what we are trying to accomplish, how important it is!" The doctor's voice had gotten louder with each question; his finger was wagging like some school teacher dressing down a naughty schoolboy. Then that finger had started to poke his chest with each point. Then at the end, he had pointed to the damned poster on his wall, as if accusing Kyle of pulling humanity from the very stars single-handedly. "Aden now thinks he is in the right. That you will protect him."

"Yes, he trusts me more now," agreed the actor as calmly as could, the growing tap on his chest making his ire slowly burn. He was a full grown man, not some child.

"No! You know he is just going to be that much more angry next time when you turn on him, all that work getting him to like you. Now you have pissed it away. Cause next time, you are going to have to try and help." The prodding grew worse with each word that finger poked, his chest getting slightly sore.

Kyle had known it was only a matter of time before he exploded back at the scientist. So, he had done the best he could, dipping into his rage early before the fire became a volcano. Cutting loose with a few pointed comments of his own. "Work?! You did nothing but feed me stupid lines . . . tell him his cage is pretty, tell him to just be happy . . . oh, and watch out for Bruno, his hugely hormonal, potentially violent brother. Yeah, you were soooo very helpful." On reflection, he could see how childish those words had been, pointless, too. All he had done was stick his face into the hornet's nest to yell; naturally, he had gotten stung.

The two had stopped listening to each other and were engaged in a full blown screaming competition when a large bucket of ice water had been thrown on them. In the form of Dr. Salter arriving to ask questions. His presence alone was enough to shut them both up. Kyle had been told to leave and get dressed.

That had been when he knew things were not going to go his way. Dr Ramon would give his version of events first. The doctor was competent enough to have gotten a position this high up in a company. You didn't get this far without knowing how to play the political game, at least a little. It wouldn't take much to swing this against the actor; after all, he was just someone they pulled in off the street, with no real skills. At least, not in the sciences. The two doctors would be able to relate.

A quick shower, and then Kyle had put his own clothes back on. He had a feeling he wouldn't be allowed to say goodbye. Sure enough, a security person had arrived, and Kyle's heart had plummeted. He didn't put up any argument. After all, what would be the point? The security officer couldn't change his fate.

A nauseated feeling had settled in his stomach as he thought of what Dempsy would say. A shiver had run down his spine when he realized that what his agent said would not be one thousandth as bad as what he did or had others do. The actor was lost in a sea of misery. It was then that a lifeline had been thrown.

Dr. Salter had been standing by the car. He dismissed the security guard with a nod. "Kyle, behavior like you demonstrated today will not be tolerated." It was a statement of fact, and the actor knew he was in no position, so he just nodded. However, hope was flowering inside him; if he was fired, then he would have never seen Dr. Salter again. The fact the man was there meant there was hope. "However, I have seen some of the recordings." Kyle tried not to wince as he thought of the edited low-lights his boss could have shown him.

"I don't necessarily agree with all of what Dr. Ramon has said or asked you to do." Kyle could almost guess the words that were coming next. "However, he does have some good points. We employed you to help keep Aden compliant and productive. I think you have shown you can do that, if you choose to."

Kyle nodded his agreement, not daring to speak lest he fuck up. Besides, he knew that the doctor would want to pontificate. If it meant avoiding the wrath of Dempsy, he could pontificate until the cows came home. Any words were good words, as long as they weren't 'your services are no longer required.'

"Tomorrow was going to be your day off, so I thought we could send you home early. A little space for you and Dr. Ramon might be the best thing right now," Dr Salter advised, and Kyle felt himself releasing a deep breath he hadn't even realized he had been holding on to. He felt like a prisoner granted a free pardon. He was not going to be fired. A small part of him realized that he would get to see Aden again. Had he not been so wrapped up in the flood of relief, he might have thought it strange that his first thought was of the horse.

"Thank you," he said, his words full of sincerity. "I really do appreciate you giving me another chance."

"Indeed, although I will be watching things more closely from here on," the scientist said in a serious tone. It wasn't exactly a surprise. Still, it was a stay of execution. At least until the next time they tried to get a sample out of Aden with him present. That would be the next big challenge.

"Understood," Kyle replied with a nod.

Dr. Salter gave the actor a slightly condescending look; like a teacher who thinks their students aren't really capable of grasping the enormity of their massive intellect. "Good, now the car will take you back to the drop off. Another will be there to pick you up Thursday at 6 a.m. Please ensure you are there promptly. It is a long journey, and, no doubt after today's display, Aden will be very keen to see you again."

"Yes, I will be there on time." That much would be the easy part. Turning up on time was simple; figuring out how to balance the needs of the job while gaining the trust of his charge, that would take finesse and some thought.

A few seconds later, Kyle had climbed inside the hovercar, and it had shot off. The actor kept his eyes on the horizon, barely noticing the sonic boom. There was no driver; human pilots made mistakes, or more mistakes than computers anyway. There were parks where people could go and enjoy the thrill of driving in a safe environment. Kyle had been a few times. It was fun; that momentary illusion that he was in control of something. However, it was a rare treat, usually after a particularly big or well-paid contract came through. Or just when he needed something in his life to make him smile.

He watched the Rockies shrink away, huge giants slowly vanishing behind him. While they did, he thought about Aden. He knew that the horse would trust him more now. There had been something between them, a spark, and he had felt it. The actor blinked as he wondered what it had meant. His clients liked his company; after all, that was why they paid him. Sometimes, he liked them, as people. Many could be kind or shy or just so very human. Yet, this had been something slightly different. It was familiar, and yet he couldn't put his finger on the feeling.

The hours passed, eaten up by the miles and miles of America that flashed before the actor's eyes. On his trip out, he had felt excited. He had taken so many pictures, just because he could. His comm bracelet had finally been returned to him on his way out. He hadn't bothered to check it; he knew what would be on there. A thousand messages from Dempsy chasing how things were going, all with a slightly friendly and yet threatening tone. Along with a couple of messages from some friends, mostly asking if he wanted to go out. Dempsy would no doubt hear how things went, hopefully not until Kyle was back working. A full week for his anger to cool would be a welcome bit of good news.

As for going out with friends, he had to figure out just what he was going to do to make sure he didn't blow things. Going out, getting drunk, or even stoned wouldn't help. No, for the first time in years, he needed to get some homework done, but, more importantly, he needed a night in his own bed. In his own little flat, where he could relax without the feeling of being on display. A wave of relief passed through him as he saw Chicago looming on the horizon.

Thousands of tall buildings, with the environmental tariffs and controls preventing urban sprawl cities, had only one direction to expand. Upwards, and they had embraced the direction like a crazed lover. Buildings had sprouted like redwoods, towering so tall and so densely packed there were areas on the ground that were in permanent darkness. Dark roads that many people didn't go down. Of course, ground level wasn't pleasant anywhere in the city; even in the light areas, the air wasn't pleasant to breathe. It irritated the throat. Living on the ground floor was a sign that you had hit rock bottom, literally.

Kyle lived near one of the commercial platforms, formed from huge concourses that linked many of the residential buildings. It was a business district, but with some cheap accommodation available. The flats there were cheap to rent; buying was not possible. The corporations owned all of the complexes, and they were not happy to sell; unless you wanted to buy the entire six hundred floors and all the issues that came with them.

The car was joined by dozens just like it, flowing in approved corridors through the city. Driving lower was not permitted, autocars work better with a full range of vision in all directions. The lower they went into cities the greater the chance of collision. Some expert in technology or risk had calculated that any travel below the top hundred floors tripled the chances of an accident. So, it was banned, except of course for emergency services. That was where the corporations came in again, each building had its own security, medical and even fire departments.

With a stomach-churning drop, the car fell out of traffic, a soft beep advising Kyle he had arrived. The actor climbed out of the car and looked out over the platform. The sun was just beginning to set, setting a red glow to the uniform white of the cars and the gray paintwork. The floor was an intricate latticework of markings, showing people where it was safe to stand and walk.

Busy, crowded, noisy, and windy; Kyle always liked being up there, though. Feeling the wind on his face, the sun unfiltered and direct. It was a pity that loitering in a travel hub was not permitted, or he would have spent more time there. Just for a few seconds, he felt like a top dweller. He had been in plenty of upper level apartments, and he knew how the top half lived. Fresh fruit, fresh air, and clean corridors. Small outdoor gardens on private concourses, residents only, many of his clients would never have seen the lower floors the actor lived on; segregation by bank account, but that was hardly something new.

Moving along the marked walkway, Kyle headed to one of the many communal lifts. He was joined by a dozen or so people; the lifts were built to carry fifty or more. There was no button pushing; the lift would stop every twenty floors to allow people to get on or off. Smaller lifts would take people to their own floors. The actor leaned against the backwall of the lift.

With a few sly glances, he played the lift game in his head. Judging his fellow lift travelers, using their hair and clothing to guess what floor they got off at. He always found it interesting that the best dressed didn't always get off at the highest residential floors, where it was more costly. In fact, some people who got off there dressed fairly plainly. The best dressed men and ladies tended to be a little further down the lift shaft, dressing for success, hoping to improve their chances of passing as one of the corporate elite.

Of course, the true elite didn't need to try; however, he could generally tell from the quality of their comm devices and haircuts. They may dress down close to home, but even their comfortable clothes were of the very highest quality, and they clearly spent money on being perfectly groomed. That, of course, was the give away, the real give away. Not just expensive looking, but high quality. There was a difference, and Kyle had been employed by enough of the social elite to spot it.

So, he got to feel faintly smug as he watched the elites and then the wannabes get off in that order. Next were the workers, people who made money but lacked the talent, ambition, and probably most importantly the contacts to get higher. Competent people, with a bit of free money but no free time. Kyle had a few clients who would fit into this class, ones with little to spend money on and less time to find social contact.

The lift continued its descent, the number of passengers growing steadily fewer. By the time it reached floor sixty, there was only a couple of people left. Kyle hadn't played the game with them. No matter how obvious it is, you never want to look at a face and know that person is living on the ground floor.

He passed quickly through the public corridors of the building and then out onto a concourse. His home wasn't as bad as a surface dweller, but there were hundreds of thousands of people who could look down on him. Looking up, he could see thousands of windows in every direction, along with many concourses and balconies. Right at the top was a small strip of the sky. This far down, the sun only managed to peek in on the dwellers around midday. A brief glimpse at the sun, somedays Kyle wondered if that made things worse, seeing what it was like but not being able to enjoy it for long.

His home was a good five miles walk away. He pulled his ad blocker out and slipped them over his eyes. Glasses and headphones, technically illegal because he was walking in a corporation-owned area for free. If he wanted to walk without the virtues of the latest A.I. software or some local restaurant being whispered into his ears and images being broadcast onto his eyes he should pay. Ad blockers reduce corporate revenue, the revenue that pays for the upkeep of the concourses.

However, he was also walking in a low-security area. His chances of mugged may be tripled, but his chances of seeing a security patrol were along the same as his chance of spotting Nessie or getting invited to Buckingham Palace for tea and crumpets. Only bloodshed would bring them down, and the vids couldn't tell an ad blocker from glasses. They had been a gift from one of his friends, an actual friend and not a client; Darwin, a low-level tech engineer and part-time criminal.

It was worth the miniscule risk of the tiny fine he would pay if caught to walk unmolested. With a couple of presses on his comm device, he triggered the music on his playlist. The sounds of the street fading away and leaving him alone in the crowd. He had selected a series of purely instrumental pieces; he had no desire to hear anyone's voice.

Eventually, he walked around the building he had just travelled down from, and he could see his home in the distance. A cross section where six concourses met, a series of small businesses had grown up at the natural crossing point. The corporations had allowed them, even encouraged them to grow, offering cheap rent for even cheaper P.R. A few small office blocks and a series of small shops, bakeries, and cafes.

The residential building just next to them suffered from the extra noise of industry as well as the lack of privacy, such as when getting out of the shower. Kyle smiled to himself as he made plans to score a free muffin the next day. Or maybe he would drop the soap and see if he could upgrade to a cupcake.

He passed out of the streets and into his own building. Getting into the much smaller lift, he pressed a button and scanned his bio-chip. As the doors began to close, he spotted someone out of the corner of his eye. His hand shot out quickly, pulling the door back open as a young lady rushed towards it.

Blonde hair, face pink with a mixture of a blush and the little trot she had just ran to get to the lift in time.

"Hi, Kyle!" Her voice positively beamed enthusiasm, and the young man couldn't help but give her a smile in response. "How are things, been on any good auditions lately? I read for a new play last week. I think they have some roles for guys, too. You should see if your agent could get you an audition."

"Hi, Claire, things are good. I've actually got a new gig, gonna be out quite a lot for the foreseeable future. I'm off again day after tomorrow," he replied, mixing lies with the truth easily as you blend honey into tea. It had been a simple misunderstanding when they met. Claire was a cliché, a young girl struggling to be an actress, an actual actress. Her parents were mid-levels but supportive, as far as she had said, and she never stopped speaking.

"Oh wow! Is it a movie role? Oh, you've got to tell me!" She practically squealed her words, dancing a little in the little elevator as it began to descend. She had moved in a year ago and introduced herself as an actress. He had introduced himself as an actor. They had both assumed they meant the same thing, only Kyle had never corrected the poor girl when he realized she was genuinely looking to star on stage or screen.

"Sorry, I've signed like a dozen non-disclosure agreements, I would be sued back to the Jurassic period if I even give you the slightest hint." At least that was true. Not to mention, he really couldn't think of how he would explain what his current role was. 'Yeah, I play Kyle, the companion and plaything of some scientist's crazy animal creation. Oh, and they expect me to start milking his balls once a day. Talk about working with demanding divas, you have no idea.'

"Oh, that is no fun, but sounds like a big role. I really want to see it. You have to tell me everything as soon as you are allowed, promise me," the bouncy little woman insisted as they walked towards their respective front doors.

"Sure, soon as it is possible, I will tell you everything." Kyle didn't even think about the lie. He knew it would be easy enough, make something up, a film that had its funding cut or something. It happens all the time, or so Claire had insisted the last time he had been away on a gig for a couple of weeks. He hadn't told the truth about that one, either. It would have been easy, too, but he kinda liked the fantasy, even if it was someone else's. Kyle the actor, struggling to make ends meet and make it to stage and screen.

Opening his front door, he sighed as he crossed the threshold, letting the door shut behind him. Home, or what currently held that label anyway. A sofa that turned into a bed, a tiny kitchen that was separated from the main room by the counter. Of course, he had never used the built-in stove; it may not actually work. He lived on processed food packages and microwaved meals (for when he felt like splurging). Fresh food and ingredients were far too costly.

A small bathroom with a shower tucked away in the corner, it called to him to go clean up again. However, he knew it would be weak and that he would be wasting some of his water ration. That was another perk of the job, and one he hadn't thought of. He wouldn't be home much, so the water and electric rations coupled in with his rent would go unused and build up.

Smiling, he pulled on his display specs and signaled his computer to start up. A screen appeared on the far wall, although Kyle knew it was actually being projected right onto his retinas. Kyle sighed, knowing he should put it off no longer. "Show all new messages." His inbox flashed up quickly. It was much as he predicted: a dozen messages from Dempsy. He dictated a quick reply, putting as much of a shine on the situation as he could. Not that it would help; you can polish a turd, but everyone can still tell what it is. He stressed that he was going back and that he would make things work.

He never even thought of lying, you don't lie to Dempsy. Expected bad news was not welcome, unexpected bad news was . . . well, the man never shot the messenger. However, Kyle had seen and experienced enough to know that honesty was the best policy, because it gets harder to lie without a tongue. Not that Kyle would expect that, not even if he lost the contract, he was too young for that sort of punishment. After all, Dempsy still needed him to make money. There were other ways to punish someone, and his agent seemed to be an expert at finding a person's weak spot and poking hard.

Darwin had sent him a couple of messages, asking if he was up to hang out. The actor smiled. The poor tech was a nice guy and certainly fun. Truth be told, the stick-thin guy had more than a little crush on Kyle. In fact, the real truth was Kyle had given him a couple of little freebies between friends. He was nice, and sometimes it just felt really good to be wanted or held. Other times, well a few drinks, and, if he wasn't in the mood, Darwin knew how to take a hint.

This was certainly more like the latter. He needed to rest, relax, and put some serious brain power into figuring out just what he would do. Not that it would help that much, he knew that he could plan and scheme, but, at the end of the day, his fate was with Aden and Dr Ramon. Either one of them could break him; all they had to do was push for it. Well, he would just have to push back. It wasn't all lost; Aden liked him and had definitely seemed open to more contact.

Yawning, he sent a message to Darwin, saying he wasn't up for hanging tonight, he was too tired from the travel. He sent a couple of images he had taken on his way to the facility, partly to share but mostly to brag. After all, what is the point in work perks if you can't rub your friends' noses in them? His mind was too tired to consider playing any games. He pulled his display specs off and staggered to what passed for his kitchen.

The cupboard wasn't bare, but it was not far from it. It was hard to imagine how much he had at his fingertips at the facility. While back in his own home, he had the choice of the three least objectionable flavors of Zack Pack food. The pathetic attempt to sound cool and edgy, or maybe it was just one of the few names not yet trademarked. The brand wasn't the worst out there, by far. However, one mouthful, and all he could think of was the packs he had at the facility. Also, the fruit, mango, watermelon, and apples. Next to real food, the semi-moist processed bar tasted like he was chewing on fifty-year-old carpet.

He resealed the foil wrapper and put it away in his cupboard. Food packs may taste foul, but they last almost forever; that was why they were made. Wasting food was a terrible thing with the world population heading towards the twenty-five billion mark. The Mars plan was supposed to have solved that problem: terraform the planet and transplant billions, more space and land. Maybe even real food.

It had still to come close to fruition. There may be over a million humans on Mars, but they lived in domed cities. Although Martian cities were like tiny hamlets compared to Earth ones like Chicago. Plus, there was no government up there. The population was effectively indentured slaves. Everyone there had to work to live. You even had to pay for the air you breathed, all part of your rent. Kyle had looked into going there once, everyone does.

The romantic notion of life on another world, of getting out from under the government, of being free. That was the carrot, or maybe cheese, they baited the trap with. It was a one way-journey unless you had some serious cash to buy a ticket back. The homes of the average Martian were less than half the size of Kyle's apartment. It took someone with a seriously deranged mind to make a combined shower, toilet, and bed. Not even a pretense at a kitchen; you ate nothing but processed food the rest of your life.

Kyle had weighed the pros and cons and realized that Earth was better, warts and all. The actor pressed a small panel, turning his sofa into bed mode, and just collapsed on the blankets. He didn't even undress. He was too tired; plus, his clothes already needed a wash. A night's sleep in them wouldn't change that.

Chapter 6

There is nothing quite like waking up in your own bed after a few days away. The mattress seems to know your body; it sinks in all the right places and supports exactly where you expect it to. Kyle slept long and sound in his bed, and, for a few blissful moments after he woke up, he had nothing to do but lay still. A day off, a rarity in his line of work. He tended to work most days. Dempsy always wanted to keep him busy. However, often it would just be a few hours. The idea of a regular eight-hour shift seemed as alien to Kyle as Kyle's job did to most people. Although the idea of a regular day off was one he could easily latch hold of.

As his clock hit nine, he decided it was definitely time to get up. For a moment, he reached for his screen specs, then decided better of it. Dempsy might have written back, why spoil the morning by reading something unpleasant? So, he got into the shower instead, lingering just a little under the hot water. It lacked the power of the one at the research facility, but knowing he had water to spare made it a little more enjoyable. There was something pleasurable about staying under the water after all the soap was washed away, just watching the water he paid for spiral into the drain.

As he got out, he made sure not to look at the window with the open curtain. He never made eye contact, just got on with drying himself. It wasn't a show if they thought you didn't know it was a show. However, something told him he could count on a free muffin that lunchtime, should he manage to get the timing right. It wasn't hard: twelve-thirty on the dot, any day he left his bathroom curtains open.

It was nice to put on his own clothes, no stupid, baggy scrubs. Something a little nicer, most of his clothes were tight. It was part of the job, after all. People were not paying him to wear baggy clothes that hid his form . . . well, most of them weren't anyway. A form-fitting t-shirt and some casual pants were pulled on, it was a nice enough day out that he decided not to bother with a coat.

Before he stepped out, he stopped by the apartment's security box, a tiny little square on the wall beside the door. It wasn't big enough to hold much, just things that you wanted to be sure stayed safe and stayed yours. A quick scan of his retina and thumbprint, along with his password, and it opened. He grabbed the only item in there and tucked it into the back of his pants.

There are some constants that just never change. Just ask any physicist or mathematician, and they will tell you. In America, there was one thing that had survived almost everything humanity could throw at it: the right to bear arms. Though the right to arm bears died a long time ago, when the world's comedians got together and realized the joke wasn't funny anymore. Kyle had a small hidden pistol that he always carried. He had felt exposed without it, travelling to and from the facility. Oddly while there, he had felt very comfortable without it. Most likely because the company wasn't likely to try and mug him, hack his biochip, and steal all his credits. Everything he owned all totaled up to something all companies wouldn't give a shit about.

Although on the other hand, their constant advertising indicated they still wanted to see if they could get their dirty hands on the contents of his account. Just before he left, he swiped the biochip in his left hand and was pleasantly surprised to see his balance had increased. Quite a lot, actually. It was roughly double what he normally made in a week. Which just meant Dempsy had made a small fortune off him and would be so much angrier if he stopped that money flowing.

Putting such thoughts out of his mind, he focused, instead, on the good news. He had a day off and a virtual wallet stuffed full for once. It was time to make hay while the sun shone. Although that particular turn of phrase always confused him; surely, hay is grown and couldn't really be said to be made. Probably, he could look up the answer, but before that, he decided he would treat himself to something a little sweet for breakfast.

The business district just outside was in full swing. A few small stalls outside selling fruit, serious prices, but, for once, he could afford it. One hundred grams of blueberries, the perfect start to a day off. The guy on the stall gave him a hard look as he picked up the small punnet, almost daring the young punk to try and steal from him. Kyle gave him his warmest 'kiss my ass', shit-eating grin and scanned his wrist across the man's till. A small beep confirmed his payment, and he resisted the urge to flip the man the bird. After all, he lived close-by and would probably see him again. Especially if the money kept rolling in.

Next, he got himself a coffee, a real fucking latte, too. He'd never actually bought one for himself, but, hell, he didn't have to worry about food for the rest of the week, so why not make his one day off a good one. His drink and food bought, he walked to the edge of the platform and hopped up onto it, swinging his legs out over the edge and sipping on his coffee as he looked down. He could see the streetlights far below and people moving down there in the gloom. Poor guys, but not his problem. With a childish giggle, he dropped a blueberry down, resisting the urge to shout 'catch'.

He could see the shocked looks on the people as they walked by. It wasn't common to see anyone staying put on the concourses, they were for travelling. Someone sitting on the edge was . . . well, if he wasn't drinking a latte and chuckling, many would have assumed he was about to jump. Many others assumed he had picked his final meal and left him to it. After, all he wasn't their problem, and they had a job to get to.

Kyle hadn't sat like this since he was a kid, when he and his sister would play on the concourses. No fear, that was the key. Back then, he had no boundaries, at least not in his mind. He would get off the lifts at whatever floor he wanted. He still remembered one day sneaking into one of the private gardens on the upper floors. His first memory of grass beneath his feet, of the touch of tree bark. Also his first memory of being arrested and dragged away. His mom had been so mad, it had been a week or so later she had told him she was pregnant with his little sister. Somehow, he'd expected everything to change after that. it sort of did, but not enough.

The sweet fruit and milky coffee didn't combine well with some bittersweet memories. He finished the food and drink and then turned to watch the people on the concourse. It was a never-ending river of humans in both directions, every size, shape, race and culture walking passed as he lazed there on a sort of sunny Wednesday morning, in the summer time.

A mother carrying a small toddler walked by. He could see clutched in the young boy's pudgy hands and his mouth was a small plastic book. A book, an actual physical copy of something. They were so rare these days, a study with full bookshelves was more of a status symbol than something anyone used. Electronic copies were easier to carry and to read, except for children. For them, they were normally cheap plastic, so they could be chewed and smashed off your brother's face. Kyle remembered being hit by more than one plastic book.

He'd loved reading to his sister when his mother was out. Anna had been easy to take care of, once he learned how to duck. Food, play, and bedtime stories, then she would go out like a light. He'd had a small collection of children's classic stories on his comm back then. His sister had adored books and stories about animals. She was desperate to have a dog, but, of course, there was no way they could afford one.

Suddenly, from the depths of his memory came a story, one he had read a long time ago. However, one that might, just might get the approval of Dr. Ramon. Even if he supported sample taking, he bet Aden would forgive him in exchange for a new book. Something new for his gilded cage. Hell, it was worth the risk. However, he knew his comm would be confiscated the second he arrived. They didn't want Aden getting a hold of such devices again.

There, of course, was a solution to that, one that was centuries old. A quick search on his comm produced an address not so far away that he might find a real physical copy of the book. He paused only to place his food containers in the appropriate recycling bins, gaining a very minor payment to his balance.

His route took him far away from his normal stomping grounds. The store was located on the two hundredth floor, a shopping area for the more well to do citizens. He had been there before once, long ago with a client. It had been an interesting day and easy paycheck, just escorting the middle-aged woman from store to store, antiquing. So many objects from across the space of human history. Unlike a museum, he had been able to touch them. Somehow, tactile contact made the history seem more real; the objects were arranged more to make the best use of the store spaces than to try and force historical facts on him. So, he would learn little snippets from many different periods.

That had been a good day, yet he remembered his confusion when, by the end of it, the woman had purchased nothing. Six hours of shopping and zero purchases. Looking back, he understood he had been company for more than a couple of lonely people since then.

Walking out onto the promenade, he had to admit it was far nicer than the business district he lived beside. The sun was shining, and, this high up, it would do so almost all day. The air was clearer, it tasted less recycled; the air down below had certainly been through more than a couple of lungs before it hit his. There were far fewer people, and no one seemed to be in a hurry, wandering from storefront to storefront just browsing.

Well, he had not come to browse, he was there to buy. The store he headed to was named The Story Palace, a rather dumb name in Kyle's opinion, but he was there to buy a book, not the shop, so he gave it the merest second of thought. Then he headed inside. The smell was the first thing that hit him. The air so dry, yet the taste of must and dust. Rows and rows of bookshelves lined the walls, creating new, narrow corridors. Kyle crept down one carefully, not sure why he was trying to be so quiet. It was as if his body naturally didn't want to disturb the silent tomes. They knew more than he did.

He spent a few minutes just wandering looking at the titles, names of authors, and stories. All of them were strange to him, stranger still because he was certain no one who had written anything there would still be alive. After all, these books were antiques, little pieces of history in their own right. A thought which almost made him chuckle as he hit the history section, a little piece of history-history.

"Are you looking for something specific, or do you just wish to browse?" The voice behind him made the actor jump. He felt himself brush up against a bookshelf, and for a heartbeat, he thought he might knock it over. "Sorry, I didn't mean to sneak up on you." The voice belonged to a young man, clean and well dressed. He had a name badge announcing his name to the world 'My name is Daniel, how can I make your experience more enjoyable?' The question on the badge clearly was someone's idea of promoting customer service.

"That's okay, Daniel. Actually, I was looking for a book," Kyle replied, giving the young guy a warm, friendly smile. It was the same smile he used to try and help new clients relax around him: gentle, innocent, and with just a hint of vulnerability.

Daniel returned the smile and waved his hands at their surroundings, "Thank God, 'cos we are all out of horses." The obscure joke took a second or two to register with the actor, leading to an awkward moment of silence. "You know, 'cos we are a bookshop . . . and I honestly don't know where the horse bit came from."

"The stables?" responded Kyle with a friendly wink. That got Daniel laughing and eased the moment of tension. "Actually, speaking if horses, I was looking for a specific story."

"Great, I can search our records and see if we have a copy, or where else you could get a copy," the young clerk replied, pulling out a small computer catalogue device. "What's the book called?"

"I . . . don't know . . ." Kyle winced as he tried to remember the book, the story he could sort of remember. "Something about a horse boy," he finished lamely, feeling the heat of a blush hit his cheeks hard.

"Right . . . What about the author?" Daniel asked, his face a mask of calm, though inside, Kyle knew the clerk was crying out 'seriously! Not another one of these types of customers!'

"I don't know, it was old. Like pre-internet old and English, definitely English." The more details he added, the more pathetic and stupid he felt.

"So, something about a horse boy, by some English author, and old?" The summary of his query sounded far worse than Kyle had expected. The look of sympathy and amusement on Daniel's face didn't help.

Deciding to just lean into the pathetic-ness and embrace the funny side, Kyle replied, "Yeah. So, you have it?" The look on Daniel's face was a picture as it took a second or two to realize the actor was joking. Then he laughed, and Kyle gave a shrug. "It's not much to go on, is it? If it helps, the horse was a talking horse."

"Well, actually, it does a bit. Look, it isn't like I have much to do today, we only get a handful of actual customers a week. Why don't we head to the customer service area, and, if you tell me what you remember, maybe we could figure it out?"

"Sounds good to me," Kyle agreed and then followed the young man through the rows of shelves to a small central area. There were several large, comfortable sofas arranged around a small table.

"Okay, make yourself comfortable. You want something to drink? We have tea, coffee, some sodas, or some draft ales," Daniel offered as he waved Kyle onto a sofa.

Sitting down, Kyle found himself sinking so far into the sofa, he began to worry this was all an elaborate trap to feed another unsuspecting customer to the sofa monster. "How much for a water?"

"They are all complimentary," the young man replied with a chuckle.

"Seriously? You get a handful of customers a week, but give away free food. How do you stay open?" Kyle asked, looking around stunned.

"Eh, Os Corp likes having shops like this here, so the rent isn't much. Plus, books are more of a collector's item these days. The last sale I made was for a first edition manuscript, seventy-five thousand credits." The clerk chuckled as he saw Kyle's jaw drop and the actor look around him. "Books are serious business. Our stock goes for between a few hundred to half a million, though I suspect we will never sell that page of one of Shakespeare's portfolios. It isn't that good."

"I . . . the Shakespeare?" The actor asked, far too shocked to say anything more erudite.

"Yeah, it is in the vault, though, I can't show you that. I could show you some first edition Asimovs if you want?" The clerk paused and then said, "Or I could just get you that drink, still just want water?"

"Ale, please!"

The clerk laughed to himself and opened a drinks cabinet disguised as a bookcase. He pulled out two chilled bottles. "I think I will join you, it is almost lunchtime, after all."

Kyle accepted the bottle of ale. It was a small one, but then a free drink is a free drink. So, he took a sip, dark, malty, and bitter as the finest dark chocolate, with an aftertaste of caramel. It was a very pleasant drink. He observed Daniel drinking down his own bottle and couldn't help but ask, "Are you okay, drinking on the job?"

The clerk chuckled and sat down on the sofa. "My Dad never comes to the store, and you are the first customer near my age this year. So, fuck it, I'm owed a couple. Now the book, more details so we can search properly. More searches on the system with a customer in the store register. So, it justifies why a few drinks may have been taken."

"Dad", the word clearly gave up so much of Daniel's life. Rich parents, probably high-up company guys. The store was more likely to be some rich guy's hobby. Which he was happy to let his son run. If Kyle was a betting man, he would put money on Daniel's old man saying the job would help build character. Which maybe it had, the guy certainly seemed affable to Kyle, though somehow, he doubted that was the effect his father was hoping for. "Okay look, it starts with this boy, he's an orphan raised by a fisherman."

"Oh, nice of him," Daniel observed.

"Not really, I think he raised him like a slave, and there's this rich . . . sultan I think who he sells the boy to. Only the boy overhears himself being sold, and he . . . steals the Sultan's horse. Turns out, it's like a magic talking horse, and they run away together."

"Right, sounds pretty cool, a bit kiddy for my tastes, but fun." As he spoke, the clerk put a few search words in. With a flick of the device, he projected a series of book titles. "Ok, for slave, horse, and runaway I have these . . ." Daniel paused as he looked at the names and the short descriptions under them. "So, a lot of these seem like porn, was that what you were looking for?"

"No, definitely not porn, I read it to my baby sister," Kyle muttered dryly and took a sip on his ale. None of the titles sprang out. "They met up with another woman and a talking mare . . . seriously not porn. I think she was a runaway, too, but like a runaway princess or something, and her mare could talk, too."

"Ok, so runaway princes, horses and . . . we have a whole load more porn to pick from," laughed Daniel as he flicked up another list of inappropriate titles. He drained his small bottle of ale. "You want another?"

"Yes, please," Kyle replied, sitting back in his chair. He certainly wasn't going to say no to another free drink, the first one had been very pleasant. A second open bottle was placed in his unresisting hands.

"Ok, so you remember anything else about it, names of characters or anything?" Daniel asked as he returned to his seat.

"Hmmm names, I think Brad . . . and Sam for the horse and guy . . . definitely something with an S and a B." The actor couldn't help but laugh as the ridiculousness of the request began to hit home. Finding some ancient book from the vague details he could remember. "This is hopeless."

"It's not like I've got anything better to do with my time. It's almost lunchtime, though," the clerk observed as he tried a few more search entries, keeping the holographic screen projected for the customer.

"Oh, you want me to leave and let you eat?" Kyle asked, trying in his mind to think of where he might find some more affordable food; his breakfast had been expensive. Plus, if they actually found the book, it might cost him a fortune. He needed it that much that he was willing. Maybe it was crazy, but if the story was what he remembered, it was too perfect. It had everything that Dr. Ramon would want in it, but to Aden, it would be a gift and another sign that he could be trusted.

"No, that's okay. Actually, if you are here, I can do this." Daniel began to pull up a few different books. The names of authors and books flashing before Kyle's eyes, each one just up for a few seconds. Asimov, Arthur C somebody, Tristan, Kipling, Pratchett . . . The list went on for a few minutes. Then the clerk stopped. "Okay, now there's a load of really expensive searches. You just became a high roller. If anyone asks, I can claim I had someone in looking to spend some serious cred . . . so I, of course, pulled out all the stops. Just wait here."

"Are you sure, Daniel?" A twinge of guilt hit Kyle. Taking perks from clients was one thing. After all, they were rich and it was part of the job. It feels good to give, so by taking a gift, you are making the client feel better. Well, that was the justification in Kyle's mind. However, if Daniel was caught, giving the expensive treats to a guy who clearly couldn't spare a hundred thousand for a book. He couldn't even afford space to put up a single bookshelf.

"Call me Danny, and sure, most customers are far too stuffy, but I can't access the complimentary stuff without one in the store. Plus, it's not like my dad could fire his son." The answer was more of a shout as the excited young man disappeared. Kyle wasn't sure how to respond. He'd met a few rich guys he could easily see firing their own son. However, it was Danny's choice, and, if he was so sure, who was he to turn down anything more.

"Alright, Danny," he called and stood up, wandering around to the nearest bookshelf. His fingers brushing over the paper, such a rare thing to feel, dry and smooth. Almost everything was plastic; paper was a rare thing to find. Plastic bags, metal cans, foil wrappers, plastic knives, plastic forks, and practically plastic people. He pulled a random book from the shelf. The cover was dark red and smelled strange, leather. Back from a day where binding your books in the hide of an animal was considered classy. He sniffed softly, letting the scent into his lungs. It was actually pleasant.

Carefully, he opened the book and ran his fingers over the words. It was strange to see them fixed, almost nailed to the page. Everything he could remember reading had been on a screen, save for some plastic books he had read to his sister, with huge letters asking if he could see Spot and his big ball. This was different. These words were permanent, they were written, and they would never change. This book was one thing, unlike his comm and the things he read there, he could access any book any time. Yet somehow, the tome in his hand felt more real than the device on his wrist. It was made to be one thing, and it would be that thing until it was no more.

"Tolkien, a good copy, too, not first edition or even close to it. It's ten thousand for that book." Kyle almost dropped it as he heard the cost, and then carefully he replaced it where it had come from. Turning, he was greeted by a wonderful sight. "We have some ham sandwiches, followed by scones with clotted cream and jam. They are really good, customer needs to be looking to spend six figures for me to break these bad boys out."

"Wow, you really didn't have to," Kyle murmured, a little embarrassed, though the embarrassment didn't even slow him down. He picked up a ham sandwich. Meat, the cost of raising cattle was insane; methane tax, land tax, and a thousand other tariffs made it a very expensive food. Clients did treat him sometimes to it, and he always relished the taste, something finer and more expensive.

"Well, I get my share. This isn't entirely altruistic of me," Danny chuckled as he grabbed a sandwich. "Now let's hit another couple expensive searches and then get back to your book."

The meal was a pleasant one. Kyle was well versed at conversation. He made Danny laugh with a few risqué stories, true ones, although embellished. While in the background, the two continued to try and search for the elusive book.

The scones and cream were devoured after the ham. Kyle couldn't stop himself licking the plate clean of jam and cream afterwards while he strained his memory to think of details that might help. "There was a lion in it, too . . . I think he attacked them. He could talk, I think he was called Alan."

Danny sprayed his with crumbs and cream as he coughed. "You mean Aslan!"

Far too excited by the name as it rang true in his memory, Kyle yelled, "Yes, Aslan!"

"Any other book in the series, and I'd have got it in seconds. You had to pick the one nobody ever asks for," grumbled the clerk, and then he gave Kyle a broad smile. "Still, if that had happened, my lunch would have been a boring apple and pear food package, eaten while I read alone." As he spoke, the clerk brought up a single book on the holo screen above the coffee table. '*The Horse and His Boy*, by C.S. Lewis.'

"That's the one!" The actor practically cheered. "I think, I mean, can I read a bit? Do you even have it?"

"Yes, we have about fifty copies of various prints. The cheapest is about six-hundred, but, with my employee discount, five-hundred," The clerk's endless generosity was surprising. Given the cost, Kyle was definitely not going to argue. That book was going to cut a huge chunk out of his last paycheck. He knew that he had to make things work if he bought the book. There was no backing out once he spent that cash. Of course, there was no option for backing out anyway, so the decision was easy.

"I'll take it, and thank you for all the help," the actor replied, standing up and waving his hand over the till to pay up.

The clerk blushed and then covered his embarrassment by saying, "I'll just go get your book." At last, things really started to make sense. Danny clearly felt a little bit of attraction to him. Kyle was shocked he hadn't seen that earlier. If he'd known, he might have pushed things a little. He certainly wasn't above trading a little bit of fun for a larger discount or more customer freebies.

When he returned, the blush was gone, and yet Kyle could see the young male tensing. He knew that any second Danny was going to ask for the actor's contact details. So, he beat him to the punch, "This was fun. Look, I'm mostly out of town for the foreseeable future. However, if you give me your info, I'll let you know the next time I am free. We could hang out or something."

With the heat of a thousand suns, the blush returned to Danny's cheeks as he stammered a "thank you". He was certainly cute; Kyle would keep his contact information. Once the job with Aden was over, he might look him up. Of course, once Danny found out what he did for a living, things would certainly end. Rich boys don't take 'actors' home to meet their parents. Until then, well, he was fun, cute, and rich; there are worse people to hang out with when you have free time.

When he left the shop, the afternoon was already half over. Somehow, his day off had dwindled to an evening off, although he had no complaints. He'd spent a lot of money, ate some really good food, and made a potential new friend. With the book clutched tightly in his hand, he headed to the lift. He didn't like to carry around such expensive objects. He certainly wouldn't be able to afford to replace it. Though it was unlikely anyone would try to steal it in broad daylight. Not on the main concourses, it was down some of the smaller side streets that things could get sketchy.

Humanity is good at finding the little gaps between civilization. Areas where the security cameras can't see and where the police rarely go. In these areas, well, things could get interesting. There were a few clubs and the like around. They tended to exist near those little gaps. It was like people knew that, to have a good time, you really needed to know your every move wasn't being watched. Well, not by the security services anyway.

Alcohol was surprisingly cheap compared to most other foods. Even cheaper if you were young, fit, and willing to flirt. Of course, his little pistol really helped if some guy or girl forgot what the word "no" meant. He cost a lot more than a couple of drinks. They could inquire with his agent if they had any doubts or the credits required. Someone had tried to mug him twice, looking to force him down and scan his biochip. One detailed scan, and they could try and hack his account.

The chips were supposed to be uncrackable; that had been the promise when they were brought in. It was the law: no more physical cash, just electronic money and transfers. Everyone over the age of twelve had a chip. The politicians promised it would end crime, make all cash deals traceable, and prevent all fraud. Governments always underestimated their peoples, especially those with a criminal mind. Within a day, there were reports of biochip theft. The first ones were somewhat simplistic and gruesome. Your chip was your access to everything. Most of the victims would survive, though a few bled out as desperate criminals severed veins and arteries as they cut the chip out.

These days, it wasn't too hard to get a scanner, an illegal one, and there were guys like Darwin who could make money disappear. Not by spending it, that was a trick anyone could do. No, to make money vanish from one place and turn up untraceable in another. Although the tech insisted he never dealt with muggers, more online fraud. A few minor tricks to get some extra credits, nothing serious. Kyle believed him. Anyone rolling in money would afford better clothing, he would bathe more. Not to mention, he would have probably purchased some time with Kyle from Dempsy. It would have been much easier than the eighteen months it had taken before Kyle just said screw it one night and gave him what he was practically begging for.

Despite the nerves at carrying such an expensive book around, the trip home wasn't bad. He was out walking just before rush hour, and the streams of people had slowed to just a trickle. Within the hour, Kyle knew the tide would come in and the rivers would flow. He hated being out at those times, barely able to move, constantly surrounded by strangers, the thousand random touches of people brushing up against him.

When he passed through the business district just outside his home, he realized he had missed out on his free muffin. Well, there was surely one in the bank for when he was ready and able. Besides, ham sandwiches with scones, cream, and jam blew a free muffin so far out of the water, it was a lonely muffin in the middle of the Sahara. Plus, he had the book; the quick glimpse he had given in the book shop had confirmed it was the one he remembered. He planned to read it thoroughly that evening over the last of the food he had in his apartment.

There was nobody around inside his building, even the lift was empty. It wasn't until the door to his room opened that he found something amiss. A figure standing in his apartment by the window, leaning over Venus. Dempsy.

Chapter 7

Kyle paused for a moment. He knew that asking Dempsy how he was there was like asking how a mountain got there. No matter the answer, it didn't matter; it was there and not moving. The man himself was far from mountainous, not even five-foot-six, if Kyle was any judge. He was wearing a suit, black and immaculately tailored. He was always wanting to look the part of a businessman, for he did business.

His hair thinning on top, not that anyone had the balls to point it out to him. Maybe even his mirror lied to him, because he seemed to have done nothing about it. His remaining hair was silver grey, Kyle wasn't sure if it was a dye job. Dempsy was easily in his forties, maybe fifties. Kyle certainly wasn't going to ask to see his ID so he could check.

Slim build, and yet there was something in his eyes. A fire burned there, behind those narrow brown eyes, and it glared out at everyone, saying simply 'don't cross me.' "Ah, there you are, my boy! How are things?" The words sounded jolly, like he had just popped by to see how his friend was doing. However, Kyle was far from believing it; for a start, people checking up on you rarely break in. Besides that, he knew what Dempsy had done, to him and others. The both did, they knew that friendship was not the word to describe their relationship.

"Dempsy! A pleasure to see you again. I'm good, how are you? You look well," the actor replied. Fighting polite lie with polite lie.

"I am doing well, although I have to admit, I was a teensy bit disappointed to hear you haven't earned a bonus on this job yet," the man replied with a slight wave of his hand as he sat down on the sofa, uninvited. As if breaking into his home wasn't proof enough of his dominance, he felt the need to show he owned the actor.

Trying not to react to the arrogance of the man, Kyle wandered to his kitchen. "Oh, well it has only been two days. It's a bit different to most jobs, they haven't actually asked me to do anything. Besides, I have only had two days with him. Really, just one, the first day was just an hour . . ."

"It doesn't take long." The words held an edge a samurai would be jealous of, they cut deep. Kyle could feel the nerves in his stomach growing. "And, gun to my head, I have to say I'm a little bit worried by the rumors that you may be on a final warning after only one day and an hour with the customer."

The actor wasn't able to stop himself swallowing a little nervously as he put on his Sunday best poker face. "It's nothing, just a little bit of a disagreement with this scientist they have monitoring my every move. He keeps telling me to say and do stupid things. Aden isn't exactly a happy client, he doesn't want stuff to be happening. So, it's taking a little bit more . . . finesse to get him to accept me."

"Well, my boy, if I know anyone who can do his job with finesse, it is you," Dempsy replied, turning his attention to the plant again briefly. "This is a fascinating plant you have. I never pictured you as a guy with green thumbs. Though I suppose it might run in the family."

Every muscle in the young man's body tensed at the mention of his family. He was aware there was a veiled threat in there. "Oh, I just looked up some instructions on them. It's not too hard, just water them and give them the right light. They do the rest themselves."

"True, plus I hear they oxygenate the room. It's good for you while you sleep and such," the man observed in a casual, friendly manner. The mention of his sleeping and breathing without actually suggesting anything. To anyone listening, they might assume it was just polite conversation. Kyle however, caught the look in the man's eye. The look that subtly hinted that maybe if things went really bad, Kyle might really struggle to breathe one night. "So, you think you can get things running smoothly?"

"Yes." The actor bit his own lip as he realized he said that far too fast. Taking a breath, he tried to return to the pretense that everything was fine. This was just an employer and employee discussing strategy and plans. "I've got something that I think will definitely get me in with Aden, assuming that dumb scientist lets me use it."

"Indeed, sounds good. I assume he can't be too dumb. I mean, they don't just give PhDs away." As he spoke, the man reached out a finger and touched one of Venus's open flowers. "Oh, it closes! How marvelous."

"It catches flies for nutrients," Kyle replied, biting back the desire to tell him to stop, that each time it bit down, it wasted vital energy, and too many false alarms could kill Venus. "There's a lot more to people than book smarts."

"Yes, indeed, and people smarts, that is why I hired you, isn't it?" Dempsy replied as he touched another flower and smiled when it closed. "Is it any good at catching flies? I don't see any."

"I haven't opened the window to let any in." The actor could feel his arms tensing as he watched the man. The mention of being 'hired' riled him more than he liked to admit. Sixteen and stupid. Easy money, easy sex, and good-looking guys. Perks every day, food, clothes, and gifts. 'Fuck you, Esteban!' Kyle thought those words real hard as he remembered his first meeting with Dempsy. Stupid little shit, way too confident and happy to be out of school, just need to sign the contract, and he would have all the work he needed. "Yes, my 'people skills' are intact. I can handle it."

"I hope so my boy. After all, I canceled a bunch of your regulars for this. If it were to fall through before I made up the money on their contracts, you might find yourself hurting for customers, and that would put a block in your cashflow." The brief pause after hurting was noted, and Kyle tried to force himself to relax. Dempsy wasn't dumb; even if things went bad with the job, he wouldn't kill him, or even hurt him physically, much.

He was an asset, and, if he did screw up, Dempsy would need someone to help him make up the financial losses. His stomach clenched as he thought of some of the tasks he knew some of his agent's other actors had been asked to do. Kyle was still in his prime: young, handsome and smooth. There was a profit to be made, and now was the best chance for it. For all the threats the man was making, Kyle knew he wasn't at too big a risk. Life would be unpleasant for a while, but he could deal with unpleasant. He'd been doing that his whole life. "I will do my best. It's a good gig, and I don't want to lose it."

Dempsy pulled his hand away from the plant and gave him another soulless smile. "Indeed, good to hear my boy. I have confidence in you."

"Thank you, sir." The word "sir" tasted like pure bile on his tongue. However, he knew he was in no position to do anything. Dempsy held his work contract. Legally, he couldn't get another job. He only had two other options; destitution followed by work camps, or Mars and a lifetime as a company slave, probably mopping floors. He doubted his other skills would be of interest to anyone on Mars. He didn't have to like the man, but he did have to work for him. Employees across history have faced the same dilemma, though not often backed up with threats by their employer.

"Well, I guess I should be going, I bet you want to relax and get ready for tomorrow. Early start, remember? Don't be late." The little man gave Kyle a friendly pat on the arm as he made for the door, and, just as it opened, he turned. "After this contract ends, you'll probably have earned enough for a holiday. I know a guy who could get you a autocar ride to Washington for a very reasonable rate."

Kyle's fists clenched, and he could taste blood in his mouth as he bit his lip. "Why do you say that?"

"Isn't that where your sister lives? What's her name . . . Anna?" The smile had dropped from the man's face now. Which was good, because had he smiled, it would have been too much for Kyle. As it was, his mind was racing, and he could feel the tingle of his pistol pressing against his spine as he leaned against the kitchen counter. "I remember reading in your file when you signed on with me, your sister was adopted by a rather well-to-do family in Washington. I hear she doesn't even live in the city, but out in the burbs. She's off to Princeton next year to study botany. You must be very proud."

"I . . . haven't spoken to her since she was adopted," the actor replied as calmly as he could. Despite his best efforts, his hatred infused every single word. Dempsy's expression was cool and unflustered, his lips ever so slightly curling up in amusement. His eyes blazed with a challenge, and Kyle got the message clearly, "go on boy, try it, see what happens . . . to her."

"You haven't seen her since you were ten? That's a shame, you really should reconnect," the man replied and then gave a shrug. "Still, what do I know? I'm just your agent. Well, I'll leave you to your evening. I do hope things go well for you this week." With that, the man left the room, and Kyle didn't say anything more. He stood like a statue until the door closed, and then he gasped for breath, his legs gave out from under him, and he slipped to the floor.

Tears had already begun to flow, the fucker had found her. He had stayed away deliberately, hoping that if he never contacted her, they would never go looking. All along, Dempsy had known everything. He knew about her adoption, he probably knew every foster home that Kyle had been sent to. Maybe even the reasons he was moved on. The fucker probably even knew about that night.

Just the reminder was enough to break down all the blocks in his mind, to show him just how fragile he was, how weak. Memories swirled around, unwanted and unwelcome, yet there and not moving; just like Dempsy. Kyle would have stayed on the floor the rest of the night, lost in his own demon-filled mind; however, a knock on the door provided the one thing he needed: a distraction and escape.

Taking deep breaths, he scrubbed his face with his sleeve, wiping away and trace of his tears. As whomever it was knocked a second time, he took a few deep breaths, steadying himself, and then looked in the mirror and forced a smile onto his face. Before giving a signal for the door to open. The visitor, this time, wasn't a surprise; Darwin.

"Hey, Kyle, I know you said you were busy, but I figured I'd stop by on my way home just to say hello." The man was a little chunky, but not overly so. Blonde, short, and messy hair almost falling down over his eyes. His eyes were blue and full of hope, which matched his smile to give him an expression which said 'please be free for some fun.' The man was in luck, because wishes just so happened to be horses right at that moment, and Kyle needed to be anything but alone.

"Darwin, good to see you! Come in, sit down, is that a bottle I see in your hand?" Kyle asked, even though he knew damn well it was and that the tech was hoping that the two might share a few drinks, and then drunk Kyle might just agree to turning the sofa to bed mode.

"Yeah, tequila, or a very close approximation," chuckled the chunky guy as he slipped inside, plonking himself down on the sofa, right in the middle to ensure wherever Kyle sat, he would be pressed against Darwin. "How'd your new super gig go?"

Kyle winced. Darwin was perfectly at ease with his profession. In fact, the tech seemed to revel in the fact he was getting some professional services for free. That made the guy a good person to vent to from time to time. Everyone needs a non-judgmental ear to rant into from time to time. "It is going okay, I guess."

"Who is the big client? Someone famous or something?" Darwin asked as Kyle sat down with two glasses taken from the kitchen. The actor grabbed the bottle from his friend's unresisting hands and poured two large measures.

"I can't discuss it, they made me sign a non-disclosure agreement or five," the actor replied bluntly, handing one glass to Darwin. Then with one quick motion, he emptied his own glass. Tequila at its very finest burned a little on the way down. This was so far from the finest, it was like a chihuahua to a wolf. There may be some distant relation, but the skinny rat still ain't getting invited for Thanksgiving.

"Damn! Take it easy," Darwin squealed, and the actor coughed for a moment.

"No time for easy, got to be up early for the job," snorted Kyle, pouring himself another good measure. It tasted like gasoline. Kyle didn't care if that was what it was; he downed the second glass, then snatched the glass from his friend and emptied it. His stomach churned at the burning liquid it was suddenly flooded with.

"Fuck, Kyle, what the hell did they do to you? That stuff would knock a horse out," Darwin gasped, grabbing the bottle away from the crazy person he was sitting next to.

"Good, then I could finally 'extract a sample.'" the actor's laugh was a little bitter as he felt the world starting to go fuzzy at the edges. It was better this way; fuzzy worlds don't have all the horrible details of real life.

"You're not making much sense," the tech said cautiously as he put the bottle on the windowsill, out of reach of the actor.

"Darwin . . . Oh, just shut up." Kyle helped his friend stop those annoying lips from flapping by launching himself at him. Kissing with desperate and forceful passion, Darwin fell back against the sofa. For a moment, the chunky man struggled, then a hand firmly groping his crotch silenced him. Kyle's tongue wriggled its way through his friend's lips, tasting him. While his hands groped and squeezed on the man's crotch. He could already feel the erection growing underneath. It felt good to know there were some things he could do right.

With a deep, lustful gasp, Darwin broke the kiss. Kyle's hands had slipped inside his pants. Desperate and yet incredibly experienced fingers working his shaft. Kyle smiled to himself, he knew he could make his friend do whatever he wanted. He could milk him of his cum in a minute, or keep him a heartbeat from release for hours; the choice was his. The actor was in control.

"Kyle . . . I." Whatever Darwin was about to say, Kyle stopped him with a hand firmly over the tech's mouth. Slipping to his feet and leaning over the trembling man, Kyle used his free hand to unfasten his own pants, letting them fall and kicking them off with the speed of a practiced expert. Without a word, he sat down, legs astride Darwin, the man's cock pressing against his buttocks.

This was something he knew, something he could do well. Reaching behind him, he grasped the chunky man's thick shaft. Darwin wasn't as long as many, but, as Kyle knew, it didn't take much, and the man had enough. A handful and more of shaft, thick, too, enough to stretch but not tear. Darwin moaned and groaned, his sounds muffled by the hand clamped firmly down on his mouth. The last thing Kyle wanted was someone talking; that would just spoil things. He didn't want to think or process, he just wanted to feel and to be in control for once.

He lifted himself up, his erect cock stroking over Darwin's slightly stained shirt. The funk of a day's work giving the tech a slightly musky scent. It wasn't bad; Kyle liked the smell of a male in his nose. Keeping his hand firmly on Darwin's mouth, he lifted the man's chin a little and then leaned forward, nibbling on his exposed neck, tender nuzzles and kisses up the salty skin. His hand stroking the thick, throbbing cock gently, feeling the hot flesh grow sticky and clammy as the excited man squealed into his hand.

"Yeah, you like that, don't you?" he whispered huskily into Darwin's ear before he sucked softly on the soft lobe. His teeth came into play, and just then, he guided the aching cock under his ass, letting the thick meat hotdog as his well-toned buttocks clenched down around it. The squeal of his lover was delicious music to his ears. He bit softly on his neck, his teeth leaving red marks in the man's pale flesh. The pain of the moment far outweighed by the promise of pleasure.

Then, with the impatience of the young and desperate, he guided the musky meat to his pucker. Without a hesitation, he forced himself down. Darwin kicked and struggled under him as his length was forced inside the actor's ass. Kyle didn't need to use normal protection; as part of his contract, he'd had a device installed for his safety and his clients. One in his ass and another at the back of his throat. Darwin didn't know, but, as his cock slid inside, it was coated with a thin film of protective filament. The device would constantly repair the paper-thin protection. To the client, it felt like going in raw, but with the full protection of the best condoms. It had hurt like a son of a bitch for weeks after installation, and, for the first few days, he had kept forgetting to turn them off before meals. Nothing was worse than eating a few mouthfuls of something expensive, only to realize you wouldn't get the benefit as your contraceptive had bagged the food in non-digestible membrane.

Grinning, Kyle took his hand off Darwin's mouth, replacing it with his hungry lips. His tongue delving inside the hot mouth, conquering it with little resistance, taking what he wanted, while his ass bucked quickly on the rod inside it. Clenching down like a vice, squeezing and massaging the meat desperately. He felt Darwin start to buck up into him, the tech's nuts smacking off his ass like a wonderful, moist drumbeat, skin on skin.

With a desperation born of a heady mixture of emotional trauma and alcohol, Kyle drove himself down to meet each thrust. His own cock unregarded between then, erect and cut, grinding over Darwin's shirt staining it with his own juices. While inside him, he felt the pleasure growing. The pain of the rough entry forgotten, he began to moan with pleasure. He could feel Darwin's heart racing under him, the man's moans and pants getting desperate.

Gasping with pleasure, he rode faster and faster, milking that hot meat inside him for all it was worth. The man under him cried out into his mouth, the thrusting growing wild and uncontrolled, the hard meat pummeling his tight hole desperately. The cries of his passion muffled by Kyle's lips as the actor swallowed every delicious squeal and moan as he forced his friend over the edge. Riding him with all the desperation of an addict desperate to get their next fix.

He felt the meat inside him throb, and Darwin's thrusting slowed as his cries reached a fever pitch. Inside him, he knew his lover was emptying. His device would contain the ejaculate in a thin, yet strong polymer coating to protect him from disease or pregnancy; he had giggled when the doctor told him that was its purpose. It had never failed him, no matter how rough or pent up his lover, the little miracle device kept him safe.

Standing up on the sofa, he felt a soft pop as Darwin's softening cock slipped from his ass. He wasn't finished yet; the moaning tech certainly wasn't done. Placing one hand on the wall to steady himself, he crouched down over his lover's face. The tech gasped as a warm black cock-tip was pressed to his lips. Kyle was usually a more passive lover, lying under him and letting him do what he wanted or sucking him off. He had never let Darwin taste his cock before.

With a moan, Darwin found his lips forced apart. He opened up, trying not to graze the invading maleness with his teeth. The member felt so hot on his tongue, the taste of musk and sweat bitter and yet moreish. He sucked gently, and then, as Kyle moaned loudly with pleasure, he sucked harder. The actor's meat was cut, his foreskin having been stolen by a mother's religious views. The tech ran his tongue over the glans, his tongue picking up the bitter tang of precum and the gentle taste of maleness.

"Mmmm, that's it, suck it!" Kyle almost growled those words, his hand landing in Darwin's mop of hair. Finger's laced through the mess, gripping it firmly and slightly painfully as he began to thrust. His cock was a good size, far longer and just as thick as Darwin's own. He thrust until he felt the tech sputtering while his cock-tip pressed to the back of his friend's throat. His knees pressed onto Darwin's shoulders, holding him down.

There was no tenderness, not this time. This time, it was him on top, in control, and Darwin, he could take what he was given. Gasping, the actor couldn't believe how quickly he was getting to the edge of his orgasm. If he had been with a client, he would have fought it, pushed it back until he thought they wanted him to cum. Not then, this was for him, and Darwin could choke on his cum when he was ready to spill it.

He fucked the man's face desperately, looking down to see Darwin's eyes closed, a slightly happy look on his face. While between those red lips, his black meat was slipping back and forth, glistening in the light with his friend's saliva. He could feel the warmth of a broad tongue with each thrust. The tech may not have known much about sucking cock, but he wasn't doing too bad a job. The moans from beneath him told Kyle that he might be able to get away with doing this more often. The confirmation of the slapping sound of a guy jerking himself off confirmed the tech was enjoying the rough treatment.

Laughing a little the actor, picked up the pace. "Yeah, you like that don't you, slut?" How many times had those words been said to him? He'd lost count. They felt so good as they slipped from his lips. The man under him just moaned in response, sucking harder on his aching meat. That was all he could take; with a deep moan, he felt his cock throbbing. He shoved his cock as far forward as he could, his hand holding the struggling man under him while he emptied every drop he could into Darwin's mouth.

Kyle held himself fully inside Darwin's mouth until he felt the tech swallow around him. The actor realized there was no way the tech had a device like his. The man had just properly drunk his first load of cum. It had been eight years since he had last properly tasted spunk. The musky, bitter fluid a taste of desire more than a good beverage. At the time, he'd loved it. Sucking and fucking his older lover had been something he'd deeply enjoyed.

With his cock beginning to soften, he pulled from Darwin's lips, squeezing the last drop out onto Darwin's lips before he dismounted from the sofa.

"Oh fuck!" Darwin panted as his airway was finally free and he could start to think about what just happened. "That was . . . intense. You feel better now?"

Not answering, Kyle grabbed the bottle of tequila and took a deep swig for it. Eventually, he responded, "I needed that, thanks."

"Fuck, anytime!" Darwin replied with a chuckle as he tucked his cock back into his pants. "You want to watch a vid or something, then maybe a round two?"

"No, I have an early start, best if you just go," Kyle responded, opening his window a little, letting some freshish air in and the scent of their rutting out.

Darwin looked slightly disappointed, but he nodded. "Alright, if that's what you want. See you next week maybe?" Kyle gave a non-committal nod, and the tech took his cue. His part was done it, was time to get out. He couldn't complain too loudly. He'd wanted to fuck, and he'd got one, albeit a rougher and quicker one than he was hoping for. He took a step towards the door and then had a sudden thought. He reached out and took the half empty bottle off the actor. Kyle resisted for a moment, but Darwin was firm. "I think it's better if I take this. After all, you have an early start."

The actor had just enough sense to know his friend was trying to help him. "Probably right." As his friend opened the door to leave, a pang of guilt made Kyle cry out. "Darwin!"

The tech turned and looked at him. "Yeah?"

"Thanks . . . I really needed someone today," the actor finished lamely.

"Glad I could help. Take care, Kyle." The man replied and then was gone.

The world was still fuzzy enough for Kyle. He had just enough sense to set his alarm. It was actually not even that late, yet he felt like he had just run a marathon. With the alcohol running through his mind and body, he just gave in to the blackness, welcoming the numbness and silence of slumber.

Chapter 8

The loud beeping that awoke Kyle was also a wake-up call to the demons inside his head. They shook themselves off and got to work, trying to dig through his forehead with tiny sledgehammers. While he groaned and cursed himself for drinking too much and Darwin for turning up on his doormat uninvited. His sleep had been fitful, and wild, unpleasant dreams had been the order of the night. Aden had been there, laughing at his pathetic attempts to befriend him. Dempsy and Dr. Ramon had been sitting in a corner, talking loudly about his inadequacies. While he had sat in the corner with a plastic book, trying to impress Aden by reading *Go Spot, Go.*

At some point during the night, he had fallen off the sofa. It hadn't even woken him in his inebriated state. So, at least there was a reason his tongue felt like a used carpet, having been stuck to one for a good part of the night. The persistent beeping of his alarm woke him just enough to get him to his shaky legs. He caught his reflection in the mirror on the kitchen and winced. The demons in his head unleashed the hellhound that was the memory of the previous night.

He moaned as he thought of his rough and rude treatment of Darwin, his friend. The dull ache of his head was welcomed as a fitting punishment; what else did he deserve? Using a friend and then pretty much throwing him out after he got what he wanted. A treatment he had far too much experience of, Kyle admonished himself that he should know better. There wasn't much time to dwell on his actions; work was calling.

A quick and ineffective shower later, the actor emerged slightly damp and still hungover. His stomach had decided that his head shouldn't get to hog all the hangover fun, so it was threatening to empty itself in protest. Kyle downed a couple of hangover cure pills and a glass of water. It would take a little while to work. They felt like a cheat anyway. He had earned his hangover, he should manfully endure it, to teach himself a lesson about trying to drown himself with tequila. However, practicality won the day. He needed to move relatively fast to pack and get to the pick-up point. Plus, once he arrived, he would need all his wits about him to deal with Dr. Ramon and Aden.

Kyle paused for a moment to examine the book. Yesterday, he had such hope and faith in the paper object. The faded, glossy cover held a picture of a young boy with a black horse behind him. Faced with the prospect of actually presenting it to his boss, of trying to get approval to read it to Aden, he had his doubts. Not that they would stop him; he had pissed away almost a full week's pay on the damned object, it had better be worth it. There was only one way to know for sure.

He tossed it into the top of his bag of clothes. As he turned to leave, his foot tapped into his pistol. It had fallen out when he had stripped. He returned it to his tiny security box. Pausing only to top up Venus's water and to leave the window open a tiny crack so she could catch her own dinner. Kyle headed out into the streets.

Feeling weak and exposed without his gun, especially while carrying such an expensive object, Kyle trotted across the concourses, dancing through the crowds. Trying not to jump as people got too close. He made it to the lift in plenty of time. He was far too preoccupied to play the game in his head as the lift rose. So, he almost missed his stop when the lift finally reached the roof. He had to shove through several people as they tried to board, just to get out.

Kyle approached one of the many parking terminals, scanning his bio-chip against it. His autocar was confirmed. The map showed where his pickup was planned, and he rushed to the pick-up terminal. The car was waiting for him as he arrived, and he chucked in his bag and sat down. Sinking back in the chair as the car took off, he felt his eyes begin to close before the car had even cleared the rooftop.

The long nap on his way back was a welcome one; not only did he arrive far more alert and rested, it kept his mind from focusing on what might go wrong. On the veiled threat to his sister. He had considered sending her a warning, only what was he to say? 'Sorry I haven't spoken to you in more than a decade, but there's some random guy who might try and have you killed if I fail at my new gig extracting semen from a half horse, half human lab creature.' She would think he was insane. Plus, he'd have breached his NDA and voided his contract. He'd send a warning if it became necessary and not before.

There was nobody there to greet him. Kyle wasn't sure if that was a good thing or not. He took the positive that they had sent the car. Clearly, they still wanted to give him one more chance to prove he could fulfil his contract.

Slinging his bag over his shoulders, he approached the security terminal. A guard stepped up to the door with a small security box. "Place all electronic devices in here."

With a friendly smile, Kyle pulled off his comm device and a few other trinkets he carried with him. For a moment, he wondered if he should mention the book, then he decided it wasn't electronic. He could always claim ignorance. Besides, he was going to hand it to his boss and ask permission, they could hardly accuse him of sneaking evil propaganda in to their prisoner. "That's everything."

The guard gave him a dismissive nod, like he couldn't care what Kyle claimed. They knew he had to walk in through scanner devices anyway. Once he passed the scanners, he entered a changing room. Stripping off quickly, he shoved his clothes into his bag and shoved it onto a conveyor belt that took it into a decon unit. When he opened the door to the decon showers, he took a deep breath.

His first time to the facility, the decon showers had shocked him. Water so hot, it was just a degree off scalding, mixed with the stench of unpleasant chemicals. Through bitter experience, Kyle knew they tasted far more unpleasant than they smelled, sitting on the tongue somewhat worse that the effluent out of the average waste processing facility. They burned his nose, and, if he opened his eyes, he knew they would sting like crazy. Walking slowly forward, he felt the jets spray into every nook and crevice he had. He'd had evenings with clients that were far less intrusive than the people who operated the decon showers.

The second wave was a little nice, the temperature cooling down to something a little friendlier as soap sprayed down from the ceiling. Specially designed to remove traces of the more powerful cleansers, more than to clean him. He scrubbed his hair and let the soap rinse out. He kept his eyes firmly closed throughout, waiting until the shower stopped. Once the flow had finished, he walked forward through the far door into the second changing room.

His bag was waiting for him, along with a selection of towels. He grabbed a couple and started to scrub himself dry. As he did so, a lab tech entered. "Welcome back. Please, can you extend your arm for a blood test?"

For a moment Kyle, thought about asking what the point was; he'd been tested far too many times now. However, he knew he was on ice far too thin to go running and jumping, so he trod carefully instead. Holding out his arm and wincing as the vampiress drained a small portion of his life blood. "Have you engaged in sexual activity while you were away?"

"No," the lie came out on automatic. There was no way for them to prove him wrong, and his devices would have protected him anyway. He had extracted a couple of small, white, squishy pellets in the morning, the result of his vigorous riding of Darwin. All safe and sound behind a thin, yet durable seal of polymers. The female gave him a warm smile and nodded as her own medical testing equipment confirmed he was still clean. "Dr. Ramon is waiting for you in his office."

"Thank you." He tried to put as much enthusiasm into his voice as he could as he replied. Although it was hard to be too happy about going to see his boss. What he was surprised to find was that he wanted to get through it, not just to get to the other side, but he was actually looking forward to seeing Aden again. The equine would surely be glad to see him, and not just because of what he wanted to do to him like most clients, or because of what they could get from him like Dempsy. Aden was lonely, that much was plain enough even to the scientists who ran the place; otherwise, they wouldn't have hired him. Someone who just wanted to see him because he wanted to see him, that was actually nice, sweet even. Although he tried to warn himself he might be reading far too much into one day and one hug.

It didn't take long to find his way back to Dr. Ramon's office. He knocked politely on the door. The door opened a second later. "Come in." The doctor was sitting behind his desk. He rose as Kyle entered and gestured at the seat opposite. "Nice to see you again, Kyle. Please, sit down." The words were formal, and Kyle's ears could easily pick up on the forced calm in those tones. Clearly, the doctor was someone who held grudges, which was just one more hurdle in the way.

"Thanks, how have you been?" Kyle replied, putting as much warmth into the tone as he could, following the doctor's instruction and sitting down. Just to show he could be a good boy and sit on command, he also knew how to roll over and get his tummy tickled. Though Dr. Ramon would almost certainly burst into embarrassed flames should the actor suggest it.

"Well, thank you," the reply was a little bit more relaxed, the actor's ease helping to calm his fight or flight nerves. Clearly, Kyle wasn't here for a confrontation, so he could relax, just a little.

"How is your sister and your . . . nephews, was it?" Kyle remembered the man had two nephews, aged six and ten. However, by letting the doctor fill in the details, he knew it would encourage him to talk a little more. To help him relax and start to share just a little more with Kyle. There was a lot of work to get back to where he had started, but Kyle knew he could do it.

"Yes, nephews. Tris and Ryan. They are very well. We had a good day yesterday. I took them to the zoo, and I must admit my sister was very grateful." The names were absorbed and stored as the actor smiled and nodded, actively listening to his boss. Dr. Ramon leaned forward and added in a low voice, "Though I was very grateful to drop them off at the end of the day, too. Oh boy, little Tris was a right handful. He kept insisting that we go see the polar bears and penguins."

Kyle chuckled along with the doctor, replying, "Nothing wrong with that, I always like the bears, myself. Them and the cats, I remember nearly peeing myself as a kid when one of the lions walked up to the window and roared." A little bit of himself shared, and another shared chuckle.

"Well, I promised to take them to the beach next week, so I can at least get to sit down for a few hours. While they play in the sand," smiled the doctor, and then he shook his head a little. "Right, anyway. We had better get on. Aden has already had breakfast, exercised, and refused to give a sample. I felt it best to get that out of the way today. However, tomorrow, we do need to try and get one. The lab has advised that they are completely through all samples taken from him. They are working with what Bruno is giving. Unfortunately, Aden has the far greater success rate. It's not entirely unexpected; he was the more refined of our subjects, the youngest and last to be born. Properly trained, it is estimated that each subject could reduce the time it will take to colonize by at least a month. Plus save two or three lives. Working on the Mars surface is not safe; a single breach of environment suit is a potential, preventable death. We really need Aden back producing."

"I will do my best to help facilitate, though I do want to try and keep my relationship with him as strong as I can," the actor replied with as much conviction as he could. "On that note, I got this for Aden while I was away, I think it might really help him listen to me if I can show I come through on my promises." While he spoke, he reached into his bag and pulled out his copy of *The Horse and His Boy*.

Dr. Ramon actually looked impressed as he picked up the book. "You actually got him an old paper copy?"

"Yes. I figured this way, he can only read the book. No chance of him finding anything but the story. I . . . the story, I think, is perfect for him. Have you read it before?" Kyle couldn't keep the excitement out of his voice as he asked.

"I'm more sci-fi than fantasy, I'm afraid. I did warn you we didn't want him reading. You might have just spent a lot of credits on nothing." The man looked at the book doubtfully, flicking through the pages.

"No! Trust me, this is a story you want him to read. It's about a horse who wants to see the world, even though he gets warned not to stray too far by his mother. He gets caught, spends years as a slave, and the book is about how he desperately tries to get home." The words came out far too fast for the doctor to interrupt him. "Just read it, you'll see. For the horses, it is all about getting home. It's perfect for Aden, it has the exact message you want, beware of the outside world."

The scientist gave him a long stare and then put the book down onto his desk. "Okay, I will give it a try tonight, and, if I approve it, you may take it in to him tomorrow. If not, then you can at least tell him you tried."

"That was all I promised I would do." Kyle had to at least admit the doctor seemed genuine in his response. He believed he would actually consider the request, which is all Dr. Ramon had promised him, Kyle spotted that a second or two later. "Well, what is the plan for today?"

The doctor smiled and pulled out a small, familiar tin, the one that held his earpiece, "We get you in to Aden quickly. He has been asking after you since we pulled you out Tuesday. I must admit, I was tempted to see if I could get him to trade a sample for your return. It felt a bit dishonest, though. I've been with him since he was born, and I try not to lie. Though I will admit, I have omitted more truths than I am entirely happy with. Sadly, the demands of the job are beyond my control."

For the first time since he returned to the facility, the smile on Kyle's face was genuine. Aden had been asking about him. He was pleased to hear they hadn't blackmailed him to get a sample; he would have had to continue that lie, and that would have been unpleasant. "Sounds good to me. You want me to change into my scrubs?"

"Please, your room is the same room. However, if you leave your clothes on the bed, I will have someone come in and clean them properly, then you would be able to feel more comfortable in your clothing." Dr. Ramon gestured at the door, as if suddenly remembering he was supposed to be acting like the firm, confident, and in-control boss everyone knew he wasn't.

"Oh, thanks!" Once more Kyle's enthusiasm was honest. The idea of a week in the loose-fitting scrubs had been unpalatable. Although he was slightly offended by the need to clean his clothes. They had already been through decon, like every part of him. Of course, arguing would be like pissing into the storm; it would achieve nothing except getting piss all over him or something to that effect. Take the good and don't bitch about that which you can't change; not the catchiest mantra but one that Kyle told himself was the one to adopt for the moment.

His hated scrubs on and annoying earpiece, complete with the annoying puppeteer, in place, he headed to the door to the yard. As he walked, Dr Ramon talked in his ear, "Aden wanted some time alone today, so we gave it to him. Although we hope he will like having you there. I've arranged for there to be nobody to bother you both, unless Bruno decides to see his brother. It's rare that he would feel like talking. He prefers to spend his time in his room with his companion when not exercising or assisting us in our experiments."

Somehow, Kyle couldn't see Bruno being allowed to handle equipment in a lab, or even scissors sharper than you give a six-year-old. The plastic sort that you just can't cut anything with, yet are prevalent in every nursery across the world and had been for hundreds of years. So, the actor guessed he was the subject of their tests, probably doing things to help prove he would be useful on Mars. Bruno would be useful on Mars, if you could keep his macho nature under control and needed someone to get something off a high shelf.

Somehow, anything more technical than that seemed a bit of a stretch.

Aden, on the other hand, seemed to think a lot more. Even though they had stopped him reading, tried to slow down his learning, Kyle had seen first-hand he was no fool. Maybe a bit naive, but then he was raised in a lab surrounded by people looking only to use him for their own ends. Yet he had already figured out the best way to show his anger. Now all Kyle had to do was make him happy so he started co-operating. Then everyone would be happy; Aden, Dempsy, Dr. Ramon, and, with any luck, maybe even Kyle could get some of that happiness for himself.

There was no hesitation this time as he walked outside alone. He knew what was waiting, and it was certainly a lot better than many of the alternatives. He spotted Aden almost immediately. The horse was sitting on the grass, resting his elbows on his knees and his head on his crossed arms. The equine's ears twitched before Kyle was even a few steps out of the door, and he quickly got to his feet.

The two approached each other, Aden looking at him and then away and back again. Kyle could see he was trying not to smile, "trying" being the operative word. If his face hadn't given it away, his voice would have, "Kyle! I was worried you wouldn't come back." Every syllable sounded sincere. Kyle couldn't remember the last time anyone had sounded that happy to see him.

"Well, you worried for nothing. I get one day off a week, and yesterday was it. So, I went home and relaxed for a bit," Kyle replied with a smile, reaching out a hand to lightly pat Aden's shoulder. The horse shuffled his hooves in the grass nervously at the actor's touch. With a smile and a wink, Kyle pointed back to the spot Aden had been sitting in. "I can tell you about it, not much to tell, really."

"Careful with talk of outside," a voice warned in his ear. However, he'd offered, so there was no way he could back out now.

"I'd like that . . . "Aden paused and leaned forward to whisper. "But maybe we could sit in a different spot."

"Your favorite spot, down by the stream, maybe?" He didn't really need to ask, but he wanted to show he'd been listening and that he could remember their first meeting.

"Yes, exactly," enthused the horse, taking the lead and walking away from the facility. Kyle followed him, noticing the horse's tail lightly twitching as he walked. Body language was something Kyle was fluent in, but Aden's body spoke a different language, and Kyle was still just learning his ABCs in it. However, he thought that seemed like excitement. He found himself smiling a little, feeling a flush to his cheeks as the warm sun bathed them both.

It didn't take long to reach the spot; the sound of running water was the first clue, a tiny stream meandering its way down the hill. It arched under the fence, around a small hillock and back out through the fence. Almost like it had no regard for the fence, or the nice, straight, lines the humans built in. On top of the small hill was a young sapling, not really big enough to call a full tree. About the height of a man, its branches spread wide. Filtering out the sunlight from the spot that Aden chose to sit in.

Kyle didn't hesitate; he sat down close to the pony, slipping right into the equine's personal space. He waited to see if there was any attempt to pull away, but, if anything, Aden seemed to move just a tiny bit closer to him. "So, what happened?"

"Oh, not a lot, really. I slept late and then did a little shopping. Treated myself to some blueberries . . ."

"Tart?" Clearly, the question was important to a fruit loving horse.

"Yes, nice and crisp, possibly a little under ripe for some; however, I liked them. I sat on one of the concourses and just watched the people pass by. It was really crowded; there's not a lot of space to spare in Chicago. It's one of the busiest, most heavily populated cities in America . . . well, I think it's ninth at the moment. Oh, I had a latte, too . . ."

"A what?" Aden asked, tilting his head, a little confused.

"It's a drink, like milky coffee, only they stream the milk first . . . erm, it's kinda bitter but creamy," Kyle explained, feeling rather silly. "They are good, but not good for you." Given the scientists control of Aden's diet, he doubted they had ever given him anything with caffeine in. A tiny part of him wondered just what a pony going hyper on coffee might be like. Though he knew he was never likely to see it.

Aden's brow furrowed in confusion. "If it is not good for you, then why do you drink it?"

"Ah, a question as old as time," chuckled Kyle. "We do it because it feels good to do something bad sometimes, and, even though we know it's bad, we can't help it." He nudged the pony in the ribs, "Don't worry, I'm not an addict."

"An addict?" The pony still looked confused, but Kyle noticed he pushed into the nudge a little. Taking a chance, he shuffled a little closer.

"Yeah, people who keep having stuff that is bad for them become addicted to it. They crave it and can't think of anything but getting more." The actor was sure this particular line of information on the outside world would meet with his puppeteer's approval, while giving Aden more of the information he craved. "Some bad things are really, really addictive. Just one hit, and you are hooked for life. Plus, when you can't get any, you feel really ill. It hurts, your body shakes, and you sweat a lot. Addicts are willing to lie, cheat, steal, and even hurt people to get another fix."

"That sounds horrible, why do they let you drink such bad things as coffee?" The horse asked, and Kyle shrugged.

"Well, coffee ain't all that bad. Most people won't knife each other for a caffeine hit. Most of the other stuff is illegal, a few aren't. Alcohol being the most common. That gets you drunk, so you can't think straight." As he spoke, the actor reached out and pulled Aden's arm around him, laying his head down on the pony's firm chest. He felt Aden's muscles tighten. However, the equine didn't try and stop it or pull away; in fact, his arm squeezed down just a little. "Then you can't walk straight, you say and do things you would normally never do, and sometimes you even throw up. A couple of times, I have been so drunk I don't even remember what I did. Though from what I have been told, I am glad I don't remember."

"Why would you do that? It sounds terrible." Aden asked. Kyle felt his hair stir as the pony sniffed his hair very cautiously.

"Well, honestly, it tastes good. Plus, it takes a lot to get you drunk. Most of the time, if you just get a little bit of a buzz going, it's okay. Things are more fun, talking, joking, and sex. All seems easier and far less stressful," Kyle answered while he reached around Aden with both arms, gently settling into an embrace. He was particularly pleased with working the subject of sex in, just gently, to hopefully get Aden's mind away from the city and down into the gutter. "Of course, the trouble is judging it right. It gets harder to stop the more you have. Logic starts to fly out the window, and then you just can't stop yourself. You pay for it the next day."

"They bill you the day afterwards?" The words were whispered with such sincerity that Kyle knew it was no joke, but he couldn't stop himself from laughing; if anything, the conviction of Aden just made it that much funnier.

"In a way, yes. The next morning, you wake up with a hangover," he chuckled as he talked. His fingers lightly tracing around the equine's perfectly formed pectorals. It was rare that he was hired for someone in such good shape. Mostly, they didn't need to pay for it unless they demanded the same sort of perfect body to play with. "It starts with a headache that is like a knife in your eyes, and all light seems to hurt. Your stomach is filled with acid, and you just want to throw up everything you ate in the last three days. It can hang around for a while if you don't have any meds for it."

"That does not sound appealing," commented the equine, his voice slightly strained. While Kyle had been talking, his hands had continued to wander, staying above the waist but gently exploring Aden's body. His fur felt oddly good running between his fingers, tickling his palms lightly.

"Believe me, experiencing one is less so. It's all part of the world out there: sex, drugs, and rock and roll." The human found himself stroking his cheek against Aden's chest as he spoke. He could feel the moist heat of Aden's rapidly growing pants on the back of his neck. His head dipped low, he could see a part the equine was interested in a lot more than just talking. He knew better than to just make a grab for it; if he touched it now, Aden would jump and possibly bolt.

"Rock and roll?"

Kyle chuckled again, his nose finding an erect nub as his cheek stroked. Stallions have nipples; he hadn't been sure as they had always been hidden. Now the pink fleshy nub was poking against his black nose-tip. "You know, music? Surely, they let you listen to music?"

"He's never asked." Kyle bit his lip as he felt himself jump. He hoped that Aden didn't notice. However, a tightening of the pony's muscles showed him that he had, or at least he knew something went wrong. The actor put a hand over his mouth to fake a restrained sneeze while he cursed Dr. Ramon for not knowing when to keep his damn mouth shut.

"No, I don't know what that is." There was something in his tone; it almost sounded like pain. Kyle realized how much the horse wanted to know.

"It's like singing, you know . . ." Kyle paused. He was a bright guy, but he had no idea how exactly you explain music to someone. It was such a fundamental part of life. It was like trying to describe the color of the ocean to someone who has always been blind. Then it hit him, he didn't have to describe the ocean, Aden wasn't blind.

"Amazing grace, how sweet the sound. That saved a wretch like me." He wasn't sure why the song came to his mind, it was ancient. He had always liked it for the message, a little note of hope. Aden jumped a little as the actor started to sing. "I once was lost, but now am found, was blind, but now I see."

For a few moments, neither of them spoke Aden's ears twitched, and he tilted his head, "I want . . . to hear more."

"Well, okay then, I know a few songs." It wasn't a regular request, and he was certainly no professional. However, everyone knows a few songs; it is something you just can't avoid. He picked a song he could remember most of the words to, maybe it was a hymn or something, he couldn't quite remember where he had learned it, and it didn't really matter. The pony listened carefully and intently to every word. Many of the lyrics were confusing to Kyle, and he knew that they would certainly baffle Aden. However, he held the tune well; it was a simple one, and he was quite shocked to see just how much of it he could remember.

When his memory failed, he let the song end. He had only managed a few verses with chorus. He chuckled and looked up at Aden. "So, that is music, or singing. Music is made with instruments, they make pleasant sounds. I am sure that we could get you some music to listen to."

"Yeah, no problem there, can't believe we never thought of music," a voice confirmed in his ear.

"We can go back soon, once you have told me what else you did after coffee," Aden replied firmly. Kyle was impressed that the equine was able to focus and avoid the distraction that well.

"Oh, well, after breakfast I went shopping to find something for you, actually, a book." There was no mistaking the shine in Aden's eyes and the smile on his face at the mention of the possibility of a book. "I spent a good few hours in a shop with a very nice man who helped me find the book I was looking for. It is going to be reviewed, and I am hoping they will let me bring it to you, or read it to you. If you would like, that is."

Kyle couldn't help but notice how the equine's ears seemed to shoot up even further. It was adorable, along with the expression on his face, like a child on Christmas Eve staring at the wonderful world of possibilities that laid in boxes under the tree. "I would like that very much."

"Okay, but remember, I need to get permission first. I did what I said I would do. I tried, I guess we'll know soon if I was successful." Kyle was glad that Dr. Ramon had at least kept his mouth shut during this. He was worried he would get scolded for mentioning the book before he even knew if he could read it. Getting Aden's hopes up, hopefully, they would not be dashed. However, if they were, he knew who the equine would go to for comfort. It was a win-win for Kyle, for once.

"I understand," Aden replied, his words full of sincerity and yet a tremble of excitement. Just as he was about to ask for more songs, his stomach gurgled.

"Sounds like someone is hungry," the human observed with a chuckle.

"It is lunchtime," the equine replied, shuffling his large hooves in embarrassment.

"We have a meal ready for you both inside," Dr. Ramon said, to absolutely no surprise of Kyle's. Every aspect of the horse's life was watched and planned, meals far more so than other things. However, on the bright side, the man in his ear had just said a meal for both of them. The free food perk was back in full force, and Kyle's stomach was ready to take advantage.

It took them no time at all to return to the facility; however, their meal beat them there. A tray of fruits and vegetables, all nicely sliced, was awaiting the hungry pair. Aden ate the lion's share, or stallion's share. Kyle kept to the vegetables. They included a few truly new experiences for him. Much like fruit, vegetables were expensive, far out of Kyle's normal price range. The idea of spending half a day's pay on a bag of carrots seemed insane. However, as he crunched down on one, he had to admit it wasn't bad.

He tried to leave the fruit for Aden, knowing the equine would prefer the sweeter treats. Aden, however, refused to take the last few slices of apple or mango, insisting Kyle had some; in his own gentle and shy way. Mostly by just observing that he was having no more. The actor caved quickly and easily, enjoying the fruit and licking his fingers clean. After the meal, Kyle stood up and said, "I'm going to see if I can find something to play some music on." He said it a little too loudly, but that was just to emphasize to Dr. Ramon that he expected someone to be ready with some music and a way to play it for Aden.

Aden rose and started to follow him. It wasn't until they reached the doors to the lab that he stopped. "I'm not supposed to go inside." It was muttered with just a hint of pleading. Kyle could pick up on the not-so-subtle subtext. Aden wanted to go with him, to the wonderful magically laboratory land. Of course, the actor knew that beyond that door was nothing but dull corridors.

"I suppose they are probably worried you might find a way to hurt yourself, though I can hardly see any harm if you were to come with me to Dr. Ramon's office." Once again, the actor wasn't really speaking to the horse, he was asking a question to the doctor.

"As long as he stays with you and it is just to my office and back, that is fine," the doctor whispered into his ear.

Approval granted, Kyle let a cheeky grin sneak onto his face. He reached out and grabbed Aden's hand, "Come on!" The actor gave Aden a wink and opened the door, pulling the equine behind him.

"But I'm supposed to stay outside," the equine replied, though his voice held a trace of a giggle, and his verbal protests didn't stop his feet from walking.

"Behold, the glorious wonders of corridor G12 dash B!" As he spoke, he waved his arms around for dramatic effect at the dull, gray corridor. Aden smirked a little, though he did look around. He'd been in the facility all his life and never been allowed through the door. Somehow in his mind, the place would have been bigger, more brightly lit, and with more colors than gray. Although the giddy thrill of breaking the rule made it all seem just a little bit more exciting; this wasn't just a corridor, this was a brand-new corridor, one he had never seen. The small yellow sign of G12-B was the first time he'd seen that sign.

The awe effect lasted a full ten, maybe even fifteen seconds before he asked, "So, where are we going?"

"Dr. Ramon's office. This way," Kyle replied with a smile, heading off down the magical, or not-so-magical corridor. A quick walk away, and they knocked on the door. It took a full minute before it opened, and then Dr. Ramon won the Oscar for most overacted role of the millennium, outshining anybody starring in their high school play and even the late, great William Shatner.

"Oh! My, Aden and Kyle! What are you doing here?" Inwardly, Kyle cringed. At least the man knew that he should play along, but he was lucky Aden had been so sheltered. A half-awake seven-year-old would not have bought that line from him, even for half a worm (the smallest unit of currency on the playground).

"Aden wants to listen to some music. Do you have an entertainment unit we could use?" the actor asked. Keeping his own voice normal was a challenge; his natural want to echo the strange overperformance was quite strong inside him.

"It that right?!" Dr. Ramon asked with such shock and awe, you'd think he had just found out Kyle and he were long-lost twins. Kyle was beginning to think the man had missed his calling. Overacting that bad belonged on a soap opera. (Where no doubt Kyle would indeed turn out to be his long-lost step cousin, who would know the secret whereabouts of the lost cursed emerald of so-and-so).

However, Aden nodded his huge head. "Yes, please. I would like to hear more songs."

"Well, I do have a small entertainment system in my office for just that. I am sure I can let you borrow it. Of course, I will need it back. Kyle can bring it back after his day with you is over," Dr. Ramon enthused, handing over a small device to the equine. Kyle could see the pure, unadulterated joy on the scientist's face, and it took him a moment or two to realize Aden had spoken to him again. Probably for the first time since Brian was taken away. It didn't help that he spoke to the huge, hulking beastman as if Aden were a ten-year-old boy.

Aden's eyes did roam around the office, drinking in every detail. They paused on the desk, staring at the book resting there, and Kyle got to see the moment of realization as the nervous smile on his face turned into an honest, full smile. The equine glanced at him. He smiled and gave a slight nod of confirmation. Showing some composure, the horse moved on, checking out the rest of the stuff in the office.

"Alright, well, I suppose we should go back now," the actor said, placing a hand on Aden's back and gently guiding him back out of the office.

"Nice to see you, Aden," Dr. Ramon beamed. Unable to resist one last moment to overact, he added. "This was a delightful surprise visit!" Kyle didn't give Aden a chance to respond, he just ushered him back down the not-so-magical gray corridor and back out into Aden's world. "We should go to your bedroom."

"Why?" The horse was confused by the suggestion.

Kyle couldn't think of a way to summarize the centuries of angsty rebel teens listening to music in their bedrooms, playing it too loud because it was meant to be loud (plus, it would seriously annoy their parents and or siblings). So, he simply replied, "It just sounds better. Plus, we can lay down and listen in privacy." Utterly private, as long as you don't count the camera in his eye and the microphone in his ear (lexicographers everywhere would scream if they knew how badly he was abusing their words).

The pony didn't seem to quite get it, but he agreed anyway and led the way to his room. Kyle was surprised by how similar it was to his own. Every stick of furniture identical, no doubt company approved. The only thing he had been missing was an entertainment unit. Kyle took the one out of Aden's hand and placed it on the small table. "I'm just going to set up a playlist of my favorites. A bit of everything, some very old and some new. A lot of songs have been around for centuries, new people make recordings of them and re-release. That song I sang you earlier, there are . . ." He ran a quick check on the device, keeping the holoscreen fairly small. He couldn't help but notice all other functions on the unit had been disabled. There would be nothing he could do with it but play music. "Two-hundred and three different versions of it on here."

"Including the first?" The pony asked, trying to look over his shoulder.

"Yes. I'll set that one to play and then just add what I think you might like. We can try a mix of stuff and see what your music tastes lean to." In his years as an actor, Kyle had learned a good deal about music. Many clients wanted him for more than just some sweaty fun; they wanted companionship and to share their likes with someone who was open to them. That had let him develop an appreciation for a wide range of styles and genres of music. "Now, just lay down and open your ears."

Aden did as instructed, laying down on the bed and closing his eyes. Kyle clicked start on the playlist and sat down on the chair beside the bed. As the music started to play, he reached over and took Aden's hand. The next few hours were amongst the most wonderful of Kyle's life. Watching Aden as his ears were opened to a world of sounds he had never even dreamed of. There were tears, both of sadness and joy, as Aden lost himself to some of the classical pieces. The two shared some laughter on some comedic songs, and Kyle introduced Aden to the voice activated 'skip' command when the pony was clearly not enjoying a song.

The afternoon passed quickly. Far too quickly for Aden, and even Kyle had to admit he felt a little sad when he was informed his time was up and that he could leave. He didn't leave straight away. He sat with Aden and listened to the last few songs on the playlist. As the music stopped, Aden sat up on the bed, his face the picture of misery. Kyle couldn't stop himself; he reached out on instinct, stroking Aden's cheek, and his bravery was rewarded with a nuzzle. "I'll be back at breakfast tomorrow."

"Do you have to take the entertainment unit?" The slight whine in the equine's voice tugged on Kyle's heart a little too hard.

"Yes, sorry, we did promise. I will bring it back tomorrow and speak to Dr. Ramon about getting you one for your room. No promises, though," Kyle whispered, leaning down a little and pressing his forehead to Aden's. It was a nice feeling, the touch of his fur, the warmth and closeness. His hand continued to stroke Aden's cheeks reassuringly.

"No promises, I understand." The two stayed like that together for a moment, then Kyle stood up. When he reached the door, Aden suddenly called out, "Kyle!"

"Yes?" the human asked, stopping and turning back to look at the horse.

"I . . . I'm glad you're my companion." There it was. Dempsy and Dr.

Ramon could go eat a dick. Kyle had done it. Aden trusted him and liked him. It was the moment he had worked so hard for, yet he couldn't understand why he felt so bad hearing that.

"I'm glad I got this job, and I'm really glad to have gotten to know you." Every word of it was true, scientists could spend decades analyzing every aspect of his sentence and not find a hint of a lie. So, he really couldn't understand why he felt so guilty as he turned and left.

Dr. Ramon was ecstatic with him when he got back to the office. Not only had he connected with Aden, he had spread a dark version of the outside world full of drug addicts and, more importantly, got the pony to speak to him again. Somehow, the scientist's joy only added to the growing pit of discomfort in the actor's stomach. He retired to his room as quickly as he could, spending only a brief time in the mess hall. He bumped into Becky, and she exchanged a few obscenities before he excused himself, grabbed a pile of food packets, and returned to his room.

The first thing he noticed was his clothes had all been taken. He hoped they would be returned the next morning. It would be nice to be able to wear his own gear. The baggy scrubs were not exactly helping him feel himself. After a scalding hot and long shower, he laid on his bed, turned some music on, and thought back on the day.

Chapter 9

This time, there were no nightmares, no dreams, only welcome blackness. Time passing but with the blink of a tired eye. Kyle awoke long before his alarm. The sunlight was red passing through his window, and, as he checked the time, he found it was just a little after five. He couldn't remember the last time he had awoken this early. However, his mind felt clear and alert, far too clear and alert for him to hope he could go back to sleep.

Instead, he slipped out of bed, the floor tiles very cold on his bare feet slapping slightly, the slightest sound seeming thunderous in the dawning hours. He pulled the blinds up and gazed out of his window to find the sky a glorious red color. The sun having just cleared the horizon, clouds dotted the blue and orange sky, many glowing orange and red with the light. It was quite beautiful, and he found himself standing there just studying the scene; like it was some exquisite painting hanging in a gallery.

The cool morning air wafted around his flesh, waking him further. He knew he would need to move and head out soon. However, he rather liked that, for a moment, he had just peace and calm. Nobody wanting him to do anything, he could just enjoy the silence and the world around him. There were no sunrises or sunsets to watch back home, not unless he went to sit on a rooftop. Then he risked being arrested for loitering, plus traveling back in the dark held its own dangers.

With a smile, he opened the window and let the cold morning air in, Kyle could feel goosebumps forming on his skin. However, that was ignored for the scent of grass, trees, and flowers. The smell of dew evaporating in the early morning sun, pollen, and so much more. The feel of the sun's rays seemed far more intense with the cold air around him, the rays kissing his naked form as he closed his eyes. Then, a soft beeping warned him that it was time to wake, he had a job to do. His body tensed for a moment, and he fought for a few more seconds of bliss.

He gave a deep sigh and gave the command for the alarm to turn off. It was time to face the day and whatever it brought him; somehow, that seemed easier. Maybe it was because of how well the previous day had gone, or possibly all he had needed was a moment of clarity and peace to calm him down. It didn't really matter which. As he scrubbed himself under the hot water of his shower, he thought about what the day would hold. Breakfast, probably with Aden, exercise, another run. This time, he would have to watch his footing.

Kyle wondered if Dr. Ramon would approve his book. Even if he didn't, he knew he'd gotten value from it. Aden had seen it and knew that Kyle had been honest with him. If it was permitted, he would read it to the horse; if not, then music and, well . . . there was the one dark cloud on the horizon. At some point, there would be a need to try and take a sample from the equine. Dr. Ramon would want him to help, and Aden would feel betrayed if he did.

It was possible that he might be able to find some middle road. A way to encourage Aden to participate while not going too far. Yet the actor knew that would not solve the problem for more than a day. Even if he didn't lose the job, Dempsy would ask him where his bonus was. Kyle pulled on his scrubs, begrudging the lack of his own clothes. There was a solution, and he had a feeling it was on the very tip of his tongue.

Opening the door to his room, he found a neatly folded pile of his own clothes. All of them clean and ready. He laughed to himself; at least he could be comfortable while he did what he knew he had to. Since he knew that Aden would exercise after breakfast, he selected some of his running shorts and a plain white tank top to wear. It didn't hurt that they showed off his body a lot more than the baggy scrubs had done.

Feeling more himself than he had since he first set foot in the facility, he stepped out into the corridor. In his pocket, he had the small tin with his earpiece, ready for action. He headed to Dr. Ramon's office, only to find the door locked and nobody answering his knocking. So, he moved on. He knew he was supposed to have breakfast with Aden. Doing so without the doctor in his ear actually seemed appealing, and it was Dr. Ramon's fault for not being up and ready as they had agreed only two days ago. So, with a smile on his face, he walked out into Aden and Bruno's compound. He wasted no time heading towards the small dining room that Aden ate in.

Aden was sitting at his table with a tray of food in front of him, a lot smaller portions than Kyle had expected. Clearly, they had not been expecting him to turn up. Dr. Ramon probably forgot to make arrangements. Of course, Kyle knew there was no going back the second Aden caught sight of him. The equine smiled and almost jumped to his hooves. Kyle gave a little gesture for him to stay there as he quickly approached. "Good morning," he announced cheerily as he sat down, his stomach gurgling a little as he knew he was unlikely to be filling it soon.

"Good morning, Kyle, I am really glad to see you again." The horse was beaming a huge grin at the actor. "Did you bring the entertainment unit? Or the book?"

Waving his empty hands, the actor shrugged. "It's a bit early for that. Breakfast, then exercise, and then fun. Plus, I couldn't find Dr. Ramon, he was supposed to arrange breakfast for me with you."

The horse moved so quickly, his arms were nothing but a golden blur as he pushed his half-finished tray over. "You can share mine!" Kyle couldn't help but chuckle; it was clear that there was one thing Aden didn't want him doing, and that was leaving to get his own breakfast.

"No, that's yours. I'm sure I can get some food packets later on." Leaning across the table, he whispered conspiratorially, "I am not about to collapse from malnourishment if my breakfast is a little late, now am I?"

Aden chuckled and pulled his tray back. "I guess not, but, if you want, you could have some of mine, just to stop you feeling hungry."

Kyle reached over and took a couple of carrot sticks off the horse's plate. "Thanks, I . . ."

"What the hell are you doing?!" The voice in his ear was far too loud, and Kyle couldn't help but wince as Dr. Ramon screamed into his ear.

"Are you ok?" Aden asked as the actor put the carrot sticks down on the table.

"I'm fine, sorry, I just need to go to the bathroom. I'll be back soon," Kyle said with an apologetic smile.

"You are never to see the subject without my knowledge!" howled the outraged scientist in his ear. The actor headed into the bathroom attached to the small test subjects' dining hall.

Once inside with the door closed behind him, there was no lock on the inside. Kyle guessed because they worried about the subjects trying to hide. He looked at himself in the mirror. "Hey, please stop shouting in my ear, you are really loud."

"Don't tell me about volume, what the hell were you thinking?" ranted the scientist, although Kyle noticed the volume was lowered slightly.

"I was thinking that you told me that I was to eat breakfast with Aden from now on." Kyle looked at himself in the mirror, giving Dr. Ramon a view of just how serious he was. "I was thinking that I needed to spend as much time with Aden as possible if I am to help you guys get him back being productive. As well as thinking that you were the sort of organized guy who wouldn't forget this sort of detail, especially considering how much importance you and

Dr. Salter place on getting Aden productive again." Kyle tried to keep his face passive, but firm. Even though he could feel a smug smirk desperate to force its way onto his face. The mention of Dr. Salter had been a particularly fun touch, he thought. After all, Dr. Ramon was very worried about his boss, and everything he had said was completely true.

"Damn it! You're right, I totally forgot we had set that up. Look, sorry for yelling, I'll get someone to bring you a breakfast tray." The change of Dr. Ramon's tone was refreshingly quick. Kyle had expected him to argue. After all, he had tried the scientist's office, the actor must have known he wasn't going to be monitored. Although given the pressure the scientist was under, he guessed he was so used to making mistakes, he no longer questioned it when someone pointed one out. That wasn't too uncommon, especially in company men. All it took was a little bit of low self-confidence and pressure, then people would believe almost anything you wanted.

"Hey, no problem. It don't make much difference anyway. I was only here about two minutes before you turned up. There isn't much trouble a man can get into in two minutes." That wasn't true, and Kyle knew it. There was a whole hell of a lot of trouble a guy can cause if alone for two minutes in the wrong place. Of course, he certainly wasn't going to tell Dr. Ramon about those occasions; they were behind him anyway.

"Alright, well look, get back out there and get on with the morning," the scientist replied, probably wanting to move on after the short exchange.

Kyle was certainly happy to move on and back out, especially when he heard food was on the way. However, before he left, he asked, "Did you get a chance to check out *The Horse and His Boy*? Aden is bound to ask about it today."

"I'm halfway through, not a bad story, really. A bit old fashioned and a tad bit . . . not politically correct in places. I can see your point, though, there is a good strong message about the dangers of straying where you are warned not to go. I want to finish it first. If the rest is like this, then I see no problem in letting Aden read it." Not the best news, especially as Kyle felt the scientist was stalling more so that he could finish reading the book than because he was going to say no. Although a yes tomorrow would be just as much use as one today.

Returning to Aden, he found the horse was almost finished his breakfast. He sat down opposite him and picked up the carrot sticks, nibbling on them slowly.

"Better?" the horse asked with mild concern. Given the sudden stop and dash to the toilet, Kyle felt slightly embarrassed when he imagined what Aden had thought his reason for being so quick might be.

"Yes, I'm fine. I guess my tummy isn't quite used to all this fresh fruit and veg," he replied, blushing slightly and waving a carrot stick in front of him as evidence and a defense all in one.

"You don't eat fruit and vegetables normally? What do you eat?" Aden asked curiously, looking down at his plate. He couldn't remember a meal that hadn't had some fruit or vegetables in. He often had oatmeal and nuts as well. However, he couldn't imagine living on just that.

"Well, processed food packs. It's the most common form of food these days," Kyle replied with a shrug as he finished his carrot sticks. "You see, food takes a lot of land to grow, and then it needs to get to the people. Plus, fresh fruit and vegetables go off, and then they can't be eaten. Well, there used to be a hell of a lot of waste. If we'd kept things like in the old days, we wouldn't have been able to support such high population. So, food is now mostly processed on the site it is grown, into small packs. They have like protein, carbs, and all the vitamins and minerals you need. Of course, they don't exactly taste as good as food, sort of chemically with all the preservatives. Fruit and vegetables can be bought, but they are not cheap. There's no way I could afford to eat them every day like you do."

As the actor explained the situation, a technician entered with a small tray. There was an apple on it along with a couple of food packs. Kyle grabbed one and opened it up. The small, brown, tacky lump was held up for Aden to see. "There, most of them are like this. Some are colored to try and make them look more appetizing. Still, these ones are pretty good, top of the range, so to speak. You want to try a bite?" Kyle half expected Dr. Ramon to shout in his ear about Aden's diet being very carefully regulated. However, once more, the scientist showed he was learning when to keep his mouth shut. After all, a good way to get Aden's mind off his wanderlust was to show some of the worst parts of life elsewhere.

The horse took the brown object by the wrapper and sniffed at the block. His face twisted a little. However, he didn't let the smell stop him; he took a small, careful bite out of one corner and chewed slowly. His face a vision of thoughtfulness. "I prefer carrots," He observed, handing the bar back to Kyle.

"Oh yes, so would most people. However, it's better than starving. Keeps you on your feet and going. Plus, it's affordable. That's my watchword for life," Kyle chuckled as he took back the bar. "If you can't afford it, don't buy it. You'd be surprised how easy it is to get into debt. A few of the other actors I have worked with, they spend too much on . . . all kinds of stuff, and, well, they get into huge debts. Then you are working more to pay your debts and try to live. I stay smart, save what I can, and don't ever spend more than I have to."

Aden didn't reply, he just looked thoughtfully at the bar and back to his own plate. The actor felt quite pleased with himself; everything he had said was true. He had to avoid mentioning that a lot of his co-workers ended up addicted to one drug or another. It was a common way to escape, but Kyle knew that escape, and it was a lie. It was better to save up, to plan, and work.

The real escape was going to be getting Dempsy to nullify his contract. Of course, it would take a large cash injection to do that, but, with each passing year, the demands for Kyle would start to fade. Everyone wanted a young, twenty-something actor. Once he hit thirty, then the man might be willing to negotiate. That left Kyle with a big 'what next' question. He had a few years left to figure out an answer for it.

He finished the food packet quickly and reached out a hand to stroke the pony's arm. "Hey, are you ok?"

"Yeah, I just never really thought about what I would eat out there, or how I would get money." The pony sighed softly and then shook his head. "I think it is time for exercise."

Something in Aden's expression sent deep pangs of guilt into the actor's stomach. He wanted to put his arms around the sad beast, to tell him that it would be okay. There were always ways to earn money and to buy food. You just had to be willing to hold your nose and do the jobs nobody really wanted. Society had developed thousands of them. Hell, that was what work really was, something someone wanted done that nobody actually wanted to do. They pay you because you would never do it for free.

Of course, the little voice in his ear would get really loud if he said anything of the sort. So, he settled for putting an arm around the horse as they walked. Aden returned the arm, his huge, muscular limb feeling quite good around him. Kyle had always enjoyed just being held; unfortunately, he didn't get to enjoy it much as they reached the small gym shortly afterwards. This time, they had beaten Bruno and Cassandra there.

Working out in his shorts and tank-top was far more comfortable than just his boxers. Bruno and Cassandra arrived a few minutes after he and Aden got onto the rowing machines. The black horse gave him a long look and then a slight nod of acknowledgement. Acceptance, it actually felt quite nice. Cassandra stopped by to exchange a few words, a professionally polite and yet empty conversation. Just making sure Kyle knew she was there and that she knew he was there.

He even managed to exchange a few words with Bruno, short ones, no more than two syllables. He didn't want to overtax the brute. Although since their encounter, the creature seemed a little bit more comfortable with him. Something told Kyle that he had Cassandra to thank for that. She had probably decided that it would be better if there was no conflict between the two. Which was a relief, although he couldn't help but notice that Bruno did seem to keep himself in the actor's eyeline.

If Kyle wasn't so sure Bruno wanted Cassandra, he might have thought the horse was coming on to him. Switching from machine to machine whenever Kyle did. Keeping himself in front of the actor as he worked out, sweated, and flexed. Although Kyle also knew it might be a subtle attempt at ensuring

Kyle knew he was no threat to the larger male. Which was the more likely scenario; however, much like Aden, the horse's very fit body was not a bad thing to watch flex and bend.

After their workout, Bruno and Cassandra disappeared into their room. Kyle wondered what they did all day. Did Bruno have the same restrictions on entertainment as Aden? He tried to stop that line of thinking before it went too far. Cassandra was like him. She would do what her client wanted, and Bruno's wants seemed pretty basic.

Kyle joined Aden on his run; this time, they took it at a far gentler pace. Jogging side by side, not saying much. Though the two did exchange a few glances and smiles. There was definitely something he actually found attractive in the horse. Maybe it was his innocence, or possibly his body. However, it didn't really matter too much; he liked him, and that just made some parts of his job far easier.

"We're going to try and take a sample after he finishes his run," Dr Ramon warned in his ear.

Kyle slowed his pace just a little, letting Aden pull ahead, and then whispered, "No! Don't, just . . . let me do it, okay?"

The silence he got in response was deafening. He was just beginning to think that Dr. Ramon hadn't heard him when he got a reply, "Okay, we'll leave the device in Aden's room." They had given him what he wanted. All he had to do now was give them what they expected, or at least wanted. He already knew what he would have to do, now he just needed to go for it and hope that Aden was receptive to more than just hugs and music.

"Are you ok?" the equine asked as the human caught up with him again.

"Yes, sorry, just a little bit of cramp. I'm past it now," Kyle muttered as the two continued to run.

By the time they had finished, Kyle's shorts and tank-top were soaking in sweat. He could see sweat glistening on the equine's coat as well as they both worked through a few cooldown stretches. "I can't wait for a shower," the actor observed, cringing for a moment as he realized he hadn't thought to bring a clean set of clothes for after his workout with him.

"My shower is just next to my room," Aden muttered, not able to look the actor in the eye. Kyle knew that was a lot more than an observation or a statement by the pony. It was an invite, quite a clear one, and definitely one that boded well for his plan.

"Maybe I could use it, too . . . if there's room for two, that is," replied the actor, looking directly at the equine. Aden seemed to be able to look everywhere but directly at Kyle; his eyes wandered the landscape. If the actor had touched Aden's cheeks, he was sure he would find them burning hot with the embarrassed blush of a teenager arranging his first date.

"It is big enough for more than just me," Aden confirmed and then turned quickly away from the actor, walking rapidly towards his quarters. Kyle had to jog to keep up, but the faster he went, the faster Aden moved. Always keeping his back to Kyle just a little, his tail swishing as his hooves clopped on the floor.

It took a moment for Kyle to figure out why the equine might feel the need to run; it wasn't just eagerness. If anything, he expected Aden to be very cautious as a lover. No, this was because he didn't want Kyle to see his front, at least not yet, and the actor had a good idea why the naked equine might want to keep the actor's eyes at his back.

Aden didn't stop or slow down until they reached his room. He trotted straight into the shower and turned the water on. Kyle didn't waste time; he stripped out of his sweat-soaked clothes and was about to step into the shower when he stopped. He reached up to his ear and quickly pulled the transmitter out, figuring it was best he didn't get it wet. Besides, there was no way he wanted anyone speaking to him during what was about to happen. Dr. Ramon could deal with visuals and whatever muffled sounds he could get. With no time to waste, he hid the transmitter under the soap dish and then turned to the shower.

He pulled the curtain open and found Aden standing with his back to the door, hot water already spraying down over his perfectly sculpted form. The huge beast seemed to shrink away from him, shuffling forward to almost hide in the corner of the shower. Kyle could see he had some work to do to get the equine relaxed to a point anything could happen. That didn't bother him; in fact, he quite liked the idea of taking his time. Especially knowing that, in his office, Dr. Ramon was probably ranting about the transmitter. It just made the moment all the sweeter. So long as he got results, he was certain that they wouldn't fire him. They were desperate to get Aden productive, and Kyle was the best person to do that job.

"Hey, you want me to do your back?" He whispered, and Aden jumped a little. Reaching out, he could feel the giant animal trembling under his fingers. "It's okay, Aden, I'm here for you, and I'm not going to do anything you don't want me to. You know that, right?"

With a nod of his huge head Aden, confirmed his understanding, and then he whispered, "I just . . . I've never . . . I don't . . . know . . ."

Kyle took sympathy on the equine as Aden stumbled over his words. Stepping closer he pressed his naked chest and body against the pony's, slipping his arms around to hold Aden's chest. "It's okay, I know you are not experienced. Is it okay with you that I am . . . quite experienced?"

Strong equine hands landed on Kyle's and squeezed tightly. Kyle rested his head on Aden's shoulder. He could still feel the creature trembling against him, yet much gentler than before; like the soft, warm vibration of a smooth-running engine beneath him. The actor just held the pony, knowing that the best thing he could do was not push. Aden wanted this, he was certain of that.

However, he was scared. Kyle remembered his own first time, the exhilaration and yet also the fear and the questions that ran through his own mind. 'What if it hurts? What if I'm no good? What if he hates me afterwards?'

"It's okay," Aden confirmed, and Kyle leaned up a little, kissing the equine's neck. Fur against his sensitive skin, yet softer than the coarse animal fur of normal horses; it tickled his skin, and he felt the huge animal exhale a deep breath. The trembling under him had almost stopped, and the hands that had been squeezing were now stroking, softly running up his arms.

"Then turn around, please." Kyle had to stand on his tiptoes to whisper that near Aden's ears. He felt the pony tense under him and heard the sharp hiss of a shocked breath. "It's okay, I just want to see you and for you to see me." The actor knew the pony had never seen him naked. He'd probably only ever seen his brother's naked body. Kyle doubted that the scientist he had replaced had ever looked to get close to Aden in this way.

For a few moments, only the splashing of water broke the silence, and then Aden began to turn. Slowly, like a huge oil tanker, his huge body almost having a gravity of its own, or maybe just gravitas. However, Kyle enjoyed the turn, his eyes wandering over the wet, furry body, taking in every glimmer of light and every flex of muscle. Then his eyes locked onto the object of his desire, jutting out at full attention and desperate to receive some of his attention.

"Beautiful!" Kyle whispered the word, and he meant it. When they'd told him what the job was, this was the moment he'd feared. He'd worried that it would be so inhuman, some strange, bestial thing. Yet Aden was so much more than his animal form. He was a gentle being, desperate to know and be known. He was a mass of power, trembling before someone for fear they might reject him. What human couldn't remember a time they had done the same? Opening themselves to rejection, praying that they were accepted.

Kyle's hands reached up, stroking up the pony's perfect pectorals, and then to his strong and long neck. His arms laced around the equine neck, and gently he pulled. It took no force at all, and Aden's muzzle came down. Their lips met. It was a strange kiss at first, Aden's lips not used to the touch and feeling different from any other lover. Then the equine stepped forward, his arms slipping around Kyle's torso, pulling him close with desperate need.

Their tongues met, and with gentle strokes, they danced while they got their first taste of each other. The equine's tongue was larger and stronger than any Kyle had encountered, yet he let the human take the lead. Strong hands stroked slowly around his back, the soft fur tickling his hot flesh. Aden moaned for the first time, and Kyle smiled, to know the equine was finally letting go.

With a shared gasp, their first kiss ended. "You really are amazing," Kyle whispered the words into the panting equine's ear while his hands stroked down Aden's chest and stomach. Feeling every smooth line and bump of defined muscle. Even under the plush fur, he could feel the well-trained physique. Although that was just the icing on the delicious cake that was Aden. The pony gave a deep, passionate moan, filled with feral need and lust, just when Kyle's fingers found what they had been questing for.

Thick and hard, and so hot to the touch, it shocked Kyle. The head was more human, and yet the length and girth, were certainly gifts from his equine heritage. Along the middle, a thick band of muscle ran, the medial ring a good half inch. Aden bucked his hips a little, soft murmurs escaping his lips as the equine struggled to speak; too lost to his first experience to form words. The shaft was mottled black and pink in color, the skin near the base leatherier.

"Do . . . do you really think so?" Aden finally managed to whisper, and Kyle smiled at his partner's nervousness. He knew that, in these situations, it was sometimes best to show rather than tell. One of his hands was pulled away from Aden's cock. He reached up and took Aden's hand from off his lower back and guided it down to his front.

The actor smiled as he heard the equine gasp, as he pushed Aden's trembling hand against his own turgid length. The fingers stroking hesitantly at first, as if not believing what he was feeling. The hand closed around the length, and Kyle gave him a deep, lustful moan as a reward, and then gasped out, "You can feel it yourself. I really, really think you are amazing, beautiful, and sexy." he whispered the words into Aden's chest. As he did so, he spied a little, fleshy nub poking through the perfect, golden chest.

"I feel it, I . . . OOOHH!" Aden cried out as Kyle's lips closed around his nipple. The little nub had always seemed a useless, inconsequential part of him. Then with his lover's first touch, it became the central part of his body, warm feeling shooting out, with each caress of the human's hungry tongue. His cock throbbed and ached, and he couldn't stop his hips from thrusting. Something deep and primal inside him was awakening, a side of himself he never knew existed. Kyle was coaxing the beast in him out, like a hunter drives out his prey before going in for the kill. "Kyle . . . ohh . . . Kyle!"

The human let his grip on the equine's shaft tighten, running a thumb over the wet glans, stroking around the coronal ridge. Aden's human-like flare fat and thick, yet small in comparison to the thick, meaty shaft that followed. While his other hand reached out to find another excited nub and squeeze, just enough to draw another squeal of pleasure from the equine. The clop of hooves on the tiled floor echoed around the tiny cubicle as Aden shuffled from foot to foot. The pleasure was almost too much for him, the feelings of his body and mind were too much. He wanted Kyle, he was desperate to have him. His nose flared as he breathed in the human's scent; even through the soap and hot water, he could smell him. Kyle smelled good. He buried his nose in the human's neck, huffing deeply.

Kyle moaned and giggled a little as the huge muzzle snuggled at his neck.

It tickled and yet felt good. Aden's hands had grown bolder, the one on his cock was jerking it quickly with the enthusiasm and vigor of a young male. Even without the experience to know exactly where to touch and squeeze, the sensation was pleasurable. Kyle thrust into the hand a little, and then gasped as the other hand grabbed his ass powerfully and possessively. Kyle knew that kind of feeling, and, from Aden, he liked the touch, the strength of the male around him making him feel both safe and somehow owned.

He could feel Aden's heart beating out a rapid staccato beat as the equine lost himself to the pleasure. Kyle wanted to ride out the moment together, to bring each other to the very peak of bliss and let that thick cock rain down the contents of Aden's heavy nuts. However, a small part of his mind was still awake enough to know he still had a job to do. Letting go of Aden's nipple, he jumped up and kissed the equine deeply and passionately.

There was no hesitation from either of them, their tongues dancing and wrestling, gliding over one another as they shared moans and gasps of elation. Then the kiss was broken. Aden sighed slightly, as if disappointed to lose such a passionate moment. Kyle felt the same, but he knew that the pony wouldn't mind in a moment. As he sank to his knees on the hard tile floor. With a soft moan, Aden's hands were pulled away from their positions.

A question was in Aden's eyes as he looked down at his human lover, on his knees before him. Kyle answered the unspoken question with actions rather than words. His hand gripping the base of Aden's shaft while he leaned forward and kissed the tip. There was no mistaking the whinny of pleasure, or the stamp of hoof on tile. The pony enjoyed the sensation, as did Kyle. He had always enjoyed the feeling of maleness in his mouth. The heat against his tongue and the taste of sweat, musk, and something more. His device was already working, and yet he could still savor Aden's flavor on his tongue. The taste of man, or beast, and of so much more. His tongue caressed over the swollen glans and then teased around Aden's coronal ridge.

He felt a jet of pre on his tongue, caught in a tiny web of polymers. He wondered what it would have tasted like. He swallowed it quickly, feeling the heartbeat of his lover radiating through his mouth. Aden was close, he knew it. He wanted to draw this out, to show the equine the true heights of pleasure he could scale. However, he knew he would have time to teach Aden all about such worldly things. For now, he knew the animal couldn't hold back that long.

Aden proved his suspicions right by thrusting forward, the cock sliding deep into his mouth until his lips kissed the medial ring. His hand started to jerk the lower shaft quickly. The other hand reached under Aden, fondling those huge dangling orbs, poor things that had not been drained in many weeks. While his head bobbed quickly, his tongue dancing and squirming over the hot horsemeat in his mouth. The sounds of water were drowned out by cries of pleasure and delight from Aden, whinnies and stamps, moans and gasps, all cut with rapid pants and the deep passion, repeated moans of "Kyle . . . oh Kyle!"

The human drank it all in, the taste, the feel, the sounds, and the emotions. Soft equine hands caressed his cheeks and then ran through his thick hair. Aden never pulled or held him; he put his trust in Kyle and was rewarded with the tongue and lips he desired. The creature could barely contain himself. He gave in to the animal inside, being absorbed by the pleasure that seemed to spread out from the warm feelings in his cock; it ran through to every fiber, dancing down his every nerve and making every touch and caress feel so much more sensuous.

With the voice above him growing weaker, Kyle could tell the equine was drawing near his peak . . . The human knew that Aden would be struggling to contain himself. He had known nothing but those devices they used to sample him. They stimulated and felt good, but it was like water compared to the finest of dark red wines. The feelings of a real, warm, live mouth surrounding you, sucking you deeper, were so much more potent and fruitful, sustaining and fulfilling. The feel of hot breath blowing into your crotch as your maleness sank into your lover's depths. Kyle knew it well, and he knew that, for Aden, this was a first, and for a moment, he desperately hoped far from the last time he would service his new client.

Looking up, he could see Aden staring down, unable to take his eyes off the human, off his cock, as it was devoured by those soft and sensual lips. Kyle's hands on the equine's heavy balls stroked and caressed, a pleasure he had never endured before, the pressure inside those orbs growing greater and greater until Aden felt they would burst. Then Kyle gripped lightly and tugged on them very gently.

It proved to be too much for Aden. He whinnied with every gasp of air as he struggled to breathe above Kyle. His hands reaching out to stabilize himself on the tiled walls. Kyle smiled as he looked up at the equine above him, lost to the carnal bliss of a real lover. As his maleness throbbed and throbbed, shooting jet after jet of cum into his hungry lover's mouth. Kyle swallowed eagerly, drinking it down as quickly as it came.

The flow had been unexpected, far greater than anything any human had ever produced. The device in his mouth had been pushed a little beyond its capabilities. Kyle could taste it on his tongue, Aden's potent juices, and he wanted more. However, most was sealed safely and swallowed, and the traces vanished as the flow began to slow. Far superior in volume than any lover Kyle had ever had. The actor wondered what it would look like spraying out, a glorious white fountain, silver spurts landing on soft golden fur.

Kyle slurped hungrily on the softening cock, making sure to get every last drop before he pulled off and looked up at the equine smiling. "Was that okay?"

Aden could barely stand straight. His shoulders were slumped as he nodded his head. "I . . . never."

"You have now," chuckled the actor, getting back to his feet, putting his arms around Aden's neck and kissing him, this time softly and tenderly. Sharing the sweet afterglow with his lover. The two stayed that way for a few seconds, their lips nuzzling one another. Then Kyle whispered, "We should probably go get dry."

"No!" Aden's reply shocked Kyle, not just for the word, but for the commanding tone it was spoken with. He stood there, confused as Aden sank before him, his mind unable to process what was happening. It wasn't until he felt equine lips closing around his manhood that he realized what was happening.

"Oh God, Aden! You don't have to," he whispered, his hands reaching down to caress the equine's mane and ears. A deep snort of derision caressed his pubic hair while Aden drove his muzzle fully down the hard length. Kyle cried out in bliss, the long equine muzzle an advantage he had never considered before. He could feel the tickle of Aden sniffing at his crotch, taking the scent of his lover deep while he savored his taste.

Then the head began to move, his cock surrounded by warmth, the squirm of the broad and strong equine tongue delightful. He'd been sucked before, even deep-throated, but this was something different. With each bob of the head, he felt himself be driven closer to his own edge. It had been a while since he felt anything with a lover. Looking down, he found his eyes locking with Aden's. All he could see there was love and care. For a moment, he forgot everything. All his worries melted, the people he knew, the things they had done. Nothing mattered but his lover and him, together for a moment.

Inside, he felt something he hadn't for too long. His hips began to thrust. He was no longer just wanting to please his client, this was about his own pleasure. About their moment. He couldn't break the eye contact, he just looked down until his eyes felt dry. His cock thrusting faster and faster. Aden's only reaction was to moan and gasp happily, his strong hands caressing the human's thrusting ass. The pony took every inch he was fed. He caressed it, loved it with whatever he could, lips and tongue.

With a deft touch learned from his lover, Aden reached out and very gently caressed the actor's swinging sac. Remembering what Kyle had done, he tugged on them lightly. It was Kyle's turn to cry out, to thrash around, lost to the bliss of his lover's lips. His black length throbbing as he unloaded everything, feeling the squeeze as his lover drank down every drop. Until with a soft gasp, he closed his eyes, feeling the muzzle slowly pulling off his meat. Soft, velvet lips kissed his soft flesh tenderly, and then Aden was standing beside him. "We should get dried now," the horse whispered into his ear, guiding his human lover out of the shower.

Kyle grabbed some towels and began to dry himself; Aden helped. The two giggled and chuckled a little, sharing kisses, caresses, and embraces as they dried each other. When Aden's back was turned, Kyle quickly snatched back the transmitter and placed it into his ear.

"I need you to come back to my office now," Dr. Ramon stated clearly the second the transmitter was in place. Kyle looked at the mirror and gave a brief nod of response.

The two left the bathroom, and Kyle picked up his sweat-soaked shorts and shirt. "I need to go back to my room and get some clean clothes; otherwise, I am going to stink all evening."

"I don't mind your smell," Aden said with a smirk and a wink, feeling the cockiness that comes with a successful first time.

"You might not, but I do. I won't be long, and I'll see if I can get an entertainment unit so we can listen to more music," Kyle replied, wincing as he pulled on his damp and smelly clothing.

"Can I come with you again?" the pony's voice held just a trace of a beg to it, his eyes looking up imploringly.

"I . . . Not this time. We already pushed it yesterday. Besides, there really isn't much to see. My room is the same as yours," the human replied, knowing that what he had to do was definitely not something he could do with Aden present. "I'll be back quickly, ten minutes tops."

The actor leaned down and gave the seated pony a soft kiss on his velvet muzzle, then turned and left. He half jogged through the facility, reaching Dr. Ramon's office as quickly as he could. The door opened as he arrived, and Kyle braced himself for a possible telling off. "Come in, I have a tech on the way." The scientist called out from inside.

Stepping inside, Kyle found the doctor sitting beside a holoscreen. It was so weird to see the office in front of him, displayed on the screen. The screen in the display showed another smaller image of the same scene, out to infinity. "There's a bucket over there, you need any help regurgitating. I can probably get some pills or something," Dr Ramon asked, turning the screens off.

A little nonplussed by the scientist's reaction, he replied, "No, I can do it for myself. You knew what I was doing?"

"Well, I have your medical files, and the camera was on . . . I didn't look much, just when I had to for confirmation." Kyle wondered how much of that was a lie, if the scientist had watched his every move. However, it seemed clear the doctor wasn't quite as stupid as he feared. Maybe that PhD was worth something after all.

Kyle picked up the silver bucket that the Doctor had pointed to. This was going to be the unpleasant bit. Normally, he would pass the small polymer bags naturally a day or so later. Though that wasn't part of his plan this time.

The door opened just as he stuck his fingers down his throat. He coughed and choked, and then his stomach convulsed, and the room was filled with an unpleasant sound and smell.

"Oh, you just had to summon me here for this, didn't you?" asked a slightly disgruntled Becky. While she stood in the corner watching Kyle hurl up several white packages, along with part of his breakfast.

"It is your job," Dr. Ramon replied frankly.

"Yes, Sir, Sperm Sucker Becky here, ready, willing, and able!" she replied with a mocking salute. The doctor rolled his eyes while she added. "Although it looks like someone beat me to the sperm sucking today."

With a smile, Kyle handed the bucket to Becky, "Here, you go, right from the horse's . . . well, you know."

"Big fat cock? Yeah, I know!" laughed Becky as she ran a device over the top of the bucket. "Not bad, a good volume. I guess our boy was backed up. They are still viable, not too much saliva in there. Way to go champ." The last comment was aimed at Kyle, who gave her a shrug and a smile.

"Great job, Kyle. Although please keep your transmitter in on future occasions. I am there to help and support you, after all." The slight reprimanding tone made something slightly rebellious inside Kyle snap.

"Oh really. I've been a contracted prostitute since I was sixteen, I am really curious on what tips you are going to give me on sucking cock." The words fell out of his mouth faster than his brain could think. Becky howled with laughter in the background, and Dr. Ramon went crimson.

"I . . . I . . . see your point," the doctor replied, unable to stop himself from smiling. "Your job is to . . ." The doctor stumbled on his words.

With a shrug of his shoulders and a wink to Becky, Kyle confirmed his job, "I'm a whore. I have sex with whorses." Making sure he pronounced the extra w for just the right comedic effect. Another howl of laughter came from the woman, while even Dr. Ramon was chuckling.

"Oh, Kyle, that was really whorendus," snorted Becky with tears in her eyes. Kyle laughed, and the doctor burst out laughing, too, finally giving up on holding back. "Hey, look, he has a sense of humor!"

"You are both whorrible at this. Now be careful, or I'll have you both whauled over the coals," retorted Dr. Ramon to both their surprise and delight. The jokes were weak, but it was all they needed to keep them laughing for a minute or two.

"You can't expect me to be eloquent. After all I've done today, I'm a little whorse," the actor replied through his laughter.

"Kyle! I am whorrified by your lack of wit," shrieked Becky as she cackled and bent over with laughter.

When they calmed down a little, Becky looked down at the bucket. "Well, I'd better get this delightful package delivered to the lab. You won't believe how excited everyone is going to be to get their hands on this treat."

"I should get changed and get back to Aden, he will be wondering where I am. Can I get that entertainment unit again?" Kyle asked, pointing at the unit on Dr. Ramon's desk.

"Certainly," the doctor replied, waving at the device. "Oh, and good job today. With Aden back producing, we can get things back on track."

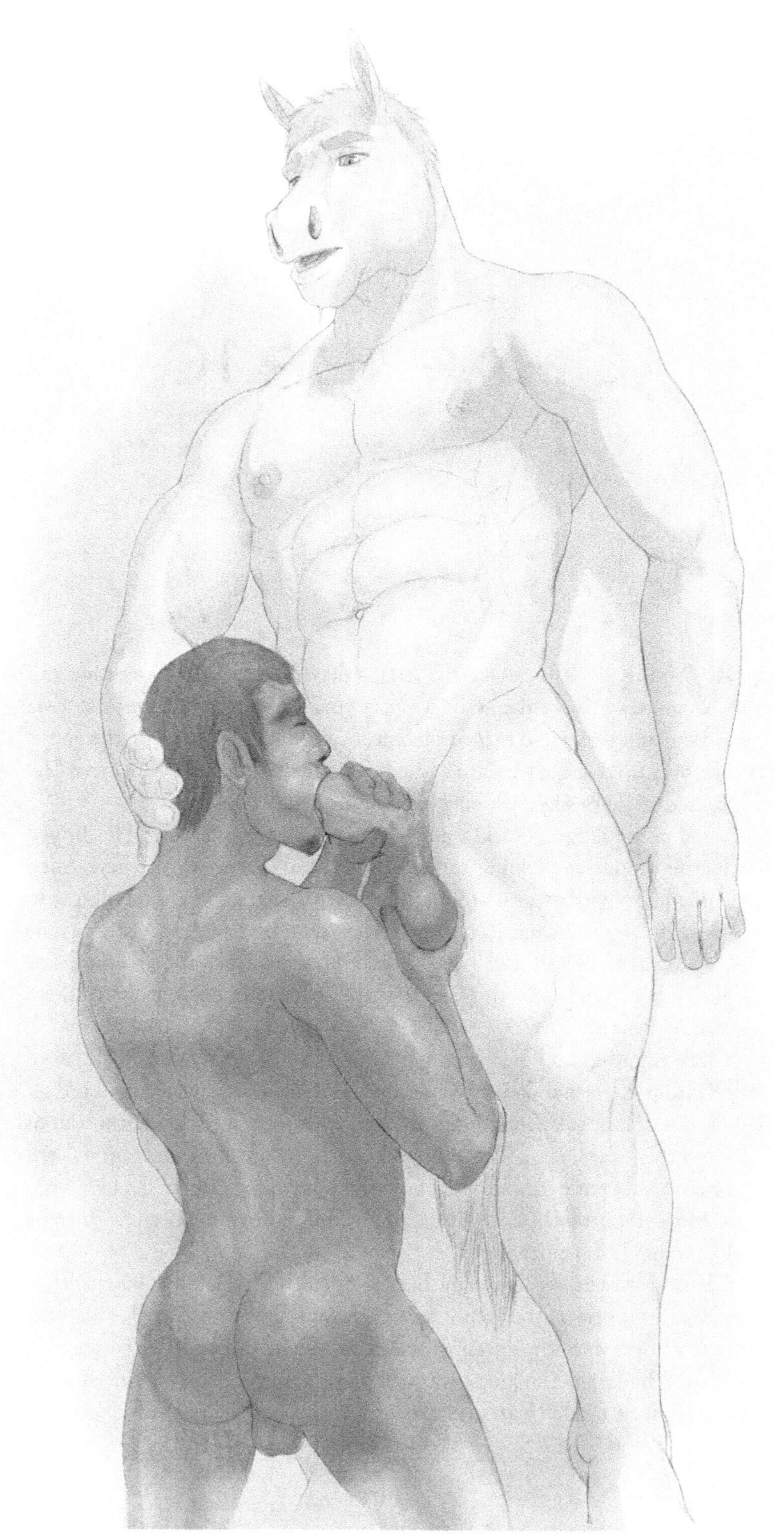

Chapter 10

When Kyle returned to him, Aden was delighted to see him, and more so to see the actor was carrying the entertainment unit. Kyle placed the unit down and turned the music on. Aden was laying on the bed as before, only this time, Kyle wasn't going to settle for the chair. "Move over," he whispered, giving a slight shooing wave of his hands.

The pony obliged quickly, and Kyle lay down beside him. He slipped both arms around the equine and rested his head on the strong chest. Aden welcomed him with an arm around him, and the actor found himself lost to the rhythm, not of the music, but the soft ba-dum-bum of Aden's heart as the two lay together, like all new lovers should. He expected Aden to want more, to push for a round two, and yet no such push came; neither one of them seemed to want to move.

Kyle found himself just letting his fingers stroke through the soft fur of Aden's stomach over and over. While around them, music played on. He'd set up a series of more classical works, no lyrics this time, just wonderful sounds to sooth the savage beast. The only question in Kyle's mind was who was the real beast? The gentle equine or the guy who was paid to extract 'samples' from him. More importantly, how savage might the gentle pony become once he realized what had happened?

However, as he listened to the beat of Aden's heart, he found his eyes closing, even the worry of the future faded away into nothing. They lay like that for a few hours until the gurgling of Aden's stomach woke Kyle. He yawned and sat up blinking. The music was still playing, but it had long since passed being listened to. Aden was snoring gently, with a rather cute smile of content on his face.

"Food is waiting for you two in the dining room," Dr. Ramon announced in his ear, breaking Kyle away from any daydreams he was having.

Reaching out, the human gently shook the pony awake. "Aden, time for some food."

The equine yawned and stretched out every muscle, giving Kyle quite the impressive display to look at as every muscle flexed and bulged in turn. He opened his eyes and looked up at Kyle with a smile. "I was having a lovely dream."

"From the sounds your stomach was making when I woke up, I'm going to assume you were having a dream dinner," chuckled the human, getting to his feet. He pulled at his t-shirt uncomfortably. "Remind me to strip off next time we do this. I hate sleeping in my clothes, feels all hot and sweaty."

"Yes, I will remind you," the pony replied with full sincerity, although Kyle thought he heard a hint of amusement in his tone.

"We should go eat," Kyle replied, offering a hand to help Aden up. The pony didn't need help, but he took the hand anyway and didn't let go after he was on his hooves. Not until they were sitting down to eat. Aden had the usual plateful of vegetables, some oatmeal, and fruit. While Kyle had food packets and a couple of pieces of fruit. Certainly not a bad meal by his standards, though he had hoped to see some meat, given the money the company was throwing around. Sadly, it seemed they didn't want to feed their stallions steak, probably for obvious reasons.

They didn't talk much as they ate, though the silence wasn't uncomfortable. In fact, it was oddly comfortable and relaxing. The doctor remained silent in his ear. It was good to see he had noticed that silence could be a good thing between two people, or maybe it was just that Aden had produced today and there was far less pressure on them all. Either way didn't make much difference; they got to eat together alone, exchanging little glances and small talk.

"Does Bruno never join you?" Kyle asked suddenly, looking around the small mess hall. It was clear that the room was designed for more than one subject. There was two tables and four chairs for a very obvious start.

"He does sometimes, but . . . well, I asked if I could get to know you alone for a week." Aden looked away, too embarrassed to hold Kyle's gaze. A second or two later, he felt Kyle's hand over his, giving it a gentle squeeze, and he looked back to a smiling face.

"I'm glad you did, it's not often I get to know people," the actor replied while he pushed his empty plate away with one hand.

"You don't?" The horse looked a little confused. "I thought on the outside, you would . . ."

Kyle shrugged his shoulders. "Not really. I mean, it's hard with my job. People tend to have expectations. As for the people who hire me . . . they call us actors because we pretend to be who you want. The people who hire me want something specific, they don't really want to know the real me. A lot of them don't want me to talk at all."

"So you are just pretending to be what I want?" The question was a bolt from the blue. It shot right to Kyle's heart. He looked back on his last statement and realized how stupid he had been, though he wasn't sure why.

Then it hit him. "No, I haven't pretended with you. You didn't want me to lie, to be someone else. So, I have been me, whoever that is."

It was Aden's turn to reach out to the human. "I'm not sure, but so far I like him."

A genuine smile slipped onto Kyle's lips, but part of his mind was still back wondering. "Does it bother you, what I have done for a living?"

"No, why should it?" The horse appeared confused by the question, his head tilting slightly, as if turning his head might bring reasoning into focus.

"I honestly don't know. It bothers most people. Most people believe you are supposed to meet someone, fall in love, and only have one partner at a time." It was a strange feeling to explain his job. It was like explaining it to a child, someone who didn't yet understand the rules of society. "People like me, we are looked down on. We have no skills or value to society, so we sell the only thing we have . . ."

"That sounds like slavery," Aden cut in, though his tone was one filled with more concern than any distaste.

"Maybe. I get paid, I suppose, enough to live on. This job pays really well. I am trying to save up to buy out my contract." Kyle leaned back in his chair and pulled his hand away from the pony. "Truth is, I am not sure what else I could do. Maybe try and get some schooling . . . it's not important right now, anyway. I have a job, and I like this contract. Good pay, nice food, and company that is both beautiful and enjoyable."

"That seems reasonable, I am glad this is a good job for you." Kyle could hear the tiny hint of pain behind those words as Aden looked away.

Kyle knew he had to do something, to repair any hurt. "The job is good, my friendship with you is . . . not part of the job. They can pay me to do what you want, what they want. They can't pay me to like you, to think of you as more than a customer. That is something that just happened. I wasn't expecting it, but I don't regret it. It is something that cannot be bought or sold"

For a moment, he worried that he had laid the response on too thick and too fast. However, Aden smiled, his eyes shining near tears and the look of pure puppy love on his face. Kyle felt more pangs of guilt, but he didn't know why he should regret saying any of it. He needed Aden to like him, more than that it was the truth.

"Do you want to go back to your room and listen to some more music?" Kyle asked, holding out his hand to the horse.

"I would like that very much," Aden's voice wavered just a little as he spoke. As the equine stood, Kyle wondered how many friends the equine had had. He'd had scientists, technicians, and Brian. One had been taken away, and the others had been the ones taking him away and stopping Aden leaving. Now he had a new friend, one with added benefits. He hoped that Aden would forgive him when he finally found out what those benefits really meant.

The two wandered back to Aden's bedroom. Kyle commanded the music to start playing, then he pulled off his shirt. Aden's ears perked up as his eyes examined the actor's body. While he lacked the physique of the pony, he was very shapely, his muscles well defined. However, it was his chest that Aden's eyes focused on.

"You looking at my tattoos?" The actor asked, sitting down on the bed next to Aden to let him have a better look.

"I didn't mean to stare. I noticed them before . . . but we were busy," the pony replied, reaching out a hand towards the tattoos. "What are they?"

"They are Celtic symbols . . . The Celts were an ancient European tribe, they didn't have technology. The star symbol on my right means wisdom, and the one on my left means luck." As he spoke, he gestured to each of the symbols in turn. "They use needles to inject ink under the skin . . ."

"Doesn't that hurt?" Aden gasped as his fingers traced over the shapes on the actor's pectorals.

"Yes, it does, some places worse than others. I got them to remind me of what I needed to remember; be smart and take advantage of your luck when you can, no missed chances." Kyle giggled a little as the horse's fingers tickled his skin.

"No missed chances, I like that," the horse replied, his paw staying on Kyle's chest. His eyes caught sight of something else, and he looked up at the black circles on the inside of Kyle's arm. "What do these circles mean?"

The question hit Kyle like a kick to the gut. He pulled his arm away, trying to hide the old wounds. "Nothing!" He almost shouted, his voice getting high pitched as his pulse began to race. "Just some old scars that never quite healed."

"Scars?" The horse asked more on reflex than anything else, Kyle's sudden change in tone and posture worrying him.

"Old injuries that never healed," Kyle explained as he forced his breathing to calm down. "I . . . got them when I was a kid. There was an accident, I got burned, and I don't like to talk about it." The words burned in his mind. He had been made to say something similar once, to his gym teacher. His fists clenched reflexively, and he forced a smile onto his face. "They don't matter." It was a lie so big, it could be seen from orbit. Yet Aden was oblivious to it, especially as the human slipped into bed next to him.

With a gentle caress, he brought Aden's muzzle down low and kissed him. At first, it was simply a way of ensuring no more questions. However, as Aden began to return the kiss he found himself relaxing, sinking into his lover's arms. Their tongues touched, and he felt a spark of electric between the two of them, of desire. He hadn't felt something like it for a long time, and he liked the feeling. Washing the painful memories from his mind, he savored the equine's taste and feel.

Under his chest, he could feel Aden's heart beating, his chest pressed to Aden's, their hearts beating faster and faster. While with each second their kiss grew more passionate, more intense, Kyle moaned, pushing his lips desperately to Aden's, yearning for more, his tongue pressed as deep into Aden's maw as it could, tasting him. The pony suckled on it softly, his own tongue caressing the human's as he savored the taste and feel.

Their hands explored each other's bodies, human ones stroking through equine fur and equine fingers tracing over smooth skin. With a gasp, the kiss was broken. Kyle looked at Aden, his eyes filled with lust, only to find the horse looking back with the same eyes. "I want you!" he whispered breathlessly.

"I know," Aden replied, his lips returning to the human's desperately, hungrily. Thick equine tongue forced its way into Kyle's mouth, tasting him and exploring. Kyle sucked on the slippery appendage desperately. Their bodies ground against each other as they writhed in growing lust and heat. Kyle could feel drops of sweat forming on his skin, the light tickle as they ran over his burning flesh.

He had made love many times, but he had never needed his lover as much as he needed Aden in that moment. His hands reached down desperately, and he cried out in joy as they closed around a thick, erect shaft. His cry was echoed by his lover, their kiss breaking once more as he looked into Aden's eyes. The human was onto his knees faster than he thought possible, his fit body flexing as he sat astride the equine's legs. His hands wrestled with the button on his pants until he managed to wrench them down.

Kicking them off, he flung them into the far corner, not caring one iota where they landed. He dove back onto his love like some starving animal onto an easy meal. Their lips met for a third passionate time. Kyle could feel the pony's thick meat pressing into his lower back. The heat of the meat radiating out, and he could feel his body quiver, both with desire and doubt. He was sure the pony was larger than any male he'd ever taken. Yet he knew they both wanted it, no more than that he needed it. He needed to show Aden how much the pony meant to him, to cement his place once and for all in the equine's life.

Forcing his lips apart from the hungry pony muzzle, he placed a hand on Aden's chest for balance and to keep Aden down. "I . . . need you to stay still for a bit, Aden. You're going to feel something really good, and you are going to want to fuck." He panted heavily as he spoke, his hot breath stirring the golden fur on Aden's chest like a stiff breeze over a field of wheat. "You could hurt me if you do it too soon or too fast, just try to listen to me. Understand?"

"Yes." Aden's voice sounded far away, unfocused, and Kyle knew what the horse was really thinking about: what he'd just said was going to happen. The equine shaft throbbed, and a thick gob of precum shot up his back. With quick fingers, he managed to scoop up several drops, his hands reaching down and smearing it over the engorged equine phallus. More pre shot, and he used it all, getting the cock as slick as he could. The feel of it as it throbbed in his hands made him ache, his fingers unable to close around the amazing girth.

Trembling a little himself, Kyle lifted up slowly, using his hand to guide the cock. He felt it touch his pucker, like two lovers kissing at the start of a long dance. With a smile, he reassured Aden, keeping his eyes locked on the pony's. Then he started to lower himself. For a second the cock, squirmed in his hand, slipping and moving as if trying to escape its fate. Kyle cried out as suddenly, the tip was through his defenses and pushing deeper inside him.

His cry was a duet with Aden, who neighed with pleasure as he felt something so tight gripping around his most sensitive flesh. Every instinct in his body screamed for him to thrust, his hands tore at the sheets, and he bit his lip as he fought for control of himself. With each second, he was pulled deeper inside that wonderful tunnel, his cock burrowing its way inside his love. The human stretched around his meat, like a tight-fitting, silken glove. His cock throbbed and ached, shooting jet after jet of pre into the human's body.

It felt like an eternity and at the same time a blink of the eye to Kyle. While he pushed down, forcing inch after inch inside him, his rear stretched beyond capacity, and yet somehow there was no pain, just the stretching sensation and a wonderful warmth that filled him. It seemed to radiate out from Aden's horsehood. With a moan, he felt the pony's medial ring kiss his stretched pucker. It was his turn to bite his lip as he forced himself down hard, stuffing that thick ring of muscle inside of him and leaving himself gasping with relief as it finally popped through.

"Kyle . . . I . . .. Oh, Kyle" Aden cried out breathlessly while he slid inch after inch deep into his willing partner. Kyle clenched down around the hot maleness inside him. His eyes locked with Aden's, and he knew that the equine was lost in the sensations around his thickness. This was a hundred times more intense than what had happened only a few hours ago, even for Kyle. He couldn't hold back his cries of pleasure. Neither one could tear their eyes from their lover. Aden's expression was of deep concentration and concern. Yet for Kyle, something strange; as he could feel a strange need and desire, it had been a long time since he wanted a lover in the way he wanted Aden. It burned inside him like a fire at his very core. All that fire wanted was for him to press down onto the length inside him as Aden whinnied out in pleasure at the feel of the mare around him, to buck and ride that thickness until the pony flooded his needy depths with his sweet essence.

Somehow, Kyle managed to control himself, biting his lip so hard that he could taste blood. The pain of stretching blossoming in his mind like a flower of clear crystal, allowing him to keep control of himself. While Aden whinnied loudly to feel warm human buttocks resting on his leathery orbs. The human's skin wet with sweat and sticking to the equine's leathery nuts.

Lifting his own voice, Kyle cried out with delight as he felt himself reaching the pony's thick hilt. The last two inches far wider than anything he ever dreamed he would take, his doughnut was burning, and yet he felt full. The fiery itch of his ring was nothing compared to the need inside him; burning with the intensity of the sun. His hands reached out, caressing Aden's muzzle and cheeks, the feel of velvet against his fingertips surprisingly clear as his body adjusted to the length inside him.

"Aden . . . Oh fuck . . . You feel . . . mmmmpph." His words failed him; how do you describe the feeling of being whole when you have known nothing but the existence of fracture, of being shattered? He couldn't say it, he barely even was aware of anything but for the need of more. With a soft buck of his hips, he lifted up an inch and then slipped back down hard. Inside him, the thick meat slid out and then rammed back hard. Each motion stroking his prostate, his own cock fully erect, rubbing against Aden's plush stomach.

Under the human, Aden whimpered, his balls aching and the tiny rock of Kyle's hips only whetting his appetite for more. His body screamed out for more, for Kyle. He wanted the human so badly, it hurt his mind. With a cry, he grabbed the human's legs tightly. While Kyle drove himself down a second time, he howled with need. The tightness around his cock unbearable, the silken depths welcoming his meat back inside.

His voice calling out with each motion, Kyle was rocking to a quick rhythm on the maleness inside him. He closed his eyes; his hands could feel Aden trembling with repressed desire. Leaning forward, he kissed up the equine's long neck while his hips drove faster and faster. When his lips reached Aden's ears, he whispered, "Fuck me, oh please, fuck me!"

Aden whinnied in response, words far beyond his abilities in that moment. He let go of any restraint, his hips thrusting up wildly with no control. His leathery nuts slapped heavily off Kyle's ass, his cock reaming the human as deep and hard as he could manage. There were no words spoken while classical music echoed in their ears, cut with the cries of their pleasure. Deep moans and gasps of pure bliss, the slapping and slurping of a cock breeding a welcoming hole.

There was no way for Aden to prepare himself for the depth of feeling that was absorbing him. He could think of nothing but the rut, the need to empty inside his mare. His body drove him to thrust faster and harder with each heartbeat. Inside, he could feel a pressure building and building. All he cared about was his release; he fucked Kyle with the brutal passion of a wild animal in the breeding season.

Kyle cried and moaned into Aden's neck, the fur there soaked by his breath. He clung onto the equine desperately, he was lost to the moment. Inside, he knew Aden would not last long enough to bring both of them to orgasm. However, he didn't care. He wanted to show Aden what real pleasure was. The equine suddenly trembled under him, the cock inside his ass throbbing just as Aden screamed out. There was no words in the scream, just animalistic noises. Warm pressure slowly built in his ass as copious amounts of pony spunk were fucked deep inside him.

With his energy drained from him, shot into his lover, Aden fell back, his thrusting slowing to a stop. He lay back, panting and gasping for air, the world around him spinning. With his world rocking so hard, he latched onto Kyle with both hands, holding the human tightly; like a survivor from a shipwreck clinging to a rock for dear life, he held onto his lover.

With soft caresses to Aden cheeks and tender kisses up and down his neck, Kyle tried to reassure Aden. His own cock began to soften, not that he cared about it. This had been about Aden, about showing the pony how much pleasure his companion could bring. He would see to his own pleasure later. Reaching down, he pulled the rapidly softening cock from his ass, carefully holding his fingers near his pucker until it closed, to stop any polymer-wrapped parcels from slipping out.

"You know your eight hours are up, I legally have to tell you we do not pay overtime. Also, your contract only allows for one bonus," Kyle winced at the thought that the doctor had watched and heard every moment of what had happened. The thought of himself being watched and heard was fine, but for Aden; Kyle couldn't help but feel your first time should be private, just between you and your chosen partner. "Should you wish to stay a while, that is fine, although we need to get that sample you just extracted to the lab ASAP." Kyle rolled his eyes at the term "sample". The guy had just watched him fuck a horse person with a first-person view, and he still couldn't say cum or simply spunk. Hell, seminal fluids would be better; extract a sample was hardly a sexy metaphor, and definitely seemed childish considering the job they hired him to do.

Not moving was Kyle's silent response. He closed his eyes and just laid over Aden, feeling the rise and fall of Aden's chest as he slept. "We are sending a tech to the dining hall to collect the sample." Kyle's teeth ground in his mouth as he felt anger rising. However, logic won the day; he knew Dr. Ramon wasn't going to let them rest peacefully, not when there was an oh-so-precious 'sample' to collect.

Moving as slowly and smoothly as he could, Kyle wriggled out from under Aden's embrace. The pony opened his golden eyes and looked up at him imploringly. "Shhh, just need to pee, I'll be right back," Kyle whispered and was relieved to see the equine closing his tired eyes again. He stepped into the bathroom and quietly relieved his bladder. When he returned to the bedroom, Aden was snoring softly.

The human snuck out into the dining hall naked. A male technician was standing, holding a metal kidney dish. Kyle vaguely recognized him as one of the many people Becky had introduced him to on his first day. The man blushed and turned his head as the naked actor walked towards him. "You here to pick up the spunk?" It was a question that didn't need to be asked, but he was annoyed and he wanted to see someone at least squirm.

"Y . . . Yes, I am here for the sample," the man confirmed, holding out the dish.

"Alright, this might take a few seconds, he really rammed it up there," Kyle replied, taking far too much pleasure in turning around and sticking his fingers inside, clenching and pushing. "Alright, there's one . . . It's a boy!" chuckled the actor as the technician stared at the wall like a man had a gun to his head. While his cheeks were so crimson, Kyle wondered if he might just ignite through sheer embarrassment. "Two . . . oh, twins! . . . No, wait, triplets!" Becky would have been proud at the level of crassness he had sunk to. As he pulled six white, wrapped, squishy parcels out from inside him. On his shoulder, a little devil was whispering that he should grab all the packages and give a quick juggling demonstration; just to see if he could kill a man through sheer social discomfort.

However, he restrained himself and just dumped the parcels into the dish. "There you go, enjoy!" The man didn't reply, he just turned and fled like he was being chased by a knife-wielding maniac. "You know you guys really have to grow up just a little if I am to keep 'extracting samples' this way," he observed, just loud enough for Dr. Ramon to hear.

"You learn a lot, studying for your degree, post grad and PhD, but there are zero training courses on polite conversation while getting a sperm sample from an . . . actor," Dr. Ramon replied in his ear, and Kyle smirked a little at the joke, although he noticed the significant pause before the word "actor".

"Yeah, I bet you can't find it in an etiquette guide, either, 'always pass the dish to the whore from his left. If he is struggling, just place it by the fish knife'." He heard the doctor chuckle softly in reply. Padding softly, the naked actor returned to the bedroom, stopping off briefly to wash his hands, for he knew exactly where they had been. Then he slipped back onto the bed, pulled Aden's arms around him, and pressed close, letting his own exhaustion take hold. His hazel brown eyes closing while looking at Aden's golden mane.

Chapter 11

A bumping on the mattress awoke Kyle many hours later. He opened his eyes just as he felt Aden's arms return around him. He hadn't noticed the pony leave, but, in the few seconds before he got back into bed, his body had noticed the lack of warm body against it and registered a complaint. He put his arms around Aden's broad shoulders and was a little surprised when the equine laid his head on Kyle's chest.

The head was unusually heavy, although that did make sense. "Trouble sleeping?" Kyle whispered.

"Oh, sorry, did I wake you? I just needed to pee," the horse whispered back.

"It's okay, do you know what the time is?" As he asked, the human let his hand stroke slowly over Aden's well-developed shoulders, feeling each muscle under his fingertips.

"Half-four," Aden replied, nuzzling against the actor's chest and kissing one of his tattoos.

Half-four in the morning, and nobody had come to get him out. Kyle couldn't help but wonder if anyone was actually watching him at that time in the morning. "I gotta pee now," he moaned and slid out from under the complaining pony. He dashed to the bathroom, the night air chilling his naked flesh, but he had to check something out. Turning on the light, he looked into the mirror and whispered, "Hey, anyone there?"

No answer came the wonderful reply, radio silence. He wondered if Dr. Ramon had just decided to walk away, or if they had someone watching him who fell asleep at the wheel. "Hello, should I come out now?" he whispered, and, once again, there was nothing, no reply at all. "Come on, I thought you guys would monitor me night and day." Still nothing but his own mischievous smile twinkling back at him from the mirror.

Reaching out, he flushed the toilet he hadn't used and looked away, turning the light off so that no shadows were cast, specifically none of his arm. He pulled the tiny transmitter out of his ear and hid it back beneath the soap dish. Then he left the bathroom and wandered back out. Grabbing his pants, he started pulling them on.

"A . . . Are you leaving?" He could hear the doubt and worry in Aden's unsteady voice as he asked.

"No, we are leaving," the actor replied with a wink and an offered hand. "We went to sleep really early, I'm wide awake, so let's go watch the sunrise. I've always wanted to do that properly. You can't see it in cities unless you live on the top floors facing east."

The equine took his hand and pulled himself to his hooves quickly. "I like the sound of that."

"Ok, but let's be quiet. I want to watch the sunrise with you and not you plus the security guys, lab tech guys, and the janitor," Kyle whispered as they slipped out into the night. The sky in the east was light orange, but the sun was not yet sticking up over the horizon. Stretching back away, it turned through a thousand shades of blue, getting darker until, in the west, it was black with stars in the sky.

They snuck out across the landscape, the night air chill and their hot breath misting up before them. Returning to the spot they had shared on the small hill, Kyle pressed up close to Aden for warmth. Kyle knew that, for the first time, he could speak freely to Aden, yet he couldn't think of what to say. So, they sat in silence watching the light grow, the tip of the sun slipping over the horizon. Kyle closed his eyes for a moment as the golden rays kissed their huddled forms.

Then he opened his eyes and looked up at Aden. The pony's mane was wafting in the breeze. Red and orange light mixed with his golden fur and his golden eyes. Aden looked peaceful and content. Kyle laid his head against the pony's shoulder and just watched the sunrise reflected in the equine's face.

It was Aden who eventually broke the silence. "This is beautiful," he whispered. Speaking loudly seemed wrong in that moment, even though they were utterly alone.

"It really is," Kyle whispered back, reaching a hand up to caress the pony's cheek. Aden nuzzled back against the hand while the two looked into each other's eyes. The distance between them seemed to melt away. Neither could remember moving, and yet their lips met. Soft and tender kisses were shared, hands gently stroking and embracing each other. Kyle knew that if he took a sample now, it would probably end up wasted. Dr. Ramon would be unhappy.

However, he didn't care, he just wanted to enjoy the moment stolen away from his employers.

With a gasp, Aden broke the kiss and sighed happily, "Would you . . . like before?" Kyle couldn't help but chuckle at the request. It wasn't unusual for first timers to want to go again. After all, they tend to spend years waiting for their first experience; waiting for the second can feel like years, even if it is just minutes. One taste is all it took, and they came back for more.

"Sure, just sit back," the human replied, pushing the pony back a little.

Kyle was shocked when Aden grabbed his wrist and shook his head. "No . . . Like before, but you inside me," the pony asked, his golden eyes looking imploringly at the actor.

The human froze. He gulped softly, "Are you sure that's what you want?" Kyle was sure that Dr. Ramon and Dr. Salter would not approve of that request. Especially as he had no way to collect a sample. Should they watch the video playback, they would know he didn't even try to take a sample from Aden.

"Yes, I want to feel what it's like," insisted the pony, spreading his legs wider and leaning back more, trying to expose himself. His cock was half hard and still impressive in size. Bathed in the golden-orange light, it seemed to almost glow. Kyle reached out and ran his hand up the shaft. A sharp intake of breath from the pony cut through the silence of dawn. The warmth of the human's fingers on his shaft was accentuated by the cold morning arm. Every touch and caress could be felt a dozen times more intense than before. "That's not . . . I mean, I wanted . . ."

"Shhh, I know, and I'll get to that, no need to rush. It'll be hours before anyone wakes. Besides, I need to get you prepared for your first time. It's not exactly as easy as I made it look yesterday." As if to prove his point, Kyle let one of his hands slip lower, stroking down along Aden's taint, tickling the musky, damp fur under there. When it reached Aden's pucker, he pushed at the entrance, which pushed back on instinct. "See? Just lay back, look up at the sky, and let me tend to you."

With Aden's worries calmed for the moment, Kyle was able to take his time. Moving his hands back up and fondling the huge, leathery stallion fruits hanging below the tree trunk of Aden's shaft. While he leaned forward, enjoying the muskiness, a night of sleeping with another had led to a far riper equine. Kyle didn't mind the musk; in fact, he reveled in it, the taste of a man, or male anyway. He had grown accustomed to it. While he was not the world's happiest employee, his occupation did have some good days. This had been one of the best already, and the sun hadn't even dragged its lazy ass fully over the horizon yet.

His hot breath kissed down along the full length as he breathed on the shaft. Mist curling and swirling around the length, the orange sunlight catching in his breath and making Aden's shaft seem to glow all the more. Aden cried out as two lips that felt as hot as coal brushed against his shaft, and yet the pain was more a lance of electric pleasure. A bolt of thunder that shot down his cock and right up his quivering spine. Kyle kissed the fat cock-tip again, fully engulfing it, his warmth surrounding Aden and making him thrust. Then he let go, and the chill dawn air came back with a vengeance, his body shivering as the air bit him with icy fangs.

Just as Aden began to reach out to his own cock to protect it from the chill, Kyle's mouth returned. Aden put a paw over his muzzle and screamed from the pleasure as the heat of Kyle's mouth drove away the chill once more. His cock was throbbing and aching while Kyle began to work the shaft with both hands, slowly and softly, but the friction of skin on skin was enough to drive warmth once more into his loins. The feel of the tongue bathing and teasing his glans, tracing around his coronal ridge, it was exquisite. Aden couldn't stop himself bucking up into the warmth.

Kyle savored the warm feeling inside him mouth, the thickness and the throb. He could feel Aden's heart beat as it pulsed down the length. However, as much as he wanted to drink a second load from Aden, the pony had made a request, and he was going to fulfil it, whatever the consequences. He reluctantly forced his mouth off the meaty length, replacing it with a hand to keep the dawn air and chill at bay.

Then the human dove, pausing on the way down to kiss and lick those sizeable, dangling pony nuts. The taste of leather mixed with musk and sweat, it was potent, like finely aged port with just a hint of sweetness. They were two big for him to fit inside his mouth, so he settled for a kiss on each. While his hands continued to stroke slowly up and down the shaft, keeping Aden excited but not driving him towards his release.

Those two wonderful orbs were just a pitstop on his way to his true target. His lips pulled back from them, leaving a healthy dose of saliva, making Aden's nuts glisten like they were covered by morning dew. He felt the heat of those nuts and their weight as his lips kissed underneath, the leather nuts resting on his cheeks as his tongue lapped at the pony's muskiest point. The taste of a pure male, a stud was alive on his tongue. It burned and stung, yet he need more, his tongue lapping hungrily, while above him, Aden cried out again and again as he was teased.

Working with the hunger of a starving man and the dedication of an Olympic athlete, Kyle kissed, licked, and nibbled his way down Aden's sweaty taint. His mouth becoming dominated by equine musk, all he could taste and smell was purebred stallion, yet he was desperate for more. The metallic taste of Aden's puckered entrance let the actor know he had arrived at his target.

His lips pushed up against the sweaty hole, and he kissed softly. Aden's muffled moans were delicious to his ears. His tongue lapped out over the tight ring and then pushed forward. The tight doughnut of muscle fought back; at the same time, Aden squirmed, wriggling under the delightful assault. Tingles running up and down his spine, he wanted more, and yet the sensations made him clenched down.

"Relax, Aden, let me in," Kyle cooed the words softly, not lifting up from his position. His lips returned to the pucker, and he could feel Aden trying to comply. This time with a little push, he felt the ring slowly opening around his tongue. The potent taste was wonderful, sweaty and musky, but clean; Kyle was grateful that they had showered earlier. He pushed his tongue in deeper, swirling it around lightly, tickling the anal ring.

Aden gasped as he felt himself stretching around the invading tongue, a familiar and yet alien feeling. It tickled pleasantly, and then, as the tongue began to move, he moaned in pleasure. Soft, gentle waves of delight were begin stroked into his muscles, the feelings making him relax further, his inner doubts and worries easing away. He sighed as the tongue wriggled further inside him, the sensations pleasurable but strange, his body pushing back against the mouth trying to feel more. He looked up at the sky. It was blue above him, with a hint of orange and gold filtering in, glowing of the clouds that were drifting lazily over him.

The human knew that Aden would need far more preparation than his tongue to be able to take him. While he was not blessed with the pony's heritage, he had a good-sized cock, a blessing many of his clients were grateful for. He knew how to use it as well, which made sure all his clients were thanking their deity of choice for hiring him. However, for a virgin entrance, it was a challenge. Fortunately, he could feel his fingers getting slick with Aden's pre as they continued to work his engorged meat.

Pushing his lips hard against Aden's pucker, he drove his tongue as deep as he could and was rewarded with the taste of copper on his tongue. The pony whinnied out, unable to contain himself as the human stroked his prostate. A bolt a pleasure shot through him unlike any he had ever felt before. The feeling lingering like the taste of fine wine on the tongue, leaving his palate craving more of the deliciousness.

Kyle pushed in again and again, swirling his tongue more as he did so. Each time, he was rewarded with a moan of pleasure and a taste of copper. He let go of Aden's cock with his right hand and let it trace slowly down the pony's taint. He knew that Aden would not be thinking of anything but the feeling inside him, of that dull ache of pleasure, that little precursor that gave the sweet promise of more and greater pleasure soon. If he told Aden his plan, he knew the equine would tense up, so he said nothing, his hand reaching his face, the stench of a ripe and virile equine shaft flooding his nose once more.

Fingers lightly tickled on his taint, but Aden barely registered them; he was lost adrift in a sea of pleasure hitherto unknown. The fingers were a tiny spice, hidden amongst a meal of hearty meat and vegetables. He knew they were there, but all they did was enhance the rest of the medley. That was until Kyle's tongue slipped out, and, before his ring could close, two slick digits were forced inside him. A sharp spike of pain cutting through the whirlwind of pleasure, he cried out in indignation.

However, the human was not put off. His fingers twisted and thrust, making sure to hit the secret spot inside Aden each time. The pleasure quickly returning, Aden laid his head back down, panting and gasping. His cock was unattended now, singing to him, begging him to play with it. As he reached out his hands, Kyle slapped them away. "No, wait . . . You don't want to cum yet."

The words seemed insane to Aden, why the hell wouldn't he want to cum? However, he wasn't going to argue, he trusted Kyle. When it came to sex, he knew far more than the pony did. The fingers inside him were slipping far deeper than the tongue, touching parts of him he never thought anyone would ever touch. The human had moved away from hitting his prostate, wanting to let Aden just relax and get used to the feeling of something inside him. It was a strange sensation. With each motion Aden felt the need to clench down and force it out; at the same time, his body cried out for more and for it to push deeper.

Kyle had unfastened his flym and his erect cock was hanging out, being stroked by a pre-soaked hand. There wasn't much else he could use as lubricant; fortunately, Aden produced the stuff in copious volumes. He could feel the tightness of the equine around his fingers, the heat clutching at him, trying to pull him deeper. Aden's hips were pushing back into each thrust, signaling to Kyle that he was ready for more.

"Ok, in a moment, I'm going to pull my fingers out. You'll feel empty, and then I'm going to push my cock against your pucker," Kyle talked calmly, trying to sound as confident as he could, to instill as much confidence in Aden as he could. "When you feel my cock against you, I want you to clench down just as hard as you can and hold it, keep clenched until you can't do it anymore. When you feel yourself relaxing, call out my name."

Aden seemed a little confused by Kyle's request. Everything the human had been doing was to relax him, to open him up. Surely, clenching down would make everything much more difficult. This, however, was a trick Kyle had learned a long time ago for taking those not so used to being fucked. The tight doughnut of muscle would exhaust itself within a minute or two, and then it would offer him no resistance. Also, the tired muscle would stretch far easier and less painfully.

The fingers slipped out from inside Aden, leaving him feeling empty as per Kyle's warning. There was a void inside him now, and he wanted nothing more than for it to be filled again. He sighed happily when Kyle pushed his cock-tip against the warm pucker. The human felt his lover clench down, the clenching pucker kissing his cock-tip in a delicious promise of what was to happen. Kyle could see Aden grasping at the grass, his fingers taking firm hold of the turf beneath them. The seconds ticked by, and Kyle wondered how long Aden could keep his muscle flexed.

Kyle knew it wouldn't be as long as Aden expected; he had been on both ends of this move. When Aden took a sharp lungful of cold morning air, Kyle knew he was fighting against fatigue already. Every lover seemed to accept this challenge, they all tried to keep it going as long as possible, to show to Kyle how absurd the request was. Maybe it was just nerves; the moment they relaxed, they knew what would happen. Your first time, it didn't matter how much you wanted it. Part of you was scared of what was about to be thrust in a place that had always been exit only. However, second by second, the ache inside would grow, the muscle would start to burn with exhaustion, and then, against his will, it would relax. "Kyle!"

There was no hesitation; Kyle had held himself at the gates to heaven for an eternity. Once his name was called, he pushed inside with everything he had. The warmth that surrounded him was almost too much, tight and moist, It clung to his manhood, not wanting to let it go, pulling him in deeper. With a united cry of bliss, the human's hips smacking into Aden's as in one motion, he hilted inside the beast. "Oh fuck . . . Aden!" he whispered as he felt the equine surrounding him. The equine looked up at him, and Kyle smiled. "Are you okay?"

A huge head nodded. "Yes, I . . . It didn't hurt. I thought it would hurt more, just a little sting."

"It only hurts if you do it wrong, or too hard. Now just lay back, and let me make you feel good." As he spoke, Kyle crawled forward over the equine, one hand grasping around the half-hard shaft, stroking it gently. While Kyle's lips found two sweet nubs, perky and erect in the cool air, extra sensitive to his licks and kisses. All the while, his hips moved slowly, grinding himself against Aden, his cock slowly stirring around inside him, letting him feel every inch and, at the same time, spreading him wider.

The sun was over the horizon now, and it wouldn't be too long before people started to look for them. Kyle knew he needed to be quick; fortunately, the pulsing rod of pony steel in his hand showed just how much Aden was enjoying things. His hips pulled back a little, sliding just an inch out before slamming it back home where it belonged. Earning a soft moan of delight from Aden. He followed that with another thrust, and then another, each one growing deeper and faster. The equine pushed into them both, showing no signs of discomfort and every indication of pleasure.

Part of Kyle wanted to stay like this for hours, to tease Aden to the edge of his orgasm and hold him there for as long as he could. To fuck him gently and tenderly until the pony begged for release, and then to take him hard deep and brutal, to fuck until the equine had no breath left, and then drive him over the edge, just to see how big a fountain he could make of Aden's wonderful member. To make his smooth golden fur a sodden, dirty, delicious mess of pure, adulterated delight. He promised himself he would another time, and that he would feast on that mess afterwards.

In the moment, he started to fuck Aden in earnest, his hips moving swiftly, rhythmically slapping into Aden's again and again. His cock driving deep and hard into the wonderful nirvana inside Aden, the world of warm, silken caresses and tight clenches. While Aden cried out with each thrust, his cock throbbing in Kyle's hand as he sent regular jets of warm pre onto his stomach. Clods of turf and earth were torn up by the equine's clenching hands. His hooves stamped hard, leaving deep hoofprints on the hill.

Aden cried out again and again. Each thrust seemed to touch something deep inside him, something pleasurable. His cock jerked and drooled to the warmth of Kyle's touch. Thrust after well-aimed thrust assaulted the equine's prostate, tossing Aden's mind adrift in a sea of pleasure. Kyle used every trick he knew to bring his lover nothing but pleasure. He wanted Aden to know nothing but the warmth of his lover's touch and the feel of his manhood inside him. As taut equine buttocks pushed back into his thrusting, Kyle knew that Aden wasn't just enjoying the feeling; he was craving it, and, for the moment, nothing else mattered. Aden reached out, trying to grab Kyle for support. Kyle grabbed his hand and pushed it down to the grass. Human fingers interlacing with equine ones, Aden opened his eyes and looked up.

Kyle was above him, framed against the blue sky, hue with warm, golden light. The human looked down into Aden's eyes, those brown eyes so intense and intent on him. Yet so full of lust and, more than that, concern. With a gasp of passion, Kyle couldn't stop himself thrusting with more and more passion. He could tell Aden was close, he could feel his lover trembling under and around him, quivering with need as the actor pounded his shaft deep inside the quivering rump. The human wanted the moment to last forever, the look in Aden's face, love and lust in a perfect blend, the feel of his warm body, soft fur against warm skin, and the air rank with the smell of their amour. Their rapid breaths turning into thin mist in the early morning air.

However, nothing in life lasts forever. Aden bucked under him once more, whinnying loudly as his insides clenched down desperately around his maleness. He felt the pony's cock throb in his hand. Looking down, he saw impressive gushes of spunk as they shot into the air. He didn't count how many jets, he just reveled in the sight. Feeling the spunk raining down on them both, he winced a little, his clothes getting a heavy dose of equine spunk that might be hard to explain . . . Kyle did not hold back, driving himself in deeper and harder, desperately breeding the pony. His own orgasm not far behind as he bred Aden with desperate, almost bestial passion and intent. Aden's thighs held him firmly, keeping his cock buried inside the equine as he bucked wildly, his throbbing cock emptying every last drop into his lover.

With his strength drained, Kyle fell forward, landing on top of Aden a panting mess. He could feel spunk soaking into his clothes, but he knew there wasn't anything he could do. The equine's thighs still held him with a vice-like grip, refusing to let his sexual partner pull out. Anyway, the warmth of the panting body beneath him was welcoming, and he found himself resting his face on Aden's panting chest.

"That was . . ." Aden began to moan as he regained his senses.

"Messy," Kyle chuckled and finished for him. "I think I just figured out how the Native Americans did a real rain dance."

"Yeah, there will be no samples taken from this," the equine muttered as his arms closed around Kyle.

Every muscle and nerve on the human tensed at once. He didn't dare look Aden in the eye. His stomach was suddenly a pit of boiling acid. Did Aden know what he had done earlier? The question blazed through Kyle's mind so bright, he could barely see or think anything else.

"It's okay," the pony whispered and nuzzled Kyle's hair. "Bruno gives his samples this way. It's not exactly difficult to put two and two together."

"You . . . don't mind?" Kyle asked cautiously. This was not how he had seen this moment going. In his mind, there had been screaming accusations, obviously heightened by the presence of an unseasonal downpour in the middle of the night, so one of them could fall to his knees in the mud and scream 'no' while the other walked away forever. A blunt 'I know what you are doing' with no anger or even pain behind. It was not something he had thought of.

"I . . . don't. I was annoyed for a moment when I first figured it out." Aden laid his head back on the grass. "I mean, I wanted to withhold until Brian came back, but, when I thought about it, I realized they are never going to bring him back. If they were, they would have done so already. Now I have you, and . . . you were willing to stand up for me, even with Dr. Ramon telling you to help them . . . you didn't. I was so worried they would take you away for defying them . . . If giving them what they want means I get to keep you . . ."

Aden fell silent for a moment, his arms squeezing the human gently. "I think it is a small price to pay. Although, I would like to keep up the pretense, let them think they are getting one over on me rather than know that I know. That is better than them thinking they broke me."

As surprised as he was, Kyle could understand the last part, 'never let the bastards see you cry'. He'd heard it a lot in his life. It rang true for everyone; sometimes, you can accept being beaten, so long as others don't know it. Just makes handling the inescapable bad parts of life a little bit less horrible. Something in his mind was nagging him, that there was more to what the pony had said. Some vital point he had missed. "I am glad, I won't let them know. I will keep sneaking out to give samples."

"And I will continue to pretend to be asleep when you do," the equine sighed and nuzzled the human's hair, squeezing him gently. "I hope we can do this every night, steal a few hours with nobody listening in."

Kyle's eyes went wide; Aden had known all along. He suddenly realized what he had heard but not taken in. Aden had heard Dr. Ramon order him to help. The pony knew he had defied orders to help him. More importantly, he had heard Dr. Ramon say that. how much else had he heard? "You know about the transmitter?"

The pony chuckled softly. "It used to amuse me, hearing the doctor give Brian orders, thinking it was secret. Even though they designed me and gave me hearing far better than any human, they still never thought to check."

"And you never told them?"

"Of course not, they would just find a way to instruct you without me knowing. This way, I know what was you and what was him," the pony replied with a squeeze. "We should go back, it is getting light now."

The human could feel the reluctance in his own body as he forced his arms to let go. The hug had felt so natural, it seemed a shame to end it. However, he knew Aden was right. He was surprised at how easily the equine had just taken charge. Standing up, he sealed his sticky cock away and winced at his clothing. "I should grab the transmitter and head back to my own room and change."

With a sigh, Aden nodded his agreement. He could see the logic, though he had wanted to go back to spend some more time cuddling. He consoled himself with the thought of getting to spend more time with Kyle soon after; it was the human's occupation, after all. When they reached Aden's room, they found the time was a little before six in the morning. Kyle placed the transmitter back in his ear and was glad when nobody replied to him. They hadn't been missed. If they checked the tapes for the night, they would find some interesting viewing, but no sound. He could always claim he hadn't noticed the transmitter had fallen out.

As he was walking out, he stepped sharply to the side, pulling Aden's muzzle down. He placed a kiss softly on those tender lips, letting them linger for a moment or two. "See you soon," he whispered as he left. It wasn't until he was halfway back to his room that he even realized he had just kissed the pony goodbye, like he was some sort of spouse or partner, not a paid actor. There wasn't time to ponder; the place was coming alive. He could hear other people moving around. Fortunately, he passed none in the corridors, so nobody saw his clothes and their cummy stains. He hoped that they wouldn't notice them on the security camera videos.

He made it back to his room and wasted no time diving into the shower, the searing heat washing off the sweat, grime, and cum of a long night. It was light years from the first time he had done this after a client. What a difference eight years makes. At least this time, he could linger as long as he needed. The weird thing was he didn't want to linger, he didn't feel that dirty. Turning off the hot water, he got out and began to dry himself. Catching his reflection in the mirror, he paused. He was smiling. So often he had to fake it, he'd almost forgotten what his real smile looked like. Of course, the moment he noticed, the smile vanished.

Aden was just a client, a nice client and a great contract. Good pay, good food, one customer, no weird shit. That was all. He was happy because, now he had things locked in, he could start making regular cash. Dempsy would be off his back, too, no more threats. He only made them when he really wanted stuff. As for Aden, well, so what if he enjoyed spending time with him? It wasn't the first time he had fun with a job or client, and that is what this was. No matter what he thought, it was that simple.

Leaning close to the mirror, he gave himself a mental slap. They could fire him at the drop of a hat, he reminded himself. 'This is a good contract, keep everyone happy and milk it, get as many bonuses as you can. Sure, enjoy it, but stay focused keep Aden happy, keep Dr. Ramon happy, and most importantly, keep Dempsy happy. Don't get too comfortable, keep your guard up and your fake smile on. Make them like you, don't start trusting them. Now stop wasting time, you have a job to do. Your client is waiting, get your ass dressed and get the fuck on with your job.

Kyle repeated those thoughts and more, over and over again, as he dressed. He fought back against questions about his feelings. They weren't important; feelings had never gotten him anything but pain. He reminded himself of the last time he had felt truly attracted to a guy. Esteban had strung him along and used his emotions. With a sigh of regret, he resigned himself. He could like Aden but he could never let it go further. After all, Aden had no control over anything in his life; letting himself get more emotionally attached than like, and then what happens when they take him away? Like they took her away. He'd been helpless, he'd kicked and cried and screamed, but they had just carried him away, and then she was gone.

His hand was shaking a little as he pulled on his socks. Several deep breaths were needed to calm down his racing heart. The thoughts of that day, even for just a moment, they were too much. Forcing his emotions back into the bottle, he stood up and placed his smiling mask back on. A good-natured, open, happy smile, unless you looked deep into those troubled brown eyes.

Chapter 12

Dr. Ramon had been waiting for him when he arrived at his office. This time, the doctor was all smiles and small talk. Things were going well, as far as he was concerned; the lab was back running, and that was all that mattered. No mention was made of the night before. Kyle could detect no sign that they had been seen. Maybe that would change, but he didn't think so. People are far less careful when things seem to be going their way, any hustler could tell you that. Make them think they are winning, and they get sloppy and confident. Besides a few hours of alone time, what could be the harm? He wasn't going to try and convince Aden to leave his gilded cage. His very livelihood relied on keeping him inside it and happy.

As he turned to leave and return to Aden for breakfast, Dr. Ramon stopped him. "Oh, one more thing..."

Kyle paused in the doorway and turned around to find the doctor holding up *The Horse and his Boy*. He waved the book at Kyle. "Here, you go, I've finished it now, and I agree; there is some good messages for Aden hidden in here. I am sure he will be very glad to have something new to read. It will help you both bond more."

The actor took the book with a nod, unable to think of anything polite to say. After all, it might have helped yesterday, but he had done it without the help of the book. Now it was just a very expensive gift, but he had it, and the two could spend a good afternoon or two reading it. Aden would like it, of that, he was sure. Of course, once he had one, there was always the next, obvious step. "If I find some more that might be good for him to read, could I bring them in?"

"Absolutely, so long as it has the right kind of message," Dr Ramon confirmed, leaving Kyle with the problem of finding another story with a message of 'stay home, the outside world is only going to try and hurt you.'

With another nod of acknowledgement, Kyle accepted the challenge. He at least knew one person who might be able to help him track down a few titles, maybe even adult ones. While at the same time, he might be able to get a few nice freebies out of him. Danny had certainly seemed open to another visit.

Aden was delighted when his human returned to him, more so to see he was armed with a book. Kyle placed it in Aden's room next to the entertainment unit he had left in there the previous night. The actor realized nobody had mentioned it at all, so he assumed it was fine to leave it in place.

The morning passed quickly. It was strange to know that Aden could hear anything Dr. Ramon whispered into his ear. In some ways, it was liberating to know nothing was occurring behind Aden's back. However, as he knew Aden could hear the words whispered into his ear, he knew that any information Dr. Ramon let slip would be with the pony. Given the doctor had access to his full historical files, there was plenty of information that he wouldn't want Aden or anyone to know.

Fortunately, with things going well, the doctor was very quiet. In fact, Kyle suspected he wasn't watching as closely or intently as he had the first few days. He had claimed to have twenty-six projects. No doubt, he had plenty of work to catch up on. It didn't matter; he was quiet, and all three of them were probably grateful for it.

Even things with Bruno and Cassandra seemed to be going smoothly. Kyle found that the odd stare and wink of encouragement at the black stallion kept him happy and secure. He even didn't object when Kyle and Cassandra were next to each other on rowing machines. Although the big brute did lumber over to some deadlifts right in front of the two. There was a little, polite conversation between the two actors, all kept fully professional. They were co-workers, and Kyle knew that is all they would ever be.

After their run, Dr. Ramon tactfully announced in his ear that there would be no attempt to take a sample from Aden today. Adding that they trusted the actor to take one for them. Taking one for the team, it was a professional requirement. As the doctor told him this, his eyes darted to Aden, who didn't react at all. The pony had never gambled, but somehow he'd developed a poker face that any professional would have been proud of. Kyle managed to stop himself from chuckling. He knew his role, but it still amused him. The scientist had watched him take a sample orally and anally and still couldn't bring himself to actually just say 'make sure to suck him off'.

As it was, he took a sample from Aden in the shower. He took the transmitter out of his ear before getting into the shower; winking to the mirror just for Dr. Ramon. Aden put up no resistance. Of course Kyle didn't expect any, they both enjoyed their shower time together. Afterwards, the two laid on Aden's bed. Kyle requested some classical music from the entertainment unit and picked up the book.

The actor laid beside Aden on the bed, the horse's strong arm around his shoulders and the other across his stomach. He felt warm and safe, and he opened the book. 'This is the story of an adventure that happened . . .' He didn't read it aloud, neither did Aden. Kyle just laid there in the equine's arms, feeling warm and secure as the two of them read on. He felt slightly embarrassed by how childish his offering was. Not that Aden showed any signs other than enjoyment.

Their afternoon was spent wonderfully and cozily, the book being quickly devoured by both of them. It had been a long time since Kyle had read it. He was surprised by how much he could remember. Some of the scenes brought up memories of reading to Anna, making roars of lions and neighs of horses and her squealing and laughing. He managed to control himself and bury those memories as quickly as they resurfaced.

It was early evening by the time they finished devouring the book. The two had read it in one long sitting, barely moving for hours. Just resting in each other's embrace, the feel of their warm bodies pressed together, almost no words spoken between them. A comfortable, happy, silent afternoon, and afterwards they had discussed the book over food. Aden enthused about how much he had enjoyed something new. Kyle said he could keep the book; after all, what use did he have for it? Other than to remind him of some happy times that stung far more than much of the sadness.

Kyle stayed the night with Aden again, extracting another sample before the two fell into a deep, comfortable sleep. The human being the little spoon and surrounded by a warm, strong, fuzzy body.

He was roused from his sleep by a gentle paw shaking him awake along with a whispering voice, "Kyle, are you awake?" A rather stupid question, but one people everywhere will recognize. Usually whispered by someone who actually means 'wake up, I have something to say, and you are not gonna get any sleep until it is said.' Some people just have to wait until three am to realize that they really, really need to discuss their holiday plans, what their work colleague said about x, or just what really happened in that movie they watched.

"I am . . . now," the human moaned softly, opening his eyes and yawning. The room was dark, he couldn't guess at the time, other than sometime after midnight.

"Sorry, I just thought you might need to go the toilet," a strange thought for anyone to have about someone sleeping soundly. Anyone listening would be baffled, but Kyle could easily catch the equine's drift, even after just being roused at stupid o'clock in the night.

"My bladder does feel a little full," he mumbled and got to his feet. He gave a couple of tests in the mirror to see if anyone there would respond and got silence in reply. The transmitter was taken from his ear and placed under the soap dish once more. Then he returned to find Aden looking a little sheepish.

"Sorry, I just wanted to talk with you again properly, without anyone listening in," Aden whispered. In the gloom of night, whispering seemed appropriate even though, nobody could overhear.

"That's okay, though we should probably be careful. Do it too much, and they might figure it out. Plus, I will get cranky if I don't get to sleep at least a couple of nights a week," Kyle replied, returning to bed. He was naked this time, and the chill of the night air made him push up close to Aden. The equine wrapped him in two powerful arms.

"I understand, maybe just every other night," the pony whispered as his muzzle nuzzled the human's neck. "*The Horse and His Boy*, it was an interesting book. Had you read it before?"

"Yes, a long time ago to my sister . . ." Kyle froze as the words just slipped out; the warm embrace and soft nuzzling had let him relax too much.

"You have a sister? What is her name?" The pony's voice raised a little in excitement, hearing a little more about his lover.

"Anna, she is six years younger than me," Kyle whispered. "I used to read the Narnia books to her at bedtime, they helped her to sleep."

"Bruno and I had a sister," Aden whispered sadly. "Isabell, she was the first of us. However, she got sick when we were very young. I don't remember much about her. She was white, and she used to laugh a lot. They never really told us what was wrong with her. I asked Brian once, but he wasn't able to find out. I suppose it doesn't matter what illness she had, but they didn't let us in to see her . . ."

"You never got to say goodbye." It wasn't so much a question as an observation. "I know how that feeling, you always wonder what you would have said and if it would have made any difference."

"Did your sister . . ." The question was left half-asked. There was little need to ask it fully.

"No, my mother did, and . . ." Kyle took a deep breath. He never talked about it.. However, for some reason, he wanted to, just a little. An abridged version at least couldn't hurt. "We had no family, so we ended up in the system."

"The system?"

"The social care system, where they put children without parents, or whose parents can't take care of them," he sighed softly. "I was considered too old to be placed for adoption. Anna was young enough. So, they found her a new family, and I was placed as a foster child with some other family."

"I do not understand, what is the difference?"

"Adoption means you get a new mom and dad, you are one of the family," Kyle closed his eyes and sighed. "Fostering means you get placed in a house with people who get paid to deal with you, as long as you are not too much trouble."

"That . . . does not sound appealing. What happens if you are too much trouble?" The horse's voice was low, and his arms pulled Kyle to him on instinct. Aden could hear the pain masked in Kyle's voice. More than that, he could feel the human trembling in his arms.

"They move you to a new house, maybe even a new city, to be someone else's problem," Kyle whispered as he tried to remember names and faces. Seven different families, he doubted he could even recall the names of all his foster parents and siblings.

"I'm sorry," Aden whispered, kissing the human's neck and cheek. There was a salty taste to Kyle's cheeks.

The warm presence behind Kyle was welcomed; the strong arms holding him felt good. "It's not your fault, I just made sure to get out as soon as I could. Signed with my agent and never looked back. I'm ok now."

"Except for your contract being permanent," observed the equine a little too honestly.

"Yeah, okay, so my plan to be independent wasn't exactly perfect," Kyle retorted dryly. "I suppose people should have expected better from the high school dropout son of a prostitute. What can I say? I chose to go into the family business." He laughed despite himself, tears still running down his cheeks. "It seemed like a good idea. There was this guy, told me I could make good money. I liked sex, it felt good, and I liked making others feel good. The guy was charming and good in bed, so I didn't read what I was signing. Not that it would have mattered, I wanted out. Stupid dumb kid that nobody wanted. My foster father at the time used to call me Rover, after his old dog, said I reminded him of Rover because no matter how hard he tried, he could never teach the damn dog to do what he said."

The silence that followed was deafening. Kyle knew he had said far too much, way more than he would have ever wanted to share. Once he had started talking, he hadn't been able to force himself to stop. In eight years, nobody had shown much interest in his past. They only cared about his present, the immediate future, and what he could do for or to them in that time. "So tomorrow, you want to shake things up a bit, run 'round the field counterclockwise?" It was a lame attempt at both humor and to change the topic.

Fortunately, Aden was able to pick up on the not-so-subtle signal from Kyle that he didn't wish to talk about things in any more detail. So, he kissed the human's shoulders so he knew he cared and replied, "If you really want to blow their minds, you could run clockwise, and I could run anti-clockwise, and we could collide in the middle."

Kyle moaned softly, turning around in Aden's arms laying his head against the broad chest, his hands squeezing the equine's strong biceps. His eyes closed on their own, and he replied, "Or we could just run back to bed. I can't think of a better way to spend a day in this place than snuggled up, listening to music . . ."

"And talking. I still want to hear more about the world, about Chicago, for a start," Aden cut in as he nuzzled Kyle's hair.

"Well, you are the customer, so I will do what you tell me," the human replied with a yawn, grinding his body into the warm equine form.

"Mmm, is that what you do for your other customers?" The question was meant as a playful joke, but it still cut Kyle a little, and he wondered if this would be the start of the pony settling into his role as customer.

"Some just want sex, many times fetish play, stuff that is hard to find a willing partner for. Others want conversation, to take me out and about, show me off before taking me home 'to get their money's worth.' A few just want someone to talk to them . . . One guy just wanted me to hug him and tell him it was going to be okay . . ."

"What was wrong?" Aden whispered.

"Dunno, I never asked, and he never told me," the actor replied and sighed. "He never hired me again. I think of him from time to time and wonder what happened, was he dying, was he suicidal . . . You tend to try not to think about most of your clients in this job. Some, you can't help but think of, even years after."

"D . . . Did you think of me? When you went back home, I mean." There was more than a hint of hope in Aden's tone as he asked.

Reaching up with one hand, Kyle stroked Aden's cheek and pulled his head down gently, their lips meeting in a gentle kiss. Kyle moaned softly, pushing closer and letting the kiss intensify, his hands stroking through Aden's mane. Then he broke the kiss with a joint sigh of content. "No, not for a second," the human snickered with adolescent laughter as the equine neighed softly in mock outrage. "Yes, of course, I thought about you. You are unique among my clients. Not just because of your genetics. Other customers know what they want from me when I arrive; even if they are shy, they have wants. With you, it was different. You didn't really have any wants beyond maybe some company. Of course, the company had wants, and I tried to keep you both happy . . ."

"Hmmm, you did. However, when they told you to do something I didn't want, you chose me," the pony whispered into his ear happily.

"Oh yeah, stupid thing to do, really," Kyle chuckled and then added, "They are paying a fortune to have me here six days a week. My agent was thrilled to get this contract; only a company could afford this kind of service."

"Pity they can't just buy out your contract so you could be here seven days a week," muttered the pony sleepily.

"Mmm, company guys get a day off, too," Kyle replied as he nuzzled his cheek into the warmth of Aden's chest. "Wish I could take you with me, show you the shithole I live in. They don't want you leaving, but I bet seeing my cage will make you long for your own."

"Your cage cannot be that bad; after all, you are in it." Aden's reply was spoken slowly and softly as his eyes closed, sleep starting to creep into his tired mind.

A soft snore above him made Kyle smile as he felt sleep starting to take hold of his mind. 'Pity they can't just buy out your contract . . .' The words leapt back into his mind, and his eyes shot open. Was it possible? No, surely, they would never go for that. Why should they? It would probably be cheaper if Kyle was to be around for years: cut the bonuses, give him a low-level company salary. Then he wouldn't have to deal with Dempsy anymore, though he would be a company guy. Was that so bad? After all, he wouldn't be a janitor, and the job they wanted him to do was pleasant enough. Maybe, just maybe . . . Kyle fell asleep, pondering the possibility, running through question after question.

The days started to pass by quickly and easily. It was strange for Kyle how comforting it was to have a routine; each day, he knew what was coming. Good food, good company, and good sex. It all added up to a pleasant day, although the fake sneaking off to deliver samples got tiresome fast. However, the secret night talks made up for it to a huge degree. They both broke the 'only every other night' agreement. It was too liberating to steal that time. It became addictive in itself, even if just an hour of talking. It was something they both craved and looked forward to.

After the third day, Kyle simply moved his clothes into Aden's room. He had slept there every night anyway and had less and less reason to go back to that part of the facility. Only really going to discuss updates with Dr. Ramon and to give over samples. Though on a few occasions, he had spent an hour or two sitting in the mess hall talking to Becky. She passed on the news from the outside world in her own unique style. She made him laugh and cringe with her abuse of the c-bomb and f-bomb.

Before Kyle knew it, it was Monday night, and his day off was looming on the horizon. That night, Aden woke him as normal a few hours after midnight. However, once the human returned from hiding his transmitter, Aden had a serious look on his face.

"Is everything okay?" Kyle asked as he slipped back into the bed. It had rained that day, and neither of them fancied walking outside in the wet grass or mud. So, the plan was to stay in bed and talk, not that there had been any verbal agreement or discussion. Kyle just knew what Aden would want, and he wanted the same.

"You are going home tomorrow night," Aden whispered in response. There was a tenseness to his body, and his voice sounded strained.

"Yes, but I will be back Thursday morning," the actor replied in his most reassuring tones, his hands stroking the equine's neck. Kyle had found that Aden's neck was a particularly sensitive spot to rub; a firm touch with both hands always made him groan with pleasure.

"Mmm oh, it is not that. I wanted to ask you to do something for me," Aden whispered with a moan and a shudder of pleasure as Kyle's fingers worked.

A flash of inspiration hit the actor. "You want me to contact Brian, don't you?"

"Was it that obvious?" The pony asked with a slight, nervous chuckle.

Kyle shrugged as he placed a kiss on Aden's fuzzy cheek. "Well, I think, after spending almost every waking moment, and most of my sleeping moments, with you for a week, I am beginning to know you really well."

"I think I am beginning to know you really well, too, and I like what I know," the equine whispered sweetly. "So, will you do it?"

"You know me so well, what do you think?" Kyle asked playfully.

"I think you are deflecting the question and might try to initiate sex to avoid giving me a firm yes or no." The statement from Aden shocked the actor. Not just because of the blatantness but the accuracy.

Taking a deep breath, he got his surprise under control. "Okay, well in that case I won't deflect, and I will be honest. I am not sure if I should, the company might be watching for me doing it. If they catch me, it would be a breach of a whole bunch of legal documents I signed before starting this job. However, even if I did I would need more than a name to find him. Brian Charles, male, and black is not enough; there could be hundreds of men, maybe even thousands, who match that search. I certainly can't risk contacting anyone who isn't him. That also raises another point of concern. I don't know Brian or if I can trust him."

"You can, he was sent away for trying to protect me. He would never do anything to hurt me!" the pony insisted, his ears twitching in restrained annoyance as he defended his friend. "I just want to know he is okay. He is thirty-two, and he said he lived in the Bronx."

"Do . . . you know anything else about him?" Kyle asked with a resigned sigh. He should say no, it would be a stupid risk to take. He could lose his job, and worse still he could seriously piss off Dempsy. However, something told him that Aden was not going to take no for an answer. Besides, Brian might have some insights he could use, so long as he was careful.

"He studied at Yale, and he . . ." The horse paused in his words, and he hung his head. "I can't think of anything else that might help. He liked classical period art, preferred mango to pineapple, and he liked to read all the time. He would read me stories every day. I remember when I was young he used to read to me in bed."

Kyle lay still and listened as Aden started to talk about his former companion. Their relationship had been very different to his and Aden's. Brian had been his companion from a very young age, and Aden quite clearly saw him as a father figure.

"He was behind me when I said I wanted to leave. I could hear Dr. Ramon in his ear telling him to tell me to stay, but he told me that he wanted me to see it all. More than just the mountains, the oceans, and beaches, other countries and other people. He even asked if I could just go for walks outside the facility. The other side of the fence, even, just to take me somewhere, down to that little town or, I dunno, a walk anywhere."

The horse squeezed Kyle in his arms and whispered, "He was the one who told me to refuse to give samples. The day after I did, he disappeared. No goodbye, no explanation, just they took him away. If you find him, will you tell him I said goodbye and that I miss him?"

"Of course, is there anything else you want to say?" the human asked, his hands stroking the pony's cheeks gently.

"That I have you now, so I'm not alone . . . I really don't know what else to say." The last part sounded like a surprise to Aden more than it was to Kyle. "I just . . . want to know he's ok and that he knows I'm okay."

"I will try," the actor, promised kissing Aden on the lips softly. "I promise I will at least try to find and contact him."

"Thank you, I . . ." The pony paused, and there was a long silence as Aden contemplated what he was going to say. "Thank you," he finished with a sigh.

The two lay in silence until the fell asleep. Kyle's mind kept him awake long after Aden as it focused on the last thing Aden has said. Aden had been about to say something, something different, and then he'd stopped himself. Maybe he was going to ask if Kyle could do something else, or ask Brian something. However, there was a very short sentence that started with an "I" that kept popping into Kyle's mind.

Chapter 13

The autocar journey back home seemed much longer this time around. Kyle tried to catch up on his sleep, but his mind kept straying to Aden and to his promise. It was a stupid thing to do, but then it wasn't even in the top ten list of stupid things he had done that year. He found himself watching the landscape as the autocar shot along above it, the tiny empty towns and villages; most of them looked intact.

Nearer to the city, he passed over small areas of suburban sprawl. Gated districts where autocars needed approval codes to land. You could walk out there, but only if you paid the environmental tariff to leave the city. A payment to make up for all the damage people made, to fund government replanting programs.

Lack of jobs, slowly increasing environmental tariffs, and increased costs had forced people out of their homes. Land had become so expensive, only companies had been able to buy it, and they had bought everything they could. There were holdouts still, but they were few and far between. People whose family had owned their land for generations, lucky ones with no need for mortgage. Growing their own food and a little to sell.

Kyle sighed as he saw Chicago approaching, home or a very close approximation. He rushed to the elevator in the growing gloom. The press of people around him felt somehow worse than before. It felt like rush hour, and yet it still looked far less full that it would be at peak times. He was too aware of people as they stepped in and out of his personal space without even looking him in the eye. His nose seemed to have grown more sensitive; the stink of dozens of perfumes, deodorants, and bodily smells assaulted him.

His heart began to beat rapidly as the lift plummeted. Each time it opened, he found himself breathing as more people got off. He shrank back further into the space that was created. When the door finally opened on his floor, he shot out onto the concourse, pushed to the edge, and stood there, taking in deep breaths. The air felt dry and yet oddly pungent in his nose, the smell of humanity piled on top of each other.

It took him a few minutes of deep breathing for his heart to calm down, for the trembles to leave his limbs. His last panic attack had been when he was thirteen and he was passed on to a new set of foster parents. They had an apartment only ten floors down, with a balcony which he could sit out in the sun. The perfect couple, or certainly they seemed it on paper. He learned very quickly that seeming was easy and being was something far different.

An accidental spill on a sofa worth more money than Kyle had earned in his whole life. His foster father had shouted at him so much, he'd locked himself out on the balcony, trembling and hiding behind one of the planters. All he'd been able to think of was the last man who'd shouted at him. It had been one of his 'uncles'. He'd been trying to keep Anna quiet, but she was hungry. He'd asked his mother for some milk to feed her, and . . . he got the scar marks on his arms instead. To make sure he learned his lesson about not disturbing mommy and uncle when they were taking their medicine.

Kyle knew what caused his last panic attack, but he wasn't sure why he had felt one on returning to the city. He tried to banish thoughts of those memories from his mind, consigning them to the tiny vault in his mind where he kept all the dark stuff locked up, where he wouldn't have to think about it. Chalking the attack up to his concerns about trying to find Brian, he started to walk towards home.

When he finally reached home, he found that nothing had changed. The sofa bed was still a mess from where he had left early. Venus was sitting alone on the windowsill. A quick check of her soil found it far too dry. Before he did anything else, he gave his plant a good drink and opened the window a crack, to let her call a few flies over for supper. Then he opened up his computer and checked his inbox.

Dempsy had sent a message; the old bastard was happy for now. Though he did hint that it was in both their best interests if the bonuses kept coming. "I would hate to lose such lucrative extras, and I am sure you would as well dear boy. Especially given the current lack of good clients. So, keep your head down and work hard. Oh, have you contacted your sister yet? You really should say hello. It is such a pity when siblings lose touch."

Deep breaths got him through the rage he felt, though he promised himself that he would speak to Dr. Ramon about buying out his contract. Maybe he'd end up stuck in a dead-end company job after his contract with Aden expired, or unemployed. However, unlike most company guys, he could survive outside them if need be. Once fired, you were blacklisted by most companies, even if you'd done nothing wrong. After all, they had millions of employees to choose from, and, if they picked to let you go, there must be a reason. Maybe your work wasn't good enough, maybe you were sick too often. Why take the risk when there are always plenty of new employees to choose from?

There was also a message from Darwin, asking if he would like to meet up for something to drink. This time, he responded to him. He said he would love to have the tech over again, though he might need some help with something. The reply from Darwin came less than a minute after he hit send, "On my way, I'll help you as soon as I get there."

It was hard for Kyle not to notice this time. The technician arrived with a much smaller bottle of wine as well rather than strong liquor. The actor welcomed his friend in and offered to buy him dinner. After all, he really needed to make it up to him for the rudeness of the previous week. That, and he needed to butter the tech up for what he needed from him.

"So, what was this favor you wanted?" Darwin asked after they had agreed on a place they could order some food from. Nothing too special, and yet something a little bit more than Kyle would normally have ordered. Some high-end food packets, with meat flavorings and a small slice of cake each. All highly processed, but still not a bad meal.

"I need you to do something with my system. I need . . . to be sure nobody can access my system, see what I'm doing. Or listen to any of my conversations," the actor whispered the request.

"Ah . . . You are aware that, by law, all activities online need to be recorded by the company providing the services. So, you know it'd be illegal for me to turn all that off," Darwin replied, though his voice was even. He didn't seem upset; in fact, there seemed to be a faint trace of a smile on his face.

"Yeah, I know. C . . . Can you do it?"

"Oh, sure, takes a little bit, just need to glitch your system. Put it slightly off kilter with the rest of the net. You'll still have access, but, for a little while, you won't be recorded." The technician was smiling broadly as he said it loudly and proudly. "I do that to my own system every time there is an update. Updates tend to put everyone back on the same level."

"Really, it's that easy?" Kyle was shocked; he'd always assumed that organizations' tech was nearly impossible to break.

"Oh no, it's not easy, and I really haven't explained half of what I have to do to get through. However, it'd take hours to explain what I would need to do, and I'm guessing you don't care that much on the how, just so long as I do it." The tech was right there; knowing the how was a luxury he couldn't be bothered with. "Now all you need to do is tell me why you want to do it? I never marked you as a criminal type. I mean, you almost kicked my ass for daring to bring a couple of fun pills into your house back when we first met. You are an honest guy, a bit more open minded than most, but honest . . . Well, as honest as anyone I mix with. That isn't too high a bar to jump over."

Kyle froze as his mind raced, and he tried to defy the accusations of honesty by thinking up a lie that would cover him. However, he could see no harm in letting Darwin know an abridged version of the truth. After all, the technician was sticking his neck out, too. What he was about to do was illegal, and, if they got caught, it would be both of them who were charged, and Darwin would likely face prison time; he already had a record. "I need to speak to someone, and I don't want anyone knowing what I said or even that I called him. Hell, I don't want anyone knowing I searched for his details. I could get into a lot of trouble if I got caught, not just from the authorities. It'd be a breach of my NDA with the company."

"So, you are about to breach your NDA?" Kyle could guess what the next question would be; however, he was damn well going to force Darwin to ask. "So, you could share some details with me?"

Rolling his eyes a little, Kyle shrugged and then gave the technician a smile. If Darwin had better instincts, he would have recognized that smile. He'd seen it on nature documentaries attached to big cats after they catch their prey. All he saw was a pretty guy smiling at him and then sitting down next to him on the sofa where a week ago he had given him the ride of his life. "I have been hired by BioCorp to help in some project."

"A corporation hiring an actor? What do they have you doing? High-level corporate retreats?" The technician asked and then gasped a little as Kyle's hands began to lightly stroke his chest and stomach.

"Mmm, I do like your bit of belly, so comfortable," Kyle muttered softly, leaning close to lay his head on Darwin's shoulder. "Are you . . . able to work with a little distraction?"

"I . . . guess I can," Darwin replied as he turned on Kyle's computer and began to give a few commands. "So, is it a corporate reTREAAAAT?!" As he asked the question, an overly eager hand stroked down over his crotch. Kyle's lips kissed Darwin's neck while his cock swelled into his firmly groping hands.

"Mmmm, I can answer all your questions," Kyle whispered his words into Darwin's ear, his fingers pulling down the technician's fly and fishing his rapidly hardening cock out into the open. "But there's something else I'd rather do with my lips than just talk."

"Oh . . . mmm, far be it from me to force you to talk when you want to do something else. Oh fuck!" The exclamation escaped his lips as a dark-haired head dove into his lap. A warm, expert mouth sealed around his uncut cock, Kyle's tongue swirling around his quivering cock-tip. He tried to continue working. However, as the actor's head began to bob, he found his focus slipping.

Kyle knew it was petty, manipulative, and unfair to do this to his friend. However, he knew Darwin wouldn't complain, and, despite himself, he did enjoy sucking cock. His tongue pushed inside Darwin's sheath, the tech's strong, sweaty musk coating it. He moaned at the taste, sucking more firmly, starting to bob his head in Darwin's lap. In his mind, he found himself thinking back to the last week, to the times he had serviced Aden.

"Oh shit!" Darwin gasped as Kyle's face was pressed into his musky, sweaty groin. His cock being forced down the back of the actor's throat, the tightness gripping his cock far better than any toy he had ever tried. Every gadget he had bought to milk his own cock was like some worthless trinket when compared to the mouth working his shaft. The tongue squirming against his hot flesh, teasing it wonderfully.

The suction increasing moment by moment, the actor's lips peeled his sheath away from his cock-tip. Fireworks erupting behind his eyes as his sensitive flesh was stuffed wantonly down the actor's tight throat. The tip being held there, worked by the constricting pipes, he couldn't stop himself. His hands gripped Kyle's head, fingers lacing through his thick black hair. With pants and gasps, he fucked up into those hungry, sucking lips.

With his eyes closed, all Kyle could see was Aden's thick length thrusting between his lips. Darwin's taste was weak compared to it, a fizzy lager compared to the musky stout of the equine. A cheap burger compared to the finest marbled steak. He sucked desperately, bobbing his head faster and faster. It was all too much for the technician, far too soon. He felt himself being pushed over the edge.

Humping up desperately into Kyle's lips, his cock throbbed, and he began to empty onto his tongue. Kyle couldn't help but notice the lack of volume; Aden's loads were always far more copious, a small amount of spunk beating his device to give him a delicious taste, just an aperitif to leave him starving for a main course. No such luck here, just several small, full, sealed packages.

He pulled off the cock as the cum flow slowed to a dribbled, leaving the softening cock to flop back onto Darwin's pants and drool stains onto the fabric. Kyle quickly pulled the packages out if his mouth and discreetly slipped them into his pocket. Then he looked up and smiled. "How are you doing with the computer?"

Darwin moaned and opened his eyes. "I got distracted."

"I thought you were a professional?" teased the actor with a slight, reprimanding tone.

"I am, but so are you at what you do," snorted the technician as he began to work again. It only took him ten minutes to finish whatever wizardry he was conducting and to wave his hands dramatically. "Voila, you are now invisible. Anything you do or say on this computer for the next few days will not be seen or heard. So, you going to tell me more about what you are doing at some company facility out in the middle of nowhere?"

"No," Kyle replied with a wink. "Sorry, I just . . . You really wouldn't believe me, or you would and you would possibly be disgusted. We have food on the way, we can just eat, drink, and forget my job."

His brow crinkling in frustration, Darwin nodded his acceptance or capitulation. For now, at least. Kyle knew he would ask again. However, for the evening and week, he had gotten what he wanted. The actor tried to be a good host this time; they ate together and drank the wine. Afterwards, he let Darwin take control for a fuck, though, after a week of Aden's impressive member, he felt annoyingly unfulfilled as the technician pumped himself hilt deep.

Of course, Kyle was used to making his lovers feel good both physically and mentally. He moaned and panted like a bitch in heat, giving every indication of enjoyment. Pushing back at the right moment, begging for Darwin to go harder and faster.

His friend left with a smile on his face and some cumstains on his pants. If they weren't the signs of a great night with a friend, Kyle didn't know what would be. It was almost midnight by the time Darwin left. Kyle wanted nothing more than to lay down and sleep. However, he turned his computer on and began to search the world for Brian Charles, thirty-eight with a degree or PhD from Yale, living in Bronx, New York.

It was surprisingly easy to find him, or someone who fit all the factors. The only way he would know for certain would be to call. Somehow, he imagined that Brian was unlikely to welcome a call this late at night, especially from not just a stranger but the guy who took his job. He thought about sending him a message but decided that it was best to leave no written evidence of communication.

Instead, he sank into his bed, thoroughly exhausted, sleep taking him quickly but not mercifully. He tossed and turned all night, rolling from one nightmare to another. Waking up after just a few hours soaking in sweat, he checked his scars one more time. Then he tried to fall back to sleep, but this time, sleep taunted him not with nightmares, but absence. His mind not able to settle, he sat, watching the light outside starting to grow. There was no beautiful sunrise, only the changes in shadow, the street lights flicking off one at a time. A fly had crawled in and fallen victim to Venus, struggling briefly against the inevitable and then succumbing.

Kyle found his mind slipping to Aden. He wondered if the horse had woken as well and if he was watching the sunrise. When the clock hit six, he dragged his sweaty body into the shower and rinsed off the sweat of the previous day and night. The idea of calling Brian this early also did not appeal to him; once more, it seemed like a bad time.

Instead, he decided to go get an early breakfast, checking his bank balance to get a rather pleasant surprise. Apparently, Cassandra was not exaggerating when she said that the bonuses for the job were worth it. Feeling extremely flushed, he wandered out into the small business area outside his building. This time, choosing to have a muffin with his breakfast latte, he ate in the coffee shop itself as a light drizzle was falling. He disliked walking out in the rain. The water seemed to pick up the dirt from the higher levels and wash it down. It stained clothing and tasted unpleasant; it packed a chemical taste far more powerful than the cheapest of food packs.

Across the street, there were several small businesses, hairdressers, massage parlors and a tattoo place. Stuff that took little space, not that much equipment, and was always in demand. Everyone still needed a haircut from time to time, or a massage. New ink was actually appealing. He hadn't been able to afford any for a long time. However, with his account flushed, he wandered over for a little browse in the window.

The owner spotted him and waved him inside. Having little else to do this early, he decided it couldn't hurt. Well, that wasn't entirely true; it certainly could sting. He spent a good hour and a bit inside and walked out a little sore and lighter of bank balance. When he emerged, he thought about contacting Brian. It was a lot more social an hour to do so. However, he also realized the bookshop would be open; Aden was expecting a new book, and he had no idea which one might be acceptable. Somehow, he thought it might be easier to get a title past Dr. Ramon. Things were going well, after all.

Deciding that he could always try contacting Brian later, he made his way back to the bookshop. There was no recurrence of his panic attack as he travelled up in the elevator. He walked into the bookshop, and this time he went directly to the middle, where he found Danny sitting with a rather elderly couple. A quick glance at their clothing confirmed they were wealthy. Real jewelry; at least, it looked real from a distance. Their clothes finely tailored, elegant, and yet functional.

Of course, the fact Danny had already busted out the ham sandwiches and port screamed that these were some rich fools about to spend six figures on some old paper. The young clerk glanced up at Kyle. The actor could see a real smile sneaking onto the clerk's business face. Kyle waved at the stacks to indicate he would browse for a while, then backed away as Danny gave a tiny nod.

He wandered through the bookshelves, his fingers tracing along the spines of hundreds of books. Pulling one out at random, he read the first line, "It was the best of times, it was the worst of times." Kyle chuckled a little wondering if that, meant the times were average. He put the book back and selected another, opening it at random and reading the first line his eyes focused on; "Twenty years from now, you will be more disappointed by the things you didn't do than the ones you did do. "Kyle imagined that, in twenty years, he would probably be disappointed to think of some of the things he did do, especially for money.

Book to book, random lines amused him. Some made him wonder, and others just baffled him. Lines out of context, they kept him busy for at least an hour before he heard a voice behind him, "Ah, you're still here, great."

"Yes, I was just . . . looking," Kyle replied with a smile.

"Was everything okay with the book?" the clerk asked, stepping a little closer and glancing at the book in Kyle's hands.

Kyle closed the book and put it away, suddenly aware it was likely to be very expensive. "Yes, actually, things went well. I came back to get another."

"Oh, well, as I said last time, we do have more of that title . . ."

"No, I mean a different book," the actor burst in with an apologetic smile.

"Okay, what title and author?" Danny asked. The expression on Kyle's face told him that he had a long morning and possible afternoon of searches ahead of him. "You at least know some character names?"

"No, but I kind of know what the story's message should be," the actor replied with his cheekiest grin, holding up his hands in submission.

"The story's message?" the clerk replied, his voice sounding like Sisyphus when the rock rolled back to the bottom of the hill and he asked, "So I have to push it back up to the top, again?" Although, at least, he could do so with nice sandwiches. Plus, Kyle wasn't bad company and certainly gave him something pleasant to look at. "And I thought last week was a tough request. Would you like a beer? I have a feeling I am going to need a few today."

"Yes," Kyle agreed on all fronts. Last week was tough, this week was tougher, and, most importantly, he would love a free beer.

The morning and most of the afternoon passed enjoyably. For all his exasperation at Kyle's rather wide scope, Danny rose to the challenge. Producing a range of potential books that all held the same core principle: "The grass may seem greener on the other side, but it tastes like shit, and people try to kill you for crossing the fence." After a few ham sandwiches and a few glasses of port, "I mean the bottle was already open, may as well have a glass or two", he selected the cheapest option. Telling Danny he would probably come back next week for another book. Which got him a happy, slightly drunken smile off the clerk.

The book he had chosen was Homer's Odyssey, or an interpretation of it. Danny had assured him the book was all about one guy's ten-year journey to get home. It sounded close enough. Kyle was more confident of it passing; Dr. Ramon wouldn't want anything to upset Aden and potentially stop him producing.

With the book firmly clutched in his hands, he returned home, getting there just as evening began to fall. There was no unpleasant visitor waiting for him this time, just Venus who had managed to trap another tiny, uninvited guest. He placed the book down carefully and grabbed a food packet from the cupboard. He knew he was out of time and, worse still, almost out of excuses.

If he wanted to, he could lie to Aden, "if" being the word he focused on. Lying was the easy way out, say he tried and failed. However, Aden would undoubtedly ask him to try again on his next day off, and again if he failed the second time. Besides, part of him wanted to see what the fabled Brian was like, inciting Aden to rebel for his freedom. For someone so smart, he had clearly not known his own limited value to the company. The second he had stepped in their way, he had been thrown away like moldy bread. His usefulness had past.

Kyle signaled his computer to start up, sitting down on the sofa with a glass of water. He recalled up the search from the previous night and found Brian Charles, Dr. Brian Charles. Lots of letters after his name, they were there to try and impress non-academics; do not match wits with me boy, I have half the alphabet after my name, I must know more than ye mere mortals, with no letters after your name.

He engaged a conversation request and waited. It took a few minutes to get a response. It wasn't an acceptance of his call, but a question in text, "I don't recognize your account, who are you?"

"A friend of Aden's," Kyle paused before he sent the message. He wondered if he should avoid using the horse's name and put something more cryptic. He mulled over a few options, but they all seemed weak; besides, if he was obscure enough that nobody reading would guess he meant Aden, then Brian probably wouldn't get it, either. So, he just hit send and hoped it wasn't a mistake.

Minutes dragged by like decades as he waited for a response. A growing bunch of knots in his stomach helped him pass the time in discomfort. Then eventually a response came through, "Call back in five minutes."

With a flick of his hand, Kyle canceled the call and sat back in his chair. Five minutes, that was just enough time to wonder exactly why Brian needed that time; was he out, was he currently setting up recording equipment, or, the most worrying, was Brian contacting the company to report the contact?

The second five minutes had past, he hit dial, and this time his call was accepted. It was answered by a middle-aged man, ebony skin, the tone almost identical to his own. Brian's hair was a match for his own style, only with a few hints of gray starting to show. His nose and cheekbones bared a mild similarity as well. For Kyle, it was like staring at a poor projection of what he might look like in twenty years if he stopped exercising. Brian had more than a couple of pounds on him, yet, much like Becky, he had obviously refused to get treatment; he wondered why.

"Hello, Brian?" It was a pretty poor opener, given that he was certain of the answer.

"Yes, Kyle, is it? You said you were a friend of Aden's, how do you know him?" He gave no time to answer his first question before the second shot out. It was clear to Kyle he was far more interested in his relationship with Aden than who he was.

"We are . . . friends . . ."

"Aden doesn't have friends, he has handlers," the man spat angrily, and, from his tone, Kyle could tell he was definitely still hurting from losing his job.

"Handlers would not breach half a dozen non-disclosure agreements to pass on a message to someone dumb enough to get their asses fired," he spat back, matching fire with fire and giving him an even gaze, daring Brian to challenge his logic. "Aden wants to know if you are okay."

For a moment, Kyle could see Brian mulling over the question, his expression still doubtful. He clearly didn't trust Kyle and was trying to figure out exactly where the trap lay. "I suppose you could say I'm okay. Black mark on my record means I can't get a fucking job mopping floors. My savings are running out, and I'm about to move back in with my mothers. Luckily, they both still have their jobs." The last sentence was said in a slightly different tone, almost like he was quoting someone; most likely something one of his mothers had said bitterly when they agreed to let the middle-aged chick back into the nest. His voice lightened up as he asked, "How is he?"

"He said to tell you he is okay, he has me for company now." He felt a bit weird saying the second half, it almost felt like boasting. "He misses you, he has talked of you a lot, though Dr. Ramon always tries to get me off 'the topic of Brian.'"

"Ah, yes, I banged my head against that particular wall until I snapped." The older man sank backwards and sighed. "It was stupid, really, telling Aden he should demand to be out. Telling him to withhold what they wanted to barter with. I was just so pissed off. He and Bruno are worse off than slaves. They have spent their entire lives inside that compound, and they will never get out. I tried contacting a lawyer after they fired me. First four refused to touch anything because of the company NDAs I'd signed. The last told me the truth: as lab animals, they have no rights, and, as livestock, their living arrangements far exceed the legal requirements for keeping animals."

It was hard to imagine Aden as an animal, livestock. Bruno maybe, he seemed to only care about filling his belly and satisfying his cock. Aden was intelligent, witty, and gentle. The idea of him as an animal had left his mind after the first full day with him. He was a person; hell, he was a lover as much as any of his friends had been, more so than some of his previous clients. "I . . . don't think of Aden that way."

"It doesn't really matter what you think," the scientist replied bluntly and then shook his head. "Sorry, that came out harsher than I meant. I am grateful to you, for taking such a risk to let me know he is okay. However, as long as Dr. Salter is in charge of that project, those poor boys are doomed to live out their lives as . . . battery ponies. A tiny pen, water bowl, producing endlessly to fit the company's needs. You know they export all successful offspring to Mars? I suggested sending Aden and Bruno there, at least they could have more freedom. All the people there are employees. The governments can't touch them, so they could actually be people there. Hell, they would be the only ones able to walk outside without a spacesuit; but animals that size have to be inspected by the government before export. They are too scared they would be seen and that someone might ask the question they fear the most: are they really lab animals? Can lab animals ask you to please stop experimenting on them?"

Kyle sat quietly as the scientist ranted. He listened carefully to what was said. A lot of it he knew or could have guessed. The destination of their offspring was a surprise. He wondered how human they looked, or if they got their looks from their fathers. "I am just paid to keep him company, I am not even a corporation employee."

The man frowned as he spoke, "So you are . . . an actor, like they hire for Bruno?"

"Yes, I am," Kyle replied evenly, holding the older man's gaze once more to show he wasn't ashamed of whom he was.

"Well, I guess that makes more sense than assigning a world class scientist to keep him company." Kyle positively brindled at the man's attitude.

"Quite. After all, world class scientists don't always think before they act and end up moving back home with their mommies," the actor retorted and reveled as the older man scowled. "Now, I contacted you because he asked me to. I have my answers, and I sure as hell don't see why I should risk my job contacting you again, so have a nice life."

"Wait! Please, I'm sorry, I didn't mean any offense." The man's tone changed from contempt to pleading and groveling so fast, his personality might have suffered whiplash from the sudden stop and reverse of mental gears.

"No, you meant offense, you just seemed to think that an actor was going to take your abuse and say nothing. I charge for that kind of service, and, judging from the state of your finances, you cannot afford me," Kyle snapped back, but he didn't hang up. He waited to see what the response would be.

"You're right, I am sorry for my rudeness. I have no right to look down on you." The man's shoulders slumped in defeat and resignation. "As I said earlier, I am grateful for you contacting me like this. It is good to know he is okay. He is . . . like the little brother I always wanted. Since he was eight, I took over from Dr. Ramon as his carer. Ten years, I was his support. I just want what is best for him. Staying in that place isn't what he needs or wants. If only we could show the world whom he is, I think the corporation would have to acknowledge that he is far more than a lab animal."

"Maybe you are right, but you know that isn't possible. Even if I was willing to try I am, scanned going in and out," Kyle replied with a shrug. "There is nothing I can do but make his life more pleasant and to make sure there are some things he does not miss out on and can explore, even inside the facility."

"I know, I remember their security procedures. I assume the deconscrub is still as intrusive and unpleasant as ever?" Kyle could spot Brian's attempt to connect with him through a joke on a shared experience. He laughed politely; he knew he had put Brian in his place, and, for now at least, he would be civil.

"Possibly gotten worse," the actor replied as he chuckled. "Although, the food is good. Look, I can't keep this call going much longer, and it may be a while before I can call again, if at all." He knew Aden would ask him to call Brian again, but he wasn't going to risk it. Not every week, maybe once every other month if the pony insisted. For now, he had once more fulfilled his promise to Aden, and that was all he cared about. "If you have anything you want to say to him, I can relay the message."

"Just . . . tell him I am okay, that I love him, and I really hope we can see each other someday." Kyle thought he could see a tear on the man's cheek as he spoke. He knew those words were heartfelt.

"I will tell him, I am certain that he feels the same." The actor put as much reassurance into his voice as he spoke. "Please, wipe any records of this conversation. If I get caught, then we will both lose him forever. Now goodbye."

He didn't wait for a reply. He just waved his hand and ended the call. Then he sat in silence, trying to process what he had just done, the risk he had taken. It was done now, but, if he got caught, then he would certainly lose access to Aden. The company would look to sue him into oblivion, and Dempsy would have to consider a fitting punishment. All because Aden had asked him to do it and he hadn't been able to say no.

Chapter 14

The journey back to the facility was quiet and uneventful; boring, in fact. Kyle found himself wondering what Aden had done without him. There wasn't a large range of possibilities, and it was mostly likely to be the same as he did with him. Although he assumed with no samples being taken. That didn't seem like much of a problem; Kyle had gotten enough samples during the week that Dr. Ramon had seemed certain the labs could keep going.

The numbers that Dr Salter. had quoted on his first day had seemed outlandish. It was weird to think that somewhere was a stable filled with mares being used to try and implant every successfully fertilized egg. People like Becky were working full shifts just trying egg after egg in the hopes of creating a few more like Aden and Bruno. People who could walk on the surface of Mars, perform surveys, build equipment. Without the risk of suit tears or life support failure.

Kyle had done a little checking on the journey. There had been thousands of accidental deaths getting Mars to have the thin oxygen atmosphere it currently held. The number ran close to a hundred thousand in the last fifty years. It was difficult to make equipment there. Most of their tools and gear came from shuttles from Earth. Meaning any breakdowns halted work for a hundred or more days waiting for replacements. Space on the shuttles was at a premium, so it wasn't cheap.

That lead to jury rigging equipment to keep things going, more risk. Human life was cheap, though, and there was always plenty of it. Of course, a few thousand people like Aden and Bruno could drastically change that, or that was Dr. Salter's theory. The actor had looked up the news reports, wondering why he hadn't done so before. There had been plenty of compelling arguments for and against. Along with a lot of religious dogma about man trying to be God.

Many people had called for the Moreau children to be terminated. Dr. Salter had argued that they held the same potential as any human child, and he would not terminate that potential. The man had fumed about religious hypocrisy of demanding he kill his children while campaigning to end abortion. In the end, he had won that battle but lost the war, retreating to Elba to plan his next assault on their values.

Kyle realized that someday more stories would be written. Their work could not stay secret forever. Brian had said the first successful children had already been sent to Mars. In twenty years' time, they would be out there doing something, fully trained. No doubt people would complain about them taking human jobs; they always complained about that.

Going through decon was extra painful, his new tattoo still very sensitive. He worried that the scrub might cause the ink to bleach or warp the design. Fortunately it seemed to survive intact. He answered the same questions, told the same lie as last time, and then went directly to Dr. Ramon's office. He placed the book down on the doctor's desk and smiled. "More reading for you and, hopefully, Aden. Oh, I was thinking, could we get a deck of cards? I know a few card games that could help keep Aden and maybe even Bruno distracted."

"Yes, on the cards, I think I can probably get someone to buy a deck this week. I won't have time to read your book, but I think I read it in college, so just take it," the doctor replied barely looking up from his computer. "Dr. Salter has decided to take a month's leave, probably had too much holiday built up. He never really takes it unless he's ill. So, while he's away, they have asked me to step in to keep things ticking along."

The actor could hear more than a hint of satisfaction in Dr. Ramon's words and could see the man was struggling to keep a smile off his face. Promotion beckoned with a chance like this, to prove he could run the facility just as well as his boss. Kyle struggled to keep the smile off his own face. The doctor would be far too busy to be watching him and Aden all the time; hel,l he might never actually hear a word from him all week, so long as things were going good.

Of course, he realized one other thing: his boss was in a good mood. If ever there was a time to try and ask for something, it was now. "Oh, well, I'm sure the place will run smoothly with you filling in." It never hurts to apply some butter to the person you want something from. Of course, as an actor, Kyle was an expert at using just the right amount of lubricant to achieve his goals. "Do they pay you any extra for this? I mean, they should, doing your boss's job and your own. You are going to be run off your feet."

"No extra money, it's what they call a developmental opportunity. Which is corporate talk for working above your grade for free while doing your own job on the side," Dr. Ramon's tone was far too cheery for Kyle to believe he was anything but thrilled to get the chance to take on this 'developmental opportunity'.

"Well, I am sure you can rise to the challenge," Kyle said with as much enthusiasm as he dared apply. "Oh, how did your day with your nephews go? Did you get to the beach?"

"Yes, thank you, it was a very pleasant day, just the right amount of sun," the scientist replied, his smile broadening, as his employee demonstrated not only interest in his personal, life but that he had been listening when he last spoke about it.

"What you got planned for next week?" The actor's questions were not entirely selfish. Kyle did enjoy seeing that some people did the kid thing correctly. Though he was still aware that showing an interest was a good way to build a bond between them. It all built Kyle up as a nice guy, and people naturally wanted to help nice guys.

"Oh, nothing much, I thought we could just spend the day inside playing games. I don't want them to get too spoiled by being taken out all the time." The last part sounded slightly defensive, as if someone might accuse him of neglecting his nephews because he hadn't taken them out.

"Ah, sometimes I think that's better than going out, a quiet day in as a family." Kyle had no idea what a day in with a family was really like. He had never had one, unless you counted the days he stayed home looking after his sister alone. Still, in his head, it seemed like a nice idea. The smile on the doctor's face told him the response was a definite hit. He decided to press his luck.

"Actually, there was something I wanted to discuss with Dr. Salter, so I guess I need to discuss it with you now. If that's okay?" Kyle asked, putting a little emphasis on the doctor's name, just to remind Dr. Ramon that he currently had the power of his boss.

"Of course, please feel free." Dr. Ramon couldn't keep a little smug smile off his face at the affirmation of his temporary elevation.

Leaning back in his chair, Kyle resumed echoing the doctor's body language as he began to explain, "Well, I'll be honest and upfront with you so you can make an informed choice." He started putting on a serious tone and keeping eye contact. "I want out of my contract. Not with you, but with my agent. I have been trying to save for a while, but it isn't easy. However, it occurred to me that there might be some advantage for BioCorp in looking to buy my contract out."

The look on the scientist's face told Kyle that he was listening, but not really liking what he was hearing. He tried to keep any thoughts of panic out of his head. "The truth is most clients hire me for no longer than a few days; however, I sense that this contract is going to go on for many months, years even. Plus, the regular bonuses that are likely to continue as Aden is unlikely to let anyone other than me take a sample from him." This got a slight nod from the scientist. "I don't know the full details of your contract with my agent, but I am assuming that you might find you could buy my contract out for less than the costs of a full year plus bonuses."

"Indeed, that would be a considerable sum, and not one to just spend without any benefit for BioCorp." The scientist was clearly feeling doubtful about the proposal. Spending so much just to help Kyle be free from his contract seemed to offer his corporation little.

"Of course, I am just laying out what I get out of the deal, so that you know what the hook is, why I am doing this. For BioCorp, you would get me as an employee on a contract for, say, five years at a much-reduced salary to my current contract, with no bonuses." The actor laid it out as simply as he could. "I don't actually know the full details of what you pay my agent. I am supposed to get fifty percent; however, I have serious doubts that I am getting it. Could you show me the details, and I could tell you what salary I would expect, then you will be able to work out the potential savings?"

"I . . . can't see any harm in you seeing the contract," Dr. Ramon conceded, and, with a few commands on his computer, he projected a copy of the contract onto the wall. Kyle felt his fists tighten and his blood boil as he looked at the numbers. He was no mathematician, but he could divide by two, and that was nowhere near what he was getting. He always knew Dempsy was cheating him. However, somehow seeing the figures on the screen was far more than a red rag to a bull; it was like fucking the bull's cow in front of him while wiping your ass with his favorite shirt.

"Twenty percent, my salary would be one-fifth of what you are paying him per week, no bonuses needed." What Kyle didn't say was that he was getting far less than twenty percent; hell, it was less than ten percent. Dempsy was fucking him harder than any of his clients had ever done.

The doctor stared at the figures, and Kyle could see him doing the math in his head. That was a big saving, depending on how much the agent wanted to buy out the contract. He could certainly see an advantage to the corporation. Though he came up with a thought, one that never occurred to Kyle. "So your contract with your agent requires fifty percent payment on your work? However, you are only getting twenty?"

"A bit less actually," Kyle muttered bitterly, his eyes still fixed on the screen.

"Would you be willing to provide a copy of your employment contract and details of payments you have received?" The doctor had a sly smile on his face, his eyes still calculating.

"Why would you need to see my contract and payment details?" the actor asked cautiously. He could feel the hairs pricking up on the back of his neck; he knew Dr. Ramon was up to something.

"So I can provide them to our lawyers, for when we negotiate the buyout of your contract. A contract he has breached, according to you." The scientist took a deep breath. "I can imagine if we try to directly buy out your contract, he is going to demand a full year or more payment up front. Even with a five-year contract, assuming we need you that long, we are unlikely to be able to afford that. However, if we had some leverage . . . well, I think we are far more likely to settle on an agreeable figure."

Kyle gulped a little. He knew he could have tried to take legal action against Dempsy. Truth was he couldn't afford a lawyer; his agent could. Plus, he knew Dempsy would have taken that sort of legal threat very poorly, and he didn't want to wonder what would have happened.

"He is clearly taking advantage of you, if you are not even getting half of your half." The scientist's words didn't help much. They stoked the fuel at the smoldering heart of Kyle's anger. "You could take some time to think of it, or we could just forget it?"

"No," the word was whispered so quietly, Kyle wasn't even sure he had spoken it. His eyes slipped back up to that number, and he thought back. Eight years of clients, eight years of working for him. How much had Dempsy taken from him? "NO! Fuck it, you can have it all." His words were more of a snarl, and he reached over to Dr. Ramon's computer unit, scanning his biochip to get his own account up. A few minutes was all it took to gather the evidence that would be needed and send it over.

Kyle didn't go straight out to see Aden; he couldn't, his entire body was trembling, with rage or fear he wasn't sure. It was done. Whatever was going to happen afterwards, whatever the price he was going to have to pay. He took a long and lingering shower, his third of the day, and yet he felt dirtier than ever. Emerging, he dressed and put his transmitter into his ear, knowing that Dr. Ramon was unlikely to be listening. Then he returned to Aden. The pony was delighted to see him.

For his part, Kyle was glad to see the pony. It felt so wonderful to be wanted, to be held, that he just laid with him all day long. Aden, sensing there was something wrong, just held him tightly and said nothing. The two passed a quiet evening together, and it wasn't until Aden woke him at after three in the morning that they really began to talk.

"Is . . . everything okay?" the pony asked, nuzzling into the human's neck and kissing his salty skin tenderly.

"I just . . . There was some unpleasantness. I might have found a way out of my contract, though. I will tell you more later. I just need to let it sink in," Kyle replied with a sigh, kissing the pony's fuzzy cheeks. "But while that sinks in, I can say I found Brian."

"You did?!" The excitement in Aden's voice couldn't be mistaken. His eyes sparkled even in the tiny amount of starlight flirting its way into the room.

"Yes, I called him yesterday, he is well. Struggling to find a job, but he has family looking after him. He . . . wanted to know how you were doing." The actor paused for a moment. He briefly considered saying no more. He didn't want to share the equine, he worried that he might be second in Aden's heart. However, as he looked at the excited, happy face, he knew he couldn't hold it back. "He said to say that he loves you and misses you."

"He did?!" Once more, the excitement in Aden's voice was so strong, Kyle could almost taste it in the air.

"Yes, I told him that you missed him and that I was sure the feelings were very much mutual," Kyle couldn't stop himself sighing slightly as he spoke. "I'm afraid we weren't able to talk long, and it will be a while before I can risk contacting him again."

"But you will try? Sometime?" Each excited word cut the actor just a little, in the most confusing way. He had never felt like this before. He wasn't entirely sure why it bothered him so much. Kyle knew that Brian could never come back, why should it matter if Aden missed him?

"Yes, I will try again, for you." He meant those last words wholeheartedly. If anyone else had asked him to do it, he would have refused or lied. Somehow, he knew he couldn't do either to Aden. All he could do was put it off for as long as he could and hope that he didn't get caught.

The excited equine made him go over the conversation in detail. Aden seemed worried by the lack of a job. Kyle tried his best to calm those worries, though he knew it was likely to be a constant for the rest of Brian's life. Once he had a black mark, and being fired was as black a mark as a corporation could put on your record, Brian's career was done. The man had sacrificed it to try and help Aden. It was hard to imagine such an educated man doing something so stupid. Did the man have more respect for his fellow scientists? Had he thought they would listen to him?

In the end, it didn't matter, and Kyle knew he would almost certainly never be able to answer that question. Even if he could, it would do little for anyone, it was all done now. There was nothing left but trying to make the best of his situation. The two fell asleep after less than an hour of talking, the actor too exhausted emotionally and physically to stay awake and talk, or anything else.

Kyle awoke with a cry, Aden looking at him in the dim light of dawn. He could see the worry and tears on the pony's eyes. His mind was filled with the nightmare he had been having, of that day. He couldn't stop himself; his eyes dragged towards his scars. He lifted his t-shirt sleeve and shuddered as he saw them. "It's okay," he whispered in flagrant defiance of reality. "It was just a bad dream."

"You . . . you wouldn't wake up," Aden whispered, the equine trembling, his hands still holding the actor's shoulders from his shaking. "You just kept screaming for your mother."

Wiping a tear away from his eye, "It was just a bad dream . . ." Kyle wasn't sure whom he was trying to reassure, Aden or himself. It was always bad to think of that day, to see her like that. Those eyes, so very much hers and yet so very alien. "Bad stuff, sorry, I don't usually get them when I am sleeping with others. I guess all the stuff with Dempsy stirred up some bad feelings and old memories."

The equine's hands slipped off his shoulders and around his back. Kyle let himself slide forward into the embrace, resting his head on the strong chest. His breathing returning to normal. "It . . . was my mother." He whispered softly, not sure why he was talking, and yet, somehow, he really knew he had to hear it. "The day she died."

Aden didn't say anything. He just tightened his arms around the human, to let him know he was there. "I remember it so clearly, she overdosed. Drug addict, she was addicted to some really bad stuff. I don't really remember much from those days. She was an actor, but not really like me. She wasn't official, at least I don't think she was. Just I know she did stuff. She'd bring home a different guy almost every night."

Equine fingers laced between his own as Aden nuzzled his neck, letting him know he was not alone. "I'd take Anna into our bedroom and try to keep her quiet . . . try not to hear or listen to what was going on. I'd tell Anna stories until she fell asleep, and then I'd play music. Just keep my headphones in, just to make sure I never heard anything."

"Then one morning, I just . . . She was right there. Naked, I remember he left her naked on the floor. I couldn't tell the police who he was, I couldn't even describe him. I never looked at them, not after one . . . burned me. Open and shut, they said. She overdosed, he panicked and ran . . . Some guy, just some guy." Kyle fell silent, struggling to find something to say. He could feel his tears dripping down his cheeks. He had never told anyone about that day, not since he had escaped the system when his mandatory therapy had ended.

"So sometimes . . . I have bad dreams," he finished slightly lamely, and then he kissed Aden's chest and whispered, "Thanks, for listening to me."

"I . . . don't know what to say," the equine whispered.

"There is nothing to say, some things you can't make better. Sometimes life is shit, you just have to live through it and focus on the days that are not shit." Looking up, Kyle tried to smile. "Like days spent with you, they . . ." They what, he asked himself. They were good? They were the best days of his life? What were they? Confused and too emotional to think it through, Kyle just accepted the warm hugs, the secure feeling of strength around him, and closed his eyes once more.

For what remained of the night, the two slept peacefully. The nightmares stayed away, kept at bay by the feelings of warm security in the tight embrace. Kyle woke up, feeling Aden's arms still holding him tightly, and he couldn't help but sigh a little with content. He nuzzled gently into the broad chest and sighed softly; as far as job perks went, it was up there with free fruit.

With a yawn and a stretch, the pony signaled he was finally awake as well. "Time for a shower," Kyle announced. A quick check told him it was well past time for breakfast. He stood up and pulled his t-shirt off, then he saw Aden's head tilt curiously. "Oh, I got a new tattoo yesterday," he said with a bit of a nervous smile as Aden stared at the Celtic horse running across his stomach. "What do you think?"

Sitting up, Aden reached out to run his fingertips over the new ink. He stopped as Kyle winced. "Does it hurt?"

"It's a little sore. I saw this design, and it made me think of you. I dunno, it just felt right," the actor said, blushing a little as he talked. He had never gotten a tattoo for anyone before. "What do you think?"

"I like it. You got it because of me?" The pony's voice was filled with awe as he looked at the design.

"Well, sort of. I mean, you definitely made me think that I liked horses, and he really fits in with the other designs." Kyle turned and gave the pony a wink. "Time for a shower, we are late for breakfast."

Aden joined him in the shower seconds later, and the two of them made sure that they were very late for breakfast. Although they were both a little giddy and breathless when they reached the dining hall. This time, they were not alone; Bruno was sitting there with Cassandra sitting opposite. They both turned to glance as Kyle and Aden entered. In front of them both were empty trays and plates.

"Good morning," Aden said far too cheerily for even Bruno to have any doubt what had just happened in the shower a few minutes earlier.

Bruno gave a nod, his eyes turning to Kyle, still a little wary. The actor saw Cassandra reach out a hand and take Bruno's, reassuring him of his place in her life. A professional smile and nod was exchanged between the two actors before they both sat down to breakfast. Salad and oatmeal for Aden, food packages for Kyle, with apples for both afterwards. Bruno and Cassandra left very shortly after they arrived, going to start their morning routine.

As they moved Kyle, called out, "Oh, I asked for a deck of cards. I thought maybe we could teach these two some games, it might help pass the time."

Bruno looked confused, but Cassandra actually smiled. "I really should have thought of that sooner," she replied, which was probably the nearest thing Kyle would get to a compliment from the woman. Maybe the ice that filled her mind when she looked at her competition was finally starting to thaw, or maybe she just really loved playing Go Fish. Of course, playing cards was a classic move for prisoners. Kyle had seen it in dozens of prisoner of war vids, or prison break films; three of them could play cards while the fourth dug for freedom using a spoon, hammer, or insert name of tool acquired through bribing a guard.

"Cards?" Aden asked as the door shut behind the others.

"Cards, just to liven things up a little. Be good, and I'll see if I can convince them to let me bring a backgammon board in. Woo boy, then the fur will really start to fly," chuckled the actor as he munched on one of his food packets.

"Like they did in the shower?" Kyle almost choked on his food as the pony spoke. He could see the mischievous twinkle in Aden's eye. The pony was joking with him again, and he couldn't help but laugh in response.

"Not quite as much fun as that, but a close . . . twentieth or twenty-fifth place after backgammon." The actor shrugged. "Maybe we could get a chessboard, too. No vids, very few books, some music. The least they can do is give us a few old games to help pass the time." After all, it wasn't as if Aden could learn to be a revolutionary or a rebel from chess and backgammon. They'd already taught him that by giving him almost nothing and then taking his only friend away, once.

Cards proved to be a big hit with the four of them. Cassandra surprised Kyle with her in depth knowledge of many different card games. He assumed she'd picked it up on the job, an assumption she confirmed by admitting that one of her old, long-time customers hired her as an escort, simply to distract his opponents as he played in various tournaments. For her, it had been hours of long, dull standing around, being pawed at by half drunken men and women. She'd learned how to play so she could at least watch the action, maybe sometimes lean in a little closer, show some cleavage at the right time to distract someone. After all, like Kyle, she prided herself on being good value for money.

Bruno surprised Kyle by learning the rules far quicker than he expected. In fact, the black horse seemed to catch on faster than he did on several of the various games. He was far more aggressive a player than the others, and Bruno managed to push that to his advantage a few times.

However, the competition between the four of them was surprisingly good natured. Even Bruno took losing with good grace and humor. Having something new to distract them all was certainly a bonus, and it certainly helped time slip by. Aden and he spent a few hours each evening reading the Odyssey and talking alone. Each day, the four of them ate together and played at least a few rounds of one of a dozen different games.

On Monday, Dr. Ramon asked Kyle to come to his office while the others went to exercise in the morning. A knot of tension built up inside the actor as he walked through the corridors alone. He knew what this would be about: his contract. In his mind, he could see two possibilities; either they had failed to reach an agreement and Dempsy was very angry with him, or the corporation's lawyers had forced Dempsy into an agreement, in which case, Kyle's agent was likely to be so far beyond angry, he could only be seen with a telescope.

Either way, Kyle would suffer. He just hoped in the end it was worth it. He could take a few bumps and bruises to have his own freedom. Taking a few bumps and bruises for a failed escape attempt was far less easy to bear, like losing his cake and watching Dempsy eat it, too. He knocked on the door and took a deep breath, pushing his emotions down and putting a calm mask on his face. Hoping that it covered any of the emotions dancing in his unsettled stomach.

"Ah Kyle, come in," Dr. Ramon said, giving a smile and then waved at his seat. "Please, sit down. I have some good news for you."

Kyle sat down and exhaled a deep breath he had been holding, good news. It could be only one thing, and he found his mask slipping, to be replaced with a dopey grin. Even with years of practice at hiding his feelings, this was one he couldn't hide. "Is it about my contract?"

"Yes, indeed, we were able to come to terms with your agent. He gets a fee equivalent to four months, your contract with him is nullified and replaced with this one." As he spoke, the doctor projected a screen up with a new contract. Kyle saw his own name attached to a rather long document. "It is a standard employment contract for a fixed period of five years, unless BioCorp decides to terminate your employment. Please feel free to take some time to read. However, we would ideally like to get it signed today."

The actor's thumb itched with desire to give his formal e-print signature. However, he remembered the last time he had signed a document without reading it and how much of his life it had cost him. So, this time, he made Dr. Ramon sit there patiently for three hours while he read every word. He asked questions about everything until the poor doctor was wilting in his chair, like a drying flower in the noon day sun.

There were sacrifices, freedoms lost. However, there were compensations as well. His pay package was actually a little higher than he had expected, or even asked for. He wondered why that was. The only explanation he could think was that Dr. Ramon had upped it out of the kindness of his heart. That seemed rather dubious; in fact, in the end, he had to ask why that was. The answer was a little surprising.

"Well, in order to be an employee, you need to be employed at a specific employment grade, and the pay rates at that grade would apply. So, based on the amount you suggested, I put you forward for the junior management contract," the doctor explained patiently. Kyle couldn't help but chuckle internally. From prostitute to management, now there was a weird career path. He doubted that many people had followed it before.

Kyle reached the end. He couldn't see anything that would stop him from signing. He knew he didn't have time, or the money, to afford to have a solicitor check it over. So, he reached out and sealed the document and his fate with a thumbprint. Dr. Ramon made a joke about signing his life away. Kyle failed to see the humor as someone with experience of it. However, he walked in a prostitute and walked out a company man . . . being paid to have sex. Progress, but baby steps.

He hadn't asked how Dempsy took the request; he knew that would be something he would have to face. Kyle knew that, on his day off, he would probably get an unannounced visit from a seriously angry small man. Threats against his sister he was sure would be nothing. After all, now there was nothing for him to lose by taking his revenge against Kyle directly. He was no longer a valuable asset belonging to Dempsy. He was one of the horse, the faceless drones of big business. On the plus side, now, if he died, the corporation would go looking for his killer. It would be a matter of pride after paying so much to get him on the payroll.

The actor told Aden of his good fortune. The pony celebrated and thanked BioCorp by giving Kyle several large samples for them to utilize. Despite draining the pony of every drop of his excitement, the actor couldn't fall asleep that night. He lay awake, wondering about what might happen when he returned home. He considered asking to stay, but he knew he would only be putting off the inevitable, and then, when it finally happened, they would make him suffer more for trying to escape it. Or worse, Dempsy might make good on his threat against Anna. There were no other options; he had to go home and face the music.

So when the afternoon rolled around, he hugged Aden goodbye tightly and tried to pretend that everything was okay. The autocar journey seemed to both last forever and be over too soon. Walking through the crowds put him on edge, the smell and the press of people around him. He jumped at every touch as someone brushed past him, expecting any moment to be dragged into a dark corner. He kept to the middle of the concourses, thinking it would be harder to get him there, surrounded by thousands of potential assailants, heroes, and witnesses.

However, nothing happened to him on his journey home. His gun was safely in his hand before the door to his flat closed. His hand was shaking as he quickly checked the bathroom and under the sofa, the only places a person could hide in his flat. They were empty. He told Darwin not to come visit. This time, the technician did as he was asked, and Kyle was glad. He didn't need that on his conscience.

He did have a mail from Dempsy. It wasn't very long.

"Dear Kyle,

I am sorry that after so long together we must now part ways. It has been a good experience having you as an employee. I appreciate that things have not ended as I anticipated; however, I am satisfied with the generous offer BioCorp has made. I wish you every luck in your new career. "

The part about things ending differently from how he anticipated it worried him. That was far too close to suggesting that the actor had stabbed him in the back. With the note in his mind and his gun in his hand, Kyle faced a second sleepless night. He did little but water Venus, nibble on some food packages, and watch the door.

CHAPTER 15

THE SLEEPLESS NIGHT PASSED without incident. The next day, the actor went out, feeling exhausted and ill. He found himself at the bookshop once more. This time, his feet took him there on automatic. The exhausted actor was shocked to see Danny greeting him happily. He was more shocked to realize in his hands were a cold latte and a large orange. There was no memory of when he bought them. As he sat down with Danny, he let the clerk talk while he tried to stay awake.

A book was picked very early on, and then the world went black as exhaustion finally claimed its victim. It had been stalking him for two days.

"Hey, time to wake up," a voice whispered, and he opened his eyes to find Danny smiling down at him. "Welcome back to the land of the living," the clerk chuckled as Kyle sat up, a blanket falling off him. He realized Danny must have placed it over him as he slept.

"What time is it?" the actor asked, a little embarrassed to have fallen asleep somewhere so public.

"Oh, it's just past six, You've been asleep all afternoon. I thought it best to leave you be. You seemed like you really needed it. Is everything okay?" Kyle could hear more than a trace of concern in the young man's voice.

"Fine, I just had a couple of late nights in a row, bad stomach keeping me awake." The lie just rolled off his tongue on automatic. He barely had to think about those sorts of lies anymore. "I had better get home."

"Oh, I was about to lock up. I wondered if you might want to . . . grab a bite to eat and maybe a few drinks? I'll pay." Danny's voice sounded full of optimism, and Kyle felt slightly bad for letting the nice guy get his hopes up. With the offer of payment, Danny was making his intentions known. He might as well have had 'want to go on a date with me? we've spent a day together for three weeks in a row and I've given you a lot of free stuff?' tattooed across his forehead, although they would have had to use a fairly small font to fit it all in. Kyle picked up on the point, but he knew that now was not the time for a pity date.

"Sorry, I really need to get home and get some sleep, maybe another time," Kyle muttered and got to see the disappointment as he dashed Danny's hope. While at the same time feel the pangs of guilt of throwing a drowning man a lifejacket, knowing it had a leak and would do him no good. In the end, he had a five-year contract with Aden, and weirdly that was the second thought he had. The first was one that he refused to acknowledge himself. That he was with Aden.

Danny seized the lifejacket as only a man that close to drowning can grab. "Great, I will hold you to that. Now go get some sleep. You need me to walk with you to make sure you get home?"

"No, thank you. I appreciate the offer, but I'm fine. I think I have napped just enough to have the energy to get home and have a really long snooze," joked the actor. If anything, the clerk's offer had woken him up enough. The journey home was uneventful, his mind still so tired that he found himself unable to worry too much. He just collapsed onto his sofa and then felt the blackness of sleep claim him.

He awoke after a good, long eight hours of sleep. Blinking, he looked around the room, only to find he was alone and that nothing in his apartment had been touched. Kyle was surprised, though more so when he realized he had gone to sleep without setting an alarm. There was no time for a shower or for careful packing. He just stuffed as much as he could into his bag and ran out.

His mind was focused on nothing but getting to the roof on time to leave. With elbows and shoves, he forced his way onto a packed lift. The occupants squeezed in until Kyle felt like they were trying to compress together into one giant human, to wreak havoc across the city. He could feel his bag being forced into his back, the clothes giving some padding between him and the very annoyed business man behind him. The tutting and annoyed exhales were almost deafening, but unless Kyle actually kicked him, the man wasn't likely to acknowledge his existence any more.

Of course, Kyle couldn't help himself turning around as he was finally able to get off the lift to give the tutting man a wink and a blown kiss. While he was laughing about that, he felt someone slam into his chest, and he stumbled backwards towards the barrier at the edge of the roof. The actor stumbled and panicked, raising his arms up to protect his face and dropping his bag. Only the find a young guy at his feet, barely in his late teens.

"Darren! I told you not to run about on the rooftop!" an outraged-middle-aged woman yelled as her son scrambled back to his feet. "Now say you are sorry to the man you nearly knocked over. Sorry, sir, he rarely gets to travel this far." The woman talked over her son's mumbled apology. Kyle could see the young man practically glowing red as hundreds of onlookers stared at the three of them.

He snatched up his bag and mumbled an acceptance of the apology. His heart was still racing as he signaled for his car. Just for a moment, he thought that Dempsy had arranged for an unpleasant "accident". Trembling a little from the adrenaline surge, he climbed into the autocar and heaved a sigh of relief as it took him away from the city once more.

It had just taken a few weeks for this job to turn his life upside down. He watched Chicago shrinking away and felt almost nothing but relief; he was heading home, to Aden. Most importantly, he was safe, and it looked like Dempsy was going to leave him be. Maybe he had better things to do than waste time punishing just one wayward former client. Whatever the reason, Kyle was glad. He could relax once more.

The journey was as quiet and uneventful as it could be. With the adrenaline surge worn off, Kyle found himself drifting off for a few extra hours sleep before the car alerted him to arriving at his destination. Yawning and stretching, he forced his limbs back to life, promising that, if they obeyed him for a little while longer, he would make it worth their while. This, of course, was a blasted lie, but it didn't matter anyway because, the second he hit the decon, every cell in his body was blasted back to full alertness.

The actor was surprised to find Becky on the other side of the decon, smirking at him in a particularly Becky way. The dumpy woman refused to take a peek at his goodies, but only because she was far too busy ogling everything as brazenly as any client he had ever had. He was a piece of meat, and she was a ravenous predator just sizing up if he could satisfy her. "Welcome back to the Ritz-Hilton. Please remember to tuck that todger away when in the public areas. You may find it distracts the other employees. How are you doing, K-man?"

Kyle winced at Becky's use of her nickname for him. It wasn't surprising; she nicknamed everyone, and he was no exception. Not liking it was just a pure guarantee that she would use it, relentlessly. "Thank you, Becky." He waited for the woman to ask him the standard list of questions for his return. She seemed to be far more interested in his chest and stomach, checking out his tattoos, or he really hoped so anyway. "Is that it, are you not going to go through a bunch of questions?"

"Oh, sure, can you make those bad boys dance? Do you have any tassels you could wear? Are you a shower and a grower, or just a shower?" The woman laughed as he pulled on his shirt as fast as he could. "Spoilsport. I assume you kept that cannon fully locked away while you were away?"

"Yes, I didn't have sex." This time, he was telling the truth, but it was statistically going to happen eventually and should not be held against him.

"Great, Aden has been missing you," the tech observed as she waved at the door. "Oh, you didn't hear it from me, but you know they say Dr. Salter is on leave. It's a lie. I heard he had a stroke or something. The higher ups are keeping it all hush hush until they know the damage. He might be back in a few months, or maybe even never."

Kyle was dumbstruck; the man he had met certainly had not seemed ill. He barely knew him, though, and he struggled to feel more than mildly unhappy to hear the news. "Oh, that's terrible, I suppose."

"Well, for him, sure. Dr. Ramon thinks it's good. I think, since he is his temporary replacement, that he will be the natural choice to replace him." The technician leaned closer and whispered, "He probably doesn't have a prayer, really. That would mean promoting him, and his only big connection is currently in a hospital bed with the IQ of a turnip. I'd bet the farm on some outsider. Course, it might just be a storm in a teacup. Dr. Salter might be fine and back in weeks."

"I . . . suppose we won't know until we find out," Kyle observed, having nothing to say about the issue, but to state the obvious and hoped it passed mustered for good conversation.

"And that will take a while. Replacing someone of his stature is not a quick thing, especially for a science-based position," Becky added, clearly not quite done sharing the facility gossip. "Hey, I heard you got onto the corporate payroll formally. Did it hurt when they pulled out your soul? I though it felt more like a sneeze."

The actor shrugged. "Five years, and I am a free man. I can walk the corporate line for that long."

Becky gave a snorted laugh, "How many times I have heard that. Everyone starts for 'just for experience'. Ten years later, they are still in the corporation. That steady paycheck, it is fucking addictive."

"Well, I must admit, I do like being able to buy things like food and shelter," Kyle joked with another shrug.

"Yeah, plus pension, medical, and dental. Addictive as fucking crack, something I assume a former actor knows all about." The woman paused for a moment and then added, "Fucking crack, that is. I was not implying you take drugs. I have seen your blood test results, and, for a ho you, are fucking dull. I mean, not even weed?"

"I like to keep a clear head. As a ho, it helps me satisfy customers. Now I better get moving, Aden will be expecting me." It was the best way he could think to end the conversation.

"Another customer to satisfy?" Becky asked, and then stopped her laughing as she looked at the expression on Kyle's face. "Oh . . . sorry . . . I was just joking. I mean, he isn't just a . . . I have to go file your blood sample." Kyle watched in pure awe as the woman who called her boss a perverted cunt actually ran from him. His fists unclenched as his muscles relaxed. He didn't even remember clenching up. Shaking his head free from the conversation, he walked off towards Dr. Ramon's office for his usual start of the week briefing.

Aden was happy to see him when he finally emerged. Kyle couldn't help but smile as the equine slipped his arms around him. He closed his eyes and returned the hug tightly, welcoming the return of that safe feeling of being held in the arms of someone who cared so much for him. The two lay together for hours saying little just resting together, their fingers slowly exploring the fine detail of each other.

Kyle couldn't remember a time like it before, no pressure and no worries. The sex felt natural, and the man in his ear was silent. Day after day passed with little happening, and yet each one somehow felt significant. Time ceased to have meaning, days and weeks flying past and, in all of it, there was one constant. One ultimate rock for him to cling to: Aden. Summer began to fade, leaves on the trees tumbling as their days slipped by.

It was a time unlike anything Kyle had ever experienced. In his heart, he knew that this was no job, it was a dream. If they asked him, he would have given up his salary, abandoned his apartment, and never looked back. Of course, change is the one true constant of life, and there was a dark cloud on the horizon. To Kyle, it looked like a little rainstorm. He was no weatherman, or maybe he would have seen the hurricane coming.

The news broke one morning. It was Becky who broke it, while Kyle handed over a sample. Dr. Salter had died. It seemed so strange at first, it was hard to understand. The man had been so distant, Kyle had only ever spoken to him a few times, yet, in a way, he knew that the scientist had changed his life. Without him, he would still be in Chicago, working towards nothing in a life that seemed like nothing more than the shadow of a nightmare, the wisps of a partial memory, a life half lived.

Aden took it harder, the equine crying over the loss of the man who created him. A distant father figure but an ever present, constant pillar of his existence had been removed. He felt the void in his heart somewhere. Kyle tried to be there for him, holding him while the tears fell. The equines were not able to attend the funeral, but Dr. Ramon arranged a small memorial at the facility. The man actually shed a few tears as he talked of the loss of a friend and mentor.

Life went on, because it knows no better and cares little for your thoughts or feelings. The work continued, and Kyle took comfort in the resumption of their daily routine. Until he returned from his day off the following week to find Becky waiting with some surprising news.

"Kazzy is gone!" The dumpy lady exclaimed. "She didn't even say goodbye, just never came back from her day off. Bruno is going fucking mental. She lasted longer than any of his previous companions."

The news wasn't half as shocking to Kyle as the sudden sense of loss he felt. A twinge or more of sadness, he had grown used to seeing her. Every day, the four of them would play cards or games. Even though things had always felt professional between the two, he had grown to respect her.

"I should go check on Aden." The actor pulled his clothes on as quickly as possible. Bruno 'going fucking mental' conjured up unpleasant images. The black stallion was far stronger than his blonde brother. Cassandra had been good at keeping his more aggressive emotions in check. Kyle's mind filled up with unpleasant images of Bruno attacking everyone, the staff, his brother, and possibly even hurting himself.

Kyle's heart began to race as he broke into a trot, passing by Dr. Ramon's office, his usual first port of call. His mind was fixed on one thought: he must get to Aden. What he found was far from a scene of bloody retribution or retaliation. No escape attempts or violence. Instead, he found Aden sitting by his brother's bed as Bruno tried to turn himself into a tiny black ball of fluff. The huge beast curled up in his bed, Aden's blonde hand standing out against his black fur as he gently patted his brother.

The actor stopped in his tracks as he looked at the world's biggest child, whimpering with his paws clutched around a pillow, his muzzle buried inside it, eyes closed. There was no need for security from Bruno, only security for Bruno in the form of hugs. "Hey, I heard about Cassandra . . ." A loud whimper emanated from inside the black ball, and Kyle found himself stepping forward. He sat down beside Aden and reached out a hand to the black form. Bruno was trembling, and all thoughts of worry were banished from Kyle's mind. "I'm sorry." It was all he could think to say; the words were filed with pure sincerity.

His response was another whimper and an eye opening to look at him. The look cut deeply, not with hate but with pure sorrow. He found himself looking into those eyes, so familiar. That look, the look of one who has little and has lost it. Of helplessness, lack of control, a child lost and alone in the dark and cruel world. He knew that look from both sides, and he knew there were no words that could heal this wound. Even time would only cause the pain to fade a little. There would be a scar in the stallion's heart forever.

Faced with such a sight, Kyle could feel tears building up, and he knew he couldn't fight them. Words meant nothing, and he knew it, so he reached out with his body and heart, lying over the huge black mess, hugging tightly as his own tears dripped. The ball moved, and, from its depths, a limb emerged, clasping around Kyle desperately tight, almost like he feared this comfort would, too, be torn from him. Deep, wheezy breaths grew louder and from the depths of the pillow came two rumbled words, "She's gone."

"I know . . ." He remembered that voice, that pain. It brought back memories so strong, and he looked into Bruno's eye and whispered, "We're here." Aden gave Bruno's mane a light ruffle to confirm his agreement.

"What's wrong with me?" A question with no right answer, because the truth was it was the world that was wrong. Matters of the heart do not care about reality, and logic means little.

"Nothing, it's not your fault," Kyle whispered softly, reaching out a hand to stroke the black, tear-soaked cheeks. "There is nothing wrong with you."

"Then why did she leave?" Another question with no answer. In fact, usually it was an easy question to answer, 'you slept with loads of other people, you got boring, your new beard itches, I can't stand your mother . . .' The list goes on. However, Kyle had never gotten a sense from Cassandra that she was anything but happy with her job. Bruno was an easy client to handle. She was determined to save up enough to buy out her contract. Hell, with the money she was earning, she could have saved up a lot more.

"I don't know," the actor whispered softly and then added, "I will find out."

A black head rose from the pillow, like a soggy black phoenix from white cotton flames. "You will?"

"Yes, I will. Next time I go home, I will find Cassandra and find out why she left," the actor replied earnestly, relieved to see the look of hope on Bruno's face.

Bruno opened his mouth to respond when the door opened and a female technician entered. She was carrying one of the devices they had previously tried to use to take samples from Aden. A basic tube with some soft, rubberish fabric. A masturbatory sleeve with a cup, though Kyle bet the scientists had some technical name to try and make it sound classy. "Bruno, it's time for your . . ."

"Seriously?!" Kyle exclaimed, rising to his feet. "Right now?!"

The woman paused. Emma, Kyle remembered being briefly introduced to her early on. She was one of dozens of scientists who seemed to fuss around all the time. She shrugged. "I know it's not ideal, but life and science goes on, just because his . . . friend has . . ."

What Emma thought Bruno's 'friend' had done, they never found out. Red mist descended and the actor covered the distance to the door in a heartbeat. He snatched the device from her hand and smashed it as hard as he could against the doorframe, shattering the plastic. "FUCK OFF!" he yelled, thrusting the shattered remains of her equipment back into her trembling hands. He triggered the door to shut, not caring if it hit the woman in the face.

Kyle said nothing more. He returned to the stunned equine and pulled his unresisting body into a hug. "You don't have to do that, not today," he whispered, and he felt a paw on his shoulder. Looking up, he saw Aden, tears on his muzzle but a proud, loving smile on his lips. Neither of them said anything. Kyle knew there would be a price to pay for his rebellion. Well, they could add it to the fucking list of paybacks he would have to make.

No more attempts to take a sample were made. With the distraction behind them, Bruno returned to weeping, holding onto them both desperately tightly. The two sat with him until he passed out from sheer emotional exhaustion. They snuck out of the room, and Kyle sighed, looking up at Aden. "I had better go speak to Dr. Ramon about what I did."

"I hope . . . I don't want to lose you, not today . . . not ever," Aden whispered, his body seeking out the comfort of Kyle's pressing together naturally.

With a gentle stroke of Aden's cheek, Kyle smiled. "Never, but I probably could have handled things better . . ."

"No! You did what I wanted to do. Thank you," Aden whispered, softly nuzzling into Kyle's neck. His hands clung on even as Kyle pulled away. He didn't want to let his human go, just in case he never came back.

"Go watch over Bruno. I'll be back soon," Kyle said, flashing his most confident smile. He suspected that Aden saw through it, but there was nothing either of them could do. In his stomach, a sinking feeling set home and sank deeper with each step. He knew he owed this place a lot; it had more than freed him. This job had changed his life forever, and he didn't want it to end. He doubted it would, but he knew it might. He had gotten violent with another member of staff, they were hardly likely to ignore that.

The door to Dr. Ramon's office was open waiting for him, like the wide-open gates of Hell inviting him in to bandy words with the devil himself. He knocked on the wall, and a stern voice said, "Come in and sit down." No please, Kyle noted immediately but with little surprise. The scientist was clearly angry.

The actor did as he was instructed. The expression on the doctor's face was angry, yet controlled. "I guess I owe Emma an apology."

"Is that all?" snapped the scientist.

"I guess you can take the cost of a replacement . . . thing out of my pay," the actor conceded quickly. If that was all it cost him, he would have gotten off cheap.

"It's not about the money!" barked Dr Ramon, getting to his feet. "You know what we are doing, how important our work is. We cannot let Aden and Bruno think that they can openly defy instructions like that."

"Why not?!" Kyle cursed himself for that comment. His rebellious side had gotten hold of his tongue for a heartbeat, and that was all it took to dig his hole a little deeper.

"Because they are too important to our work. You know what we are trying to do. We need them happy and productive . . ."

"And taking away their companions, then demanding they jerk off into a cup while they are crying, is the best way to do that?" Once more, Kyle couldn't stop himself. He just couldn't understand how they could not have just given Bruno a day or two. The equine had never stopped producing, but he was hurting, and he needed time.

"Cassandra leaving was . . . unfortunate. I also regret Emma going in. That was my mistake, I didn't give clear instructions. I said we would need to restart manual sample extraction." Dr. Ramon kept his tone firm, but he was at least willing to admit his mistakes. That helped calm down the raging volcano inside Kyle.

The scientist sighed, "Can I show you something?"

Kyle gave a nod of agreement, and the scientist reached into his desk and pulled out a framed picture. It took Kyle a second or two to recognize the person in the picture. It was a very young Dr. Ramon; his face didn't have the worry lines he had now. His eyes didn't look so tired or heavy. He was standing upright with what looked like a baby in his arms. A closer look showed it was no ordinary child. A black muzzle was protruding out of the swaddling cloth. "Bruno?"

"Yes, I have pictures of all three. I was there the day each of them was born. I watched them grow." The scientist took the photo from the actor and gazed at it. "I spent my entire career with them. Bruno's first word was 'Dada', and he said it to me. I was there when they took their first steps. They grew up before my eyes. You think Bruno is a handful now, you should have been there when he hit puberty."

The scientist laughed with happy nostalgia. "I know I do not spend much time with them now. It is not by choice. This project is not cheap. We have to compete with hundreds of other projects each year to justify our spending. The first second generation of the hybrids was a huge win, proving that we could breed them true. Getting the offspring up to Mars, it allowed the project to go forward. Though I had to admit I felt some sadness to see him go. I would have loved some more foals around the place."

Dr. Ramon put the picture away. "What I am trying to say is, don't think that I don't care for them. My whole life is built around Aden and Bruno. However, the best thing I and you can do for them is ensure this facility continues to be productive. Now, please, when you return to them, pass my apologies along to Bruno. Let him know we will find him a new companion as soon as we can."

"Why did Cassandra leave?" Kyle asked as he got to his feet to leave.

"I can't discuss the private details of another contract. However, it was her choice. I am sorry it hurts Bruno so much. Please be assured no one will try to take any samples from him this week. Though we do need Aden to keep producing," Kyle nodded at the last part. It was a very clear message, 'if you want time for Bruno, don't forget your real job.' Whatever moment of humanity had held Dr. Ramon had past; now he was back to being Kyle's boss. The guy who quite literally ran the place. "Oh, and I will dock your pay for the damage you caused."

One last parting shot. Kyle felt better for it, though. He liked to pay the price upfront; he didn't like being in any form of debt.

CHAPTER 16

THE DOCTOR KEPT HIS PROMISE, and nobody tried to take anything from Bruno. A few days later, Emma actually apologized to the recovering equine. Kyle's apology to her had been public; the actor had found her in the mess hall. Becky had sworn at him a lot, carpet bombing the room with c- and f- bombs. The actor had absorbed it all quietly, given Emma a heartfelt apology, reiterating it three different ways. None of which was truly accepted; there was a distinctly defensive 'she was just doing her job' air about the staff at the facility.

Kyle couldn't help but feel they protested a little too much, like a thief protesting that it was his victim's fault they had made it too easy so he hadn't been able to stop himself. A drunken man's excuse that held no real water, it just made him feel better. It was a bitter pill to swallow, but Kyle knew how to do that better than any. Pride was edible; it could be swallowed at need, and he needed to get his apology out so that things could move on.

In the end, he retreated, having said all he could. For a few day,s the staff barely acknowledged his existence. He noted the lack of any food but food packets in the meals they brought him. Kyle never said a word about it. Although he was moved when, halfway through their evening mea,l a black hand reached out and placed an apple on his plate. Bruno never said a word, but Aden gave a knowing smile as the actor picked up the fruit.

When his day off rolled around, Kyle kept his word, searching for Cassandra. It wasn't too hard to track down her contact details. He knew her name and employer; however, his calls went unanswered, as did his texts. As evening started to draw close, the actor decided to try a different approach.

Calling Cassandra's agent instead, the call was picked up almost instantly. "Estelle and company escorts, how can I help you?" asked a female and far too friendly sounding voice.

"Hi, erm, I was wondering if . . . I could book Cassandra," Kyle asked, slightly nervously. He wondered if his customer felt so strange when they called up looking for his services. What did you say to the receptionist, 'I'm horny send me a hot person to bang?'

"Okay, sir, can I take your details? I am sure we can find an appropriate companion. This is your first time with our agency, I take it? Have you hired an escort before?" the female replied, glossing quickly over his request.

With a few gestures, Kyle sent his profile to the agency. Thankfully, with the money he had earned recently, he looked like a semi-reasonable client, or he hoped so. "Yes, first time hiring. Is Cassandra available?"

"Well, please, wait a moment. I am just checking your credit and criminal records. Standard procedure I'm afraid," the female replied calmly. Kyle held his breath, waiting for the response. He'd not had any convictions; however, if the credit check looked back further than a month or two, his balance would seem distinctly thin. "Okay, that's cleared. Now I can send you over a selection of . . ."

"No, I know which I want. A friend introduced me to Cassandra and, well, I know she just ended a long contract. I've been waiting months." A lie mixed with enough truth that he hoped it would taste like the truth.

"Sorry, Cassandra isn't available. However I have . . ."

"When will she be available? I can wait," insisted the actor quickly. The last thing he wanted to see was a list of escorts. All he could imagine was the number of people browsing through a catalogue from Dempsy, pointing at his picture and saying he would match the new sofa for the evening.

"She . . . no longer works for this company; however, I can assure you . . ." The woman was clearly trying to remain calm and push for a sale, just like a good sales clerk. Of course, Kyle wasn't really looking to rent or buy, so even the best salesperson in the world would have failed.

"Where does she work now?" he demanded a little too loudly.

"I do not have that information, and even if I did I could not pass it on to a random person. Now, can I help you find an al . . ." Kyle didn't let her finish. He cut the call off and sat back on his sofa. Well, Cassandra had been looking to buy out her contract. She might have just up and left. However, no matter how he rolled the idea around, it didn't sit right with the image of Cassandra.

She was cool, confident, and professional. Cutting and running without saying anything to anybody just didn't feel right. The way she had acted with Bruno, alright, she was paid to be his companion. However. he had been in the business for eight years. He could spot even the best phony affection. That wasn't what he saw when he thought of the way she acted with Bruno. There had been genuine like there, maybe not love or anything deeper. However, she would have said goodbye.

Hell, for that matter, the confident woman he had met wouldn't have dodged his calls. She would have answered and spoken to him, even if it was to tell him not to bother her. No, there was something wrong. He could feel the hairs at the back of his neck sticking up. He wasn't sure what was going on, but this was not just as simple as she quit. However, he had no idea of how to find out. Everyone involved who might know would almost certainly not want to share that information to him just because he asked.

When he returned to the facility, it was as a failure, or he certainly felt that way. The look on Bruno's face when he told him that he hadn't been able to contact Cassandra was enough to reinforce just how much of a failure he was. Although Bruno did thank him for trying, he seemed a little stronger than before. There were no tears, and he even consented to give a sample when one of the female technicians came to extract one.

Dr. Ramon promised that they would find him a suitable replacement companion soon. Although, at Kyle's insistence, he agreed to wait a few weeks more to give Bruno time to heal and get over the loss. The scientist said that was probably for the best. Their budget review was coming up, and, with no expensive companions on the payroll, things looked a lot better.

"How is it looking?" Kyle asked conversationally and wishing instantly he hadn't. Just the mention of it had made the scientist cringe, and he could see a drop of sweat forming on the man's forehead.

"Honestly? I think we could be in better shape. The board hasn't assigned a replacement for Dr. Salter, that . . . well, I'm sure it's going to be fine. We might get hit with a few cuts, but this program has been running for over twenty years . . ." The actor recognized the voice of someone trying to convince themselves that red was in fact black. "We'll find out in a few days, and then I will be able to get some sleep. I am a scientist, I never really liked board meetings."

That little exchange stuck in Kyle's mind, Dr. Ramon's expression as he tried to lie to himself. Kyle could taste it; there was something in the air. The company guys scuttled around heads down, getting their jobs done. Business as usual and yet not so. Every interaction seemed slightly off. He had a whole conversation with Becky where she didn't swear or insinuate something sexual.

It felt like everyone was poised ready for attack, scientists squatting in foxholes ready to defend their work against the evil accounting department. Would they come today? How many? Who would still be sitting at a lab bench at the end of it, and who would not? Dr. Ramon seemed to be everywhere, Davy Crockett trying to rally the troops. One more defense of their projects, that was all he asked. Keep calm, remember your thesis, and you will survive! No research project would be left behind, damn it!

Aden and Bruno seemed to sense it, too; they were quieter than normal. Routine suddenly seemed all important, one day echoing the last exactly. Kyle knew it would not last forever, but he wondered if this was normal. Was this what being a company man was like? Were all those little perks to pay for the drama of the budget review? Every year, you lived happily save for the week or two before budget approval . . . or denial.

The board met on Friday and on Saturday. Kyle was instructed there would be a meeting in the mess hall for all staff. He guessed that included him. He certainly had no intention of missing it. One week of this pressure had been far too much. He needed resolution much like everyone around him. So, he kissed Aden goodbye and joined the throng of staff in the mess hall.

It was strange to see them all together; security, catering, scientists, technicians and even a couple of custodians of the porcelain bowl. All gathered, a soft murmur of a hundred whispered voices, nobody talking aloud. Kyle remembered a client taking him to church once. It had the same feeling: nobody wanting to raise their voice too loud for fear the gods might hear and smite them down.

Eventually, Dr. Ramon arrived, the high priest ready to bless or curse. Kyle felt his guts tighten as he looked at the man's face. He looked pale, almost green. His eyes seemed slightly too red. Was it just late nights or had the man been crying? Kyle couldn't be sure which. However, he was sure this was not the face of a man bearing good news. Around the actor, others seem to be noticing the same. The whispering intensified for a moment or two and then stopped.

Dead silence deafened them all as the scientist tried to compose himself. Then he stepped up onto a chair, hundreds of eyes boring into him intently. "Hello everyone," he announced, his voice starting off far too quiet and then slowly raising. "I am not going to draw this out any more than I have to, so I'll start with the good news. Nobody is being let go . . ." A collective sigh of relief rushed around the room. Kyle swore he could feel a breeze in his hair. "However, there will be some changes."

The actor felt his stomach tighten again. He could see the man struggling. Whatever he had to announce, Dr Ramon knew it was a bitter pill, and he didn't want to swallow it. "Several projects are going to be shelved, the staff within it reassigned . . . The most notable one being the breeding program has been terminated . . ." The whispers of before returned, almost deafening Kyle as every single person seemed to be expressing their disbelief to their neighbors. While Kyle felt a chill down his spine, he was only there because of the breeding program. He noticed the doctor was looking right at him. There seemed to be a tear in his eye. There was definitely something more going on, he was certain. Even if he was to be fired, he couldn't imagine Dr. Ramon crying over it.

"What about Aden and Bruno?" Kyle called out as he felt himself beginning to sweat.

"They . . . their . . . contributions are no longer required. The board feels that, with one-hundred and thirty-two viable offspring already relocated to Mars, the sensible thing to do is wait until they are old enough to start the next phase, to assess if they are viable on the surface . . ."

"But what about Aden and Bruno?!" the actor barked the question a little more urgently. He disliked when people didn't answer questions. It usually meant they knew you would really hate the answers.

"Well . . . given the cost of keeping them here . . . financially, it was decided that, given they are no longer needed . . ." Kyle felt as pale as the scientist looked. A bead of cold sweat dripped down his neck; he felt like every drop of his blood had drained from his body. While Dr. Ramon continued, "They will . . . be retired. Right, please, any more questions, you can ask your supervisors. More details will be sent directly, including specific reassignments for those who have been reassigned."

Moving with surprising speed, Dr. Ramon jumped down off the chair and pushed his way out of the room. The whispering from before erupted into full blown voices. Everyone had an opinion and was voicing it fully. Except for Kyle. He was pondering the word "retired", and, less than a minute later, he pushed his way out. He went directly to the doctor's office. The idea of knocking didn't even begin to form in his mind. He opened the door and entered to find a nervous scientist behind his desk.

"Don't worry, your contract is still valid. I got you a spot on . . ."

Kyle hadn't given a second thought to his own position; there were far more pressing questions on his mind. "What do you mean, retired?!" he demanded, placing his hands on Dr. Ramon's desk and leaning over it, holding the scientist's eye with his gaze, daring him to try and avoid answering.

"Well . . . you see, they . . . I . . . Fuck." The swear word surprised the actor a little. The man slumped back, his shoulders drooping in submission. "Legally, these creatures we created are not people. The only reason we cannot euthanize one is if there is value they can contribute to our research."

A million responses erupted in Kyle's mind, many of them single words; murder, evil, and heartless were some of the softest ones. He couldn't manage to make his mouth work. His fists clenched, and his entire body began to tremble. "That was my argument ten years ago, when Isabel was ill . . . She was first, you see. We got it slightly wrong. She was never going to make it to ten years old. Tumors, benign on their own, but they kept growing. We tried everything. She was in so much pain. We kept her apart from Aden and Bruno for a year."

Tears shone in the electric light on the scientist's cheeks. His voice was breaking and yet high pitched. Yet he continued, as if a dam was breaking inside him, and everything he had held back was flooding forth. "I couldn't take it . . . They told me I couldn't end it, and I told them she was just a research animal . . . I could end it, and there was no value left. I . . . I just wanted to take the pain away, you have to understand. Every breath was agony, she couldn't . . . We had her on so many drugs, and it was never going to get better . . . I never thought they would use it like this. My own arguments, my own words . . . The precedent I set, the legal advice I got that confirmed it would not count as murder, or manslaughter. Fuck, it's not even animal cruelty!"

Kyle felt like the words were coming from a distant room; he could hear them and understand, and yet, for some reason, he couldn't react. His body just stayed put, staring at the weeping man, unable to respond in any way.

"I am fighting this every way I can think of. I'm not ready to give up just yet. However . . ." Dr Ramon's voice trailed off as he couldn't bring himself to say it. "It would probably be best if Aden and Bruno were not told of what . . ."

"That you are planning to put them down?" Kyle spat, suddenly able to move, as if freed from quicksand. "That they are just lab rats and you have finished running them through mazes? That their lives have a monetary value and it is no longer the same as their upkeep?" The actor could feel every muscle in his body trembling.

"I never . . ."

"Bullshit, you have kept them as research their entire lives. Given them food, enough exercise to keep them fit, and just enough entertainment to stop them from trying to escape. Now they are no longer needed, you are putting them down. Look me in the eye and tell me this is right? That they are just animals." He grabbed the doctor's lab coat. "Look in my eyes, you bastard, and tell me it's okay to just kill them because of a legal technicality."

"It wasn't like they gave me a choice. I begged, I fucking pleaded with them. All I got was the board's decision is final. This is the best financial decision and will save a few hundred jobs. For the greater good, we have been told to terminate the project," the doctor spat the words out with more bile than Kyle expected from the defeated, weeping man. "They said if I didn't do it, they would force the issue. They could, too; fire anyone who gets in their way and have them escorted off site. I thought . . . it would be better this way, with people who care about them."

"I . . . I can't go in there and lie to them. I can't just stand by and let this happen. I won't let you do this!" The actor bellowed his final sentiment and then let go of the doctor.

"I'm willing to listen to any ideas," Dr Ramon replied. "If we refuse, they will simply replace us with people who will see Aden and Bruno as nothing but unwanted lab animals. They won't introduce themselves; they will terminate them without a second thought."

"Then we don't refuse. We break them out. If we can't work within their system, we ignore it," Kyle replied, and, for a moment, he wondered if it had been a mistake. The scientist could have him escorted off site easily. Maybe he could fight his way to Aden and Bruno, warn them. That would do no good; security would be there. Even if by some miracle he got them outside, they couldn't get far before they were run down.

"They will hunt them down. It's not like they can just cut their mane or grow a beard and hope to blend in," the doctor replied, shaking his head. Kyle realized the scientist had already put a little thought into that. He might be able to talk him around if he could come up with a plan.

"Maybe not, but there is a lot of empty countryside out there. Places they could hide . . . I dunno what, but it has to be better than the alternative." The actor knew his argument ended weakly, but he could see in Dr Ramon's face that he wanted to agree. "Just give me some time. We can figure something out."

The doctor pulled open his desk draw and took out two pictures, the one of him and Bruno and another of him sitting with what could only be a tiny Aden bouncing on his lap. "Okay, if we can figure out something, someway. You know . . . That'll be it for you and me, too, right? If we do this and get caught, the company will wipe us out financially. We will almost certainly end up in prison."

"If we don't do this . . . I can't live with knowing I did nothing. I'd take a handful of pills or a dive off an upper tier concourse." Kyle shuddered, and he meant every word. By most people's standards, his morals were extremely pliant. However, to just let two innocent beings die . . . No, he was better than that.

"Ok, I just wanted to know you were sure. We . . . shouldn't tell anyone. Not even Aden or Bruno. If someone reports us, well, that's it for both of us and them," Dr. Ramon replied, accepting the consequences of his decisions without further thought. "They want them to be terminated by the end of next week. I will continue to push the board to see if I can change their mind."

"I am going back home," the actor replied a little hesitantly as he tried to figure things out in his mind. "I have a friend or two who might be able to help. I need to figure out a place to hide them, and I can't do that here. It's probably best if I just go. If I see Aden right now . . . I don't think I can hide anything from him."

"Good luck. I will have someone explain to them that you had to leave to attend to something unexpected but you will be back soon." The doctor took a few deep breaths, composing himself as the actor left.

Kyle felt strange leaving without saying goodbye to Aden. He knew it was the right choice. If he let them know what was happening, they might panic. He certainly would in their place; he'd make a break for it without a plan or a chance. That was what he'd always done, taken the first option out his entire life. Figure out the buttons of his foster parents and push them until they couldn't take it, sign up with Dempsy, sign up with BioCorp . . . Now he was going to take his first exit out of the corporation. At least, this was for the right reason. It was the harder choice as well. He could have stayed a company man, let the horses die, and continued on in whatever role the doctor had secured for him.

As he watched the facility shrink away behind the autocar, he knew he had made the right choice this time. Aden was worth it, they deserved a chance. Any life he could find for them on the run would be better than sitting in their cage until they died. If he got to be with them, well, that would be a worthwhile life. Whatever happened, he knew he would not regret this choice.

His apartment was just the same as when he left it. For the first time in weeks, he felt relieved as he entered. He had lived there for years. It had been his tiny castle, a defense against the world outside. Venus was sitting on the window, and it appeared she had caught another fly in his absence. Before he did anything else, he topped up her water. Looking over her carefully, he found that she had a few new buds coming through.

Picking her up, he walked out and across the hall, knocking on one of the doors. It opened to reveal Claire. She gave him a surprised smile, which was not entirely unexpected; in the four years she had lived opposite, he had never knocked on her door. "Heya, Kyle, it's been awhile since I saw you. How is that job going?"

"It's . . . coming to an end, I suppose. However, they want me to be on site for the next few weeks straight. I was wondering if you could look after my plant while I am away?" he replied, putting on his most earnest smile, holding out the plant like he was offering her a baby.

"S . . . Sure, I can look after it . . ."

"Her!" Kyle insisted a little bit too loudly and quickly for his own liking. "Sorry. It's silly, I know, but I talk to her . . . practice my lines."

"Oh, of course. I do that, too," Claire replied with a broad smile, taking the plant from his hands. Just for a moment, he held on, and she had to tug slightly to pull it free. "I generally use the mirror, though, so I can check my expressions, too."

"Well . . . she's a good listener, too, easy to care for. Just leave the window open a crack and keep the soil damp but not waterlogged." It felt strange, it was just a plant. However, Venus was his. She had been his only real responsibility for years, and he found it strangely difficult to let her go.

"Great! Well, I have been accused of having a black thumb, but I am sure I can keep her alive for a couple of weeks," the actress replied with a good-natured chuckle. "Would you like to come in for a drink or something?"

Kyle felt his fake smile fading, and he shook his head. "I'd love to, but I have a really busy day tomorrow and for the next few weeks. Maybe after I get back?" No harm in throwing out the invite; he knew he was not going to be back, and this was a nicer way to say no.

"Sure, I will hold you to that, neighbor," she replied with a chuckle as she swallowed the sweet lie whole.

"I am sure you will, but it won't be hard," he replied, turning on the charm a little more and winking. Her skin flushing as she blushed and giggled, brushing her hair behind her ear. "Well, I had better go . . . Thank you again, I owe you one for this."

The apartment felt empty without Venus. She had been such a permanent fixture for so long. The room smelt wrong without her, but it was too late to do much that night. He sent Darwin a message, asking if he could speak to him sometime tomorrow. He had no idea exactly what he was going to say to his friend. Maybe he could just ask to trade some services. Something told him that Darwin would want details. Before that, he wanted to speak to Danny. The guy had family high up in a company. If anyone might know how to change a board decision, they would. It was a long shot, but he would take every shot he possibly could and hope that some deity up there or down below would guide his aim to the right target.

Laying himself down on his bed, he found it hard to fall asleep. His mind filled up with thoughts of Aden. He wondered if the pony was thinking of him. He was sure he would be worried about his human. A strange thought, but he knew it now; he was Aden's human. That had become clear the second he had heard what the company had planned for him. Now he just had to wonder if Aden felt the same in return, or if he was simply the only option.

Eventually, his eyes began to droop, and he fell into an uneasy nightmare-filled dream. He awoke in the middle of the night, the lights from the city outside casting shadows around his room, many familiar and several very unfamiliar. His heart froze as he heard a deep voice rumble out, "Mr. Dempsy is very upset."

Chapter 17

Dempsey only hired professionals; they took little pleasure in their actions, it was a job. One they fulfilled with the cold and dispassionate nature of true experts. Kyle was sure they were experts because they had started with a boot to the chest, knocking the wind out of him. They kept clear of his head, not for fear of injury, but to stop from dazing him and to make sure his senses were fully awake. Dempsy clearly wanted him to feel everything he had sent his former client's way. Kyle's pathetic attempts to retaliate were shrugged off.

A boot to his leg, and he was down on his knees again. Another one to his stomach, and he could taste blood in his mouth as he curled up on the floor. Closing his eyes, there was no thought in his mind beyond that he hoped they had not come to kill him. A sharp kick to his back made him whimper. He could hear someone calling for help, a weak, straining, pathetic voice. It begged and pleaded for them to stop, pausing briefly to cry out in pain with each blow.

Then, as quickly as the assault began, it was over, the men leaving without another word. While Kyle cried and whimpered on the floor, his eyes closing as he receded gratefully into his world of nightmares. At least these ones couldn't really harm him.

The sun was quite high in the sky by the time he awoke. He whimpered deeply, regretting being stupid enough to wake up again. His body reminded him of how bad a decision that was as he tried to get to his feet. Somehow, he managed to struggle to the bathroom. His chest, sides, and back were covered in bruises. His horse tattoo seemed to have footprint over the horse's head.

His skin purple and black, swollen and tender.

Struggling to the shower, he screamed as the hot water hit his aching body. Breathing seemed difficult. Dried blood washed away quickly, and he leaned against the tiled wall, gasping for breath. He didn't attempt to dry himself when he stepped out, not caring for the water that dripped onto the floor or the wet footprints he left as he shuffled. He opened a cupboard in the kitchen and pulled out a small packet of painkillers. It wasn't much, but it was all he had. Popping a couple, he grabbed himself a glass of water and waited for them to take effect.

As he felt the sharp edge of pain dulling, he checked over his bruises with his hands. Working around each bruise, many of them felt very sore. Yet he could feel no broken bones. He would recover in a few weeks. If only he had the luxury of that time. Biting his lip, he pulled some clothes on, grabbed his pistol, and tucked it away. Walking gingerly, he emerged, limping along the halls and out into the city.

Danny's bookshop had never seemed so far away. Each person that brushed past him brought sharp lances of pain right through him. However, he pushed through both the pain and the crowds with a determination he never knew he possessed until he finally reached the bookshop and his friend.

The clerk seemed a little surprised to see him, although not unhappy. "It's been a slow day," he said as he ushered Kyle to the center of his shop. The man had one or two customers a day. Kyle couldn't help but wonder how much slower it could possibly go. Although any thoughts about that slipped from his mind as a friendly hand touched his back and he inhaled a sharp breath as pain blossomed forth. "Jesus, are you okay?"

"Yeah, I just . . . I don't want to get into it, honestly. I'm not here to buy a book. I need to ask you a few things. I need your help." The pain made thinking harder, and the truth took a lot less thought than a lie. Plus, he didn't have the time to mess about. He needed to know if there was a chance to change the board's mind. Dr. Ramon had said he wasn't ready to give up on that. Then had promptly agreed to help him break Aden and Bruno out, so Kyle figured the chance was slim. The doctor was probably just trying out all options before he flushed his life down the toilet. Kyle was going to do the same, though he knew his options amounted to little more than a desperate grasping in the dark.

"Oh, well, can I still offer you a beer?" The clerk's voice was heavy with disappointment along with a hint of worry.

Alcohol; it sounded like the best idea at that moment, especially when mixed with all the painkillers he had taken. "Fuck yes!" He sank gratefully onto the soft sofa and drained the bottle of beer in a single swallow.

His friend sat down nervously, a little nearer to him than he normally would. Danny's hand placed down on the sofa next to his leg. "So, what can I help you with?" There was so much misplaced hope in that face and voice that Kyle couldn't stop himself from smiling just a little.

"Your father and grandfather were high up in some corporation, right? You know anything about how to change a board's decision?" As the alcohol mixed rather worryingly with the cocktail of painkillers he had bought and taken on his way to the bookshop, Kyle's mind began to wander to strange places.

"You don't. I mean, I've heard most of my family bitching about some bad decision the board has made. However, it is like getting instruction from God; they speak, and you fucking follow it. There might be some wriggle room in what they have asked you, so you might look to work your way around it that way," the clerk replied, taking his hand off the sofa and sitting back, picking up on Kyle's lack of acceptance of any gentle hints.

"What if they tell you to kill someone?" Kyle blurted out directly.

"That would be murder," Danny replied bluntly, taking a swig from his bottle of beer. "They can't order that without all facing prosecution for it."

"Yes! But what if legally it wasn't?" the actor replied, looking around. "Is there a chance of another beer?"

"I think you've had enough," Danny replied, putting his own bottle down far away from Kyle's reach.

"I've only had the one," protested Kyle, pausing a little to analyze himself. His mind seemed to be tingling, as did his skin. "I think I probably should have checked my medication before drinking that."

"Kyle, what is going on?" Danny asked, leaning forward again and trying to hold the actor's wandering and dilated eyes. "You turn up one day, desperate to find a book you had never heard of, come back week after week looking for books on a very specific theme. Then a couple of weeks, you don't come back. Now you turn up, clearly beaten, and ask me how you change a board's decision to murder someone."

"I . . . Can I invite someone else? I have to explain this to a friend later, and I am just too tired to do it twice. Also, can I get some water?" Fortunately, it had been a small bottle of beer. He knew Danny was right a second bottle would be a bad idea. The first had clearly been a terrible one. Kyle hoped that it would pass through his system quickly. He needed to concentrate and hope like hell he wasn't about to make a mistake.

"Sure, I think you could probably use more than one friend right now. I'll get that water." While the clerk was away, Kyle sent a message to Darwin, asking him to come to the bookshop as soon as he was able to. By the time Danny returned, he had dozed off on the sofa.

He was awoken by a gentle shaking some time later. Danny was sitting next to him, and he could see Darwin sitting opposite. The technician had a clearly concerned look on his face. It was mirrored by Danny. Kyle guessed the clerk had caught the technician up on their earlier conversation. There was a glass of tepid water on the table in front of the sofa. He yawned and reached out for it, draining it quickly. The fuzziness from the beer and pills had worn off, the pain returning, bringing with it a welcome clarity.

It took a long time and many questions from his friends, but Kyle tried to explain everything that had happened over the last few months. He told them everything: about the facility, Aden and Bruno, Cassandra, and even Becky's foul mouth. Kyle broke every single one of his non-disclosure agreements; that gave him a surprising satisfaction. With his story finally told, he slumped back in his chair, as he could feel his chest throbbing in pain. All that talking had done nothing to help the growing ache.

Danny and Darwin sat, looking at each other a little doubtfully. It was Danny who spoke first, "So . . . you're a prostitute?"

Kyle laughed out loud and regretted it as pain shot through his body. "Everything I told you. Animal human hybrids, secret research facilities, and people killing sentient beings to save on budget, and that is the first, biggest question you have?"

"Well I . . . I just . . . You didn't seem like one," the clerk mumbled in embarrassment.

"They don't exactly wear badges lad," chuckled Darwin. He had seemed a little more at home with everything Kyle had said. He never trusted corporations, and the idea of secret research and immorality were easy ones for him to swallow. "So, they are just going to put this Aden to sleep, like a racing hound after his racing days are over? Heartless fucks!"

With his mind mulling over the question of what exactly he should look like after choosing a career as a sex worker, Kyle only half listened to Darwin. "Yes, heartless. Now I just need to figure out a way to stop them. Danny, you said that boards never change their mind?"

"Yes . . . Well, actually, there is one thing that can change their minds. Public opinion, massive public opinion. Just look at what happened when BioCorp announced their birth. The church rallied the public behind them in outcry and boom, government changed the law. Plus, BioCorp got kicked in the teeth financially from it; a lot of people switched to their competitors," Danny replied and then added, "If we could get a short clip up on the net, spread it around, and let more people know what was going on, they might back down. It'd be the best financial decision."

"Don't be daft, they'd just deny it. Kill them and say it was some elaborate hoax. They'd ask everyone who do you believe: a decent company that has stuck to the new laws ever since they were made, or a prostitute?" Darwin shook his head in disgust. "Look, you want to save them, you need to get them out. Now I might be able to help. I mean, I can cobble together some gear for you easy enough. It ain't that hard to hijack an autocar. I could have it drop you off anywhere. The only trouble would be it'd have trackers in it. They'd know where you landed, so you'd have to run for it and hope they can't track you down."

"It wouldn't be too hard to escape. Security is so focused on keeping people from getting in, I don't think they are expecting anyone to break out. All I'd need to do is find something in the lab that would cut through the wires." The idea certainly had some merit. If they were quick and quiet, they could cut through the fence skirt around the facility to the car park and steal and autocar. The big question is where to go. If they went to a city, Bruno and Aden would be spotted instantly. There really was no hiding human-equine hybrids that were well over six foot tall. Even if they could, their lives would be no better than they were in the facility, hiding in some tiny apartment the rest of their lives. Besides, if they could figure out where they went, it wouldn't take too long to track them down, city or countryside.

"If you land in the country, you could probably find some abandoned houses to hide out in, maybe even some food to forage. Old gardens and stuff, I dunno," Danny muttered, thinking out loud. Food was something Kyle hadn't even considered yet. Two hungry ponies and two humans, that was a lot of food to find while running from pursuit.

"That's if we can find an abandoned town. I'd need to know the coordinates for the autocar to . . ." Kyle paused mid-sentence, and a smile spread across his lips as an idea sprung fully formed into his mind. "I think I have a plan, a place to hide and avoid being chased. At least for a day or two."

Kyle laid out his idea, and, while it was far from perfect, it was better than the other options. If they were lucky, it might work long enough for them to get a serious head start. Darwin said he could have a slicer device ready for him by morning, and Danny wished him luck. The actor limped home, or to what passed for home. The blood stains from the previous night were still on the carpet, and the actor just couldn't sleep. Not until he took a few more powerful pain meds. They knocked him out.

Waking up was painful, but it was becoming something Kyle was used to. Pain was a part of life, or his life anyway. There was no sense in denying it, and he knew it wouldn't stop him or slow him down. In the end, Dempsy may have done him a favor. He knew he could use that pain to drive himself forward. After all, failure would only mean more pain.

He was surprised by how little he felt as he packed his bag. There was little to no chance he would ever return to his home for the last eight years. His first days there had been something fun with Esteban. As the new and youngest on the books, he had been popular. Esteban had gone with him for his first appointments, keeping things fun.

It wasn't horrible: good money (or so he thought as a stupid kid), sex, and freedom. Then later, okay money and freedom (the sex was still there, but he learned quickly his pleasure was the last thing on anyone's minds). Eventually, he had realize he had just enough money to keep him where he was, no freedom to do anything, and the sex was a job, not a perk.

There had been good times. He struggled to think of any shining examples as he looked over the wreckage of his life. Steady food at least, he'd learned quickly how to find the perks in any job. He slung his bag over his shoulder, wincing at the pain. Then he left and didn't look back. A life on the run; no security, no perks, maybe no food . . . But freedom wonderful and terrible freedom. A smile spread across his lips as he walked towards the carpark.

Darwin met him on the roof, slipping a small device into his pocket while the two discussed the weather as if they were spies trading secrets. The technician wished him luck and then was gone. Kyle took a brief moment to look out along the skyline and then called for his car. Inside his bag was a smaller satchel. It held his pistol and as many food packets as he could squeeze into it. He added the device Darwin had given him. The tech had told him it was simple plug-and-play technology; once inserted, it would fly the autocar to a small town several thousand miles away. A journey of a few hours.

He stashed the satchel in a corner of the facility car park behind some old car parts. Masking his actions by pretending to struggle with his bag. It wasn't well hidden, just obscured from view of the facility. Anyone walking into the facility from the carpark entrance might spot it. However, he had no time or opportunity to hide it better without arousing suspicion. He knew it meant that they would need to try to escape very soon. The longer they waited, the greater the risk of it being found.

Kyle was pleasantly surprised to find that the decon scrub was not needed. "New orders from on high," the security guy told him. The actor suspected Dr. Ramon had canceled them to keep up the appearance of going through with Aden and Bruno's retirement. After all, it saved time, money, and there was no need to protect assets that had been declared surplus to requirements.

His bag was subject to a quick scan, so he was glad he left the satchel behind. Some security procedures the scientist clearly couldn't justify removing. With no health survey or need to redress, Kyle was inside the building and at Dr. Ramon's office in record time. The two didn't exchange hellos. "Did you have any luck with the board?" Kyle demanded the second the door shut behind him.

"None, all I have had is my own arguments thrown back at me and a lot of veiled threats about my future looking bleak if I can't be a proper facility director and instigate important board decisions." The scientist spat the last part out in disgust and asked, "How about you?"

"On changing the board's mind, no joy. However, I have a device that we could use to hijack an autocar, get it to head to a small abandoned town thousands of miles from here. Plus, some food and a gun stashed in the carpark."

He knew there was no point hiding anything from the doctor now. They were well past the point of no return. They had to trust each other and hope like hell it wasn't a mistake. "We just need a way to cut through the fence . . . "

"There is an alarm wired into the fence," Dr Ramon replied flatly.

"Shit, I didn't think of that. We can't take them through the building. Even that late, someone will spot them on the security cameras," Kyle replied, the sinking feeling returning to his stomach. "Can you get to security tonight, stop them raising an alarm?"

"What do I do, ask them very nicely not to raise the alarm?" snorted the scientist desperately and far too sarcastically for Kyle.

"I did say there was a gun stashed in the carpark. Say you are just stepping out, grab the gun, and take the security team hostage. We'd have to do it anyway if we are going to do this." The shock on the doctor's face was a mirror of the shock Kyle was feeling at his own words. However, he knew he was right. "For this to work, we can't have witnesses or someone reporting us too quickly. Nobody needs to get hurt. They aren't going to expect the head of this place to point a gun at them. Just make them lock themselves in a closet or something while we make a getaway. It'll be over in a moment."

"There has to be another way," Dr. Ramon almost whimpered, looking around nervously as if they could be overheard.

With a shrug, Kyle sat down, wincing in pain as he did so. "I can't think of one. Can you?"

"What's wrong with you?" The doctor asked, clearly trying to change the subject.

"The severance pay from my last job turned up at three a.m. the other night. I will be fine, just some bumps and bruises. Nothing that will stop me, assuming you haven't changed your mind." The actor leaned forward and added, "This isn't a robbery or some stupid attempt at corporate espionage. We are trying to save two lives. I am willing to go to prison for the rest of my life to save theirs. I thought you were willing to do the same."

The doctor got to his feet and shuffled to a small cabinet. He pulled out a small kit and selected a syringe from inside. "This isn't yet available publicly, but should help with the pain long term and promote healing." Dr. Ramon turned and said, "Roll up your sleeve, please."

Kyle paused. For a moment, he suspected the doctor might be trying to betray him. However, he couldn't think of a reason why. Why go through all they had done so far just to have him arrested? Surely, the company had better things to do than trick employees into trying to break the law; so he complied. "You haven't answered me."

"No, but I have not changed my mind. However, I need this escape to have a realistic chance of succeeding. Even if we get in that autocar, the company will track us down. It won't take them more than a few days to run us to ground." The scientist sighed and shook his head as he injected Kyle. The actor felt a sharp sting, and then, after a few moments, he felt the pain easing. "Better?"

"Yes, actually, much," Kyle replied, bending over a little, testing out the results. The pain was still there, but dulled much more than the painkillers had managed to.

"A first successful human trial. What a pity I can't document it," the doctor replied with a smile and a laugh as Kyle glared at him. "You said you were willing to go to prison. I assumed you were willing to be a guinea pig."

"Yes, well, you also assumed we'd be in the autocar, and you are wrong about that, too," snorted the actor. "That is just a red herring. We cut out our biochips, stick them in the ca,r set it off. They will assume we are making a run for it. Even when they track the car down, they will just find it empty, save for our biochips. It might take days or weeks for them to realize their mistake. In the meantime, we hide in that empty town down the hill, and tomorrow night I have a friend who will pick us up and take us somewhere else. After that, I dunno what we will do. Try and figure out a new life, I suppose."

"That just might work," conceded the scientist. "Assuming they don't catch the autocar before it lands."

"That is why we need to take security hostage and erase any security footage. A few hours head start, and, by the time they realize we never got in the car, we will be so far over the horizon they will never track us down." The actor put as much confidence as he could in his words, knowing he had to sell the idea or everything would be lost.

"Ok, that seems like a good plan. I mean, as good as can be expected given the lack of time and resources we have," the scientist agreed and took a deep breath. "I have never fired a gun before."

"You don't have to. Just point it at them and seem like you mean it." Kyle reassured him, "We are doing this to save lives. I am not going to lose any sleep over putting a couple of guys in a closet for a few hours."

"Alright, alright, you have convinced me. I'll do it!" A smile crept onto the scientist's lips, partly through nerves and partly relief at a tough decision made. "Somehow, I always expected that, when I finally got a promotion, it would last a little long. Maybe enough to get out there, meet someone, and have kids of my own."

"Look on the bright side. If we get caught, you will probably meet someone in prison. I mean, they will be bigger, hairier, and kids are unlikely, but at least you won't be alone," joked the actor. "Of course, for me, it'll be just like going back to my old job. Hell, it might even be a little nicer. No agent to worry about, just a three-hundred-pound gorilla named Alfonso."

"Alfonso?" Dr. Ramon laughed despite himself.

"Hey, nobody disses my imaginary prison husband but me!" snorted the actor through painful laughter.

"Knowing my luck, I will end up in a cell with a tiny accountant put away for fraud who will expect me to look after him. On the plus side, I'm sure I can make him my prison bitch, Bernice," laughed the scientist.

"Bernice?!"

"Hey! Anybody dissing my prison bitch is getting shived!"

The two laughed together for a minute before being dragged back to reality kicking and screaming. "Are you going to tell them now?" Dr. Ramon asked.

"No, I'll tell them before I go, and, since we are pretty much fucked after today, I have two questions I was hoping you could answer," Kyle replied. He had thought of telling Aden, but with their hearing, Bruno might find out. He trusted them both to want to escape. He knew they wanted to live, but he didn't trust their acting ability. By which, he didn't trust Bruno's acting ability. Aden had demonstrated a poker face that would have allowed him to be a master poker player.

"Ok, ask away. I guess we have no secrets left."

"What happened to Cassandra and all of Bruno's other companions?" The scientist looked like he had been hit with a brick and, given some of what Kyle knew about the things that had gone on, he wasn't entirely undeserving of that fate.

Dr. Ramon shrugged and sighed, "Look, you know those contraceptive devices that you guys have fitted?" Kyle nodded, noting the description of prostitutes as 'you guys'. It was nice to be typecast once more. "Well, Aden and Bruno are a bit more productive than the average human. In honesty, they just weren't up to the task . . ."

"They all got pregnant?" the actor asked flatly. For some reason, he wasn't surprised. Maybe because he had tasted just a hint of seed each time he had gone down on Aden. It made sense, he supposed; a creature that was mostly human might crossbreed.

"Yes. Turns out the hybrids are capable of cross breeding with both parent species. Although, with humans being by far the larger part of their DNA, they were much more susceptible to conception." The scientist pulled open a draw in the bottom of his desk and pulled out a bottle of scotch and two glasses, pouring two generous measures. "Oh shit, you can't drink on those meds," he mumbled and emptied one glass into the other while Kyle sat fuming slightly at missing out on a bottle of fifteen-year=old malt.

"Dr. Salter bought this for me the day Isabell was born. It would cost you a month's wages, and I would never have bought it for myself. I figure it's only right I should finish it before I leave." Kyle had heard plenty of addicts explain away their need for the drug. Right then, though, he wanted answers. "Three of them chose to abort the child, the others . . ." The scientist tilted his head back and looked up.

"I really hope you are not saying they are in heaven!" The actor warned, his heart racing.

"No! We're not monsters. They are on Mars. Cassandra would still be en route now. They accepted a very lucrative payment to bring the child to term and even serve as parent until ten years old." With a large swig from the glass, the scientist gave a shrug. "Technically, there is nothing in any of the legislation about breeding a new hybrid this way. Of course, unlike eighteen years ago, we were not going to be so arrogant as to announce it to the world and let them fix the loophole. So that, I believe, answers question number one. You said you had two."

"What's your first name?"

The doctor actually burst out laughing in surprise. "All these months, and I never said?" Kyle shook his head in response. "It's Scott, Scotty to my friends . . . Well, friend, I suppose. Top secret research isn't exactly conducive to a full social life."

"Well, Scotty, see you tonight. Please don't down the rest of that bottle tonight. Bring it with you. We can have something to drink while we wait to see if we get caught." Kyle winked as he got to his feet. "It'll keep the edge off the suspense."

He heard the scientist laughing and the splashing sound of liquid being poured back into the bottle. Maybe he wasn't the most honest man, but he seemed to be a good man, or good enough anyway. It wasn't like Kyle had much choices; partners in crime were hard to come by, and now was not the time to quibble over their bad habits.

Chapter 18

Aden had been delighted to see him back. The equine had sensed something was up and didn't seem to want to leave him alone. Bruno was happy to see him as well. He complained that Cassandra was still missing. The big lug was still hoping to see her again. Kyle wasn't sure how he would break the news to him, that she was on her way to Mars and pregnant with his child. That seemed like the sort of sensitive conversation to have once you are finished running for your life.

He kept the details of what was going to happen to himself. Dr. Ramon called him away briefly, and he picked up a pair of wire cutters. Kyle didn't ask where they had come from; technically, Scotty ran the entire facility, and that meant, if he wanted to take wire cutters, who in their right mind was going to say no? It was weird to finally have a name for him; all the months they had worked together, he had never cared to ask. Now . . . it seemed important to know the name of the guy when you are putting your life and two others in his hands. Kyle really hoped the scientist didn't have butter fingers.

As night fell, he encouraged both equines to take an early night. Aden took that suggestion eagerly, his tail perking up and swaying in a cute way. Kyle had noticed the equine always did that when he felt frisky. As soon as they were inside their room, he found himself locked in a powerful equine embrace. Aden pushed his muzzle into the human's neck and took a deep breath. The warm, moist breath caressing Kyle's flesh tantalizingly. "I missed you a lot," the equine whispered as his velvet lips nibbled softly on the nape on his neck.

The warm sensation echoed out, and Kyle found himself relaxing. Closing his eyes and leaning against his lover, enjoying the strong embrace. For a moment, he forgot everything that was coming. All that existed in the world was Aden, his touch, his scent, and his warmth. "I missed you, too," He sighed with content; he had never meant anything as much as he had those words.

"I don't like it when you go away," moaned the equine softly, his paws starting to slip under Kyle's shirt. "Especially when you don't say goodbye and you . . ." The words died on Aden's lips. His eyes stared in shock at the human's stomach, just where he had lifted the shirt. "What . . ."

"It's nothing!" Kyle snapped, pulling his shirt down hard, blushing deeply. "I just . . ." Kyle paused, unable to finish the sentence. 'I was just beaten to a bloody pulp by three men on behalf of my former employer. But the doctor gave me a magic injection.' Somehow, he didn't think Aden would find that comforting.

"Kyle . . . please, tell me what happened," Aden whispered, his eyes glassy with forming tears as he looked at his lover with concern.

"I just had to pay the price," the actor replied with a shrug. "So much wonderful stuff has happened. I got out of my contract, and I . . . met you. Life doesn't let things stay that good for long." He pulled up his shirt to show the purple, puffy skin. "Dempsy sent some guys around to let me know he was upset when I left. I know it looks bad, but it's done now, and I am free. If this is the price of being with you, then I will pay it gladly. I would pay any price . . . to stay with you."

Aden looked away, his ears twitching. Kyle knew that was a sign of nervousness. "I . . . would do anything to be with you, too," the equine whispered and then turned to look at him, his eyes shining pools of molten gold. They seemed to swallow him whole, and, once more, the world seemed to drop away, no worries and no escape. Just Aden and him in a tiny universe a few meters wide, just enough for them to be together. Their lips met once more, and Kyle kissed Aden with a desperation he had never known. Inside him, he felt a burning need and desire. This might be his last chance. In a few hours, they would be free or they would be . . .

He wanted to be with the equine he loved just once more. Their torsos met, and pain flushed forth, but he ignored it. Focusing on the sensation of the warm velvet caressing his lips, the strong, dexterous tongue dancing with his, and the flavor of sweet fruit and hay in his mouth. His breathing grew rapid, and, before he knew, it his shirt was discarded, his pants following. He fell to his knees before the equine and smiled up as Aden flushed with desire.

Before him was the mottled flesh of sweet equine perfection. His hands ran up the pony's thighs, dancing through his fur as he leaned forward and kissed the tip. Then he stopped and turned his head. He reached a finger into his mouth and turned off his device, turning off both with a double-press. There was no need for it now, and, just once, he wanted to taste his lover without anything in the way. Nobody was going to come and collect a sample, so he could enjoy himself.

Above him, the panting breath paused, and he knew Aden was confused. He provided clarity with his lips to the equine cock-tip. The flavor washed over him, so much stronger and muskier than he thought it would be. A deep, pleasurable moan erupted from inside him, and he found himself hungrily devouring his lover's maleness. Gulping down the thick meat, tasting the sweat and grime of the day. It was like feeling Aden for the first time. The equine's hot flesh was addictive; he couldn't get enough, forcing the cock deep and down his throat.

With a whinny and a stamp of his hoof on the floor, Aden signaled his delight. His hands grabbed Kyle's head, equine fingers running through his black hair, caressing and yet not holding him down. Kyle bobbed his hungry mouth on the hot length quickly his hands reaching up to find two heavy swinging orbs in their leathery sack. They were damp and hot to the touch. A light squeeze made Aden whinny again.

There was no holding back. He was looking up, trying to memorize the moment. The sound of Aden's cries, the feel of his hot flesh sliding between his lips and filling his mouth. He swallowed the equine's taste and inhaled his scent, losing himself in Aden's being. Kyle sucked desperately, firmly, bobbing his head without mercy or pause. He could feel Aden's heart beating through the pulse on his tongue. The pony's heart was racing, and Kyle knew why; he could sense his lover was already near the edge.

Kyle had no intentions of stopping or holding back. This was something he wanted more than anything he could remember for a long time. He milked the shaft between his lips, his tongue dancing around the medial ring. His hands giving gentle tugs on the pony's nuts. The sensations mixing with the feel of his mouth. Aden was lost in a world of pleasure. He could feel his orgasm taking hold, and he didn't fight it.

The first jet surprised Kyle; he knew it was coming, and yet to actually feel Aden's essence in his mouth was something so strange. The silky warm and thick fluid jetting into his mouth so powerfully, the slight pause was all it took for his mouth to overflow. The white fluids dripping down his chin and onto his chest, the warm droplets forming little streams running down his body. While the thick rod continued to pulse and throb, he tried to swallow, and yet there was just too much. The stallion milk kept coming and spilling down his body.

He could feel the warm drops on his own cock. They tingled and almost burned on his skin. His cock ached with desire, and yet he couldn't take his hands off Aden. Kyle was desperate to give Aden everything and to take everything. His head bobbing slowly on the aching meat, milking it for every drop, until the softening member pulled from his sloppy lips with a slurping sound and the actor fell back panting, the warm cum starting to dry on his trembling body.

"You . . . the . . . Won't they want . . ." Aden panted as he looked down at the human.

"No, fuck them. Never again," Kyle whispered and looked up at Aden, his eyes filled with desire. He pulled himself up the equine's body, the cum on his skin making Aden's fur stick and tickle more than ever before. He pressed his lips fiercely to the equine, sharing his taste. Aden returned the kiss hesitantly at first. However, Kyle would brook no hesitation. His body ground against the equine, his bruises aching, and yet nothing could stop him. Aden was his, and nobody could take him away. "Fuck them!"

"Fuck them!" Aden replied, giggling with the giddy thrill of rebellion. His paws gripping Kyle tightly, possessively, and he whispered, "I want you . . . Just you."

"Then take me," Kyle replied, his hand taking Aden's and placing it on his pert buttocks. He kissed those velvet lips once more passionately, both of them moaning and gasping with bliss before the kiss was broken. "Make me yours." With that, he fell backwards onto the bed, landing with a thump, lifting his legs up just enough to expose himself. His desires could not have been clearer, even if he had "fuck me" tattooed across his chest.

Aden's desire was also clear, thick, erect, and dripping-ly clear. The equine pounced down onto his lover, their kiss rejoined with renewed vigor. they tried to devour each other, tongues and lips battling for supremacy. While Kyle felt a hot thick cock-tip trace tantalizingly up his inner thigh. His body was screaming and burning with desire, the need to be taken. The pain from his bruises somehow only made the need so much worse. He cried out as Aden found his mark, his hands gripping the equine's strong back desperately tight, as if fearful he might try to get away.

"Please, oh, please. I need you," he whispered desperately, begging Aden for what his body was demanding. With a soft whinny, his lover replied and then punctuated that response with a firm thrust. Pain spasmed from Kyle's chest and back. There was a burning feeling inside him. The equine had thrust in raw. With his device turned off, he felt the thrust fully. He cried out, welcoming the sensation, knowing he had never been this close to anyone. The equine's touch inside him far more real than anything he had felt in the last eight years.

His fingers clawed desperately against Aden's back, holding him and yet trying to pull him closer. Aden was like a mountain, unmovable and dominant above him. The equine's hungry lips were on his once more. He devoured the human's every cry and whimper as he thrust into the tight, twitching depths. Never before had it felt so good. Somehow, every motion was far more sensuous, the pleasures dancing up and down his cock. A burning need consuming the pony's mind. The need to breed, to rut his mare and drain his very being into his lover.

"Aden!" Kyle's desperate cry echoed around the room as his body writhed up against the firm body of his lover. He forced himself up into each thrust, desperately trying to get more inside him. The soft, leathery slap of Aden's balls drumming off his ass gave a deep staccato rhythm to their love. Hips pounding against ass, fur on skin. Hands clawing each other desperately as they fucked.

"Oh, Kyle!" Panted, breathless words sounding so sweet in the actor's ears. He could feel his lover around him, above him, and inside him. All he wanted was to be right there and nowhere else. Never before had he felt that. He knew that feeling, strange and yet familiar. It consumed his mind and yet protected it, too.

Kyle could feel the build-up, that familiar pressure inside him. With each thrust, Aden forced more pleasure into him, driving him nearer to the edge. He looked up, his eyes desperate with need, and he found those golden eyes looking down at him with love and burning desire. "I . . . love . . . you!" He screamed those words, and he meant them. He had never said them to anyone and meant it.

The words were like a spur in Aden's mind. He was desperate to respond, and yet he couldn't. His body did the talking for him, showing the human his love with deep powerful thrusts, his maleness working its way fully inside as he bucked and whinnied out like a feral beast. Their mating reaching peaks he never dreamed existed. Below him, Kyle cried out, and the human's depth became desperately tight, almost forcing his maleness out.

Aden's nostrils flared as Kyle felt the animal inside his lover respond, breeding him with the passion and strength of a stallion breeding a mare. Instinct alone was all either of them had left. Kyle pushed back as Aden railed home hard and fast, fucking his mare with desperation born of love. Kyle's ears rang with the cries of his lover, while inside him, Aden's cock began to throb. In the full grip of his orgasm, Aden rutted with pure desperation, rutting with every last ounce of strength he had as he emptied himself into the human. Kyle gasped as Aden ran out of strength, collapsing down on top of him and gasping in his ear, "I love you, too."

Wrapped in each other's embrace, they held together, panting softly and dozing in the blissful afterglow of their union. Tender nuzzles became sweet kisses and more. Kyle found his mind slowly slipping away from the bliss and onto the future. He knew their happiness could not last forever. Soon, he would need to break the news and explain the plan to Aden. He clung to the equine desperately, wanting to prolong this time with him for as long as he could.

There was no knowing how Aden would take the news. It was not an easy thing to hear, or say, for that matter. Sorry, your use as a lab animal has ended, and next week they plan to put you to sleep. If it helps, they want your end to be painless. Oh, it will save a few hundred jobs, and they will push the funds from this to the Mars research program to enhance the terraforming efforts.

Eventually, he knew he could put it off no longer. Aden was softly snoring into his neck, and he gently shook him awake. Sitting up in bed, Kyle slipped to his feet while Aden looked up at him curiously. "Is everything okay?"

Kyle gave the worst answer you can give to that question, "No, nothing is okay." The human took a deep breath and sighed, "I have something to tell you, and it's not good. It's terrible, in fact, and I just don't know how to say it."

With his eyes going wide with fear, Aden shot to his feet, his hands reaching out for Kyle. "You're not leaving me, are you?"

Unable to not smile, to hear the pain in that voice, causing pain was not good, but the feeling of love that must have caused that filled him with warmth. It gave Kyle strength, and he reached out, taking Aden's hands and shaking his head. "Never! I promise, as long as I live, I am never going away!"

A nervous smile returned to Aden's face as he sighed in relief. "Then whatever you have to say, it can't be that bad."

"It is pretty bad, though." Yhe human paused for a second. "I really can't think of a way to say this. You and Bruno, you need to leave tonight."

"Leave? You mean run away?" the pony asked, stepping back a little, as if afraid for a moment. "Why?"

"There was a decision, a board decision, when they were looking at the funding for this facility . . ." Kyle paused. He knew Aden only had the most basic concept of money from his talks on contracts and pay. It wasn't like the equine had ever been able to pop to the shops to pick up a couple of food packs and a couple of bottles of beer. "This place, it costs a lot. Yhe food they feed you, staff who watch over you and take the samples and process them. Well, they have decided that they have enough offspring from you to go to the second phase of the project, when your and Bruno's children grow. They . . . don't need you anymore, and this place costs a fortune. So, they are closing down your project."

"What about me and Bruno?" Aden's voice quivered, and he took another step back from Kyle, as if fearful that the words that came would hurt him.

"They . . . think you are too expensive to keep, and, if they let you go, well, the public might not be happy to find out what they have been doing. So, they decided the best course was to terminate you both." The actor hated himself in that moment. All he could see was pain and confusion in this love's eyes, and he knew it was he who was bringing such pain. He stepped forward, reaching out, but Aden stumbled backwards, confused and hurt, tears streaming down his face. Kyle stopped advancing, trying to let the pony absorb the details. "That is why you need to escape tonight, with me. I will be with you, no matter what!" He backed up a little, giving Aden space, feeling the wall press into his back as Aden pressed himself into the other wall and slumped to his knees, his legs no longer able to hold him.

"I don't understand," whispered the blonde pony, his eyes full of fear and confusion. "Why do they want to kill me?"

"No, they don't want to. At least, it's not as simple as that," Kyle replied, his back sliding down the wall as he slowly slumped down to the floor opposite the pony. "None of them want to kill you, it's not personal. That's what makes it so much more evil. A bunch of people have gotten together. They have conducted cost benefit analysis and decided that the best course of action for everyone is to stop paying for your upkeep and to terminate you. Maximize profits, everyone benefits, their shareholders, their employees . . . Hell, in their minds, the entire human race. They don't hate you, they don't want you dead, it's simply better this way. In their minds"

As he spoke, he could feel the tears on his face, "You know there are machines and robots that can do almost everything a human does. There is no reason why a human should pick up litter, scrub toilets, or clean the house. We lie to ourselves that humans do a better job, but we all know that actually robots would do it better. I used to tell myself that the companies wanted to keep people down, that by forcing the working man to scrub their toilets, the executives got some sort of crazy power trip . . ."

Kyle sighed and looked down at his hands, examining the fingers closely. "That's just the bullshit the working man says about those with money. They don't care enough to want to keep us down. The real reason is far more sinister: it's cheaper. Humans are the cheapest, most plentiful resource left on this world. Biological life forms. They maintain themselves, they control themselves, and, in time, they produce their own replacements, the next model, so to speak."

"The people who decided to do this to you, they believe they are doing the right thing. Maybe they feel a little guilty, but they think it's right." He couldn't keep the bitterness out of his voice if he tried as he continued, "They will argue the advances to our colonization efforts of producing a new, more able biological source of labor will enhance humanity immeasurably, justifying every aspect of their project. They will have gone home, feeling proud of themselves. They made a hard decision, kill two sentient beings, to enhance the lives of billions by a fraction of a percent. Death by committee for the greater good." He spat the last of his words with more venom than a cobra, punching the wall in impotent frustration.

"I . . . I . . . don't want to die," whimpered Aden, pushing closer to the human. Suddenly the warmth of another's touch was far more needed than anything.

Kyle was desperate to put his arm around the horse, to kiss him and tell him it would all be okay. However, he knew Aden had taken his fill of lies, and he didn't think he had another one in him anyway.

"Neither do I, and I will do everything I can to keep us both alive," the human whispered. It was the truth at least, although nowhere near as comfortable as the lies he could have spun. "The best part is . . . it won't work. In the end, they may produce a new race of people, a sub species. However, life doesn't work like machines. No matter how well they teach them to behave, to want to be captive, no matter how gilded their cages, they will want the one thing that they can never give: freedom. It's not personal.

"Ha! You know, I once read that the meaning of words changes over the years. It's not personal, they say it like that makes it better. Maybe hundreds of years ago, it made some sense. To me, it would be better if it was personal. At least then, they would be killing you for something beyond the numbers on some spreadsheet. Death by committee, fuck them, fuck them all." Inside, Kyle felt it, the boiling pit of rage that had been simmering away his entire life, the pressure rising until he felt like his entire body would explode. His shoulders shook as he felt the sobs coming. However, there was something more, something far stronger than hope, of freedom. It was pure hatred. "They won't fucking get you, or me, I will find a way, I don't care who I have to kill or what I have to do . . . I will find us a way."

Strong arms wrapped around the human, and he slumped, weeping into a sea of golden fur. Nothing in his life had ever been fair. Life wasn't fair, and he knew it. With nothing left but love and hate inside him, he would make it unfair in their favor, or more likely die in the attempt. They clung together and wept for their situation, and yet, even in the deepest, blackest pit of despair that they found themselves, there was the light of the other. It shone out to them both, and their tears dried, and crying turned to kissing.

Kyle reached up and wiped Aden's tears away as equine fingers stroked the tears off his own cheek. "I have a way out and a plan. They might want you dead, but there are others who want to help you. Dr. Ramon and my friends. We are going to do everything we can to save you both. It is getting late, we need to go. I have to dress, go wake Bruno and . . . tell him Cassandra is okay, she is on Mars. Let him know we are getting out and why."

The black pony took it better than Kyle thought he would, hardly a tear. Mostly, he was confused, and he kept asking, "What did I do wrong? I did everything they asked." Kyle's heart ached to see the faith Bruno still had in the people around him, those he had grown up with. His family, how easily they had turned. Kyle and Aden reassured him that not all of them had and those who hadn't were willing to risk everything they had, including their lives, for him.

That more than anything reassured him, enough that he was willing to follow Kyle. The actor pulled his transmitter out of his pocket and placed it in his ear. "Scotty, you there?"

"I'm here." It was weird, the relief he felt hearing that voice in his ear. For so long, it had been nothing but a source of frustration. Now it was one of hope. "Making my way to the car park, I suggest you get to the fence."

"Understood . . . good luck," he replied and looked at the two who nodded. They had both heard the response and knew what they had to do. Kyle pulled the wire cutters from his pocket and walked briskly into the night.

The sky was crystal clear, the crescent moon hanging just above the mountains. Stars dotted out into the infinite black, their breaths forming little puffy clouds as they stalked through the grounds. There was no sound, just the soft thumps of feet and hooves in the grass as they jogged quickly to the fence. A soft crack spat out in the night, not loud yet strange, and Kyle paused. "Scotty, you there?" There was no answer, and Kyle felt panic rise in his chest. "Scott, Dr. Ramon, answer me, please. We are almost to the fence."

There was nothing but silence in response, and the actor looked to the two scared ponies. What if the doctor had been caught? They had no chance, but he'd try anyway. They were done regardless. He could at least give them a good run. Make the bastards earn it. As these thoughts began to fill his mind, he got his response, "Sorry . . . I'm here. The fence alarm is off." There was something wrong with the scientist's voice. It seemed distant, shaken. Kyle hoped it was just because of the adrenaline. The noise worried him, though. It was muffled but closely resembled a gunshot, though it was hard to be sure.

While he clipped the wire, he kept looking back at the facility. It remained quiet and dead. No alarms and no lights. No security guards chasing them down. So far, things were going according to the plan. He worked as quickly as he could, cutting a small hole low down in the wire, just enough for them to slip through. Aden went first, then Bruno, and finally Kyle. He noticed both of the equines looking out at the world, the world with no fences. Welcome to the land of freedom. Hopefully, you'll still be alive to enjoy it in the morning. Words he kept to himself. Instead, he signaled them to follow him. They skirted the fence quickly, jogging single file until they reached the building.

The windows were almost all dark, but he signaled the two to be quiet anyway and ducked under each one. Taking things a little slower, he didn't want the thump of running feet to disturb some light sleeper or late-night reader who might come and investigate. He could see the end, and he focused on that, watching it draw nearer inch by inch. His body trembling as, any moment, he expected to hear the cries of outrage or surprise. However, they never came, and he reached the entrance to the car park. A single autocar waiting for them.

"Wait here," he whispered to the two ponies. "If I shout to run, just run and keep running" The two brothers grasped at each other for support, their eyes wide with terror. They were so far beyond the world they knew, even if it was only a few meters, it was like another planet to them.

Kyle crept into the carpark, his eyes fixed on the security station window. He could see nobody in there. His heart was beating rapidly. He reached his satchel and grabbed it; his gun was gone. So that at least had gone according to the plan. "Scott?" he whispered, and the silence that answered was deafening.

The man crept closer, right up to the security station, pushing open the door. A chill ran down his back as the air inside was thick with a sickly warm scent. One he knew too well: blood. Then his eyes spotted two feet sticking out from behind a desk. Knowing that he had no choice, he had come this far, he had to go. Kyle stepped forward. Moving around the desk to find the owner of the feet. It was a security guard, one he had seen a few times. Young and cheerful, only not anymore. His eyes were closed and would never open again, the gaping, bloody hole in his chest was testament to that.

"He . . . wouldn't, and I . . . I didn't . . . I just wanted him to listen." The voice was no longer in his ear; it was behind him. Kyle turned to find Dr. Ramon behind him, pressed to the wall, as if trying to push through it to get away from the body. There was no color in his face. His eyes were unfocused. Kyle's pistol was lying at his feet.

Stepping closer, Kyle nodded. "I understand . . ."

"No! You don't . . . He, I just . . . The trigger," Scott shouted, his voice trailing off. "Welcome to Wonderland, I wrote that on a card. Raymond, he had a baby girl, they called her Alice. He said I made his wife's day, she loved that book and . . . and . . ."

The actor could tell Dr. Ramon was in shock. It wasn't hard to guess the details of what had really happened. The doctor had tried to threaten the young guard. Raymond had refused to back down. From how Scott was trembling like a leaf, he guessed a nervous man and a pistol with a hair trigger made for bad companions. Raymond gave ghastly testimony to the truth of that.

Moving up to the man, he grabbed him by the shoulders, forcing him to look into his eyes. "Scott! We don't have time! It was an accident, we have to go!"

Jumping and squirming, the scientist pulled from his grasp. "No! I can't go, I . . . I have to face up to what I did. It's my fault, don't you see? I shot him, I widowed his wife and took Alice's father from her. There is no running away from that!" the man ranted, waving his hand at the corpse on the floor. Kyle could see Scott's eyes wild and full of tears. A man of science he had ceased to be. He was lost to his grief and guilt.

"You can't stay here! They will put you away!" the actor hissed, firmly trying to grab his wrist.

The scientist pulled back. "I have done so much, don't you see? Creating Aden and Bruno, hiding them. I rode the very edge of morality my entire career, told myself it was okay. Kept them like pets. When Dr. Salter fired Brian, I did nothing. I took away everything that was helping them grow, because I was told to. There is nothing I can do to take that back now, but I can face up to this."

"You don't have to . . ."

Rounding on him with the look of a wild animal just before it charges, the scientist shook his head and replied, "Yes, I do! Maybe it's stupid, maybe not. I don't know. Right now, it feels like the right thing to do. To stand up and own up to something for once. If I don't, then . . . what good am I as a man? I'm a scientist, an uncle, and a good brother. If I leave now with you, I will always be the man who murdered someone he barely knew and then ran away."

The two men stood silently for a moment, Kyle struggling to think. His body wanted him to run. Every moment, he was aware they might be discovered. Aden and Bruno were counting on him, and he knew if he let them down, he would get no chance at redemption. After the longest minute of his life, Scott turned and said in a steady voice, "No, this is better. I can throw them off from the inside. Make sure they chase the car. In the meantime, I can start deleting stuff. Pay my debt."

"Deleting what?"

"Everything! We only published a tiny fraction of the research on Aden and Bruno. If I delete enough before they stop me, they might reconsider terminating them."

Kyle took a sharp intake of breath as his mind spun with what the doctor was saying. It spanned right past the chance for the board to change its mind to something else. "Why didn't you mention this earlier? A way to save Aden and Bruno without an escape."

"There's no way to know if it would work. Even if I deleted it all, I don't know if it would change anything." Scott looked up with a half-smile. "Besides, it's my life, you know. My legacy, Dr. Salter's, too. He was no saint, but he was a brilliant man. His techniques were a cut above. It seemed wrong to just erase them. However, I guess he will always be remembered as the guy who went that one step too far. It would be nice if people think that I am a man who eventually stepped back over that line. However, it doesn't really matter. It is a chance, and I owe it to Aden and Bruno to take it. Two lives for the price of a few files, that seems like a bargain to me."

Standing slightly taller than Kyle could ever remember him doing, the man gave him a nod. "It has been an interesting time getting to know you. Something tells me that we are unlikely to see each other again, unless we end up in the same prison. Beside the console is my bag. I had some supplies in there and a few other things. I suggest you take them with you. Good luck."

As Scott turned to walk, Kyle replied, "Thanks, for everything, I guess. I'm really sorry it had to end this way, I know you didn't . . ." The actor's eyes scanned down to the ghastly scene on the floor and back up to the scientist. "I hope you find whatever it is you need. If we get away and I can figure out some way to contact you, I will."

The scientist paused for a moment, and Kyle thought he might say something, and then he continued and was gone. Kyle found the bag and grabbed it, then he accessed the computer console. He had a message to send. He felt guilty prolonging their time there. Each moment that past increased the odds of their capture. This was something private and in many ways selfish, but he took a couple of minutes to record a message and sent it anyway.

Then he turned and ran. Pausing at the autocar, he pulled a small knife from his own satchel and put the straps of the handle between his teeth. His hand trembled a little as the blade neared his wrist, but he knew he was long past the point of no return. A little pain had been part of the deal. His muffled screams echoed in the small carpark as he cut deep and then reached in with his fingers. Pulling out his biochip, the little green thing looked so small and inanimate in his hand. He'd expected it to flash or beep, or something. However, it looked just like a little lump of jade. Inside it was Kyle: his history, bank accounts, every message he had sent or received, everywhere he had been, and everything he had bought. His entire life in a tiny pebble, floating in a small pool of his congealing blood, in the palm of his hand.

Closing his eyes, he flicked his wrist, and the biochip landed on the autocar seat. He plugged the device Darwin had given him into the car and shut the door. A second later, the vehicle sprung to life, rising up and driving away. Kyle wrapped a small bandage around his wrist and dashed outside. He slung Dr. Ramon's bag at Bruno. "Here, carry this, we have to go."

"Where is Dr. Ramon?" Aden asked, looking in through the car park.

"He . . . isn't coming. He is going to try something else that might just save you if we get caught," Kyle replied as he started to walk briskly down the hill. The skyline in the east was already a shade of navy blue. Morning was coming, and they needed to be inside before the sun was up and the facility awake. "We have got to move!" he grunted as he began to run. A second of two later, he heard hoofbeats as the two equines began to follow him.

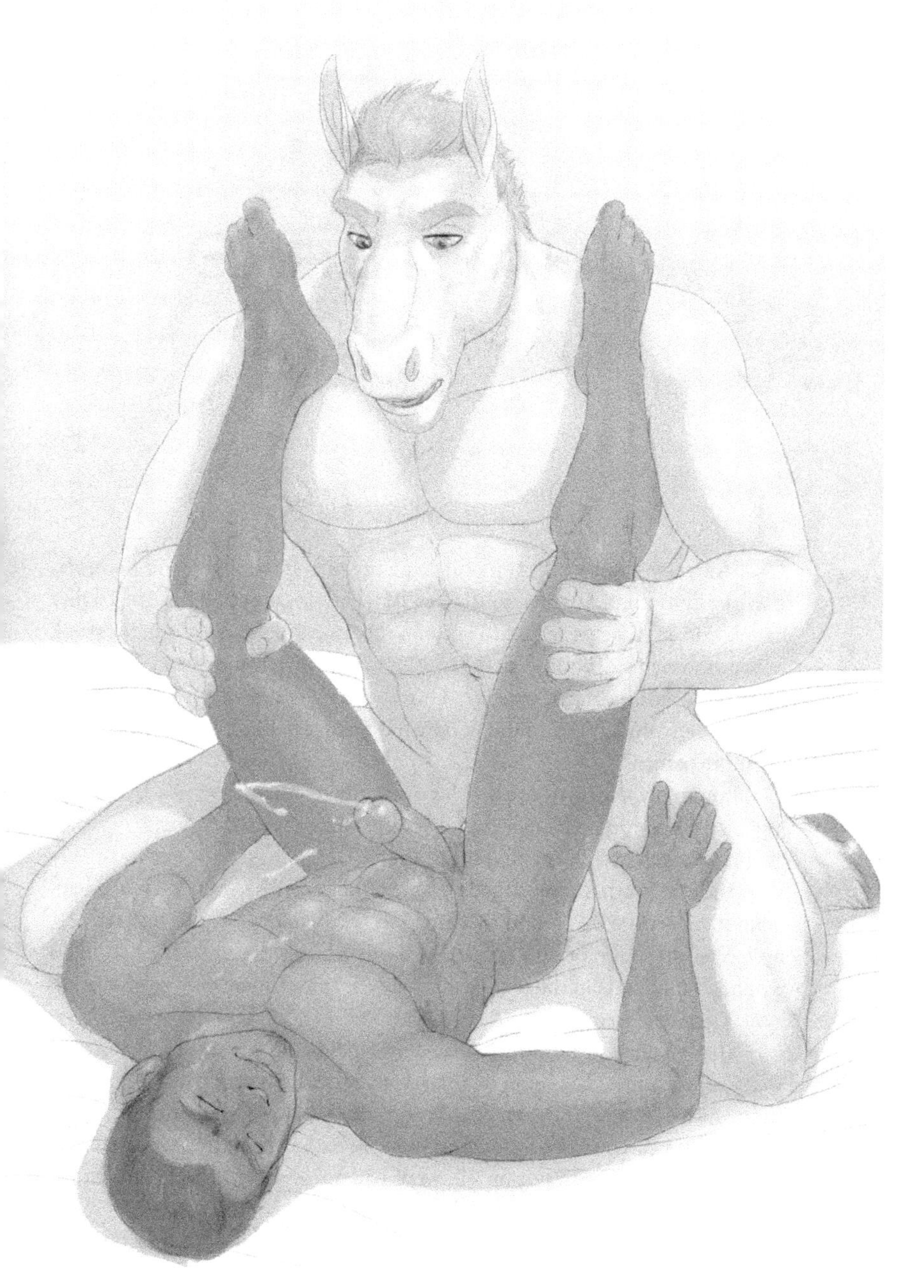

Chapter 19

The town proved to be further away than he thought, and there was no smooth road down to it. Clearly, when it was populated, the facility hadn't existed. Kyle struggled to keep up the pace. Aden and Bruno overtook him in moments. The injection Dr. Ramon had given him seemed to have worn off, or maybe it just wasn't made to handle the sort of stress he was putting his body under. Each moment, he fell further behind, breathing becoming more painful.

Eventually, Aden stopped. Bruno stopping a second or two later. They jogged back to him. and Kyle found his legs turning to jelly. "Sorry, I . . . Just go, on I'll catch up." He panted breathlessly.

The two brothers exchanged a glance, and, before he knew what was happening, his arms were around two broad sets of shoulders. While his feet were no longer on the floor, the two equines worked together to carry him like a wounded soldier from the battlefield. Kyle was in too much pain to argue. His eyes began to close.

They opened again hours later, only to show he was sitting against the wall inside a house. The room had clearly once been a nursery. It had little cartoon animal images in the wallpaper pattern. All around him, little children danced with cartoon dogs, cats, and mice. For a moment, he wondered who the wallpaper had been put up for, what had become of them. However, the return of his chest pain put an end to any such speculation.

The room was empty, the floorboards thick with dust and hoofprints. With a groan of pain, he pulled himself slowly back to his feet. "Aden? Bruno?" he called out into the silence.

"Down here!" came Aden's prompt reply.

Kyle winced as he walked. If he ever spoke to Dr. Ramon again, he would have to discuss the definition of long term when it came to pain control medication. Although, he was still feeling a lot better than when he woke up the previous morning. It was as he looked down the stairs it hit him, just how much had happened in the last twenty-four hours. He was grateful the plan for the day was to sit around and wait.

He walked out onto the landing of the house they were holed up in. Much like the bedroom, the place had been stripped, all apart from the wallpaper. A nice flowery pattern, faded and tattered from many years of neglect. Small, darker squares on the wall showed where once pictures had hung for years. Aden was standing by what was clearly the door outside on a tiny scrap of material. Kyle smiled to himself as he could see faded words on the ancient doormat, 'welcome, now wipe your muddy hooves, this isn't a barn'. Apparently, the owners had had a sense of humor. He wondered if Aden or Bruno had noticed the appropriateness of the message.

"How are you feeling?" the equine asked, not even trying to hide the concern in his voice.

"I've had better morning and softer beds. However, no complaints, all things considered," Kyle replied, limping down the stairs. Aden stepped forward as he reached the bottom, and they embraced tightly. "Well, you finally got to see this place. I hope it isn't too disappointing."

"Well, I'll admit I imagined a bit more of a friendly welcome. Fortunately, there are some new residents who are very pleasant to be around," the pony nickered softly into his ear as they embraced.

"Where's Bruno?" the man asked, looking around the empty hallway.

"He's out scouting the neighborhood," the equine replied, stepping out of the hug. "This was the first house we came to. The door wasn't even locked."

Looking around, the actor knew why: the former owners knew they weren't coming back, and they had already taken everything. Except the doormat to warn any visitors to wipe their dirty feet. "He shouldn't be out during the day. If anyone from the facility sees him, they . . ."

"He knows that. He is keeping behind buildings and trees. We just wanted to see if we could find somewhere more comfortable or something to eat or drink." As he said the last part, Kyle groaned. Drink! How had he forgotten something as basic and vital as water to drink?

"Damn, I totally forgot something to drink." He limped through into what had at one time been a dining room, he guessed. It was hard to be certain, but the wallpaper had a fruit pattern that would have seemed out of place in a living room. It was surprising how much a man who lived in a single bed flat knew about how people decorated full houses. Although, he had seen the inside of far more houses than most people, and he'd never decorated them or been asked his opinion on the furnishings.

There was a kitchen on the far side, counters covered with decades of dust. He could see hoofprints on the floor, and several of the cupboards were open. He guessed Bruno and Aden had gone rummaging. By the door, he could see his satchel and the bag Dr Ramon had given him. He limped over and rummaged in his bag, pulling out the food packets. "We may not have much to drink, but we are not going to starve. It's just for one day. Hopefully, when we get to the next place, we can find something to drink. Darwin might bring some in the autocar, too. Did you look through the other bag?"

"Yeah, just food and a couple of devices. I told Bruno we shouldn't use them," the pony replied, and Kyle smiled proudly. Choosing not to use tech was a smart decision. Most tech automatically connected to the net, and, if there was anything that could identify the owner there, then it wouldn't take someone looking for them too long to track them down.

However, Dr. Ramon knew what they were doing, and he was smart enough to only bring what was needed. So, Kyle snatched up the other bag and started to pull out the contents. A few more high-end food packets, no doubt stolen from the mess hall. Next, he pulled out a few mobile data storage devices. He wasn't sure what was on them, and he knew he wouldn't get time to look. Maybe when Darwin arrived, they could check them out.

The next thing he pulled out made him stop. It was the picture of the young doctor holding the tiny infant Bruno. There were two more, and Kyle found himself staring at them all. Aden did, too. "He wasn't a bad guy in the end," Kyle said quietly. "Maybe he could have done better for you, maybe someone else would have done much worse."

"I remember when we were young he used to play with us, and Isabell," Aden whispered the words, his eyes fixed on the photo. "He used to carry me around on his shoulders until Dr. Salter caught him and told him off."

"Endangering an expensive lab resource," the actor said the words with a sigh. Maybe that hadn't been the term used; however, he knew something like it had been.

Just then, they heard the door open and the clear echo of hooves on wooden floor. Bruno appeared a moment later, his arms clutching his haul while his mouth was chewing, "Apple trees, just a few hundred meters away. They are a bit tart, but juicy."

A breakfast of freshly harvested apples went down very well for all. Especially given their water situation. Kyle tried the kitchen taps just in case, by some miracle, the place was still getting water pumped it. All that came out of the tap was a rather startled spider.

After they had eaten, Kyle returned to the bag, pulling out the last few devices. One was a comm device, mobile and quite powerful. A quick check confirmed that the device's location software had been disabled. A chip had been burnt out; apparently, the doctor had found time and a soldering iron to do what he had to do. It would come in useful, though logging into his account to check messages would certainly not be wise. Radio silence was called for. His mail account would certainly be being monitored now, as would everyone he had had contact with.

He did flick it on and did a very quick scan of the news sites. Not a whisper of their escape. Of course, the corporation was unlikely to announce that. They wanted the people to forget about the Moreau children, let them be no more than a footnote in history. For now, anyway. Eventually, they would have to come out, once they had proven they could really do what they were made for. Once they were a success, then they could be rolled out into full production. On Mars, where even the government couldn't stop them.

As that thought rattled around his head, it knocked loose an idea that Danny had put forward. The one thing the boards would care about, when they finally showed Aden's children to the world, would be the opinion of the people. Governments could only act based on laws, but when they had the people behind them, even corporations had to back down.

"Aden, Bruno . . . I have an idea," he said, turning the device's camera on. "All your lives, they have tried to hide you from the world. All people know is what they saw when you were born: abominations, animal-human hybrids. Well, let's show everyone who you are, not just what you are."

"Are you sure that's wise?" Aden asked in a whisper, looking at the camera nervously as if expecting a torch-wielding mob of villagers to spill out of it and assault the abominable animal-human hybrids.

Kyle shrugged his shoulders. "We really don't have much to lose. We don't know how long we can run for . . . If enough people speak out against what they want to do to you two, maybe, just maybe, someone will stop it."

The black stallion looked over at his brother and shook his shoulders. "What should we say?"

"Just say what you feel," the actor replied. He was no speech writer, and he couldn't help but think that a speech from the heart, even if flawed, had to be better than something rehearsed.

"Well, I guess this is where I have to try and explain things." Kyle's own voice trembled a little as he thought of what to say. While he framed a good shot of Aden and Bruno next to each other, looking at the camera nervously. "I hope you'll forgive me, but it's not what I'm best at. If you are old enough, you may remember these two. They were quite famous when they were born. BioCorp had them engineered to help the terraforming effort on Mars. They have been kept in a laboratory facility their entire lives."

"A few days ago, the BioCorp board reviewed the project and pulled the funding. They gave the head scientist an instruction to terminate the lab animals. After all, they are just laboratory animals, aren't you?" With a press of a button, he zoomed in on Aden and Bruno. He could see their eyes already glassy with tears. He could see the confusion and doubt as the two looked at each other and back at him, unsure of what to say.

It was Aden who took the lead, trusting Kyle. "I guess we are," the blonde equine whispered. "We were made in a lab, then raised in one. I think we could be more. There is so much more I would like to do. I want to see the world, or maybe Mars. We were made for there, they wanted us to help, we can survive on the thin atmosphere. We are willing to help . . . We will do whatever you say. Please, we don't want to die."

"Bruno, do you have anything to say?" Kyle asked, moving the black equine into shot.

"I don't understand. We did everything they asked us to. I . . . Why? What did we do wrong? Please, just tell us. We can be better, we can do better. Just tell us what we did." Kyle's stomach tightened as he filmed. He could see glistening lines on those black cheeks; Bruno was crying while he begged for his life. The sound of their voices was anything but animalistic. Surely, anyone who watched would feel the same. The world wasn't so far gone that people could look into the eye of an intelligent being begging for his life and feel nothing. However, Kyle wanted to show them more, though he knew he didn't have long. Too long a video would possibly be too much for people. They liked their information in short bites that were easy to swallow.

"Bruno, who was Cassandra to you?" Kyle's asked, his voice cracking as he spoke through his own tears.

"Cassandra? She was . . . my friend. She made me happy. She would talk to me, tell me stories, and keep me company. Like you do for Aden. They took her away, too. I don't know why. I want her back, I feel wrong without her, incomplete, like a part of me was missing." The stallion wiped away his tears and took a breath, trying to steady himself. "I just want to see her again, to know that she is okay."

As the black equine broke down in tears, Aden put his arms around him protectively. He gave the camera a glance. "Please, we just want to live and work. I know we are not exactly human, but is that really a reason to kill us?"

Kyle couldn't take any more. He could see the pain in both of their eyes, and it hurt just to look at, to know them and to think how casually someone had ordered their euthanization. "We're on the run right now. BioCorp is hunting us down. I don't know how long it might take them to find us. I do know what'll happen when they do. I'll go to prison for theft, breach of contract, and any other offences they can make stick. As for Aden and Bruno, escapee lab animals, they have no rights beyond those of a lab rat. They will be put to sleep humanely. We have nowhere else to turn to for help, so we are asking you. Please, share this video with anyone any way. Let people know what BioCorp is doing and has done. Or this will just get worse. BioCorp has been using Aden and Bruno to breed more of their race. Their children are on Mars right now, growing up. Only question is, what will they grow into? You can't even call them slaves because a slave is a person. They are beasts of burden, to be used and then terminated when they are no longer of use. Help us and them now, please."

He ended the video with a close up on Aden hugging Bruno. It was the most human thing to him, one brother comforting another. The actor quickly drafted a very short message and forwarded it to Danny, then, after a second though, he sent another copy to everyone in his address book, even Dempsy, and then every news site he could think of.

Kyle turned off the device after sending that message. He was sure it was tracked. He hoped that at least Danny had received it. He was the only person that knew what was going on, and he was sure he at least would try and send it on. The others . . . Well, there was always some hope they might send it on. Darwin had been left off the mail. It might have made the company look to him. It would probably make the company look to everyone. Most were innocent enough that Kyle knew they would be fine. Others, well, if his last, desperate act caused Dempsy a legal headache, then that would give him something to smile about.

After the tears had stopped, they had found time to just sit down together and actually get some more sleep. There was nothing else to do anyway, though thirst was definitely an issue. Kyle really hoped Darwin would bring something for them all to drink. The rest of the apples Bruno had harvested were munched on. Kyle and Aden ate a food packet. Bruno refused after a single bite, saying he would rather wait until they found out where they were going and what the chances were on getting better food.

Eventually, the sun went down, and the house became extremely dark. They relocated outside. With the darkness to cover, them there was little fear of being spotted. Kyle still kept glancing around, expecting any moment that something would go wrong. Dr. Ramon had no doubt been caught by now. He was a far from stable man, and it wouldn't take an expert to crack him.

They observed a couple of autocars flying in and out. The facility seemed to be a hub of activity. Then they spotted a car on the wrong trajectory, one that wasn't aiming for the lab. Kyle scrambled to his feet, groaning softly at the pain. "Okay, I hope this is our ride," he whispered. Even though they were miles from anyone, somehow, in the dark during an escape attempt, whispering seemed right; logic didn't matter so much.

The car set down on the far side of town. The three ran to meet it, none of them saying a word. Aden and Bruno stopping as they saw the car and a man standing beside it. Kyle didn't stop; the light from inside the car was just enough to let him know it was Darwin. "It's ok, he's a friend!" he whispered loudly back at them, waving for them to follow him.

"Did someone order a cab?" Darwin asked with a broad smile as the three approached him.

"Darwin! I am so glad to see you," Kyle replied, giving the man a bear hug. He never thought the plan would work this well. Now they were just one step away from true escape. They were going to set down in some town in the middle of nowhere, with no way for the company to track them. Even if Dr. Ramon told them the plan, he didn't know where they were heading. "This is Aden and Bruno. Aden and Bruno, this is my friend, Darwin."

For a moment, there was an awkward silence as the three exchanged glances, then Bruno stepped forward and offered a hand. "Thank you for doing this."

Darwin glanced down at the hand just for a moment, and Kyle could almost see him working it over in his mind, 'should I really shake hands with a horse-man'. It lasted only for a moment before the man grabbed the hand and shook it firmly. "My pleasure to help you guys out. If it pisses off some corporate bigwigs, then so much the better."

He shook Aden's hand next and then waved at the car. "Let's get the show on the road, or flight path, shall we?"

They all bundled inside, and Kyle sighed as the tension eased out of him. "I really didn't think this would work," he muttered out loud as the car rose into the air.

"Well, it did, ain't worth thinking about. Now, who wants a beer?" The engineer grabbed a six-pack of tin cans from the floor.

"What is a beer?" Aden asked, eyeing the tin.

"Is it as bad as a food packet?" Bruno chimed in quickly.

"It is . . . what makes eating food packets seem like a good idea, at four in the morning," snickered Darwin as he opened a can and handed it to Bruno, then another and gave it to Aden. He opened one more for himself and lifted it up. "Here's to liberty. May she never be taken from you again, huh?"

The two equines stared at the lifted can while the engineer looked at them expectantly. "He wants you to clink your cans together as a toast. It's sort of a formal . . . thing people do."

"Why?" Aden asked.

"Tradition," Darwin replied, clinking his can to Aden's the Bruno's and taking huge chug from his can.

Aden sniffed at his open drink doubtfully while Bruno put it to his lips and took a sip, then a gulp. "It's not bad. It's no apple juice, but it's not bad."

"Apple juice! Oh my God, I should have brought you guys some cider!" laughed Darwin as he took another swig from his can.

It wasn't until Kyle opened a can that Aden finally took a sip. He didn't seem to like it much, but after a day without water, they were all far too thirsty to refuse a drink. Kyle was a little sad that this journey was made in the dark.

He would have liked to have shared the American landscape with them. Eighteen years inside a tiny facility yard, their entire world a few rooms. At least, when they arrived, they would be free, maybe free to starve in the countryside if they couldn't find food, but still free.

Whatever happened, he would be there with them, and it would be better than the humane end the corporation had planned for them. Hell, it was probably better than the ending he would have found if he had stayed with Dempsy. For a moment, he thought what might have happened if he hadn't gotten this contract. He knew he would still be in that tiny square flat alone, with an occasional free muffin the highlight of his week. Looking at Aden, his face reflected in the window, eyes wide with wonder as he stared out into the black night at the lights of nighttime America. Kyle shuddered to think how easily he could have missed out.

He slid up to Aden and put an arm around him, leaning his head on Aden's shoulder and sighing with a moment of contentment.

"Hey, what's on these?" Darwin asked, and he glanced over to find his friend holding up the data storage devices he had found in Dr. Ramon's bag. "I was just looking for something to snack on, but why are you carrying datarods?"

"I don't know," Kyle replied with a shrug. "The guy who helped us escape gave me that bag. He never really mentioned their contents . . . but he had things on his mind." Darwin raised an eyebrow at that last comment. For a second, Kyle thought he would push for more information, and then he just nodded.

Of course, Darwin couldn't put them down. He fished a device out of his pocket. "Well then, let's see what we can do with whatever is on here," the engineer muttered as he accessed the first device. "Huh, it is mostly just pictures and videos," he said, slightly disappointed, casting images up on a projection. Young equines of every age peered out at them all.

"They are pictures of you two," the actor said with a smile as he waved through several images. Selecting a video to play, the four of them watched as a young Scott encouraged Bruno to take his first steps.

"I like this video better than the one on the net," Darwin observed with a smile and a celebratory sip of beer.

"Our video, the one we sent to Danny? You've seen it?" the actor asked desperately. It had made it to Danny at least.

"Oh yeah, I have it along with a few thousand others. Damn thing is going viral. Though a lot of people are saying it is a fake. Others? Well, there are dark corners on the net where the real scum thrive, and I won't say more on their thoughts." The engineer shrugged and drained his can, reaching down for another.

"Dump this all up there!" Kyle demanded, his eyes moving from image to image. "Show them everything."

"Ha! Not a bad idea kid. It is hard to kill a guy when you just saw a video of him as a baby having his diaper changed." Darwin almost spat out his beer as the diaper-changing video played and laughed louder when young Bruno chose that moment to relieve his bladder. Scott's shrieking, delightful horror would bring memories to any parent.

"D . . . Do you have to show everyone that?" a quiet voice asked in an embarrassed whisper.

"Yes, oh sure, it's embarrassing, but people will love it. They will love them all. It will remind them of their own kids," the actor insisted, and Darwin was already working on it. Uploading image after image and videos, linking in what he could to Danny's original video.

Then the autocar shook as it took a sudden, unplanned course change. "What the fuck?!" Darwin exclaimed as he dropped the data device, a second after Bruno's embarrassing video was uploaded. He dove to grab the hacking tool he had used to take over the car. "Fuck, fuck, FUCK! How the shit did they find us?"

It hit Kyle like a punch to the jaw, "Your account, you were uploading from your account! Your biochip!"

Darwin gave Kyle the sort of look a marine biologist gives some hitherto unknown organism just extracted from around a deep sea volcanic vent; he was mildly disgusted, intrigued, and just trying to figure out exactly what it was. "Kyle, do I look like some fucking amateur? I used your damn account."

"Oh," the actor deflated a little, slightly worried that he had just accused a friend, who had risked everything to help him, of being stupid. Then something occurred to him, "Wait, you accessed my account? How? Citizen's accounts are the nearest thing to unhackable."

"Yes, well . . . nearest thing means not actually unhackable," the tech replied with a smirk. "This ain't my fault. I can probably override easy enough. Trouble is, they now know where we are and where the autocar is. They can follow us wherever we go."

"One thing at a time. How did they know where we were? I checked the tech we had. Do datarods have tracking?" the actor replied, partially to gain a moment to think. In the back of his mind, he knew this was it. They were caught, they just weren't actually in cuffs yet. It was all a matter of time, though.

"No, I checked them and the rest of the tech. You sure they didn't slip a transmitter on your or something?" Darwin said, looking up and down Kyle, then to the two silent, worried equines. "Or on these guys? You know corporations, eyes and ears everywhere."

"EYES!" Kyle screamed and smacked himself, placing his hand over his eye. "I had a camera in my eye, replaced every week. Dr. Ramon, he wanted to watch what I was doing . . ."

"Pervy fuck," snorted Darwin with disgust.

"No, he just wanted to make sure I didn't do anything stupid. Like convince his test subjects to make a run for it, while leaving an active camera in my eye. I was inside all day until you showed up. They must have seen the car reg or something," wailed the actor as he looked to Aden and Bruno. "I'm sorry, it's my fault. I can't believe I could be this stupid."

Aden looked at Bruno who nodded and then back at Kyle. "It's not your fault. You tried to help us. We know that you, Darwin, and Dr Ramon are going to be punished for this. I . . . didn't want things to end this way. However, if they have to end, I would rather die trying to escape than to have just stayed there. I just hope . . . you are not punished too harshly for . . ."

"Got it, I have control back. What should I do, order the car to just put down here? It might take them an hour to get here. We could make a run for it." Darwin announced, cutting across Aden's speech.

Kyle reached out to hug Aden anyway, kissing his lips softly and then turning to Darwin. "No, take us home. They want to kill them, let's make it big and public. Chicago, the Lincoln Park car park. That's a big one, and get that camera running. We have one more thing to upload."

"Alright, we are on our way." the tech grabbed his can and lifted it in salute. "Well gentlemen, I was hoping for a long and relaxed friendship with you all. I will take short and interesting. Cheers!" He drained his can and then pointed the camera at Kyle, sandwiched between the two equines.

"Well, looks like we have run almost as far as we can. We are about to land in Chicago at the Lincoln Park car park. No doubt, we will be arrested the second we touch down. In about an hour . . ."

"One hour twenty-seven," Darwin shouted over him.

"If you want to help us, if you believe that these guys shouldn't be killed for the crime of no longer being financially viable, please, be there. Don't let them take us." As he finished speaking, Kyle nodded to Darwin, who took the hint. He ended the video and uploaded it once more.

"Wow, the original video has seven million hits so far," he observed. "The diaper video has eight hundred comments so far."

"With fifty-seven billion people in the world, I wonder how many of those hits are in Chicago," muttered Kyle as he leaned against Aden, his arms tightly around him. He rested his head on the equine's shoulder and whispered, "I love you, no matter what."

"I love you, too," Aden whispered in reply, nuzzling the human's hair and sniffing his scent.

Ever the diplomat Darwin looked at the tender scene and then at the lonely Bruno. He winked and said, "I sort of like you as a person, no matter what."

The equine grinned broadly and grabbed the last remaining can, giving Darwin a wink in return. "I sort of like you as a person, too."

"You guys are assholes," snorted Kyle and then laughed. There was nothing left to do. The car sailed on towards the rooftop in the latest city he had called home. With Aden's arms around him, he snuggled down tightly and tried to soak up every moment before it might all be torn from his grasp.

"Twenty million views," Darwin observed.

"From seven to twenty in just a few minutes? That's really impressive!" Kyle observed.

"That wasn't on the original video; that was on the one we just uploaded, twenty-one million . . . shit! I have seen something go viral before, but this is something else. Twenty-one and a half,." observed the engineer as he stared at the counter flying up.

"What does that mean for us?" Aden asked quietly.

"I really don't know. I hope it means a rooftop full of people who want you to live. But it could just be . . . just internet buzz. Those people might be thousands of miles away," sighed Kyle as he squeezed the equine in his arms. "Whatever waits for us on that rooftop, we'll face it together."

"Twenty-two"

"Twenty-three"

"Twenty-four . . ."

The End

EPILOGUE

"PRISONER T-K FOUR Twenty-one, step forward," prison warden Dyson Carlos announced. It had been a long day, but then they all were long days. This prisoner had been a model one, a bit of a celebrity when he came in. Of course, that hadn't made things easy for him. Everyone loved a celebrity inmate, especially in a maximum-security prison. He had been popular, and not really in the good way.

The man had tired eyes and unkempt hair. Shuffling forward in his old and tatty jumpsuit. Ten-years was a long stretch, though, from what Dyson had heard, the guy got off easy; if not for public pressure, the judge could easily have just thrown away the key. T-K Four Twenty-one didn't look up at the guard; that was encouraged, physically when required, don't eyeball your betters. "Yes, Sir."

"I am here to escort you to your cell. Grab your stuff. The parole panel has decided to release you early, good behavior," the guard announced. There was no moment for the prisoner to gather his thoughts. Dyson had a busy shift, and he certainly wasn't waiting around for some God damned celebrity releasee to gather his thoughts. He would have plenty of time to think outside and off Dyson's damned, tired, and dirty hands. "Move it! Don't make me write you up for disobeying a guard, it'd get you another thirty days."

Whips may work wonders, but that threat was far more motivating than any pain or pleasure the man could be offered. His scrawny body shuffled along at full speed through the maze of the joint. "What was it you were famous for, T-K Four Twenty-one? Something about fucking animals, wasn't it?" snorted the guard as he shoved the whimpering man into his cell. "Doesn't matter, you have two minutes. Grab whatever crap you want to take with you. I will wait outside, two minutes, and then I drag your scrawny ass out, ready or not."

T-K Four Twenty-one nodded. He rushed into his room and grabbed his toothbrush; even in 'the joint', there was no reason to be an animal. He reached under his mattress to take out a couple of data rods, letters from the outside. Just enough to remind him of what he was missing, keep him going when the idea of making a noose out of his sheets grew in his mind. He wondered what the world outside was like. He knew he had changed. He hoped that maybe, just maybe, it had changed too.

He had been given two minutes, but, after ninety seconds, Dyson opened the door. T-K Four Twenty-one was all ready to leave with a smile on his scruffy, bearded face. His eyes twinkling with mischief, he knew the guard had wanted to drag him out unprepared. Guards like to maintain order by setting rules they never obeyed themselves, to keep the inmates off balance. For someone as smart as T-K Four Twenty-one, it had been something easy to adapt to. The other inmates, well, that was a different and darker story.

The prisoner was matched through the maze once more, seeing faces. Some smiled to see him going, others scowled. None of them would he miss, though some he would no doubt see again in the depths of the night, when he was soaked in sweat as he tried to stop himself falling asleep.

Arriving at the processing center, a box was brought from storage. "Your belongings." The prisoner opened the box. He pulled out a nicely tailored suit. He'd worn it to his trial. What a day that had been. A real media circus, he wondered how many of those reporters remembered his name after so long. Stripping in front of the guards felt natural to him now, far more than on the first day. He was a prisoner; he had lost the right to modesty. His prison jumpsuit was discarded and replaced with the suit, the smooth material feeling so good against his skin.

Dyson stepped forward and placed a small datarod on the table. "Your biochip has been credited with enough credits to get you housing for a month at any of the half-way houses listed here. You will also find the name of your parole officer and the details for your probation within. Prisoner T-K Four Twenty-one, the exit is that way, now fuck off!"

There was no need to say it twice. He resisted the urge to flip the guard the finger as he left. No need to risk a farewell beating and get his suit bloody. He pushed at the door and stepped outside. In pure defiance of every prisoner movie he had seen, the outside world was not bright, the sun not warm and beautiful, nor was there a storm raging for him to tear his shirt off and howl at the injustice. It was in fact gray, with a drizzly mist surrounding everything, getting his suit soaked, without the decency to be a dramatic downpour.

Not really caring about the rain, he strode clear of the joint and out into the city. He had only just cleared the facility's front gate when a voice behind him said, "Well, fancy meeting you here!"

Scott turned to find a familiar face standing under an umbrella behind him. "Kyle!" the former prisoner cried out in utter joy and surprise. The tall black man stepped forward. He had a few more worry lines on his face, but he was still holding his youthful good looks well. Before Scott could gather his thoughts, he found himself locked in a hug.

"Welcome back!" Kyle announced, "I have a car waiting just down the road to take you to your sister's. Your nephew and niece are eager to see you. Aden and Bruno, I'm afraid, couldn't make it. It is not easy to get here from Mars, and all of us leaving at once was too much."

"You came back for me?" The former scientist's voice broke as he spoke, tears streaming from his eyes.

"Of course! We've been helping your sister fight for your freedom since day one, we all wrote you . . ."

"I got your letters! Every single one, I think . . . I have them here." Scott waved the datarods almost defensively in front of him. "They only let me send one a month, so I had to write to my sister. However, I did ask her to . . ."

"She passed on every word, and we looked forward to them. I'm sorry it took so long to get you out. Manslaughter, even with the circumstances, it was hard to get them to let you go," the former actor replied as they reached an autocar and he opened the door for Scott.

Inside, he smiled. "Your sister is going to cry when she sees you."

"What about the kids on Mars?" Scott asked desperately.

"Well. Cassandra is looking after the school, we have another three teachers as well. Though there is a space for you. When you are ready," Kyle said proudly with a smile. Things had gone a lot better for him than he had ever dared hope. The outcry they had created had been huge. It had shaken Bio-Corp to the very foundations. The governments had smelt blood in the water; like a shark, they had risen from the depths to feed.

First had been new rights given to Aden, Bruno, and their offspring. Then they had turned their eyes skyward to the colony they had ignored for so long. Corporations no longer ruled there. There was a council on Mars in charge of progressing not just terraforming, but the establishment of a new state.

It had been natural for Aden and Bruno to be drawn there. Bruno had left a few months after they were arrested on the rooftop by the actual police. Protective custody while people tried to figure out what to do with them all. The black stallion had charged off after Cassandra and found her, heavily pregnant with his child. One of many.

Aden and Kyle had travelled, using their celebrity status for a little bit, attending dinners and functions. It was fun, though, for Kyle, oddly familiar, being treated as more as some curious art piece than as a person. He'd given a few speeches, mostly about freedom and equality, nice crowd-pleasing stuff.

Humans, of course, grow bored with their new baubles quickly. When they had sensed the end coming, they had headed skywards. Aden and Bruno both found jobs easily as engineers, well trained and very well paid. They were doing what they were created to do, establishing equipment and facilities on the red planet's surface far faster than humans confined to bulky environment suits ever could.

While Kyle had spotted a growing problem, "growing" be the operative word. All the children that Bruno and Aden had fathered, all bar the few with Bruno's former companions as mothers, were removed from the corporation facility they were being raised in. They had been given to families instead. Kyle had petitioned the council to start a nursery for them, and that request had been granted. Somehow, he had ended up in charge of it.

Now, of course, the children were far beyond nursery and growing fast. He looked forward to the next few years as hundreds of headstrong equine children entered puberty. The future was anything but smooth, but, for once, Kyle looked forward to the challenge. His sister had gotten in touch shortly after his arrest. She had received the message he had sent her from the security office. She told him she had been one of the ones sending the link around. She had networked every friend she had to help her big brother.

Scott looked at him with tears in his eyes. "I'm not a teacher."

"You're a scientist, and I have hundreds of equine kids to help teach. Who else on this planet knows as much as you do about dealing with adolescent ponies?" Kyle asked with a grin and a wink.

"Well, I suppose not many. Maybe, after I have spent some time with my family. Once my probation is over," Scott replied and let out a deep sigh of content. "For now, I hope you don't mind, I think I will have a nap."

"You're not going to miss Bernice, are you?" the former actor asked with a cheeky grin.

"Bernice?" The former inmate looked confused for a moment, and then his memory triggered. "Naw, I shived that bitch years ago. She was more trouble than she was worth!" The two laughed as the car sailed onwards. First stop, a tearful family reunion for Scott. A few days later, Kyle returned home to his husband, Aden.

About the Author

Sisco Polaris has been writing with a furry focus for over ten years. He's a quiet guy who likes nothing more than snuggling up with a good book or a good book reader. He loves stories, both writing and reading and has a special fondness for erotica (otherwise known as the whole story, just with extra fun bits).

www.ingramcontent.com/pod-product-compliance
Lightning Source LLC
Chambersburg PA
CBHW051457170626
46811CB00002B/522